One Way
Or Another

Also by Rhonda Bowen

One Way or Another

Get You Good

One Way Or Another

RHONDA BOWEN

Dafina
Books

Kensington Publishing Corp.
http://www.kensingtonbooks.com

DAFINA BOOKS are published by

Kensington Publishing Corp.
119 West 40th Street
New York, NY 10018

All Kensington Titles, Imprints, and Distributed Lines are available at special quantity discounts for bulk purchases for sales promotions, premiums, fund-raising, and educational or institutional use. Special book excerpts or customized printings can also be created to fit specific needs. For details, write or phone the office of the Kensington special sales manager: Kensington Publishing Corp., 119 West 40th Street, New York, NY 10018, attn: Special Sales Department, Phone: 1-800-221-2647.

Dafina and the Dafina logo Reg. U.S. Pat. & TM Off.

ISBN-13: 978-0-7582-5959-2
ISBN-10: 0-7582-5959-X
First Kensington Trade Paperback Edition: March 2012
First Kensington Mass Market Edition: March 2014

eISBN-13: 978-1-61773-039-9
eISBN-10: 1-61773-039-4
Kensington Electronic Edition: March 2014

10 9 8 7 6 5 4 3 2

Printed in the United States of America

*For the Bowens, the Ramsays, and the Rhodens.
There is nothing like family and I would be
incomplete without all of you.*

Acknowledgments

I wrote this book when I was far away from the people who matter most to me. But in my heart it was as if they were always there. I thank God for giving me the chance to do this again, and for the wonderful people He has put in my life to hold me up while I do it.

Vonnie and Clive, thank you for your unending love and support. Kevin, thank you for being my brother, my manager, and my comic relief.

Kemi, Steffi, Mika, and Naps, thank you for being sounding boards for my what-ifs.

Rhonda McKnight, "thank you" is not enough, but it will have to do for now. I am so grateful for your friendship and your support. Thank you also to all my writer friends for your inspiration, encouragement, and check-ins.

Special thanks to my editor Mercedes Fernandez for being patient with me through our long-distance relationship. You and the Kensington team have made this a wonderful experience for me.

Thank you to all the reviewers and outlets that supported *Man Enough for Me,* including Tyora Moody and the Tywebbin Team, Urban Reviewers, APOOO, Readers With Attitude Book Club, and Tabitha Vinson. If I forgot to mention you, it's not because I don't appreciate you. I pray that the messages behind my books stay with you long after the publicity is over.

And of course a huge thank-you to all the readers who picked up *Man Enough for Me.* Special thanks to those readers who took the time to drop me a note and let me know about it. Your stories and messages came at the times when I needed them most. To those of you who will read this book, I hope that it will be more than just another reading experience for you.

And to my Thai family: *Phra Jiaow wai pon.*

God bless you all.

Chapter 1

The metal felt icy and unwelcome as the cuffs snapped tight around Toni's wrists. She grimaced. This was not how she had planned to spend her Wednesday night.

The burly police officer dragged her to the cop car, placing his hand on her head of long, dark, silky hair as he lowered her into the backseat. At least he was being civil. The same couldn't be said for the one manhandling Afrika.

"Get your nasty hands off my butt, you perv," Afrika snapped, shoving him away with her shoulder.

The short, dull-looking cop stumbled back a bit, seemingly surprised at her force. Yeah, he didn't know. Afrika might look tiny but you didn't want to mess with her. More than once Toni had seen her friend take a chunk out of her pro-basketball-playing ex-boyfriend Tyrone. She was nobody's victim.

For once though, Toni wished Afrika would take it down a notch. It was bad enough that the cops had caught them snooping around the mayor's premises.

No sense encouraging the Atlanta PD officers to find a creative way to actually charge them.

Toni's mind scrambled for a solution as she sat in the back of the cop car on the way to the station. The clock on the dash said 10:34 p.m., leaving her with barely an hour to file her story and get out of this mess. She thought of all her possible lifelines, including her brother, Trey, and her sister-in-law, Jasmine. But none of those options were appealing. Her brother's smug look she could deal with, but she would rather spend the night in a cell than get another lecture from Jasmine, who seemed to forget that at twenty-seven she was the same age as Toni and not, in fact, her mother. That left only one person. Unfortunately, said person was sitting beside her, just as helpless as her, and a lot less cooperative.

By the time they got to the mini-precinct, south of downtown Atlanta, Toni realized that she was on her own.

"So, Miss Shields, you want to tell us why you were in the area of the mayor's residence tonight?"

Toni smiled at the large man who had been the one to handcuff her earlier. "Just taking a walk, Officer Powell."

"I'm looking at your file here, Miss Shields, and you seem to like taking walks near the homes of well-known people in this city."

Toni shrugged. "What can I say? I'm a fitness buff."

She hoped Afrika was holding up okay. They had been separated, and the other officer was questioning her in another section of the station. Toni could see her but couldn't hear what was going on.

"And what about that camera you were carrying?" he asked, an eyebrow raised.

"I like photography too. It's a new hobby."

Officer Powell rubbed his eyes. "Where's the memory card, Miss Shields?"

"Memory card?"

"Yes," he said. "You know, that little thing that records the pictures? There was none in the camera. And we didn't find it when we searched your things."

Toni shrugged. "I don't know what you're talking about."

Officer Powell sat forward, his forehead wrinkling. "Miss Shields, you were caught wandering near the mayor of Atlanta's home in the dead of night with a very professional-grade camera and a major zoom lens," he said. "I personally think you might have even been on the mayor's property, but unfortunately there's no way to prove it. Do you expect me to believe that there was no card in this camera?" he asked. "Now, either you produce the card on your own or we're going to have to search you."

"But you already searched me," Toni said innocently.

The officer glowered. "A full body search."

Toni pursed her lips. "You can't do that. Full searches can only be conducted by someone of the same sex. And I'm looking around and all the officers I see on duty tonight are men."

He rubbed a hand over his head tiredly. "Then you can be someone else's problem." He closed her file and stood. "My shift is over anyway."

Toni looked at the wall clock. 10:45. Right on schedule.

"Okay, please tell me you have a plan to get us out of here," Afrika hissed into Toni's ear moments after Officer Powell seated them beside each other in the holding area.

"Sort of." Toni turned her head left and then right as she tried to work the kinks out of her neck. The back of that cop car had not been good to her.

"Sort of? You're gonna need to give me something better than that." Afrika twisted around in her seat, giving Toni full access to her glare. "I can't go to prison, Toni. I may act hard, but I ain't no criminal. I can't go down like this!"

The hysteria in Afrika's whispers went up a notch at each statement, and Toni had to bite her lip to keep from laughing. Afrika would definitely not see the humor. And with Toni's hair looking a shaggy mess, she couldn't afford to have her best friend and hair stylist not talking to her.

"Afrika, we weren't caught doing anything wrong," Toni said, hoping her even tone would mellow her friend out. "They have nothing to charge us with. All they can do is detain us for a couple hours."

She left out the part about what could happen if they searched her and found the memory card in her bra.

Afrika narrowed her eyes at Toni. "How long is a couple?"

Toni shrugged and glanced away. "Maybe four or five."

Or seventy-two, she thought.

"A lot could happen in four or five hours," Afrika murmured.

Toni saw her friend glance out the corner of her eye at the thick red-skinned woman who had taken up the entire bench across from them with her size ten frame and size twenty attitude. The bottle blonde had skewered them with her bloodshot eyes when they first came in, before going back to the production of picking her nails, which were so long they seemed like weapons themselves. A darker skinned woman of indeterminable everything lay buried in multiple layers of clothing on the only other bench, snoring.

"Don't worry. It's usually pretty quiet this time of night," Toni said, leaning her head back against the wall.

Afrika scowled but didn't say another word. Toni knew her friend was still mad, but she was glad that Afrika had calmed down. It would be a long twelve minutes if she had to sit there and listen to her whine.

"Well, well. Looks like it's ladies' night up in here."

"Mikey?" Afrika had a puzzled expression on her face. "What you doing here?"

"Hey, cuz." Mikey chuckled and unlocked the door to the holding cell. "I work here. What you doing here?"

"Keepin' bad company," Afrika said, throwing a nasty look Toni's way.

"Toni," Mikey said. Her name on his lips sounded as oily as the chicken grease that had stained his uniform. There was no doubt he'd had a three piece for dinner.

Toni forced a smile even though she really wanted to gag. If he was any other cop on any other day, Toni would have given him a piece of her mind for the way his eyes were roaming all over her. But she needed this *Good Times* reject, and he knew it.

She got up off the uneven bench and followed Afrika out of the cell, feeling the heat of Mikey's gaze on her behind. She scowled. She was used to guys raking their eyes over her five-foot-four frame, particularly her generous behind, but it still disgusted her.

"So it says here that you aren't charged but you need

to be searched," Mikey said, a toothpick in the corner of his mouth as he flipped through Afrika's and Toni's files.

"Don't even think of putting your nasty hands on me," Afrika warned.

"Easy, cuz." Mikey laughed. "The search would have to be done by another woman."

He turned his eyes on Toni. "Unless you want to waive that right."

Toni fought her gag reflex again. "Thanks, Mikey, but you can already see we don't have any weapons. Plus, like you said, there are no charges. You're gonna let us out in a couple hours anyway. Why not save yourself some time?"

Mikey raised an eyebrow and Toni sugared up her statement with a smile. He laughed again. She wasn't sure if that was good or bad.

"I guess you have a point there," he said a moment later, stepping forward and removing the cuffs from Afrika's wrists.

"It's about time." Afrika scowled. "Where's my stuff?"

Mikey pulled a small plastic tray of items from behind the station desk and slid it over to Afrika.

Toni held up her wrists toward him expectantly.

He glanced at her hands but didn't reach for the keys. "You've been in here an awful lot lately. Maybe you need to sit in a cell a couple hours and cool off."

Toni scowled.

"Or maybe you could help me change my mind," he suggested. His eyes swept her frame again and she noticed his voice had ducked to a whisper.

"How about dinner again?" He leaned forward to drop the last words. "This time at my place."

Toni resisted the urge to step back as the slightly

rank smell from Mikey hit her. She would bet anything that homeboy had been rocking the same frowsy uniform all week. Nothing short of a gun to her head was putting her anywhere inside Mikey's place.

"I don't think so, Mikey," Toni said, just as she heard the doors to the station open behind her.

He glanced up and nodded to the newcomer before moving around the desk and away. "Well then, I think I'm gonna have to take a little more time writing this release," Mikey said stiffly. "I don't want to miss anything important."

He looked past Toni at the person behind her. "How can I help you?"

"I heard one of my kids was here. Rasheed Roper?"

"Oh yeah," Mikey said, turning back to the desk and flipping through the stack of reports. "He got picked up with some other youngbloods near the old Bankhead Courts. Residents called it in—said they were a bit noisy. We found a little weed on a couple of them, but your kid was clean."

Toni tapped her foot impatiently as she listened to the exchange. She glanced up at the clock—11:00. The Thursday morning edition would go to print in the next hour with or without her story. And if the latter was the case, all the crap that she had gone through tonight would be for nothing. She wasn't having that—not after she'd had to beat out the other Metro section reporters for the front page.

"Let me get him and then you can sign him out." Mikey turned away.

"Mikey"—Toni grabbed his arm before she lost him completely—"the cuffs?"

"Toni, we going or what?" Afrika asked from the door, a sour look plastered on her face.

"What did you say your kid's name was?" Mikey looked past Toni as he started moving toward the back again.

"Rasheed Ro—"

"Come on, Mikey," Toni whined, slapping the desk in frustration with her handcuffed palm. "You really gonna do me like this?"

"Like what? Girl, I never told you to get your behind locked up. You the shizzle up at the *Atlanta Journal-Constitution*. Tell your boss to come bail you out."

"Do I look like I have time for all that?" Toni shot back.

"Uh, hey, you think you could get Rasheed . . . ?"

Forget Rasheed.

"Can you just hold on? Your kid will still be a criminal in five minutes," Toni snapped, swinging around to glare at the stranger who kept interrupting.

Her anger died on her lips when she saw exactly who was behind her. As she craned her neck to take in all of his six-foot-something frame, she couldn't help but think of the fence she nearly broke her neck scaling less than an hour earlier. Now here was a brother who did not need a boost. And with his I-do-real-work-every-day arms he could have probably hoisted her over without breaking a sweat.

However, the expression on his gorgeously angular face told her he wasn't inclined to do anything for her at that moment, except maybe help Mikey put her back in the holding cell. The slight downward turn of his full lips and the tightness in his strong jaw confirmed the irritation.

But, boy, did he make ticked off look good.

* * *

She was trouble personified.

Adam could tell before she even opened her pouty mouth. It was in her flushed cinnamon-toned skin, the dark inquisitive eyes, and the legs that he was mad at himself for looking at. Women with legs like hers shouldn't be allowed to wear jeans that looked like they had been painted on. It was just wrong to mess with a brother's head like that. Especially when he was trying to keep it PG-13 upstairs.

He felt bad for staring. But she kept looking at him with those huge eyes and he couldn't turn away.

"You don't look old enough to have grown kids," she said after a moment.

"I think you got bigger things to worry about," he said. "Like making it out of this place tonight. But it looks like you already have a plan for that."

The big beautiful eyes turned into slits. "Maybe you shouldn't be so quick to judge, seeing that I'm not the only one at the police station in the middle of the night."

"Only one of us is wearing cuffs," he shot back.

"It takes one to raise one," Toni said. "In your case I'm sure the blunt wasn't rolled far from the weed."

"Whatever." Her tongue was sharper than an army knife. He had nothing.

He didn't even know why he was getting so riled. Maybe because he was ticked off that his day had had to end with him in a police station picking up Rasheed. But more likely it was because the woman in front of him was stealing more of his attention than he wanted to give. And the joker in the too-small uniform sexually harassing her was working his last nerve.

"All right, here he is," Mikey said, returning from

the back with a cross-looking Rasheed only a few steps ahead of him.

Adam felt the corners of his mouth drop into an even deeper frown. He saw Rasheed visibly tense when he saw him.

"Yo, Bayne, I wasn't even doing anything!" he protested.

"I don't wanna hear it, Rasheed," Adam said, shaking his head. "Go sit over there, till I get through with this mess.

"You got something for me to sign?" he asked the sloppy officer.

Mikey nodded and began pulling together a sheet and clipboard for Adam.

"Toni, I'm calling a cab, and I'm leaving."

So her name was Toni. Adam glanced back at the young woman standing at the door. She looked even more annoyed than he felt.

Toni turned back to the officer. Desperation and frustration fought for position on her face. "You really gonna make her leave me, Mikey? You know if I don't get back and get this story in I'm done."

Mikey shrugged as he handed Adam the clipboard.

"Say the word and you can be out of here right now," Mikey answered.

Adam found himself hoping that Toni turned down whatever homeboy was offering. Instead, she stomped her foot, and uttered a word he used to use quite frequently before God put a noose on his tongue.

"Fine, I'll do it," she hissed through her teeth.

"Really?" Mikey said, sounding surprised. "I never actually thought—"

Mikey stopped short when he caught her glare. "So eight on Friday then?" He tried to whisper but Adam still heard him. Adam shook his head in disappointment.

"Whatever," Toni said. "Just get me out of these."

Mikey grinned as he fumbled with the keys and freed Toni's hands from the restraints. With a look of pure annoyance, she snatched the release form from Mikey's pudgy fingers and examined it. She probably wanted to make sure that whatever she had done didn't end up on her record.

Adam frowned but began to scan the form in front of him. He just wanted to sign Rasheed out and be done with it. The night had gotten too weird. However, when Mikey leaned in a little too close to the woman, Adam couldn't help but look up again. And when the rent-a-cop put his hand on Toni's behind, Adam didn't even think before he reacted.

"Brothah, you need to back up," he said, stepping forward angrily. Who did this toy cop think he was?

But before he acted on his temptation to handle matters in a less verbal manner, the petite woman turned around and kneed the officer hard in a place so close to the groin that it made Adam shudder. Mikey hollered like a five-year-old and doubled over in pain.

"You think you feel something now?" Toni hissed at his bent over form. "You lucky I never put my foot where it really wanted to go."

"Oh man, she got you!" Rasheed hollered with a laugh.

"If you ever put your hands on me again, you'll be sorry you ever met me, you got that?" Toni snapped angrily in the officer's ear.

Rasheed was still hooting in laughter as she stuffed the release into her pocket and grabbed her stuff out of the tray on the table. Adam stepped way out of her way as she stormed past him and through the door, pulling her friend behind her.

He glanced at the cop, still crouched over and holding on to the table for support, then at the door where Toni had just exited.

Yes. That woman was definitely trouble.

Chapter 2

"Toni, boardroom now."

Gordon didn't wait for a reply, and as Toni replaced the phone receiver, she knew it wasn't going to be a good morning.

"Come on, kid, let's go," Naomi said, tapping her pen on Toni's desk as she walked past it on her way to Gordon's office.

With a deep breath, Toni got up and followed her editor down the hall. They both knew the routine. They had gone through it every time Toni wrote a story that was a little too edgy or ruffled the wrong somebody's feathers. Gordon was about to read them the riot act.

"Okay, Gordon." Noami seated herself in front of the paper's publisher and nodded at the seat beside her for Toni to do the same. "What's got your knickers all knotted up today?"

Toni knew that only Naomi could get away with talking to Gordon like that. The slim Caucasian woman barely reached Toni's height and was probably a hundred pounds soaking wet, but there were two things

Toni knew: no one could work an Anne Klein suit or a news story like Naomi.

"I think you know what," Gordon snapped, not bothering to sit down. He flung the morning's edition on the table in front of them.

"What's this?" Naomi glanced briefly at the paper over the top of her Prada glasses, as if she had not seen it roll off the presses herself some seven hours earlier.

"It's our Thursday edition," Naomi exclaimed. "In fact, I think this is the lunchroom copy. Looks like there's some coffee stains on it. . . ."

"Naomi, don't play games with me." Gordon's pale freckled face had already started to turn an unnatural shade of red. "The story, Naomi. How could you print this on the front page?

"And you, Toni." He turned his furious eyes on her. "How could you write this? What happened to responsible journalism?"

Toni opened her mouth, but Naomi stood up before she could say a word.

"This *is* responsible journalism." Her voice had lost its earlier mock cheerfulness in favor of a sharper edge. "It would be irresponsible not to print it. It was a darn good story, Gordon, and you know it."

"What I know," Gordon said, yanking off his glasses to glare at Naomi, "is that the mayor's office is threatening to sue us for libel and slander, and Brenners is threatening to pull all their advertising and support from the paper."

"Let them keep their partisan support. Maybe then we can go back to having a fair and balanced paper," Naomi retorted stubbornly.

"And what about the lawsuit? Should we let them do that too?"

"Please, we've had lawsuits before and we'll have them again," Naomi said, her hands on her hips. "Besides, we didn't print anything that wasn't true."

"How did you even get that photo?" Toni flinched slightly as Gordon's glare zeroed in on her. "Was that what you were doing when you were crawling around on the mayor's premises last night?"

Toni rolled her eyes. She should have known Gordon would find out. He was more connected than the CIA.

"Technically I wasn't actually on the mayor's premises," she pointed out.

Not when she got caught anyway.

"But regardless, he's a crook, Gordon." Toni frowned. "Who's gonna blow the whistle on this dude if we don't?"

"That's not an excuse for committing a crime and putting this paper in legal jeopardy," Gordon growled, pounding the table with his fist.

"How did that photo make it to the front page anyway? I thought they took your camera when you got caught?"

Toni glared at Gordon and the vein in the middle of his forehead that was growing bigger by the second, but said nothing.

"Our information comes from credible sources," Naomi said, filling in for Toni.

Gordon crossed his arms over his skinny chest and cocked his head. "And who are these sources?"

"Come on, Gordon, you know that's protected information," Toni said.

"Only until there's a court order for them."

"Oh, please." Naomi rolled her eyes. "You know the

law protects us on this. They don't have any right to that information."

Toni looked back and forth between the two power-houses of the newspaper squared off on either side of the table. They always seemed to be at loggerheads about something. In fact it sometimes seemed as if Naomi purposely provoked the fifty-six-year-old publisher of the newspaper to see how far she could push him. He had run the *AJC* for almost thirty years, but Naomi was one of the most sought after editors in the region and even beyond. He knew that they would be foolish to get rid of her and so did she. But Gordon was still their boss. It made for an interesting game.

"That may be the case, but this time things have gone too far." Gordon put his glasses back on. "Toni, you're being reassigned from Business and Government."

"Gordon, no!"

"You are now back in the pool with the other general assignment reporters." He sat down and began to shuffle papers as if he had not just ruined her life. "This week you can go dig something out of city court."

"City court?" The words fell from Toni's mouth with disdain.

"Yes." He glanced up at her in confirmation. "And you will send me the first draft of your story before it goes anywhere else."

"Gordon, this is not fair." Toni stomped her foot. "I'm your best Metro reporter. Who is gonna cover the lead-up to the November elections?"

"We'll find someone."

"But it's already May!"

"You did this to yourself." Gordon folded his hands on the table in front of him. End of discussion.

Toni wanted to scream. She couldn't believe this was happening. Not after five years at *AJC*. She had covered the last local election and had written more Metro front page stories than she could remember. This was supposed to be her time to get a leg up. To get a chance at running with the big boys. And now she was being demoted to general assignment? Thrown into the pool with freshie reporters who couldn't smell a scoop if they stepped in it?

She turned to her editor. "Naomi, you can't let him do this."

She already knew that if she got dumped into general assignment Gordon would make sure she got nothing but crap stories for the rest of her *AJC* career.

"Toni, would you excuse us, please?" Naomi kept her eyes on Gordon. "I need to have a few words with our publisher."

Toni glanced at Gordon again before sighing and heading toward the exit. As soon as the door closed she heard their voices. They were definitely going at it again but she couldn't tell who was winning. She crossed her fingers and hoped it was Naomi. Because if it wasn't, Toni wasn't sure she could handle what came next.

"Remind me why we're here again instead of at K and K's?" Afrika asked as they walked up the driveway of 25 Wicker Way.

"Because Jasmine wanted to show us something," Toni said.

Toni heard Afrika's stomach growl.

"She couldn't show us at the restaurant?" Afrika rubbed her middle longingly. "I haven't eaten all morn-

ing. After last night's drama a sister had to skip breakfast just to catch up on some sleep."

At the other end of the wide, cobblestone driveway,
they found the double doors to the huge two-story
home slightly ajar. As they slipped inside they could
hear Jasmine's voice echoing off the high ceilings and
open walls.

Afrika gave an appreciative whistle from behind
Toni. "This place is nice."

"Mmm-hmm." Toni's eyebrows knotted. "Too nice."

Jasmine came from money. Old money. So it was no
surprise that when she and Toni's brother, Trey, had
started looking for a house, her tastes were more on the
high end. It seemed like Jasmine had forgotten, again,
that her father's credit card was no longer the source
from which all blessings flowed.

"Chicas, I thought you would never get here!" Jasmine beamed as she appeared from around a corner,
her six-month-pregnant belly showing up before she
did. Toni wasn't sure how such a tiny woman managed
to carry around such a round belly.

"Well, it does take a while in midday traffic to come
all the way to Ansley Park," Toni said, referring to the
almost upper-middle class neighborhood where Jasmine had asked them to meet her. "It's not really on our
regular route."

"Well, you're here now." Jasmine clapped her tiny
creamy hands. "You've got to see this place; it's amazing!"

She looped her arms through Toni's and Afrika's,
pulling their reluctant forms forward.

"Don't you love this huge two-story foyer and this
amazing floor? It's hardwood throughout, you know,
except for the bathrooms, of course. But can't you

imagine Trey and I having the best Christmas parties in here?" She tittered. "The foyer, of course, not the bathrooms."

"I don't know, Jasmine," Afrika began, unwrapping a stick of gum she had rummaged out of her purse. "Trey doesn't really seem like the fancy Christmas party type. Some chicken wings, sodas, and a pool table seem more like his flow."

Toni bit back a laugh as she watched Jasmine visibly shudder. Better from Afrika's mouth than hers.

"Well, it's not anymore," Jasmine said matter-of-factly. "Besides, who wants chicken wings when you can make the most amazing tapas in this fantastic oversized kitchen?"

Jasmine was off again, not waiting for either of them as she gave the full tour of the nearly three thousand square foot property, including the living room, the beautiful den off the kitchen, and the three massive bedrooms.

As Jasmine glided through the second kitchen with them trailing behind, Afrika caught Toni's eye. "Aren't you gonna say something?" Afrika mouthed.

"You know I've been trying to stay out of Trey and Jasmine's business," Toni whispered, shaking her head.

"I know, but are you seeing all of this?" Afrika whispered back "This place must cost a mint. I know your brother makes good money, but I didn't know it was *this* good."

"Girl, please, we're in a recession," Toni muttered dryly. "Ain't nobody's money this good."

"So, what do you think?" Jasmine asked as they stood in the front foyer again at the end of the tour. "Think this is the house for me and Trey?"

"Too fancy-pants for me," Afrika said, blowing a

bubble with her gum. "But hey, I'm just a little black girl from Grove Park. What do I know?"

Jasmine rolled her eyes and turned to Toni. "Well?"

" 'Well' what?" Toni hedged.

"Well, what do you think of the place?" Jasmine asked with exasperation. "Could you see me and Trey here?"

Toni sighed. *Maybe if your dad kicked the bucket early,* was the answer she had on the tip of her tongue.

She was a speak-the-truth-and-speak-it-immediately kind of girl, which was what got her in trouble most of the time. And if she said what she really thought, this time would be no different.

"What do *you* think of the place?" Toni deflected.

"I love it." Jasmine's eyes were brighter than the floodlights in the soccer-field-sized backyard. "I think Trey would love it here too. He really appreciates high quality in a home."

Toni wrinkled her nose.

"What?" Jasmine said, her tone changing. "You don't think he'll like it, do you? 'Cause you know so much more about what Trey likes—more than me, his own wife, who he comes home to every night."

Out the corner of her eye Toni saw Afrika shake her head and give her a don't-go-there look. Too late.

"I actually don't think Trey would like all this." Toni folded her arms. "And I don't know why you think he would. You know how mellow Trey is. All the bougie stuff just makes him uncomfortable."

Jasmine narrowed her eyes. "You mean my bougie stuff."

Toni shrugged. "Hey, you said it, not me."

"Why are you always trying to class down your

brother? You think just because you have to be everybody's homegirl that he wants to be ghetto too?"

Toni turned to look at Afrika. "Did she just call me *ghetto*?"

Afrika rubbed her eyes tiredly. "T, she probably never meant it like—"

"Oh, she meant it like that." Toni glared at Jasmine. "She still thinks she did our family a favor by marrying Trey. Like we weren't doing fine on our own before she tried to spend my brother into debt."

"Excuse me?" Jasmine stepped back, hands on her hips. "So because I want nice things I'm spending *my husband* into debt? In case you forgot, I work and make my own money too. But I guess I'm supposed to wear Walmart clothes to make you feel better."

"Please, Jasmine, you couldn't find a Walmart if it was in your own backyard," Toni replied. "And nobody's saying you gotta be cheap, but sometimes you gotta bring it down. Everything can't be the Ritz all the time."

"But it isn't," Jasmine protested.

"Really." Toni smirked. "So tell me, what's the price on this house?"

"Huh?" Jasmine stuttered, caught off guard.

"What is the price on this house?" Toni spoke slowly and deliberately. "You know, since you're not high-end *all* the time."

Toni folded her arms as both she and Afrika turned to Jasmine. She shook her head as she watched her sister-in-law spin her wedding ring on her finger, then fiddle with the ends of her long dark hair.

"It's not much, just a couple hundred thousand."

"Really." Toni could smell Jasmine's lie. "How many is a couple?"

"Just a couple," Jasmine said, getting in a huff as she shouldered her purse and turned toward the door. "Are we going to eat or what?"

Toni and Afrika exchanged amused looks as they followed Jasmine to the door. Toni noticed a sheet of paper sticking out the top of Jasmine's open purse and snatched it from behind. It was the listing.

"Hey!" Jasmine protested. "Give me that!"

But Toni turned away so she couldn't reach it. Her eyes widened when she saw the asking price.

Afrika, who was peeping over Toni's shoulder, swore loudly. "Five hundred K?" she squealed.

"It's just an asking price," Jasmine said, snatching back the paper and stuffing it into her purse. She made sure to zip it shut. "We can negotiate."

"Down to what?" Toni retorted. "Four-fifty? That price doesn't even include closing and negotiation costs! Jasmine, there's no way Trey can afford that!"

"How do you know what Trey and I can afford together?" Jasmine snapped. "Why don't you just mind your own business?"

"Why don't you stop trying to send my brother to the poorhouse with your high-maintenance self," Toni snapped back.

"Okay, okay!" Afrika said, stepping between Toni and Jasmine. "That's enough!"

"Why's she always in the middle of my marriage like a third wheel?" Jasmine snapped.

"Okay. Firstly, Jasmine," Afrika said, "*you* were the one who invited *us* here to see this place that you were considering. *You* were the one who asked *us* our opinions. So don't get mad if you hear something you don't like."

"And before you start gloating, Toni, you know you

need to fall back and let Jasmine handle her business with her husband. I know Trey's your brother, but she's his wife. She comes first."

Toni and Jasmine had a brief eye-rolling standoff.

"Now can we get some food?" Afrika whined. "I'm about to pass out."

"You two go ahead." Toni slipped on her sunglasses and pushed past them. "I'm not that hungry anymore." Toni wasn't sure she could deal with Jasmine right then. She loved her sister-in-law but sometimes she really didn't like her.

"Toni, wait!" Jasmine caught up with her just before she got to the end of the driveway.

"Look." She took a deep breath. "I'm sorry I went off on you. I just really like this place, and sometimes I feel like you shoot down everything I do. Like the things I want for Trey aren't good enough. It's not easy being a wife. But you have to know I'm just doing things the best way I know how."

Toni sighed as Jasmine turned her large sad eyes on her. Her sister-in-law pouted a little and Toni shook her head.

"Is that the look you use on Trey to get him to do what you want?" Toni asked, grudgingly.

"Yes." Jasmine nodded. "Is it working?"

"Maybe." Toni tried to maintain her annoyed look.

Jasmine grinned widely and Toni knew that she couldn't stay mad at her.

"Okay fine." Toni rolled her eyes and cracked a small smile. "I'll try and zip it more often."

Jasmine grinned and threw her arms around Toni in a hug.

"Okay, can we wrap up this Lifetime moment so I can get something to eat?" Afrika asked, tapping her foot impatiently as she stood by the car door. "I can't believe we're gonna have to spend another half hour battling through traffic to get somewhere decent."

"Actually, there's a little bistro at the corner," Jasmine said. "We could leave the cars here and just walk down to it."

This time Jasmine caught the look that passed between Toni and Afrika. "I know what you're thinking, so don't worry," she said, . "I've been there before with a friend. It's not expensive."

"Okay, fine." Toni put her keys back in her bag. "But if I have to spend more than fifty dollars on lunch, you're paying."

Afrika snorted. "Make that thirty for me. I'm self-employed and it's hard out here for a pimp."

Toni side-eyed her friend. "Bet you paid more than thirty for that piece of rock hanging 'round your neck."

"Hey!" Afrika grabbed her wooden beaded necklace and pendant and held it close to her chest. "You know it was my only indulgence this month. You were with me when I bought it!"

"What's with you today?" Jasmine glanced over at Toni as the three of them walked together. "You're a little more acidic than usual."

"She's right," Afrika agreed, still fingering her jewelery, a hurt expression on her face. "That was below the belt."

Toni sighed. "I'm sorry. It's just been a really bad day, that's all."

"What happened?"

Toni frowned. "I got reassigned."

"What?" Jasmine asked, surprised. "When?"

"This morning."

Toni scowled as she remembered her boss and editor in chief Naomi's words after she had left the meeting with Gordon, the newspaper's publisher. Gordon's decision had stood. She was back to being a general assignment reporter.

"Umm-hmm. It's 'cause of that foolishness from last night, ain't it?" Afrika cut her eyes at Toni.

"Girl, I'm still mad at you about that. You're lucky my cousin Mikey could pull some strings to get us out. You know I ain't built for that kinda mess."

"What mess?" Jasmine looked back and forth between Toni and Afrika as she rubbed her oversized tummy.

"Is this where we're going?" Toni asked, as she pulled the door open to a small café-style shop. She stepped ahead to be seated, not waiting for the girls to catch up.

She didn't want to talk about last night. Afrika might have been mad about being locked up for less than an hour. But Toni was still mad about Mikey's nasty hand on her behind. Plus she would be lying if she said she wasn't just a little bit worried about what might come out of her kneeing him in the stomach. If that wasn't enough, she kept having random thoughts about Mr. Hotness, and his chocolate eyes.

"So anyone gonna tell me what happened last night?" Jasmine asked once they were seated. She looked back and forth between Toni and Afrika, ignoring the menu the waitress had placed in front of her.

"Your sister-in-law got us arrested," Afrika said grudgingly.

"Seriously?" Jasmine sighed. "Again? This is what, the third time you've been picked up?" Jasmine shook her head. "They must have a special spot for you downtown now."

"Not downtown," Afrika said, her lip curling in disgust. "Just in the mini-precinct near Bankhead where my cousin happens to work."

She turned to Toni. "Why are you and him so familiar anyway? Mikey's my cousin and all, but I know you ain't messin' with his nasty behind."

"Of course not," Toni said with disgust.

"So how're you getting him to pull those kinda strings for you on a regular?" Afrika asked.

Toni picked up a menu and yawned. "I let him take me out one time. He probably thinks there's a chance for something more. So sue me if I dangle the carrot a little."

"Dios mío." Jasmine looked up at the ceiling.

"Well, you make sure that all you do is 'dangle,' " said Afrika, picking up her own menu. "Otherwise I might have to end this friendship quick."

Toni laughed and handed her menu to the waitress as the tiny young woman took their orders.

"So how did you end up getting reassigned from this?" Jasmine asked after the waitress had left. "I thought you had the one boss in the world who doesn't care if you have a record."

"It was Gordon," Toni said, her mood souring again. "He caught some heat from the city over my story."

"I'm guessing the mayor wasn't happy about this morning's photo-op?" Afrika asked, scrunching up her narrow caramel-colored face as she wrestled her long black dreadlocks into a ponytail.

"No, and that coward Gordon demoted me to assignment reporter." Toni pouted. "Can you believe it? I've been working major stories for over a year and now they want to dump me on random assignments.

This week I'm supposed to be covering city court. What am I? A first year intern?"

"Well, you knew something like this was going to happen eventually." Jasmine took a sip of the drink the waitress had just put in front of her. "You can't keep blowing up all the big names in the city and think you can get away with it forever.

"Don't worry too much about it, though," Jasmine added. "I know you, and even you can find a good story in courts."

Afrika snorted. "Don't hold your breath. My niece Jamelia, who works in booking, says it's pretty dismal over there. But there are some hot lawyers."

Toni rolled her eyes. "Please, they're probably as corrupt as the criminals they represent. Plus you know I don't do lawyers."

"Or doctors . . ." Jasmine added.

"Or politicians . . ." Afrika piped in.

"Or CEOs . . ." Jasmine dropped.

"Or pro athletes . . ." Africa noted.

"Or anyone who wears a suit or a uniform to work," Jasmine and Afrika finished together.

Toni rolled her eyes again. "Hey, I have standards for a reason," she said. "It's so I don't end up with soul-sucking basketball players or spineless investment bankers," she finished, referring to Afrika's and Jasmine's ex-boyfriends.

"Okay, okay." Jasmine waved away the memory with a flick of her wrist. "Before you burst a blood vessel, I actually might have a story for you."

Toni sighed and bit her lip. She had heard Jasmine's story ideas before. And it made her even happier that her friend had chosen psychology and not journalism as a career.

"Is this another conspiracy theory piece?" Afrika asked wearily as the waitress came back with their food. " 'Cause I gotta get back to the shop in about an hour."

"No, this is real," Jasmine said, ignoring Toni's skeptical look. She wiggled her eyebrows. "And it's really good."

"Okay." Toni took a mouthful of tuna and vegetables in pita bread. Now that she was actually being fed, she was feeling a bit more generous. "Let's hear it."

"So there's this kid down at the center where I volunteer on Tuesdays," Jasmine started. "Apparently he was involved in some stuff and got caught by the police. But instead of sending him to prison, they sent him to the center, where he more or less works off his time."

"Is this a touchy-feely story?" Toni grimaced. "You're not going to tell me that he cleaned up and now he's going to Harvard or something."

"Please, I know your heart of stone isn't into all that." Jasmine pursed her lips. "The story is that he's been at the center for two years, but now they're trying to make him serve the original term in prison, even though a judge already allowed him to serve his time at the center."

Jasmine shook her head in disgust. "That poor kid doesn't even have a good lawyer to help him fight the charges. In fact, right now it looks like he's gonna end up serving a double term if the prosecutors have their way."

"Wow, that's messed up." Toni paused to take another bite. Her lunch was better than she had expected. "Can they do that?"

"Looks like they plan to," Jasmine answered.

"You should look into that," Afrika said between hearty bites of her chicken sandwich. "That sounds like something you could stretch out into a couple stories. You know, interviewing the kid, getting viewpoints from either side, that sort of thing."

Toni raised an eyebrow at her friend, who had heard so much about her job over the years that she probably could do it herself if she wanted to.

"What?" Afrika asked when she caught Toni staring at her. "I'm right, aren't I?"

Toni didn't answer but pondered the thought as she chewed on the head of a broccoli spear. If she was going to be stuck in general assignment she might as well make it interesting. It couldn't hurt to look into Jasmine's story anyway. At the very least it would get her sister-in-law off her back and earn her some Brownie points with her brother.

"Okay," Toni said reluctantly. "I guess I can check it out. When can I come by?"

"Maybe early next week. I'll talk to the guys at the center, find out if it's okay, and give you a call," Jasmine said.

Toni turned her attention back to her pita sandwich. "What's this kid's name anyway?"

"Jerome Douglas."

Toni spun her motorcycle into the parking lot of the Jacob's House Young Men's Center. She shut off the engine, removed her helmet, and looked wearily up at the three-story building. She had spent the last few years actively avoiding the group home that was connected to her brother's church, Immanuel Temple Atlanta. It's not that she had anything against the place. It was just that she heard enough Jesus-talk whenever she was around Jasmine and Trey, who were heavily involved with the church. She didn't need to be preached to at Jacob's House as well.

Jasmine had been a Christian all her life. Toni had had the pleasure of learning this the first time she met her when Trey brought her home for Christmas. At that point Toni was almost positive that her brother's relationship with the high-society Latina woman wouldn't last. Both Trey and Toni had given up on the Christianity thing for various reasons.

But either Jasmine didn't know this or she didn't care, as she never stopped trying to get them to come to church with her. Toni had resisted. Trey hadn't. But Toni had always suspected that her brother had only done it because he knew he wouldn't have had a chance with Jasmine otherwise. But somewhere along the way he had changed, and by the time he had married Jasmine they were united in their campaign to save Toni for the Kingdom—whether she was interested or not.

With a sigh, she pocketed the keys to her bike and trudged up the front steps. She tried not to laugh as the two young men in headphones sitting on the steps gawked at her. She was used to getting that look every time she showed up somewhere new with her Honda CBR250R. It was her second motorcycle, definitely an upgrade from the scooter she'd had before. And she loved every second on it, even though it kept her brother and sister-in-law on heart medicine.

She winked at the boys before slipping through the double doors into the main lobby where Jasmine was already waiting.

"Hey, mami, you got here quickly!"

Toni grinned at her sister-in-law, who was looking stylish in black slacks and a white wrap blouse. Her long, thick black hair, left hanging loose, was curling slightly around her face, contrasting with her smooth olive complexion and making her small nose and full lips look even more Latina than usual. She might not agree with Jasmine on a lot of things, but she had to admit, that was one beautiful woman her brother had married.

"Time is money," Toni said, accepting Jasmine's warm embrace.

"Ugh, don't tell me you rode that thing over here." Jasmine flicked at the helmet in Toni's hand.

"You know, Jasmine, you might love it if you give it a try," Toni teased. "And think of how sexy Trey will think you are on the back of a bike."

"Please," Jasmine scoffed. "There's nothing sexy about being dead, and that's exactly what's going to happen if you don't give up that thing soon. Especially with the way you ride."

"Yeah, yeah. Heard it all before," Toni said, looping her arm into her friend's and changing the subject. "Show me your office. I can't believe you've worked here for almost two years and I've never seen it."

"Well, technically, I don't really work here—I volunteer," Jasmine corrected as the two ladies turned into a wide open corridor with large windows that opened up to a field on one side, and doorways to what looked like classrooms on the other.

"And my office is actually a common room used by all the staff."

Toni followed Jasmine into a large room that looked more like a staff lounge than anything else. Several school-teacher desks that had seen better days with similar looking chairs were set up strategically at the front and at one side of the room. At the other end of the room two battered couches and a coffee table created a makeshift lounge area. Beside the lounge area was a door that led into what looked like another office. From what Toni saw through the slightly ajar door, it was pretty tiny. Definitely nothing to write home about.

"Geez, this place is tighter than our newsroom at the *AJC*," Toni murmured.

Jasmine chuckled. "I know." She guided Toni toward one side of the room. "But none of us really spends a lot of time in here anyway, so it's not that big a deal. Plus if we have less, it means the boys can have more."

"I guess this is your desk?" Toni asked, sinking into a battered chair at the side of a desk that looked like it used to be mahogany.

"How'd you guess?"

Toni pointed to the picture of Jasmine and Trey. "You must have made a hundred of these and stuck them up everywhere," Toni said, shaking her head at the picture. "It's your own personal Jasmine-was-here stamp."

"Whatever," Jasmine said, shrugging, even though Toni could see the redness staining her cheeks. "For your information, I share this desk with my husband. That's why the picture is there."

"Mmm-hmm," Toni said, knowing better. She had seen that exact picture in Jasmine's office at the clinic, in her car, and also in her purse. Her friend wasn't fooling anyone. Nonetheless, Toni thought it was cute that Jasmine and Trey were still crazy in love after five years of marriage.

"Okay, so who's the dude who gets that piece of real estate?" Toni asked, nodding toward the one solo office.

Jasmine looked up from the files she was gathering. "Oh, that's our director's office. He pretty much runs things at the center."

"Hmm," Toni murmured.

"Yeah, in fact, we need to talk to him," Jasmine said, biting her lip. "He has to give the okay for you to do the piece on Jerome."

Toni's head snapped up. "Jasmine!"

"What?" Jasmine asked, avoiding her friend's eyes guiltily.

"You told me on the phone that the whole thing was okay!" Toni groaned and covered her face. "You know how much I hate the politics of these things. I thought everything was already set for me to meet this kid."

"It is," Jasmine insisted, glancing away. "Sort of."

Toni folded her arms and glared at her fidgety friend.

"Look, he was a bit skeptical," Jasmine conceded. "But I am sure once he meets you and you give him your pitch for the story, he'll be all over it."

Toni groaned and buried her head in her hands.

"Come on, it won't be that bad," Jasmine cajoled, springing to her feet and dragging Toni with her. "All we have to do is find him."

Toni sighed. This was why she picked her own stories. She should have known better than to get Jasmine of all people involved.

"Oh, here he is now," Jasmine said brightly. "Adam, this is the person I spoke to you about earlier. Adam, meet my sister-in-law, Toni. Toni, this is our director, Adam Bayne."

Toni turned around and let out a laugh. It was Mr. Man from the station.

"This is your friend?" he asked, an eyebrow raised as his delicious eyes glanced at Toni and then back at Jasmine.

Toni took up her purse and helmet, already knowing the end of this particular story.

"We already met." He smirked. "And my answer is the same as before, Jasmine. No."

Chapter 3

"So I hear you met my sister today."

Adam grimaced, faked Trey on his left, and dribbled past him on the right side before doing a clean layup at the basketball net.

"Yeah. For the second time," he said, tossing the rebound back to Trey, who was still panting a few feet south of center court. "Remember the girl I told you about from the other night when I picked up Rasheed?"

Trey let out a laugh. "No way!"

"Oh, yes. It was her," Adam said, shaking his head.

"Oh, man. Jazzy told me you met her." Trey dribbled the ball while he tried to catch his breath. "That's our Toni," he said. "Also known to the newspaper world as T. R. Shields."

Trey tried to dribble past Adam with the ball. But Trey was weak on his right side, and Adam knew it. Blocking him hard on the left, Adam forced him right and then easily stole the ball. By the time Trey caught up with him the basketball was already swishing smoothly through the net.

Trey rested his hands on his knees, panting. Adam shook his head at his friend, who was so out of breath that he could barely call "time."

"Man, look at you," Adam chided mockingly. "You're a disgrace to men everywhere."

"Hey, I'm not as young as I used to be," Trey said breathlessly, even though at thirty-one he was only a year older than Adam. Staggering, Trey followed Adam over to the bench by the side of the court. "The spirit is willing but the flesh is weak," Trey panted.

"You mean *your* will is weak," Adam teased, grabbing his bottle of Gatorade from off the bench behind the center. "I've been to your house. I know what Jasmine's been feeding you. You just can't say no."

"Hey, no blaming the wife," Jasmine called out as she walked toward them from the back doors.

"Baby, did you see how Adam was whopping my behind out there?" Trey called out. "How you gonna let him do me like that?"

"Sorry, hon, I got my own battles to fight with this one," Jasmine said, sitting down on the bench beside Adam.

"Before you say another word, Jas, I'm not changing my mind."

"Come on, Adam. You haven't even given her a chance," Jasmine whined. "You know she's a really good reporter. I've heard you say so yourself."

"She's a criminal in the making," Adam said, wiping his face with a towel. "You forget that I saw her assault a police officer?" A serious look came over Adam's face.

"I don't need Jerome picking up her any-means-necessary attitude. We're tryin' to instill certain values in these boys—so they know how to come correct in every situation."

"Don't you think that you're making too much of it, though?" Jasmine asked. "From the way she told it, that officer was pretty out of line. If he had done to me what he did to her, I would've probably gone off on him as well."

Adam knew that she was right. After all, he had almost taken matters into his own hands.

"All she wants to do is talk to Jerome, find out his case, maybe write a story about it," Jasmine finished.

What Jasmine said sounded innocent enough. But even though Toni had been disrespected that night at the station, it was hard for Adam to forget everything that had gone down before that.

"Your girl was still caught doing something shady," Adam said, shaking his head. "That's how she ended up at the station bargaining for her freedom in the first place. Plus the way she went off on me while I was there . . ."

"She can be a little rough sometimes," Trey admitted.

"Hey! You're supposed to be on my side," Jasmine said, whopping him with his towel.

"Oww . . . But, baby, it's true," Trey said, rubbing his arm, a wounded look on his face. Adam grinned at the two of them as they fussed with each other. They were one of the most functional married couples he knew. Though he had no immediate plans, Adam knew that whenever he tied the knot, it had better be as real as Trey and Jasmine.

"Adam, come on," Jasmine tried again. "Have I ever steered you wrong?"

Adam sighed and began stuffing his high tops into the gym bag at his feet. "Jas, I know you're pretty sure about this, but I gotta do what's right for Jerome."

His eyes darkened as he thought about the seventeen-year-old young man, and even the warm afternoon sunshine streaming through the maple trees surrounding the court couldn't lighten the air of solemnity that seemed to fall over the three of them.

"How did things go today?" Jasmine asked, referring to Jerome and Adam's visit to Legal Aid earlier that morning.

Adam shook his head. "Not good. We spent almost all day downtown and I feel like we keep getting the runaround. You would think that since they know us there they would give us a break and get us through the system, but sometimes I feel like they make it harder on us, just because."

"So still the same lawyer," Trey said with an air of disgust.

Adam nodded and Jasmine hissed her teeth.

"Have you even heard from him?" Jasmine asked, her distaste obvious.

"Not since he showed up late to court for Jerome's hearing three weeks ago," Adam responded dryly, leaning back against the picnic table portion of the bench. "We've tried calling and leaving messages but I guess we're not high up on his list of priorities."

Adam's brow furrowed as he remembered the frazzled guy who had been assigned to Jerome this second time around. The guy hadn't even known Jerome's name before he entered the courtroom. If only they could have had Jerome's original lawyer, Wallace. But he had left Legal Aid and moved to Alberta, Canada, to open up his own labor law practice a year earlier. And since there was never a dull moment between oil workers and mining companies over on that side, Adam doubted that he would see the dedicated court officer on this side of the border anytime soon.

"There's got to be something we can do," Jasmine said, shaking her head. "We can't let this happen to Jerome, not when he's come so far."

"I talked to his teacher last week. She said he finished at the top of his class this past spring. So are you telling me the kid's gonna go through all of that just to serve five years in prison?"

Adam wished he could tell Jasmine that wouldn't be Jerome's story, but he had seen too much happen with the boys who came through this place to be optimistic. Jerome's situation bothered him more than the others though. Maybe it was because he had seen the kid grow up before his eyes. Maybe because he knew Jerome was bright, and deserved a second chance. Maybe because Jerome reminded him of himself, and it didn't seem fair that he should have been able to start over and this kid couldn't.

"What are you thinking?" Jasmine asked, her brow furrowed as she peered at him.

"Nothing," Adam said, pushing the thoughts of his past out of his mind. The look she gave him told him she knew he was lying. But he had not told Jasmine and Trey about his past, and he wasn't about to start now. He hated when she shrinked him.

"Look, maybe I can make a few calls and see if we can find someone," said Trey, who had been silent for a while. "We really should have a lawyer on volunteer staff here."

"Like we should have a gym, and a computer room with more than five machines, and a few tutors," said Jasmine dryly. "There's no money for any of that either."

"God gives us what we need when we need it," Adam said, standing up and slinging his gym bag over his shoulder. "Let's give thanks for that."

But the words were more for himself than for his friends. And as he walked toward the center's back doors with Jasmine and Trey trailing him, he couldn't help but hope, like they did, for a little more.

"So how'd it go yesterday?" Afrika asked, following Toni into her office and plopping down in a chair beside Toni's desk.

"It was a bust," Toni said, as she recalled her run-in with Adam at the center. She dumped her purse, iPhone, and portfolio on her desk. "Remember the guy from the station the other night?"

"The sexy one with the kid?"

"Yeah, him." Toni raised an eyebrow. "You thought he was sexy?"

"Yah, girl," Afrika said, her eyebrows going up in confirmation. "All six-plus feet of him. And did you see his—"

Toni raised a hand to stop her friend before she could go into details. "He's the director for Jacob's House."

Afrika whistled. "Sometimes I forget how small the ATL is. Guess that story's a wrap."

"You got that right," Toni said, sitting back and grimacing. "He was not happy to see me at all."

"That's too bad," Afrika said, resting a manila folder on top of the junk on Toni's desk. " 'Cause from all accounts this one looks like it could be a front pager."

"Really," Toni said, not hiding her skepticism as she powered up her laptop with one hand and flipped Afrika's folder open with the other. "What did you find?"

"Let's just say, you owe me big time for this one," Afrika said with a smug grin.

Toni shook her head. Afrika was good at hair, but the truth was she should have been a private eye for the way she could dig up information. Not only did she seem to have a cousin, aunty, neighbor, or friend in every single area of the city, but somehow she had a knack for uncovering the most unattainable pieces of information. God bless the day Toni walked into Banyan Tree Salon and reconnected with Afrika. Who knew her old high school friend would be more connected than Atlanta's finest?

"Okay," Toni said, swiveling her chair toward Afrika. "Convince me."

"Well, it looks like this whole case is less about the kid and more about what the city is doing with the police."

Afrika dropped her voice and leaned in toward Toni. "So you know this kid got charged for grand theft auto, right? Well, apparently, two months ago the city cut the number of officers working in that area."

Toni shrugged, not particularly impressed. "So what? They reassign officers all the time. What's the big deal?"

"The deal is that once the insurance associations heard about it they got into a fit," Afrika continued. "Of course, the city ignored them so they leaked it to the opposition, who plan to use it as a campaign tool against the current city government. And guess what year it is?"

"Election year," Toni murmured absently, as the gears began to fit together in her mind. "So they're using Jerome and his case as an example of how they are not ignoring auto theft, but making their unit more efficient."

"Exactly," Afrika said triumphantly.

Toni leaned back in her chair, rolling her pen between her palms absently. This was definitely something she could work with. In fact, she already knew at least three different angles she could approach the story from. Afrika was right about her initial suspicion that they could wring at least three headlines out of the whole thing, if they did enough digging.

"Aren't you glad I talked you back into this story?" Afrika asked, crossing her legs in satisfaction. "With all the work I've done too, you better show a sister some appreciation."

"That's if this story ever makes it to print," Toni said, sitting up straight again and pulling up her contact list on the computer. "If Adam Bayne doesn't let me talk to Jerome, then there won't be any appreciation for any of us."

Afrika stood up. "Well, maybe someone needs to bite the bullet then and get to begging."

"First of all, I don't beg for anything," Toni said pointedly. "Secondly, why should I have to convince some glorified juvenile parole officer to give me a story that's going to help his kids?"

"Because I know you, girl, and there ain't nothing you love more than a front page story," Afrika tossed behind her as she sashayed toward the elevator.

Toni scowled, but even as she did, she picked up the phone and started dialing. If she really wanted this story it was clear that she would have to make it good for Adam.

"Hey, Dwayne? It's me, Toni," she cooed in her best voice through the receiver. "Remember when I delayed running that story on your client so his stock wouldn't fall before his big sale, and you told me you owed me big time? Well, I'm ready to collect. . . ."

Chapter 4

"**K**nock, knock."

Adam looked up from his desk at the head of long, silky black hair that had stuck itself inside his office door. He grimaced.

"Now, that's no way to greet your guests," Toni said, slipping inside and taking a seat before he could say a word.

Adam rubbed his temples. There were things he could deal with today. Like the past-due energy bill sitting on his desk and Dexter's failing report card. But Toni he didn't have the energy for—even if her vanilla-scented perfume brought a welcome change to his office.

He watched her smooth out the nonexistent wrinkles in her black slacks and fold her hands in her lap expectantly. He took a deep breath and inhaled another whiff of vanilla. Guess she wasn't going anywhere.

"How can I help you, Miss Shields?"

"It's Toni," she said brightly. "And actually I've been thinking there's a way we could help each other."

She smiled and Adam wondered if this was the same person who had taken out an Atlanta PD officer less than a week ago. He glanced at the morning's copy of the *Atlanta Journal-Constitution* sitting to the side of his desk. A few hours earlier he had skimmed over her latest article about the shortage of legal aid at city court. It was a lot milder than most of her other pieces—not that he followed her stories.

Something told Adam she wouldn't leave until he heard her out, so he put down his pen and clasped his hands together resignedly. "I'm listening."

"So you know I want to talk to Jerome about his case. . . ."

"You already know how I feel about that," he interrupted.

"Yes, but I think it might help everyone if we were to work together on this," she added quickly.

Adam raised an eyebrow. "I suspect it would help you more than it would help me, Miss Shields."

"I disagree. And it's Toni."

"Well, *Toni*, I think we're going to have to agree to disagree."

"But you haven't even heard what I have to say yet." She narrowed her large dark eyes.

"Given what I've already seen of you, I'm not sure I want to," Adam said.

Toni's mouth fell open. "That's not fair! You don't even know me."

"Yes, but apparently the Atlanta PD does."

"That is so judgmental. . . ."

"But true. Right?" Adam challenged.

"Look, are you going to fight me all morning or are you going to at least hear me out?" Toni asked, losing the brightness.

He couldn't help but smirk. "I was wondering how long it would take for the real you to show up."

"Well, here I am." She let her glare reinforce her words. "So let me know if I should leave now, or if we can have a civilized conversation like two grown adults."

Adam glared back at Toni. He was doing it again. Picking a fight with her. Something about her seemed to unsettle him, and the quicker he could get rid of her the better. Unfortunately it seemed like the only way to get rid of her would be to hear her out.

He frowned. "Okay, I'm listening."

"For real this time?" Toni challenged.

Adam bit back what he really wanted to say and settled with "Yes."

She took a deep breath and for a moment Adam saw that she was a bit nervous. He was surprised.

So she did have feelings.

"I know you're trying to protect Jerome." Her voice had mellowed out to an even tone. "I can understand that and I'm not trying to exploit him. But I do think there are people out there who are."

"What do you mean?" Adam asked, his brow furrowing.

"Your people downtown don't really care about Jerome," Toni said flatly. "They're just using his case to hit the opposition at elections."

Adam listened, stunned, as she explained what Afrika had told her about the changes in the auto theft unit and the way the opposition wanted to use it against the current government.

"They're planning to make an example of Jerome," Toni said. "They want to use him to prove how well the system is working, even though they cut the budget.

When he goes to prison, Jerome will be the poster boy for how committed they are to fighting crime."

Adam leaned back in his chair and rubbed a hand over his face. So Jerome was just a puppet. And everyone knew it. That's why no one at Legal Aid would touch the case. It was a suicide mission—failed from the get-go.

"How do you know all this?" Adam asked.

Toni offered a tight smile. "You don't really wanna know."

Adam sighed. "This is not good."

"That's not all," Toni said, her eyes tainted with something that looked to Adam like pity.

His eyebrows rose. "What do you mean?"

She bit her lip. The pause before she answered only served to increase Adam's apprehension.

"If you lose the case with Jerome, chances are they're gonna start reopening all the cases on all the boys here."

"What?" Adam asked, the lines in his forehead deepening as he sat forward.

"There's already a list of the ones they're thinking of looking into first," Toni said.

Adam closed his eyes.

"Listen, they haven't started looking into any of the others yet," Toni followed quickly. "It might not even come to that, but I thought I should let you know."

"So is this how you're helping me?" Adam asked dryly. "By letting me know the Jacob's House program is falling apart in slow motion?"

"No," Toni said sincerely, shaking her head. "I was just explaining the situation.

"But I do know someone who can help," she continued. "I have a friend who's a lawyer who would be willing to look at your case."

"We already have a lawyer."

Toni chuckled. "Not a good one."

"So I guess you've been talking to Trey."

"Well, he is my brother, so yes," Toni answered, her sarcasm thinly veiled. "But I also know Emmett Green, and trust me when I tell you, he's not trying to help you out. You'd be better off defending yourself."

Adam grimaced. They had already figured out that part on their own.

"Look," Adam said. "It's nice that you're taking an interest, even though it might be opportunistic of you. . . ."

Toni rolled her eyes.

". . . But we can't afford a big-time lawyer. Look around," Adam said, nodding to the peeling walls and aging ceiling. "We're barely getting by as is."

"Adam, my sister-in-law and brother both work here. Give me some credit," Toni deadpanned. "I know money is tight. The lawyer I spoke with is willing to do this pro bono for you. He's got a quota he has to fill for his firm.

"Besides, he's just gonna look at the case and let you know what Jerome's chances are and what kind of representation you're gonna need," Toni finished.

A small spark of hope lit up inside Adam, but he squelched it before he could get too optimistic. "So you're saying there is an actual criminal lawyer who is willing to work with Jerome on this case, free of cost?"

"No," Toni said with a small smile. "There is an actual top-notch criminal lawyer who is willing to work on this case, free of cost."

Adam tried not to smile, but the muscles in his face were already relaxing.

Okay, God, I see you.

Suddenly his eyes narrowed at Toni. "So what do you get for your part in orchestrating all this?" he asked suspiciously.

Toni smiled sweetly. "I think you already know what I want."

Adam cocked his head to the side and considered her, wondering all the time how someone so beautiful could be so calculating. So this was how Samson got caught.

"Call your lawyer friend." Adam let out a sigh, shook his head. "Is this how you get all your stories?"

Toni grinned as she reached across the desk to use his phone. "Only when I'm being good."

Chapter 5

"So why you so interested in talking to me any-way?"

The lanky young man draped his almost six-foot frame over the chair and glanced at Toni. With his two neck tattoos, two-inch afro, and two-sizes-too-big clothes, Jerome almost seemed older than his seven-teen years. But his sleepy copper eyes, which shone brightly in the blanket of his deep mocha skin, were what gave him away.

"Maybe 'cause everyone else is so interested in making sure I don't," Toni said. "Kinda makes me feel like you know something worth knowing, you know?"

Jerome laughed and stuck a fry in his mouth. The two of them were sitting across from each other out-side a McDonald's on a hazy Thursday afternoon. Adam had finally caved and let Toni talk to the boy, but he had insisted on it being a supervised session. Toni had insisted that was stupid. So instead they had come to a compromise that involved Adam sitting one table away, pretending to read the paper while Toni chatted with Jerome.

Toni looked across at Adam. "Is he always that uptight?" she asked.

"Pretty much," Jerome said.

"Too bad," Toni said, her eyes lingering. "He might have been a lot of fun."

"He's all right," Jerome said, taking a bite out of his cheeseburger. "You just gotta get used to him."

Toni wrinkled her nose. "I'll pass."

She looked back at Jerome, who had completely finished the cheeseburger in about three bites, and stifled a laugh.

"So you ready to talk now? Or do I need to bribe you with another one of those?" she asked, an eyebrow raised.

Jerome licked some ketchup off his fingers. "Not now," he said, grinning mischievously. "But maybe later. So what you wanna know?"

Toni leaned back and shrugged. "How 'bout you tell me how you ended up at Jacob's House in the first place."

Jerome took a large sip from his soda. Then he told her his story.

It wasn't an unfamiliar one to Toni. He had grown up in what used to be Bankhead Courts before it was demolished in the Atlanta Housing Authority public housing wipeout.

There were two of them, both boys, both with different fathers whom neither of them knew. His mom worked two jobs and was never home, and so he followed his older brother and his brother's gang around on the street.

"They never really told me anything, you know?"

Jerome said, all the ease long gone from his features. "I was just Jamal's kid brother. Wherever Jamal went, I went.

"So, one day, we're just hanging out as usual, me and Jamal and some other dudes, when we end up downtown. There's this car parked on the side of the street, and Rico says, this is the one.

"I'm asking Jamal what he's talking about, but he just tells me to shut up. So I do, 'cause I know these dudes, and if they tell you to shut up, you shut up. So I'm just standing there, and then I see Rico pull something out of his pants and start trying to boost the car.

"So, I'm like 'Yo, Jamal, what are you doing?' He tells me to shut up and go watch, make sure no one's coming. I tell him no, but he says if I don't do it, he's gonna make sure I go down with them when they get caught."

Jerome's eyes narrowed in anger. "My brother, my blood. And he's about to sell me out for some niggas who don't give a sh—"

He stopped midway, and suddenly looked across, as if sensing Adam's eyes. Toni looked across and found Adam glaring at him.

Jerome cleared his throat. "Uh, sorry."

He took a sip from his soda and seemed to relax a notch. "So anyway, I go out and watch the corner," Jerome continues. "At first it's all good, but then I see five-oh cruising down the street, like they on patrol or something. I try to tell Jamal we need to bounce, but Rico's got him in the driver's seat tryin' to start the thing. I don't know what he does, but the alarm suddenly goes off and that nigga Rico takes off down the street. Jamal gets out the car, we start running but somehow we end up splitting up, and since I don't know downtown like they do, I'm the one who gets caught."

Jerome slumps back in his chair, a ticked off look all over his face. No doubt still angry about everything that had happened. Toni would have been too if her brother had ditched her and let her take the rap for his mess.

"What happened after the cops got you?" Toni asked after she had given Jerome a moment to calm down.

Jerome's eyes grew darker. "I was in lockup for a while before I could see a judge. That was some other sh—" He paused again. ". . . Was messed up. 'Cause I wouldn't tell them who the others with me were, they charged me for trying to steal the car, and then pinned some other boost on me 'cause they said it looked like the same crew. It was probably Rico who did that other job, but I wasn't even there. Didn't even know nothing about that other mess, but I was the one who took the rap.

"Since I was fifteen, they said I would probably end up in juvie, but then my lawyer told me about this program with Jacob's House where I could live there and go to school and whatever, and if I kept clean, then at the end of my two-year sentence, they would clear my record. Since my moms didn't want nothing to do with me, and I wasn't feeling the juvie scene, I figured a free bed and grub, why not? So I signed up, and here I am."

"Just like that, huh?" Toni asked.

"Nah," Jerome said, his eyes going cold. "Not just like that. This is better than what could have happened to me, but it ain't no fairy tale. My moms still won't talk to me, and I can't go anywhere near where I used to live. If I do, I go straight to juvie. If I miss curfew, I go straight to juvie. If I jaywalk, I go straight to juvie. It's not prison, but ain't nobody free."

Toni watched him carefully as he fiddled with the wrapper of his burger. "So what happens now?" she asked.

"Now they want to put me in prison. Real prison. Gen pop, with the rapists, the triple murderers, and a bunch of other coldhearted brothahs."

"Why?"

Jerome scowled. "They say I didn't really serve my sentence. That the state was too easy on me." He snorted. "I wanna meet the person who came up with that mess. Let them spend a week at Jacob's House. Let them see how easy it is."

Toni glanced at Adam, then dropped her voice. "Jacob's House—do they treat you well over there?"

Jerome nodded. "Yeah. Bayne, Dr J, Shields, Walters, Gonzales, they're good people. But like I said, it ain't no fairy tale. We got chores and work and school, and some of us got jobs outside of that. And of course church is a must, and if you break any of the rules, that's it."

Toni looked across at Adam. He had switched to a book Toni had never heard of. She took a sip of her own drink and turned back to Jerome.

"Anybody ever get dropped from the program?"

"A couple," Jerome said. "Not everybody is in it for the right reasons, you know? Some dudes think it's a free ride."

Toni smirked. "But of course you're in it to change, right?"

Jerome's eyes turned to ice as he looked her up and down. "What do you care, you just trying to make front page."

Toni heard a cough from her right. She didn't need to look to know Adam had heard everything.

"Well, I gotta write something to sell your hard-luck story," Toni shot back.

"Write what you want, I don't care," Jerome said. "It ain't gonna change nothing. Nobody cares about me or any of us except Bayne and the rest of them. You think your little story is gonna change that?"

Toni scowled. "Guess we'll have to wait and see."

"Yeah," Jerome said, dismissing her with his eyes as he stood to his feet. "I ain't holdin' my breath.

"Yo, Bayne, can we bounce?" Jerome said, with an air of distaste as he ignored Toni. "I'm done here."

Toni caught Adam's eyes as he stood, and the look there was clear: Jerome was done talking to her, and she was done talking to Jerome too.

Chapter 6

"Got a second?"

Toni watched from the door as Naomi looked up from her computer. She spotted Toni, sighed, then looked back at the screen. Her fingers flew across the keyboard, not pausing for a second as she spoke. "Sorry, kid, I got an appointment in two minutes."

"I know." Toni came fully into the office and closed the door behind her. "I'm your appointment."

Naomi's fingers stopped moving as she glanced at Toni skeptically. Toni watched nervously as her boss swiveled her chair around to check her desk calendar.

"You're interviewing to be the new local arts reviewer?" Naomi asked, cocking her head to the side.

"Well, I might as well be, with all the great stories coming my way." Toni hoped her sarcasm had hit the intended mark. "And it doesn't help that my boss, who used to be my number-one fan, won't even give me the time of day."

Naomi sighed and motioned to the chair across from her. "Have a seat."

Still holding on to her attitude, Toni sank into the seat across from her boss. As she did, she noticed for the first time the age lines etched into Naomi's pale skin, as well as the streaks of silver that seemed to punctuate her auburn hair more than before. It seemed like her boss had aged ten years since the last time she had seen her, which in all honesty was probably over a week ago.

Ever since the fallout with Gordon over Toni's article on the mayor, Naomi had been a lot less visible. She still came in at her ungodly hour of 6:45 a.m. and left at 7:15 p.m. However, unlike before, she was more often in her office than around the office. In fact, other than when Naomi came and went for meetings, Toni barely saw her. Which was why Toni had had to resort to unorthodox methods.

"If you're slick enough to sneak yourself onto my appointment calendar without me knowing, than I guess you deserve the time you stole," Naomi said with a small smile.

"I'm sorry." Toni bit her lip. "There didn't seem to be any other way. And I really need to talk to you."

"Okay." Naomi put down her pen and leaned back in her chair. "Let me hear it."

"I'm really mad about being demoted to a regular assignment reporter," Toni said, her forehead wrinkling in a move of its own. "I love my job, and I am really good at it. You know that. I feel like I'm suffocating here."

Naomi took off her glasses and rubbed her eyes. "I know." She sounded as frustrated as Toni felt. "And, Toni, it hurts me more than it hurts you, because I know you are one of my best reporters. But like I told you before, I had no choice. It was either this or a pink slip."

Toni felt the breath leave her body for a moment. "They were gonna fire me?" she squeaked.

Naomi's lip curled in distaste. "That's what the mayor wanted in exchange for making his absurd base-less lawsuit go away. I had to convince Gordon to keep you on. The only way to do that was to promise to keep you off the front page."

Toni fiddled with the clasp on her watch. If that was what Gordon really wanted, then this was going to be harder than she thought.

"That might be a problem," Toni said, measuring each word. " 'Cause that's exactly what I'm here for."

Naomi groaned and closed her eyes. "Toni . . ."

"Come on, Naomi," Toni whined, sitting forward. "You know I wouldn't come to you on this unless I knew it was good."

Toni watched her boss roll her pen between her palms as she sat back. "Okay," Naomi said, the appre-hension still apparent in her voice. "Let me at least hear what you got this time. Although I can't make any promises."

That was all Toni needed. She spilled out the entire story of Jerome, his case, and Jacob's House to Naomi, who listened carefully but said nothing. When she had explained her angle for the story, Toni pulled out a USB memory drive and handed it to Naomi.

"What's this?" Naomi asked, even as she plugged the stick into her computer.

"It's the first draft for the story. I've been working on it on my laptop and didn't want to save the files on our hard drive here." She smirked. "You never know who isn't minding their own business, you know?"

"Yeah, I know."

They both remembered more than one story they had been working on that had been shut down halfway by Gordon, or had had its sources dry up without explanation. After that Naomi and Toni had practiced keeping the more high profile stories as independent of the office as possible.

Naomi's expression was pensive as she read through the piece Toni had spent hours putting together from Jerome's interviews and information from the case she had been able to find in public records downtown. Toni was always nervous when she had to watch her boss read her work—even when she knew it was good. This time was no different.

When Naomi leaned back and nodded, Toni knew she was done. But she had gone back to the pen-rolling routine without saying a word.

"Well?" Toni probed when she couldn't wait a moment longer. "What do you—"

Naomi's hand in the air made Toni stop short. Naomi swiveled her chair around to the window, her back toward Toni. Toni tried not to fidget as she watched Naomi go through what she knew was her mental routine for evaluating a story. Usually Toni never had to sit there as she did it. But the silence forced Toni to evaluate the situation herself. What if Naomi wouldn't use the story on the front page? What if it got cut down to a three-paragrapher below the fold on the second page of the courts section? What would she tell Jerome? Adam? They already didn't think much of her. This definitely would not help.

It was just a story. They were just players. And when it was all over, everybody would walk away and go back to their life. So why then did the thought of disappointing Jerome twist her stomach into knots?

"Okay," Naomi said, swinging around. "This is good."

"Good?" Toni perked up. "How good?"

"You already know how good. Front page good."

"Yes!" Toni squealed, bouncing in her chair. "I'm back!"

"No you're not." Naomi's voice had too much caution for Toni's liking.

Toni deflated instantly. "What do you mean?"

"I can't publish this in your name, Toni," Naomi said matter-of-factly. "It would be the absolute last straw. Gordon would have us both out on our behinds before the ink could dry on the first copies."

Toni fell back in the chair and covered her face. She wasn't sure how much more of this she could deal with. "I can't do this, Naomi." Toni shook her head and stood. "I can't live like this. If I can't write stories that I care about here, then I might as well quit, and find something else to do."

Naomi rolled her eyes. "Sit down, Miss Drama Queen. I said we can't publish this under your name. I never said we can't publish it."

Toni blinked and sat down, not quite sure where her boss was going with this, but willing to hear her out. "What are you thinking?"

Naomi leaned in closer and lowered her voice. "Would you consider publishing this under a different name?"

"As in giving it to another reporter?" Toni almost choked on the words.

"No!" Naomi's face contorted in horror. "You know

I don't believe in that mess. I mean publishing under a moniker." Naomi sat back. "I was thinking about something like Ann Armour."

Toni cocked her head to the side. She hadn't thought of that. "Who would know?"

"That's the thing," Naomi said. "You couldn't tell anyone. You would have to work on this as a freelance writer, do it on your own time, still keep up your other reporting from your beat and get paid for it separately. You and I would be the only persons who would know."

Toni chewed on her lower lip. She wasn't sure about this.

Naomi sighed. "Look, Toni, I know this will be different. You won't get the glory and won't be able to talk to many people about it. But this is the only way this story gets played out here. So think about it. What matters to you most, telling this kid's story, or keeping your name on the front page?"

Jerome's face flashed through her mind. It was a no-brainer. "The story is what's most important." Toni folded her arms in her lap. "I'll do it."

The first smile for the day broke onto Naomi's face and for a moment she looked like the editor that Toni knew. Toni grinned along with her.

"You have no idea how glad I am to hear you say that." Naomi sat forward, looking energized. "Now we can really flesh this out."

The smile slid from Toni's face. "Flesh it out?"

"Of course," Naomi said brightly. "Now that you are a contracted freelance author, Miss Armour, we have to decide how far we're going to take this story. I won't publish it unless we have two follow-up pieces. For one, we really need to get into crime as an election issue, and talk about all the manipulation happening at city hall around it. If you can get some insider scoop and drop some names, we could have a bombshell on our hands."

Toni nodded, starting to understand how Naomi was thinking. It looked like she might get to cover the elections after all. She couldn't help but grin.

"Plus we need a human interest feature piece on this home."

Toni's face fell. "The home?"

"Yeah, this place where the kid is serving his time," Naomi continued, skimming her computer screen again. "What's it called?"

"Jacob's House." Toni's lips felt heavy as she supplied the name. Doubt began to spring up like weeds inside her.

"Can't we just run this piece and see how it goes?" she suggested with a fraction of her earlier enthusiasm.

Naomi laughed. "Toni, honey, I didn't get to where I am without some well-honed intuition. That intuition is telling me that we had better have two more stories waiting in the wings to follow this one. If we pull this off, we could become a number-one choice for coverage of the elections. Do you know how many issues we will sell? Do you know what that will mean for getting interviews with both parties during the entire process?

"This is a good story, Toni, but it can be better."

Naomi swivelled back to her computer and began typing again. "Let me look over this once more. In the meantime, get me a piece on that home. Find out about the other boys there. It's been around for what, twenty-five years? There must be a few big names that've been through it. Find out who they are."

Toni pulled herself out of the chair and headed for the door. Wasn't this what she had expected anyway?

So why was she surprised that this was happening? And why did the thought of going back to Adam for more information make her stomach turn?

"Oh, and one more thing."

Toni paused to look back at Naomi, her hand on the doorknob.

"Interview that guy, what's his name?" Naomi's eyes scanned the computer screen. "Adam Bayne."

Chapter 7

"Bayne, I don't think this is working."

"Yeah, man. It's supposed to look like the rest. That don't look like the rest."

Adam sighed and sat back on his heels, looking at the roof shingles in front of him. Tarik and Sheldon were right. Something was wrong. He just didn't know what. They had been trying for the past hour to fix the leak in the roof over Tarik's bedroom that they had delayed addressing all spring. June and the end of the school year had finally rolled around so they could get to it. But with three of them on the roof, and three others on the ground, they still hadn't been able to figure it out.

"Yo, Bayne, I'm not trying to say you can't do this," Tarik began easily. "I seen you fix the plumbing in the bathrooms, and even Ray-Ray's bed after he popped it down with his heavy self. But ain't none of that ever taken two hours, and we been on this roof for two hours. You get what I'm tryin' to say?"

Adam got exactly what he was trying to say. He

rubbed his hand over his face. What he wouldn't give to have a roofer appear right now.

"Hey! What's going on up there?"

The three of them looked over the edge of the Jacob's House roof to where the voice was coming from. Adam grimaced. This woman had a knack for showing up at the worst possible times.

"Hey, it's the honey who was here for Jerome the other day. What up, shorty!" Sheldon called down from the roof.

Tarik socked him in the arm, and they both looked over at Adam, who was glaring.

"I know you can do better than that," Adam admonished.

Sheldon scowled. "Sorry." He leaned back over the edge of the roof. "How are you today, Miss Toni?" he asked, enunciating each word for Adam's benefit.

Adam could hear Toni's laughter below. "I'm good. Tell your boss to come down so I can talk to him."

"I'm kinda busy," Adam called out as he turned away to focus his attention back on the roof in front of him. He couldn't waste any more time. There were still three other parts of the roof waiting for similar attention.

"Busy doing what?"

"Tryin' to fix this roof," Tarik answered dryly. "Too bad he don't know nothin' 'bout what he doin'."

"Maybe if you quit runnin' your mouth and got your behind over here you could help me figure this out," Adam threw back.

"Let me take a look," Toni called out. All three heads on the roof and those on the ground shifted to look at Toni.

For the first time that day, Adam grinned. "You want

to take a look at the roof," Adam said, the amusement in his voice poorly disguised. "For what?"

"Maybe I can help," Toni called back, cocking her head to the side as she stared up at him from under huge sunglasses.

"I don't think so," Adam said. But before the words were properly out of his mouth, Toni dropped her bag on the grass below and took off her tiny belt. Adam watched in horror as she kicked off her shoes and slipped the oversized dress shirt she was wearing over her head. She tossed it on the ground in the pile with the rest of her stuff, all to the background sound of the boys' whistles and catcalls. He thought about reprimanding them, reminding them of the importance of respecting women. But what should he expect? They were street kids, and an attractive woman had practically stripped down to her basics right in front of them.

She seemed oblivious, however, and Adam almost forgot the purpose of the whole show until she slipped on some work boots and climbed the ladder to the roof, clad only in the boots, black leggings, a tank top, and her sunglasses. He knew instinctively that the image of her slim, curvy body would leave a scar on his brain. At least nothing was see-through.

"Jerome, come hold this ladder so I don't break my neck," she called out, even though she was already halfway up.

"For what?" Jerome argued, eyes narrowed. "Ain't nobody send you up there."

Toni paused on the ladder and turned to look at Jerome. Adam couldn't see her face, but whatever was there did something, for Jerome slunk his reluctant form over to the ladder to steady the base.

"You can't be up here," Adam said testily, when she

finally made it past the three stories to the roof. "If you fall off or get injured, you're not covered under our insurance."

"Please." Toni smirked as Tarik and Sheldon helped her onto the roof. "You're more likely to fall off than I am. Okay, let's see this leak."

Toni crawled over to a section of the roof that met a higher attic wall. The shingles had already been pulled away from where Adam had attempted to start some work. Adam gritted his teeth as he watched her. Was she serious? Did she think she could just go wherever and do whatever she wanted? What was with this crazy chick?

"Toni, this isn't a joke," he began.

"No, but this flashing is." She pulled at the metal piece that sat at the corner between the roof and the wall. "Nothing's wrong with it, really. It's just not installed properly. Come, let me show you." She motioned for them to come over.

Sheldon and Tarik got there before Adam. He wasn't sure if it was their enthusiasm to learn, or to get a closer look at Toni.

"Look, Adam," Toni said, beckoning him closer. "The flashing is supposed to overlap and fit under the shingles. But here it's just sitting on top. We just need to pull it off and reinstall it properly."

"Toni . . ."

She turned to look at him. Then she took off her sunglasses and he realized she was serious. "I know what I'm talking about. Just trust me," she urged.

She turned back to the problem in front of them. "Now, we can get this fixed in no time, we just need some tin snips, a hand brake, a hammer, a couple nails, and some rubber sealant. Oh, and I'm gonna need some gloves."

"I got you," Tarik said, disappearing down the ladder to collect the supplies she requested.

Adam gave her his own gloves and watched, amazed, as she pulled off the shingles from the section of the roof near the attic wall and removed the metal flashing that was in place. She was about to replace it when she peered closer and frowned.

"What?" he asked with apprehension. He was almost afraid to know. He had been in this house long enough to expect that when you pulled away the source of one problem, you often found several others hiding underneath.

"Uh, well, the felt under these shingles is damaged," she said. Glancing over her shoulder, he saw that the fabriclike material that was supposed to act as a layer of protection was torn in several areas.

"Guess we need to replace that too." Adam sighed. So much for thinking this was going to be a quick and easy repair. "Sheldon, you're gonna need to help Tarik bring the roofing felt up from the ground."

"Don't worry." She placed a hand on his shoulder. "It won't take as long as you're thinking. And on the bright side, I think this part is the worst of it. Your other leaks are probably just missing shingles and damaged felt."

To Adam's surprise, she was right. But then, why wouldn't she be? She clearly knew more about roofing than he did.

In twenty minutes they had fixed the leak near the attic wall. After that, she showed the three of them how to fix the other leaks and then left them to it while she checked the flashing near other sections of the roof. In an hour and a half they were descending the ladder to the ground.

"Yo, Miss T, you the man," Sheldon said, giving her dap.

Toni laughed. "I do what I can."

Adam watched as she sat down on the grass and stretched her long, slim legs. He still couldn't believe she had crawled up onto the top of the house and fixed the roof like it was no big deal. All the women he knew, and a lot of men also, were too afraid of heights to clean their roof gutters. But not this one. She was something else.

"Do I even want to know why you know how to fix roofs?" Adam asked, sitting down beside her on the grass. The boys had long abandoned them for the kitchen.

Toni leaned back on her elbows and grinned. "I used to date a guy who did roofing part time. When he found out heights didn't bother me, he would let me hang out with him on the roof while he did jobs."

Adam raised an eyebrow. "Aren't there rules against that sort of thing?"

"Of course." Toni wiggled her eyebrows. "That's what made it so much fun."

Adam turned to squint at her. "So you just break the law for kicks?"

Toni shook her head. "Not for kicks. Sometimes a little bending of the rules is necessary."

"Is that what you were doing that night when you ended up in jail?"

Toni turned to look at him. "Yes. And I have no apologies. It was for a worthy cause, and I would do it again if I had to."

Adam smirked. "And you wonder why I didn't want you around Jerome."

"Oh, come on, Adam." She sat forward, folding her legs Indian style. "Even you must admit that there are occasions where breaking the rules is justified."

He wrinkled his nose. "I'm drawing a blank."

"Okay, what about Rosa Parks?" Toni challenged. "Wasn't she breaking the law when she refused to give up her seat for white passengers, even though the laws of segregation said that blacks were supposed to? And Irene Morgan did the same thing before her."

"Okay, hold up, Miss Civil Rights," Adam said, stopping her. "Those people broke the law for good reason, to stand up for their civil rights and freedoms where they were being denied. The only freedom you were standing up for that night at the station was your own."

"First of all, I was standing up for the rights of the Atlanta people," Toni said, holding up one finger. "They have a right to know what their politicians are up to and sometimes we have to go to extreme measures to bring them that truth."

Adam opened his mouth to protest.

"Second of all." She held up another finger, cutting him off before he could get a word out. "That was very judgmental of you, Mr. Bayne. You just assumed I was trifling without any facts to back up your argument."

She squinted at him. "Aren't you a Christian? Aren't you supposed to be accepting and loving and all that? I'm not feeling the love, Mr. Bayne."

Adam shook his head and smirked. "Very smooth," he said. "I almost bought it. You can get down off your soapbox now."

Toni winked at him and grinned before reaching for her shirt. "Hey, I'm just trying to keep it real."

He watched thankfully as she slipped her shirt back over her head, covering up the snug-fitting tank top and leggings.

"Speaking of keeping it real," Adam began, "what's this spontaneous visit about? I doubt you felt divinely compelled to come down here and repair our roof."

Toni paused for only a moment. But it was long enough for Adam to get suspicious. His brow furrowed as he waited for her response.

"I actually need a favor."

"Why doesn't this surprise me?"

"Hey," Toni protested, slapping his arm lightly with the back of her hand. "I just fixed your roof up there. Can you cut me some slack for a minute?"

Adam folded his arms. "Okay, you're right. I should at least hear what you want before I say no."

Toni opened her mouth to protest, but then closed it and sighed. "I need more for the story."

Adam chuckled and stood. He grabbed the tool bag and scraps of roofing items that the boys had left behind. "No way." He headed for the inside.

"Come on," Toni complained, grabbing her things and following him. "You haven't even heard what I want yet."

"Don't need to."

He reached for the door but she beat him to it, slipping easily into the small space between him and the door. She was so close he could feel the heat radiating off her skin. There was that vanilla again. He stepped back to clear his head.

"I just fixed your roof." With her hands on her hips and her body pressed against the door, she effectively blocked his way inside. "Do you know how much a professional would have charged to do that? Plus I got my lawyer friend to not just look over your case like he initially agreed to, but to take it on full time. Do you know how much money his time is worth? Do you know how I had to twist his arm to get him to do it?"

He saw a vein near her temple stand up. "But I did that all for you. For free, I might add, out of the goodness of my heart. . . ."

Adam coughed. "Goodness? Heart? You know what those things are?"

"I gave up my time to help you," Toni continued, ignoring his jab. "The least you can do is hear me out." Her eyes burned into his, daring him to say no.

"Well?" she demanded after a moment when he didn't respond.

He raised an eyebrow, and she visibly backed down a notch. He bit back a smile. "Okay, what do you need?"

He saw her relax a little.

"I just need to talk to a few more kids from the center, maybe talk to whoever it is that you work with from the church to make this happen. . . ."

She paused and bit her lip. "And I need to interview you."

"Me?"

"Yes." Toni rolled her eyes. It was clear that she was equally annoyed at the proposition. "My editor thinks that we need to get your outlook on what brought you here, and where you see the center going."

Adam shook his head. "The other stuff, maybe I can pull. But I don't do interviews."

Toni smirked. "You don't do interviews? Who are you? Kanye West? You gonna refuse to be photographed next?"

Adam glowered. It was amazing how easily she could push his buttons. "Not the way to get what you want, Toni." He reached past her for the doorknob.

"Okay, okay, I'm sorry." She quickly slid her body over the door handle as a last attempt. There was a hint of desperation in her eyes. "I just really need—"

He held up his hand to stop her as he pulled his vibrating cell phone from his pocket.

"Hello?"

"Adam. It's Tina."

Adam turned away from Toni to talk to the fellow Jacob's House administrator. "Hey, what's up?"

"It's about the trip over spring break," the woman said. "I just called Sabrina and she says she's not going."

"What do you mean she's not going?" Adam asked before his brain could modulate the irritation in his voice.

"She says she can't believe you still expected her to go after . . ."

Tina trailed off and let Adam fill in the blanks.

After they had broken up.

"Yeah, I know," Adam said with a grimace.

"So we're short one volunteer." Adam could hear the worry creeping into her voice. "And you know we can't go legally unless we have four."

"I know."

"Adam. We only have a couple weeks left."

"I know."

"Adam . . ."

"I'll find someone," he said, even though he didn't have a clue where.

Adam ended the call and looked up to the sky. *Okay, God. What now?*

"Hey, I'm still back here," Toni said in the relaxed tone of someone who had not just been handed a big problem.

Adam laughed. *No way, God. That's Your idea?*

Adam sighed and turned around to face Toni.

"You okay? That sounded like a rough call." She didn't even bother to look up at him as she dug through her purse for something. A moment later she pulled out a piece of gum.

Adam smiled. "I'm fine. And you can have your interview."

Toni's hands froze on the gum wrapper and she looked up. "You're gonna let me interview you." Her eyes narrowed. "What's the catch?"

Adam took a few steps forward until he was only a couple inches from her. This time when the intoxicating scent of her perfume hit him, he was ready for it. "I'll give you your interview, let you talk to anyone at the center, and even put you in touch with our chaplain from Immanuel if you do one thing."

Toni looked apprehensive. "What?"

"Come with me and the boys to Mississippi."

Toni raised an eyebrow. "Gee, Adam, we just met and you're already asking me to go away with you?"

"We're taking a dozen of the boys and a couple staff to Mississippi to work on a Habitat for Humanity project," Adam began, ignoring her sarcasm. "One of our volunteer staff bailed on us, and Jasmine can't go again for obvious reasons.

"Be our replacement, and I'll give you the story."

"When is this trip?" Apprehension was still written all over her face.

"End of June," Adam said.

"Adam, that's in three weeks!"

"I know," Adam said. "So is that a yes?"

"No!"

"You didn't even think about it!" Adam said, trying hard not to sound as desperate as he felt.

"Why do you want me anyway?" Toni asked. "You forget that little speech you made about me being a bad influence? Aren't you afraid I'll corrupt your little reformed gangbangers?"

"No, I'm not," Adam said easily. " 'Cause you only get your interview after the trip, and I know you wouldn't risk it by convincing the boys to do anything stupid."

Toni narrowed her eyes. "How do I know you won't change your mind after you get what you want?"

"I'm not like that." He was surprised at how naturally suspicious she seemed. "All I've got is my word. So if I say I'm gonna do something, I do it. Ask Trey, Jasmine, or any of those boys if you don't believe me."

She seemed to consider him for a moment. Then she relaxed. Adam let himself hope.

"So what's it gonna be? Are you in?"

"No way," Toni said, looking at him as if he had just lost his mind.

"Fine," Adam said, shrugging. "No trip, no interview."

This time she didn't try to stop him as he opened the door and went inside. He had hoped that she would. Hoped that she would walk down the hall, give him her usual scowl, and then agree to do it. But she didn't. In fact, when Adam finally dared to look back, the hallway was empty and she was gone. He couldn't deny the tiny sting of disappointment that lingered with him. Now he had to go find some other volunteer.

He stuck his hands in his pockets and made his way to his office. So much for that.

Chapter 8

"Jas, Trey, I'm here!"

Toni turned her key to her brother's town house and pushed the door open. When she got no answer, she shoved it closed behind her, kicked off her shoes, and made her way to the kitchen. She had almost bailed on coming to see them, but she had left work late, and since she knew her fridge was empty, this would be a quick way to score some food and avoid face time with her stove.

Toni grabbed a banana from off the kitchen table and headed down the hallway. She was about to holler again, when she turned the corner to the living room and stopped short.

There were people everywhere, sitting on Jasmine's special-order cream couch, lounging in her Crate and Barrel wing chair, curled up on the carpet. In fact, it looked like everyone from Jasmine and Trey's church was crammed in there. And she should know; after all, it used to be her church too, before she quit going ten years earlier.

Toni stomped her foot, barely biting back a four-letter word. It was Wednesday night. She hadn't realized. And now she was caught in Jasmine and Trey's small group meeting. Although *small* probably wasn't the best word to describe it anymore.

Suddenly her stove was looking very attractive. She tiptoed backward slowly, hoping that everyone was too busy in discussions to notice her. She was still hungry, but there was only so much she could endure for free food. This was definitely above her threshold.

Her foot hit something that wasn't carpet. Toni let out a tiny shriek as she lost her balance and began to fall backward.

"Whoa, easy," a voice said from too close to her ear. She felt firm arms steady her from behind, even as fourteen pairs of eyes turned to look at her from the living room.

So much for a clean getaway.

"You okay?"

She turned around and grimaced. "I'm fine." She glared at Adam even as she pulled out of his grasp.

"You're mad at me?" he asked incredulously. "I just saved your behind from hitting some hardwood."

"Maybe if your eyes hadn't been *on* my behind you wouldn't have walked into me," she snapped.

He shook his head. "You're crazy."

"Toni! You came!"

Toni forced a smile as Jasmine ambled across the room to embrace her. There was no getting away now.

"Yeah, I guess I did." How could she not realize it was Wednesday night? She never came over on Wednesdays. *Never.*

"Come on." Jasmine all but dragged her across the room. "We're halfway through, but you can still join in."

"Lucky me." Toni glanced behind her, but Adam had already wandered off, joining a group of three guys and two girls sitting on hassocks in the corner.

"Hey, everyone, I want you to meet Toni," Jasmine said, introducing her to a group of three young women sitting on the sofa. "Toni is Trey's sister and one of my good friends."

"Toni, this is . . ."

". . . Camille and Susan," Toni finished. "What's up, girls?"

"Nothing much," Camille said with a smile so bright Toni wanted to reach for her sunglasses. "Haven't seen you in a long while."

"Yeah, well." Toni sat down on the sofa as she resigned herself to her fate. "You know how it is sometimes."

Camille smiled but said nothing.

"Well, it's good to see you anyway," Susan finished. "Hope it won't be the last time."

It was Toni's turn to nod and smile.

"So I grew up with these two, but I don't think I've met you," Toni said, turning to the third woman, who made up for her lack of pigment with her amazing silky auburn mane that fell to the middle of her back. Toni had felt more than seen the woman's gray eyes watching her since she had joined the group.

"Toni, this is Sabrina," Jasmine said. "She joined Immanuel a couple years ago."

"So you're Trey's reporter sister," Sabrina said. "I read your stories in the *AJC* all the time. You're good."

Toni smiled. "I just get lucky, that's all." She gingerly shook Sabrina's tiny soft hand, afraid she would break it.

Jasmine clapped her hands together, clearly done

with the chitchat. "Okay, so we were talking about for-giveness and mercy. . . ."

Toni listened for a while, but got distracted as her eyes wandered around the room. When had the small group gotten this big? The last time Trey and Jasmine had tricked her into coming had been about two years ago and even then it was no more than five or six peo-ple. Now it seemed to be almost three times that num-ber. And half the people Toni didn't even know.

She glanced over at Camille, who was nodding in-tently at something Sabrina was saying. She couldn't believe Camille was still in church. When they were teenagers, no one had been wilder than Camille. She had been the one who snuck Smirnoff into their hotel room on their class trip to New York. She had been the one who had taken her mother's car out of the garage, crashed it, and then reported it stolen. And Toni wasn't sure how many people knew it, but Camille had had an abortion before she was eighteen.

But here she was. Living the holy life. All chummed up with God like she was Mother Teresa. Well, better her than Toni.

Toni stifled a yawn and glanced at her watch. She was missing *Law and Order*.

"Okay, guys, so you know we're all glad you were able to come for small group tonight," Jasmine said from the front of the room a few minutes later. "As usual we have snacks in the kitchen and you're free to hang out for a bit. Our home is your home.

"And speaking of homes," Jasmine said, her face seeming to light up as she spoke, "we have a special announcement to make."

Toni rolled her eyes as she watched Jasmine beam at everyone excitedly. She couldn't imagine what her sister-in-law had to announce. But drama was her middle name, so it could be anything. Toni's stomach grumbled and she wished they would get on with it already.

"So you know that our family is expanding," Jasmine began. "And this little old place won't be enough for three of us. We've been praying, and God brought us to a place. Somewhere that's very dear to us, and somewhere we hope that we can soon call home."

Toni watched Trey grab Jasmine's hand and whisper something to her. She seemed to brush him off slightly and continue. His brows furrowed. The look on his face told Toni that he had not been let in on whatever it was Jasmine was about to announce.

This would be entertaining.

"Trey wants us to wait till everything is confirmed, but there's no harm in letting you guys know, especially since some of you know how long we have been looking," Jasmine said. She clapped her tiny hands together and bounced on her toes as she paused dramatically. "We're moving back home! We're buying Trey's parents' old house. Isn't that amazing?"

Cheers went up from the room as if Jasmine had announced she had just found a cure for cancer. Toni couldn't believe her ears. In fact she would have sworn there was some confusion, except Trey's eyes, which she now realized had been watching her through the whole announcement, confirmed every detail.

Toni grabbed her purse and stumbled toward the front door, her whole body shaking. She was down the steps and halfway across the yard before her brother's voice even registered.

"Toni!"

She kept walking, and fast, her blood pressure increasing with each step she took.

"Toni!"

"What?" she screamed, whirling around.

He stood at the top of the steps, looking frustrated. "It's just a house, Toni," he said weakly. "It's been ten years."

It was just a house?

Toni squeezed her eyes shut and tried not to scream. She could not believe the words coming out of her brother's mouth.

"What's your problem, Toni?" Jasmine asked moments later as she marched out onto the steps, her eyes flashing in annoyance. "You come to my home, you're rude to everybody, and then you just walk out after we share with you something that's really important to us? What's wrong with you?"

"Me?" Toni stepped forward, her eyes widening. "What's wrong with *me?* Are you freaking kidding me, Jasmine?"

"Toni, come on," Trey began, holding out his hands helplessly. "Can we just . . . can you—"

"Can I what, Trey?" Toni said, challenging him to finish his sentence. "Can I calm down? Is that what you want to say?"

"Yes, Toni, can you calm down?" Jasmine said, hands on her hips. "We have neighbors, you know."

"I don't flipping care!" Toni shot back, her hands balling into fists. "Don't tell me to calm down. How could you do this, Trey? How could you buy that house? And then you tell me like this? In front of all those people?"

Her blood felt like it was literally on fire and her ears were ringing so loudly she could barely hear herself, much less anything else.

"After everything . . ." She swatted at her face, annoyed at the tears that were blurring her vision. "How could you?"

"Come on, Toni. That's not fair," Jasmine began.

"Shut up!" Toni fired back. "Don't tell me what's fair. You've never had to live fair in your whole privileged life."

"Is that what this is about? Our money?"

Was she really that dense? Was Jasmine really that out of touch with reality that she thought this was about her stupid money?

"I don't care about your freakin' money, Jasmine," Toni said. "You and your money can kiss my—"

"Toni!" Jasmine's hand flew to her stomach, and she grabbed Trey's shoulder to steady herself.

Toni shook her head. As she watched the two of them, she knew that Afrika had been right. Jasmine was first. And at this point, what Toni thought or felt wasn't even secondary. It didn't matter at all. Trey had been all Toni had left. And now she didn't even have him anymore.

She backed away toward her motorcycle.

"Toni."

His voice sounded tired and defeated as he called out to her. She was almost tempted to turn back. Almost.

"What do you want me to do, Toni?" he continued, a bit stronger. "Do you expect us to just give up the house?"

So it was *us* now. Trey and Jasmine. Both of them got to make the decision about the house that had swallowed Toni's childhood and Toni got no say in it.

"Do what you want, Trey," Toni said. She got on the bike and gunned the engine. "I don't care."

"Toni," Trey jumped up from the steps, alarm ringing clearly in his voice. "Don't go off angry like this."

She put on her helmet.

"Toni!"

She revved the engine louder, then roared off down the street, pushing the gas as far as her anger would let her, until she was breaking every speed limit home. It was only when she shut off the motorcycle in the parking lot behind her apartment that she realized her hands were still shaking. She rested her head against the handlebars and cried.

Chapter 9

" *T* oni. Toni, sweetheart."

Toni was pulled from her sleep by the light, musical voice calling her name. Her eyes fluttered open reluctantly, to find a pair of beautiful copper ones staring back at her lovingly.

"Momma?"

Her mother smiled, her eyes lighting up at the sound of Toni's voice. Warmth flooded through Toni at the feel of her mother's hand against her cheek. She felt her heart lurch and tears spring to her eyes. She opened her mouth to speak, but her mother was already standing up from the edge of the bed.

"Wait," Toni said desperately as she sat up quickly.

Still smiling, her mother stopped at the doorway and looked back at Toni. Her eyes beckoned her daughter to her. Slipping out of bed, Toni heeded her mother's call and followed her into the hallway.

By the time she turned the corner, her mother was already on the stairs, her long, curly jet black hair floating lightly behind her as she made her way down-

stairs. Toni stumbled as she tried to move faster to catch up with her mother, the grogginess of sleep still wrapped tightly around her every facet.

Light streamed generously into the kitchen Toni had grown up in. Something smelled good, like fresh, hot pancakes, with strawberry syrup ladled all over them. Toni's stomach growled noisily. She looked around the kitchen from the bottom of the stairs. The griddle was hot, with two freshly poured pancakes working away on it. Another stack sat invitingly on the counter with the syrup bottle only a stretch away. The radio on the counter that always stayed tuned to Praise 97.5 was streaming gospel hits into the kitchen. But her mother was nowhere to be seen. It was as if she had just poured the batter, and then gone to do something else quickly before it was time to flip them.

"Momma?"

Toni walked slowly through the kitchen, then out into the dining area, the music fading away behind her. The room was spotless like it always was. Pictures of Toni and Trey hung on the wall behind the dining table. There were also a couple of her parents together, and a large family picture from when Toni was twelve. She grimaced. They really should take another one of those.

She heard shuffling in the living room and quickly moved toward it.

"Momma!"

Why was her mother not answering her? It was irritating. She was about to call out again when she tripped over something. She grabbed the edge of the living room chair to keep from falling, and looked down for the offending object.

"Oh God!"

Her blood ran ice cold in her veins when she saw the feet of her father. She began to shake as her gaze traveled up his form to his chest, the point where his body met the pool of his blood lying on the floor. It soaked through his shirt, turning the white fabric a disturbing shade of bright red.

Oh God. Her father was dead.

She couldn't breathe, and her head began to feel light. She gripped the back of the recliner for support but she felt her body begin to give way. At the first sob, she felt gentle arms wrap around her.

"It's okay," her mother breathed soothingly into her ear. "It's okay, honey, it's okay."

Toni buried her head against her mother's chest and began to cry. Wetness soaked the front of her shirt. She looked down and began to shriek when she saw the blood staining her mother's dress. Where did that come from?

"Momma, you're bleeding!"

Her mother stepped back and looked down at the wound in her abdomen as if seeing it for the first time. Her eyes saddened and then she looked up at Toni.

"I'm sorry," she whispered.

Toni looked at her in a mix of confusion and fear. "Momma, wha—"

There was a loud explosion and Toni's body jerked as she felt unimaginable pain slice through her shoulder, and radiate through the rest of her body.

Toni screamed and sat up in bed, a cold sweat trickling down her back and dampening her forehead.

She grabbed her left shoulder to feel for the injury, but there was nothing there. Even the scar had faded.

"It was just a dream," she repeated to herself over and over. "Just a dream."

But it had felt so real. She had smelled her mother's perfume as she hugged her. The one that smelled like a cross between amber, vanilla, and brown sugar. The one that Toni still wore every day. She had felt the warmth of her mother's arms around her, the stickiness of her blood against her fingers. And the pain. The pain had been so real that Toni almost seemed to have a lingering sensation of it even now, when she was sure she was awake.

Toni looked over at her bedside clock. 2:20 a.m. She sighed and ran her hands through her sweat-dampened hair. She had barely been asleep two hours—even less than the time she had been asleep the previous night, before a similar nightmare had awakened her. It seemed like they had intensified since Jasmine's little announcement a week ago.

Toni crawled out of bed and padded barefoot through her apartment to the kitchen. She didn't turn on the lights. The moon cast a stream of light through the living room that was bright enough.

She opened the fridge, poured herself a glass of homemade ginger beer, and took a long sip, letting the scorching liquid shock the last of her senses back to reality. With the last few drops came the inherent knowledge that she would not get anymore sleep that night. She walked back into the living room and powered on her laptop, which was sitting on the tiny desk pushed up against the wall. If she was going to be up, she might as well get something done.

She pulled up the story she'd drafted on Jerome and reread it. She shook her head. That kid had had a tough life. When he got arrested he was suspended from

school, and essentially from his mother's house. There
had been nowhere for him to go. He had been completely alone, at the mercy of a system that didn't care
much about black people—especially black boys from
the projects. She knew how that felt—the being-alone-
and-at-the-mercy-of-the-system part. It was no wonder
Jerome had mistrusted her initially.

Toni opened up her work e-mail in-box and scanned
through the seventy-plus unread e-mails. Most of them
were spam. But there were a few that caught her eye.
Halfway down the list she saw one from Patricia Kentie.
Tricia was a second-year student at Emory's School of
Law who sometimes did research for Toni. Because of her
legal connections, Patricia could often get hold of information that Toni didn't have access to.

She opened the e-mail and sat up a little straighter
when she read the contents:

Hey, Toni:

You asked me to find out what I could about the
legal arrangements between Jacob's House and
the city. I've attached a couple documents on
the initiation of the project from its pilot days and
how the city's been supporting it over the years.
I had no idea this place had been around so
long, and I'm guessing you didn't either. It actually opened up more than twenty years ago with
about ten kids, and has been expanding since.
Anyway, I'll leave you to read all the juicy details
yourself.

I've also done a check on all the staff. Everything looks normal, but I am still waiting for some

info on Adam Bayne. I got something else for you, though, that will make your toes curl. Check out the attached list of all the people who've gone through Jacob's House. You might recognize a few names. ;)

Tricia

Toni ignored all the other files attached and went straight for the list. It was more than two pages long with almost one hundred names. It included not only the dates when each person entered and left the program, but also a note on what each person was doing currently. That column was the most interesting for Toni. A broad smile lit across her face when she saw the name Silver Maxwell halfway down the list. Jackpot. Tricia was definitely going to get a bonus for this.

Satisfied with her find, Toni began to go through the rest of the research, which though not nearly as interesting as the first document, was just as enlightening. After forty-five minutes of just reading, Toni stretched and walked around the room. Then she sat back down and pulled up a new document.

Her fingers flew across the keyboard as she typed. She had initially planned to write a technical piece on how Jacob's House operated as a supporting institute of the Atlanta Justice System, but somewhere along the way it became more of a historical feature piece, outlining the start of the institution and the many great men of Atlanta who had passed through its doors. She included a number of the names of persons on Tricia's list whose stories she knew personally, except for the parts about Jacob's House. She already planned to try to score an interview with a few. Her mind began to spin at light speed as she thought of all that could come from this one piece. This could be an opportunity for funding for Jacob's House. That could help them increase their capacity, hire more staff, fix their aging roof and edifice.

Toni couldn't wait to tell Adam about it. He would be thrilled. And it would score her some Brownie points so that he would maybe do that interview with her. It turned out that Jacob's House wasn't as bad as she thought it would be. In fact, she was almost getting attached to the place.

When she finally stopped typing and looked up, it was quarter to five. She got up and stretched again, this time walking over to the kitchen for something to drink. As she sipped on another glass of ginger beer, the mail on the table caught her eye. Flipping through, she tossed the bills she had paid into the trash, while sticking the ones that had just come in the day before on the fridge. At the bottom of the pile she came across a pink envelope with her name neatly printed on it. Without opening it she knew what it was.

Jasmine's baby shower invitation.

Her jaw tightened as she opened the envelope and scanned the contents. She wanted to toss the whole thing into the bin. But she knew her brother would call about it sooner or later. And if he asked, she knew she would have to show up—even if she didn't want to. Darn that connected-by-blood thing.

She sighed and glanced at the date again. It was set for the end of June. Her eyes popped open. It was set for the end of June! And if she was already away, on something more important than a baby shower, then she couldn't go, and she would get no guilt trip from her brother, or even Afrika. She smiled as her plan formed in her mind. Maybe a week with the boys wouldn't be so bad after all. It would also mean a week with Adam, but quite frankly, he was the lesser of two evils.

She shook her head as she walked back to her bedroom to change into her running gear. It looked like Adam would get his way after all.

Chapter 10

"Okay, I'll do it."

Looking up from Romario's homework assignment, Adam saw Toni leaning against the doorway of the empty classroom. Though she was all business in a sleek gray suit, her eyes were red and he could see creases in her forehead from where her brow must have been furrowed. She looked exhausted.

"Who's that?" Romario asked, nodding toward her.

Instead of answering, Adam handed Romario the pencil. "Finish this up, doing what I showed you, and then leave it on my desk. I'll look it over and get back to you before curfew tonight."

The thirteen-year-old nodded, but still watched Toni curiously.

"So you gonna tell me what I have to do, or do I need to research that too?" Toni asked impatiently.

Adam stood up, his jaw tightening. For some reason she seemed more annoyed with him than usual. He could already tell that her attitude was going to be a joy.

"Romario, stay here and do what I said."

"Yes, boss," Romario answered.

Adam turned toward Toni. "Let's take a walk."

She rolled her eyes but followed him anyway. She didn't speak and neither did he, until they were outside Jacob's House.

"Where are we going?" she finally asked as she followed him toward the sidewalk.

"To a place where you're calm enough for me to have a conversation with you," Adam threw behind him.

"And where is that?"

"However far we have to walk for you to calm down."

Toni hissed her teeth and stopped walking. "This is stupid," she said stubbornly.

"Is it?"

She scowled and turned to walk away. "You know what? I've changed my mind. Forget I even came by."

Adam grabbed her arm before she could take a step. She pulled away but he grabbed it again. This time she didn't pull away. In fact, she stopped walking, seemingly surprised at his persistence.

"What?" Irritation still laced her voice.

"You tell me," Adam said, frowning in concern. "What's going on with you?"

"Nothing."

"Really," he said suspiciously. "Because last week I couldn't pay you to go to Mississippi but now you're volunteering to do it. What's with the sudden change of heart?"

Toni pursed her lips. "Guess I got really desperate for that story."

Adam narrowed his eyes at her curiously, seeing

through her hostility. "No," he said after a moment. "It's more than that."

"It isn't," Toni said.

"You're lying," Adam said simply.

"How do you know?"

"Because I live with teenage boys who lie to me every day. I know what it looks like."

Adam watched as Toni deflated a little before him, the fight seeping out of her like a balloon with a leak.

"Does this have something to do with Jasmine's baby shower?" he asked.

"Why would you ask that?"

"Your brother told me you got into a fight about it this morning."

"Do you guys talk about everything?" Toni asked incredulously. "You're worse than girls."

"You didn't answer my question," Adam said, ignoring her tangent. "Is this because of the drama between you and Jasmine?"

"No." She folded her arms stubbornly. He peered at her and she sighed. "Maybe." When he kept staring, she rolled her eyes. "Why does it matter anyway?"

"Because I don't want you to do this because you're mad at Jasmine," he said. " 'Cause next week when you're not mad at her anymore, you'll back out again."

He trained his eyes on her to make sure she understood. "You want to bail on me? That's fine. But these boys are depending on you. If you say you're going to do this, you've got to do this for real. One hundred percent. No halfway. It has to be for the boys."

Adam watched Toni chew on her lip. He knew he was taking a risk in even considering letting her come along. And even as he stood there watching her contemplate what he said, he couldn't help but contemplate whether this was really what God wanted him to do.

"Is Jerome going?" she asked.

Adam nodded. "Yes."

She looked down at the ground for a moment, then back at Adam. "Okay." Adam caught the resolution in her eyes as she spoke. "I'll do it. I'll go. For real."

"You sure?"

"I'm sure."

"Why?"

She shrugged. "I like Jerome. He's kinda grown on me."

Adam stared at her for a moment, to make sure she was serious. "Okay," he finally said.

"Okay," she echoed. They started walking down Winslow Street, away from Jacob's House.

"So you gonna tell me what I have to do?" she asked after they had been walking for a bit.

"Only if you tell me what that Jerry Springer moment at Trey's the other night was about."

She didn't miss a beat. "None of your business."

"Okay," Adam said, not fazed. "Maybe tell me then why you're so exhausted."

Adam expected her to give another dismissive response. But when she paused a bit before answering, he glanced over at her. She was biting her lip again. That was her giveaway—the thing she always did before she went and did something totally out of character. Like answer honestly.

"I have trouble sleeping."

Adam's brow furrowed. "Why?"

Toni shrugged. "I just do," she said. "I never really sleep through the night."

That would explain a lot of things. Like why she was on edge all the time.

"Has it always been like that?" he asked.

Toni kicked a twig off the sidewalk with her shoe. "Not always, but for long enough. Ever since . . ."

She paused as she seemed to rethink what she was going to say. "Just a really long time."

Adam wasn't quite sure how to respond. He didn't know much about Toni. She was Trey's sister, and he had been best friends with Trey for almost four years. You would have thought they would have met at some point during that time. But Adam had come to realize that Trey and Toni lived extremely different lives. They were also both very private persons. He knew their parents had died some time ago, but Trey rarely ever talked about it. And on the few occasions that he did talk about it, he made little reference to his sister. The only thing he said was that it had changed them both—but it had affected her more than him. In fact, according to Trey, Toni was a lot different now than she was when they were growing up.

As Adam watched the sullen woman walking beside him, he couldn't help but wonder what she had been like before.

"That sucks," Adam said. He immediately wished he could take the words back. What kind of stupid response was that?

Toni smiled. "Really eloquent, Mr. Bayne. I couldn't have put it better myself."

He smiled ruefully and rubbed the back of his neck, embarrassed. "I couldn't think of anything else to say."

"I get it," Toni said, slipping her hands into the pockets of her slacks. "You don't really understand, but you're afraid that if you press me any further I'll rip your head off."

He snuck a glance at her and saw the smile playing at the corner of her lips. "Yeah, pretty much," Adam said sheepishly.

They both laughed and Adam felt the tension ease.

He suddenly realized that they were quite a ways away from Jacob's House. In fact, they had walked so far that they were almost at the bottom of the street where Winslow ended in a cul-de-sac. He was about to suggest they turn back when Toni stopped suddenly.

"What?" he asked, looking at her curiously.

"Isn't that Rasheed?" she asked, nodding to a point at the end of the road. Adam followed Toni's eyes to the park just beyond where the cul-de-sac ended. Two figures were standing under a tree, a few feet back from the road. He squinted a little and saw that it was indeed Rasheed.

"What's he doing down there?" Adam asked, taking a few steps further. He was almost sure the other person Rasheed was with was a girl from his high school. He had spotted the girl near Jacob's House a couple times before.

Toni grinned, her eyes still fixed on Rasheed and his female friend. "I think he's getting his game on," she said mischievously.

Adam shook his head. "I don't think so." He stepped forward.

Toni grabbed his arm before he could get far. "Where are you going?" she asked.

"To get Rasheed," he said. "He has no business hanging out alone with that girl like that."

He began to move forward again, but Toni pulled him back, this time with even more force. He raised an eyebrow, surprised at the amount of strength in her deceptively tiny hands.

"Come on, Adam." She tilted her head to the side. "Don't you think you're overreacting? Rasheed is a kid! You think he's gonna jump her bones out here in broad daylight? Cut him some slack."

Adam was on the verge of thinking that he had indeed overreacted, until he turned around again and saw Rasheed and his female companion making out against the tree—in broad daylight.

Toni's eyebrows arched in surprise. "Whoa, Rasheed, didn't know you had it like that."

Adam felt his jaw tighten. "Guess he's bolder than we both thought."

But before he could move off again, Toni jumped in front of him and placed both hands on his chest, blocking him from Rasheed and his antics.

"Toni!" he growled. "This is not a game."

"I know." She gently pushed against his chest, causing him to back up. "But remember how you told me I needed to calm down a couple minutes ago? Well, now you need to calm down. If you go charging down there like the infantry, disrespecting Rasheed in front of his girl, he's gonna hate you. And then you won't be able to get him to do anything."

Adam glowered angrily. She had a point, but he still wasn't happy about what was going on.

"So what am I supposed to do?" He glanced behind her at Rasheed, who was still going at it. "I can't just leave him there."

"No." Toni turned him around gently and pulled him forward toward Jacob's House. "Does he have a cell phone?"

"Yes."

"So call him." She made it sound like the most obvious thing in the world. "Tell him he needs to be at the house in the next five minutes and then you talk to him when he gets there."

Adam frowned, but pulled out his cell phone and made the call anyway, even as Toni slipped her arm into his and lead him back up Winslow toward the house. By the time he hung up, they were crossing the yard onto the basketball court behind Jacob's House. They were too far away for Adam to see if Rasheed had made a move. But the mere fact that Rasheed had actually answered the phone when Adam called was a good sign. Maybe Toni knew something about kids after all.

"See? Everything's working out fine." She dropped Adam's arm once he had calmed down. Adam immediately missed the warmth of her touch.

"We'll see, once he shows up." He opened the door and let Toni walk in ahead of him.

"He'll show up," Toni said confidently as they walked back to his office. Adam didn't say anything. He wondered how she could be so sure when he wasn't.

He pulled a couple of forms from his desk and handed them to Toni with instructions for her to fill them out and bring them back to him as soon as possible. She tucked them carefully into her huge oversized purse before turning to leave. She was almost at the door when she turned back to look at him.

"What?" he asked, after a moment when she didn't say anything.

She sighed. "Are you sure you want me to do this?"

"Are you trying to—"

"No, I'm not trying to back out," Toni said, holding up her hand. "But come on, Adam, you already know what I'm like. I'm not really good at following rules and I prefer to do things my way. Are you sure you're willing to take that for seven days?"

Adam shrugged and looked down, shuffling the papers on his desk. He had thought about everything she had said more than a few times. He would be lying if he said he wasn't anxious about putting this no-holds, no-limits woman in charge of kids who more than anything else needed holds and limits. But even though she hadn't been around the boys at Jacob's House that long, they seemed to have taken a liking to her. Plus there was that feeling that he had that he was supposed to ask her.

"I've thought about that," he said. "And I know that we'll probably spend the majority of the trip arguing with each other. But maybe that's okay.

"I'm really tough on the guys because I think they need that. But maybe every now and then I need someone to tell me when I'm being too tough on them."

Toni grinned.

"That doesn't mean I'll always listen," he said quickly. "I'll still make the final decision."

Toni saluted. "Got it, captain."

"Hey, Miss Toni. Hey, boss, you wanted to see me?"

Adam looked up in surprise at Rasheed, who was standing at the door. He looked over at Toni, who was grinning at him smugly, as she made her way to the door. He knew exactly what she was going to say.

"Told you so."

Chapter 11

Toni pulled her motorcycle into the last one-hour parking spot in front of Westpoint Medical Center. She barely had time to secure her helmet and grab her purse from under the seat as she hurried inside. It was 11:10 and she was already late for her appointment—one that she'd had to beg for in the first place.

"I am so sorry, Camille," Toni said sincerely as she rushed up to the desk where Camille was standing, filling out some forms. "My boss had me in a meeting and I couldn't leave, and then I got stuck in traffic downtown."

"You still getting everywhere late, aren't you?" Camille said.

Toni saw the hint of a smile on her face and relaxed a bit. "Well at least I'm consistent," Toni said with a smile of her own. "I really am sorry though."

"It's okay," Camille said, waving Toni's apology away. "The doctor's running behind anyway. I'll let her know you're here."

Toni smiled gratefully. "Thanks, Camille. And thanks for setting this up for me on such short notice."

"No problem," Camille said, smiling warmly as she retrieved the forms from the desk. "Have a seat and I'll let you know when they're ready for you."

Toni took a seat in the half full clinic and looked around. She had never been to Westpoint before, but she had heard that it was one of the better places. Adam said it was where all the boys going on the trip had gone to get their trip medical insurance done, but because Toni had joined the group so late, she had missed the opportunity. He had recommended she talk to Camille. But given the way things had ended with Camille and Toni's friendship, Toni had been more than a little apprehensive.

They had been best friends growing up, but a lot had happened in that last year of high school that had pushed them apart. She had figured that Camille would have been hostile toward her—and she would have been within her right. But she hadn't been. Toni was still wondering why.

"Okay. She can see you now," Camille said, sticking her head around the corner and motioning for Toni.

Toni watched Camille as she walked ahead of her. The young woman had put on some weight since high school. It looked good on her. Toni had always thought she was too thin. But her loser boyfriend Gary had always told her otherwise and that had gotten stuck in her head. As long as they had been together—and they had always been together—Camille had been on some endless trip to become a size zero. She had grown her hair out now too and it looked more natural. Toni was beginning to like this new Camille. Maybe more than the one she remembered.

Camille stopped at an open door at the end of the hall, allowing Toni to go in ahead of her. "Give me a shout when you're all done," she said.

Toni nodded.

"You take good care of this one, Dr. Ramikie." Camille pulled the door closed. "She's a friend of mine."

So she still considered them friends. Toni couldn't explain it, but for some reason she was glad to hear that.

Thirty minutes later, rubbing her sore arm, Toni thanked the doctor and made her way out to the waiting area. She heard a laugh behind her and turned around to see Camille grinning.

"Don't worry, it only hurts for a little while," she said.

Toni pouted and looked down at the three red spots where Dr. Ramikie's huge needles had massacred her. "I'm finding that hard to believe right about now," Toni grumbled. "I thought they had orally administered booster shots nowadays."

"Not the kind you need," Camille said, leaning against the nurses' desk in the waiting area. "If it makes you feel any better, Adam's so jumpy it took him almost ten minutes just to get one."

Toni smiled.

"Don't you dare!" Camille warned when she caught the glint in Toni's eyes.

"What?" Toni protested in mock innocence.

"You know what," Camille said knowingly. "I can already see you plotting how you are going to tease the poor man about it."

Toni shook her head. "I can't believe you would think that of me, Camille," she said in mock indignation. She clutched her chest dramatically. "Is that the kind of person you think I am?"

Camille rolled her eyes. "Please. Go try that on someone who hasn't known you half your life."

"Okay, you got me," Toni said, grinning mischievously. "I promise I won't tell him I heard it from you. But that's the best I can do. This one is too good to sit on."

Camille shook her head and laughed.

"What you doing now?" Toni asked after a moment. "I got an hour. You want to get some lunch?"

"Sorry, I gotta be across town at my hairdresser to get my ends clipped." Camille glanced at her watch. "Shoot," she said, stomping her foot. "I'm already late. And with the midday traffic, I'll never make it over in time on MARTA."

Toni shrugged. "I'll take you," she said. "It's probably my fault you're late anyway."

Camille looked up at her hopefully. "Can you? You would save my life. If I miss this appointment, I won't be able to see Tracey again for like a month."

"It's no problem," Toni said, shouldering her handbag. "Grab your things and let's go."

"Okay, where's your car?" Camille asked, slipping on her sunglasses as they stepped through the glass doors of the hospital and into the bright midday sunshine.

"I don't own one," Toni said, walking toward her motorcycle.

Camille's mouth fell open as she watched Toni remove her helmet. "No way," she said, shaking her head and taking a step backward. "I am not getting on that thing."

Toni grinned. "Come on, Camille. It's just a motor-cycle, and I've been riding for almost six years. I promise I'm a good driver."

"Toni," Camille moaned.

"You'll love it, I promise." Toni said, handing Camille her helmet. "You'll probably want to get one of your own too."

Camille sighed but put on the helmet anyway, and got on behind Toni. "I doubt it."

Toni turned the key and pushed on the kick-start with her foot. The motorcycle roared to life and Camille screamed.

Toni laughed. "Hold on, girl!"

She took all the back roads she knew and broke a few speed limits but it still took them fifteen minutes to get to the Divine Hair Salon. And when Camille walked out of the salon after only five minutes with a dejected look on her face, Toni knew that the effort hadn't been enough.

"What happened?" Toni asked, still straddling the motorcycle.

"She thought I wasn't coming," Camille groaned. "She gave my appointment to a walk-in."

"Well, can't you come back tomorrow? Or later this week?"

Camille shook her head. "Tracey is booked up solid on weekends and after work. And my schedule is so tight I can't take time to come in the day." She bit her lip as she held up her hair ends for inspection. "Maybe I can clip them myself in the mirror."

Toni's eyes widened and she pulled out her cell phone. "Let's not get carried away," she said. "Remember when you tried to cut my hair in high school and how it turned out? There's a reason you didn't go into cosmetology."

"Well, what else am I supposed to—"

Toni held up her hand to stop her. "Hey, girl," she said into the phone. "I got a hair emergency. Can you squeeze me in now?"

Toni rolled her eyes as Camille watched her, puzzled.

"You can eat your lunch anytime, and they rerun *Days of Our Lives* on the soap channel," Toni said. "I'm coming over. We'll be there in ten minutes.

"Okay, get on," Toni said, clicking her phone shut and starting up the engine.

"Where are we going?" Camille asked as she slid on behind Toni.

Toni smiled. "To someone who can work hair miracles."

Only ten minutes later Toni was pulling up in front of Banyan Tree Salon.

"What is this place?" Camille asked, getting off and removing her sunglasses.

"You remember Afrika Keswick from high school?" Toni asked as they walked toward the front doors.

"That girl with the dreads and the funky jewelery collection?" Camille asked.

Toni nodded. "Yeah, her. This is her salon."

Camille raised an eyebrow.

Toni laughed. "Don't worry," she said, pushing open the door. "She does my hair every other week. She's really good."

Toni loved going to Banyan Tree. It felt more like an urban oasis than a hair shop. The front area served as a lounge for waiting guests, and was painted in earth tones and decorated with lounges woven from bamboo, large palms in clay pots, and other foliage in woven planters. The exposed wooden roof, and wooden louvered doors and windows, added to the natural atmosphere of the place and always made Toni feel relaxed and at ease.

As Toni caught Camille admiring the terra-cotta tiles, she knew her friend was on the way to being won over as well.

"Hey, Roxanne," Toni said, calling to the girl who was making some blended concoction in the small juice bar to the side of the lounge area. The young woman waved. Roxanne did gorgeous braids, but she also made amazing smoothies for the guests when she wasn't working.

"Hey, you said ten minutes!" Afrika called out from the back of the salon. "How'd you get here so fast?"

Toni waved at two other girls working in the salon as she and Camille made their way to the back. Afrika was curled up in her salon chair, sipping a large colorful drink, her eyes fixed on the huge television screen on the rear wall.

"It's been ten minutes," Toni said, laughing as she fell onto the couch at the back near Afrika's station.

Afrika sighed and reluctantly spun her chair away from the television. "Okay, so where is this emergency?"

Toni nodded toward Camille. "Afrika, Camille; Camille, Afrika," Toni said, making quick introductions. "Camille went to high school with us."

"Yeah, I remember you," Afrika said, snapping her fingers as a light seemed to go on in her head. "You were the skinny girl dating that guy on the basketball team. What was his name . . . ?"

"Gary?" Camille supplied.

"No, no," Afrika said, shaking her head. "What was his name . . . Pee-wee!"

Toni burst into laughter.

"What!" Camille looked shocked. "That wasn't his name."

"It was for us," Afrika said with a dry chuckle. "He tried to step to one of my girls, but she cussed him out good. He got so mad, he started yelling at her. And the madder he got, the more his voice came out in this high-pitched nasally tone. So we started callin' him Pee-wee." Afrika laughed out loud, slapping her thigh. "It was hilarious."

Toni tried to cover her mouth, but it was impossible to hide her laughter. Especially because she remembered exactly how Gary's voice used to go up when he got mad—and he really did sound like Pee-wee.

Toni felt bad for Camille though, even though she and Gary had been done a long time ago. But even Camille couldn't keep the smile off her face, and when Afrika began imitating Gary's angry voice to perfection, none of them could stop laughing.

"I'm sorry," Afrika said when she recovered. "I hope you aren't still with that loser."

Camille shook her head. "No. That was over a long time ago."

"Good," Afrika said, getting up and patting the chair for Camille to sit. " 'Cause I might have to run you out of my shop if you were."

"Please don't," Camille said, sitting down in front of the mirror with a sigh. "I don't think my hair can go another day like this."

Afrika wrinkled her nose as she pulled Camille's hair out of the black hair band that was holding it to-

gether. "You ain't lying, girl. When was the last time
you had a hair treatment?"

Camille bit her lip. "I don't remember?"

"Mercy," Afrika said, shaking her head. "Your hair
ends are split halfway up the shaft. You would be better
off cutting a couple inches good so it can grow back
healthy."

A petrified look formed on Camille's face.

"I won't do it if you don't want me to," Afrika said.
"But you have good hair, and it's a shame to see it
looking a trashy mess."

Camille glanced at Toni, with a look that Toni read
perfectly. A feeling of déjà vu washed over her as she
thought back to the many times growing up when
Camille had looked at her in that same way when she
had a decision to make. They had always trusted each
other's opinions completely—sometimes to each other's
detriment. But Toni felt warm inside to think that even
after so many years, it still mattered to Camille what
Toni thought.

Toni looked down at Camille's hair and then at
Afrika, who had transformed her own tresses the first
time she had sat in her chair. She nodded at Camille.

"Okay," Camille said, turning her eyes back to her
own reflection. "Do it."

As Afrika went to set up a sink to wash Camille's
hair, Camille turned her eyes back to Toni and grinned,
wiggling her eyebrows. Toni couldn't help but laugh,
and even as she did, she felt a rush of nostalgia. She
missed this. The laughing with her best friend. It was a
part of her life that she had given up after her parents'
deaths, along with many of her old friends, her church,
and her relationship with God. She had thought she
hadn't wanted any of those anymore. But just a few

hours with Camille had made her start thinking differently.

Maybe being around the things of her past—the things that she had shared with her parents—wasn't as bad as she thought it would be. Maybe she didn't want to give up those things anymore.

She sighed dejectedly. Too bad she didn't know the first clue about how to get them back.

Chapter 12

It was still dark outside when Adam reached over and hit the snooze button on his alarm. It was 4:00 a.m.—a lot earlier than everyone planned to be up. But it was their first working day at the Habitat for Humanity project, and Adam knew he needed the extra time to mentally prepare.

The last time he had come to Mississippi was with a group from the army to do some relief work after Hurricane Katrina. Adam and his fellow troops had done all they could. They had brought supplies. They had helped to rebuild where possible. Some of them had even given away their personal belongings. But instinctively he had known that it had not been nearly enough. He had been depressed for two weeks after that. But his outlook on life had also changed. That was when he had started thinking seriously about what he would do when his time with the army was over. And all his prior plans for using his business degree solely to line his own pockets had seemed juvenile.

The house barely stirred as he moved quietly through

it and onto the back porch. From there the land opened up a few more yards before sloping downward toward the coast. His eyes traveled the vast stretch of natural landscape before him. As he scanned the beach his gaze fell on a figure standing near the edge of the water. Adam squinted to get a better look, wondering who would be out there at this time of morning. The wind shifted again, lifting long locks of silky hair off the shoulders of the curvy figure. Adam shook his head. He should have guessed.

"Trouble sleeping?" he asked a few minutes later when he was standing behind her.

"No more than usual," Toni answered, not turning around. "You?"

"I wanted to get an early start," Adam said.

Toni glanced down at her watch, then turned to look at him. "Four-thirty? That's pretty early."

Adam knew he probably should have responded, but the minute she turned to look at him every thought left his head. She looked almost ethereal with the glow from the moon framing her in soft light. Her large eyes, which looked like balls of copper fire in the dimness of the early morning, seemed to look right into him as she spoke. He had to blink several times and take a step back just to focus.

"Uh, yeah," he said, clearing his throat and looking away. "I, uh . . . I need to make sure my head is in the right place before I start the day."

Toni nodded as if understanding.

"How long you been up?" he asked.

She shrugged and turned back toward the sea. "Since three. I only came out here half an hour ago though."

"Guess it beats staring at the ceiling," Adam said.

Toni smiled. "It sure does."

She didn't say any more and Adam was fine with that. A comfortable silence fell between them, punctuated only by the sound of the sea as it washed in gentle waves onto the shore before pulling back again.

As Adam watched the water move in and out, smoothing out all the ridges and pathways in the sand, erasing all the unevenness and making everything level, his mind seemed to settle into a hypnotic calm. For a brief moment, he forgot everything: the people in Mississippi, the boys sleeping a short distance away, the things back at Jacob's House that he would have to handle a week later, even the things in his life that he had been avoiding taking care of. For just that fleeting moment on the Gulf of Mexico, he had peace.

He let out a deep cleansing breath and wondered what it would be like to stay in this place forever.

"Want to talk about it?" Toni asked.

Adam made an amused sound. "You wouldn't want to hear it," he replied.

"Don't be too sure," Toni said, turning slightly toward him again. "Which reminds me, you owe me an interview."

Adam stuck his hands in his pockets. "Yeah," he said, turning to look at her. "At the end of the trip."

"Come on, Adam. I'm already here. It's too late for me to back out." She tilted her head slightly. "How about now?"

Adam raised an eyebrow as he stared at Toni questioningly. "Now? Don't you need to get ready?"

Toni smiled sweetly. "I'm always ready."

Adam knew instinctively that she wasn't just talking about the interview. He watched her pull out her cell phone from the back pocket of her cut-off jeans and start surfing through it.

"I have a voice recorder on this thing," she clarified.

"And what about your questions?"

"All up here," she said, tapping her temple with one finger. She sat down on the ground and patted the space beside her, inviting Adam to join her.

He watched her make herself comfortable on the sand, his eyes drawn to her long bare legs like the waters of the Gulf to the shore. It wasn't like he didn't try. He did really, but she was wearing shorts and he was already having problems keeping his eyes off her on a whole as it was. He would find himself on his knees for where his thoughts were going.

However, in spite of how inviting she appeared, he was still apprehensive about being interviewed by Toni. Something about the way she looked at him whenever they were together made him feel like she saw right through him. He wasn't sure how much he wanted her to know about who he was, but he had a feeling that once she started asking questions, he wouldn't be able to keep himself from answering.

He sighed and sat down anyway.

"It won't be so bad," Toni said teasingly. "I promise to be gentle."

"You don't know how to do gentle," Adam said dryly.

Toni tilted her head to the side thoughtfully. "Okay, you have a point there," she admitted. "I'll do my best."

She switched on the voice recorder. "How long have you been at Jacob's House?"

Adam squinted as he tried to remember the exact date. "Three and a half years."

"What made you go there?" Toni asked.

Adam shrugged. "I had just finished my tour with the army, and I wasn't sure what I wanted to do. I talked to the chaplain on our base and he told me about Immanuel Temple and how they had this home for delinquent boys called Jacob's House. He made a few calls to Pastor Reynolds and I ended up there."

"Did you have any experience working with young boys?" Toni asked.

"Not past the squad I was in charge of in the army," Adam said, resting his arms on his bent knees as he looked out to the ocean.

"So why did they think you could be in charge of twenty-one boys in the equivalent of a juvenile hall?"

Adam shrugged. "I guess I didn't realize what it would involve. Maybe if I had, I wouldn't have agreed to it."

"Tell me about your life before the army."

Adam felt his body tense involuntarily. He looked at Toni, who was watching him innocently.

"I grew up in Baltimore in the projects with my sister and six older brothers," he said. "My mom and pops were solid from as far back as I can remember, and they tried to keep us out of trouble.

"But I guess raising seven boys in the projects isn't easy. I got into a little trouble with my brothers every now and then, and when I turned eighteen my mother decided that the best way to save me was to send me away. So she made me enlist."

"Were you the only one in your family who enlisted?" Toni asked.

"Yup," Adam said with a nod. "Everyone else pretty much got their act together by the time they graduated high school. But my grades weren't the greatest and going to college without a scholarship would have been impossible. As well as keeping me out of trouble, the army was the only way I could afford an education."

Toni nodded and looked out at the sea. "You said you used to get into trouble. Tell me about that."

Adam swallowed a lump in his throat and tried to think of the best way not to lie. "You know what the projects are like." He hoped he didn't sound as vague as he was trying to be. "There was always a gang or three to get mixed up in. It was pretty hard to avoid them. My mom wanted to make sure I didn't end up . . ."

Adam's brow furrowed as he caught himself. "She wanted better for me than what Baltimore offered to young black men." He looked away from Toni. "It's the same thing with the guys. I know what their community, the police, even their own families expect to happen with them. They're supposed to drop out of school, get some low-paying factory job, have a bunch of babies with a bunch of different women, and end up either selling drugs or going to prison or both. But that doesn't have to be their future. They can choose another option. God wants more for them than that, and I want them to want more for themselves.

"That's why I got mad when I saw Rasheed mackin' on that girl the way he was. 'Cause if he keeps going that way, then he's gonna end up with some kid he didn't plan for, and his life will be a lot more difficult. He should already know that."

Adam forced himself to stop. He knew he was getting worked up about things, but the constant fear of seeing the boys fail always hung heavy on him like a lead vest. Theoretically he knew that he couldn't save them—only the Spirit of God could set their minds on the right path. He knew that he could only give them the best options and after that it was on them to choose. But somehow in his heart he always felt responsible when they chose wrong. He took it personally when one of them ended up back in prison or dropped out of school. He felt like he had failed them all over again. It made him think of others he had failed in the past.

"You feel like your success and failure is tied to theirs, don't you?" Toni said, reading his thoughts perfectly.

He felt her eyes boring into him, seeing more of him than he wanted anyone else to see, getting too close to the things that Adam had tried to hide away from everyone, even God.

Out of the corner of his eye he saw her hit the pause button on the phone recording.

"You shouldn't do that," she said quietly. She reached over and touched his shoulder. "You'll burn yourself out. Those boys are smart. They know what will happen to them if they mess up. You've given them all the opportunities you can. Stop feeling guilty because of the choices they make. It's about them—not you."

Her last words made him look up at her. She was watching him with concern. She hadn't intended to insult him or put him down. She was just telling him the way it was.

He sighed. "I know," he said after a moment. "I guess that's the control freak in me that you and Jerome like to talk about."

Toni's mouth fell open a little bit. He grinned, loving that for once he had been able to catch her off guard. He knew she and Jerome had thought no one had heard them while they were talking about him in the back of the orientation session the previous day.

"You weren't supposed to hear that," she stammered.

"Maybe both of you shouldn't talk so loudly during orientation then," he said.

"Let's get back to the interview," Toni said, turning the phone back on, and still a bit ruffled. "What does the future of Jacob's House look like?"

A thousand thoughts sprang to Adam's mind but he looked down at the sand and said nothing for a moment. "I don't know," he said finally. "I would love to see the place expand, accommodate more boys. I would love to have more staff, and more equipment, and see the program do more for the boys once they get to the age where they have to leave. A lot of these guys are really talented, but they don't know the first place to go to get direction. I would love to see some sort of extension program that helps with that." He watched Toni nod as if understanding.

"What about your future?"

He shrugged. "I don't know. If you had told me seven years ago I would be doing this, I would have laughed, but here I am. I am learning to take things day by day as God leads."

"Final question," Toni said, stretching and sitting up straight. "Any regrets?"

Images from Adam's past flashed before his eyes in quick succession, bringing with them the heart-wrenching emotions that were so tangible they often kept him awake at night. He looked out at the vast horizon, which seemed to go on into eternity. It seemed endless, like the pain that he had carried with him for so many years. He knew about regrets. Knew lots about them.

He could feel Toni's eyes on him again, waiting for his answer. But he was tired of answering questions. He stood to his feet and brushed the sand off his pants. "I think you have enough for your piece," he said, reaching a hand down to her.

She looked at him curiously for a moment before grasping his hand and letting him pull her up into a standing position. She held onto his hand a moment longer, forcing him to turn his eyes on her. The expression there held him in place and sent a chill through his bones. Even moments after she let go and wordlessly began the trek back to the house, her last look haunted him.

It was impossible, but for a moment, it had felt like she knew everything.

Before that morning Toni thought she could handle anything. But the moment she stepped out of the van that brought them into the community of houses that HFH would be building, she realized that she was out of her depth. She had seen the pictures of what Katrina had done on the television, had watched the reports. She had even heard some of her fellow journalists talk about what they saw when they visited the affected areas. But there was nothing like seeing it firsthand. Toni couldn't believe that even after so long there were still places like where she was standing. Places that looked like the hurricane had just passed through some days earlier instead of some years. What was worse, there were actually people living underneath these piles of board and dirt.

"Pretty bad, eh?" murmured Tina from beside her.

Toni didn't remember whether she nodded or not. In fact, she remembered little of what she actually did that day—even though her muscles burned from the manual labor, and the heat of the sun sucked every ounce of strength out of her. She felt like her efforts were useless.

She had no concept of time, except that at some point she noticed the sun dipping down behind the horizon and realized that they probably had been out there most of the day.

The work teams, which included several other groups from inside and around Mississippi, broke up for the day and got on the buses that would take them back to the house. Toni rested her head against the window and sighed as she looked back at the work site, which in her mind's eye only looked mildly better than it had when they had arrived that morning.

"How you feeling?" Tina asked, falling into the seat next to Toni.

Toni sighed again. "Useless."

Tina laughed. "I know," she said. "We always feel that way on the first day. Especially the first time out. But you'll feel different soon."

"Look at all these houses, Tina," Toni said, nodding to the other dilapidated structures they passed on their way out of the community. "When will all of these get rebuilt? What will happen to the people who live here until then?"

"You have to take it one day at a time, chica," Tina said, putting a reassuring hand on Toni's. "This community wasn't built in a day. We can't rebuild it in one day either. But we do what we can. We build one house at a time until it all gets done."

"And when is that?" Toni asked. "It's been years."

Tina sighed. "I know. That's the hard part. But you know what? It's just like these muchachos. They come to us at fourteen, fifteen, sixteen, after years of bad influence. We can't fix everything in one day. We can't fix anything in one year. But does that mean we don't try? No. We have to try. We have to do a little. If we help one, then it is all worth it. It is the way God feels about us. Some of us take a longer time to fix than others, but it's worth it for Him.

"It might take a long time, but it will get finished," Tina said confidently. "I am sure of it."

Toni forced a small smile but said nothing. She wished she could be as sure as Tina, but she knew better. Maybe God fixed some people. But she was pretty sure that there were some who had to work out their lives on their own. She was one of them. And she was fine with that. At least she had no one to blame but herself. And if things didn't work out, well, the only person she could be disappointed in was herself.

She watched as another house passed by her window. From afar it looked like it might be okay, but a glimpse through the door hanging open showed that inside was a mess. The walls were rotted and there was no floor. It reminded Toni a little of herself.

Tina was wrong. Everything didn't eventually get finished. Not everyone got fixed. She was living proof of that.

Something was wrong with Toni.

Adam wasn't sure how he knew but he just did. The problem was he couldn't figure out what it was because for once she was doing exactly what she was supposed to when she was supposed to be doing it.

It was the last working day on the project. They had completed the houses they originally came to work on two days earlier and had joined with another project to help finish it up. Things had gone better than Adam had expected, and he was already seeing a huge change in attitude for a lot of the boys. He just hoped that it was real, and not just the effects of the exhaustion of working six days in the Mississippi heat. He wanted to believe that the same exhaustion was what had gotten to Toni. But as he watched her move a paint roller up the side of the house they were working on, he sensed it was more than that.

"Hey, you okay, Bayne?" Sam asked, setting down a pail of cement next to Adam. "I think I see three new wrinkles in your forehead."

Adam barely managed to crack a smile at the only other male staff member from Jacob's House along for the trip.

"Yeah, I'm good," Adam said, glancing up at Toni again as he poured cement for the walkway. "Hey, let me ask you, you notice anything strange about Toni?"

Sam shrugged. "Nah, not really," he said distractedly. "Although, she does seem quieter than usual. Not chatting it up with the guys as much as she used to. But then most of these guys are so wiped out by the end of the day they're not in much of a talking mood either."

Adam nodded. He knew that was true.

"Why you ask?" Sam asked curiously, as he emptied the rest of the cement in the pail onto the walkway and got on the other side to help Adam level the surface.

"She's just been very cooperative and low-key, that's all," said Adam. "Very un-Toni."

Sam laughed. "Well, maybe she's just worn out like the rest of us. Although Tina did mention that she freaked out a little yesterday."

"Oh yeah?" Adam said, looking up.

"Yeah," Sam said, not pausing from his work. "Apparently she was acting all weird when the bus pulled up here—almost like she didn't want to be here. And then when they handed out work assignments, she switched with Tina so she wouldn't have to work inside the house."

Adam frowned. "She didn't want to work inside?"

Sam nodded. "That's what Tina said. I don't know what her problem was. If I got to work inside and be out of this killer sun, I would not be giving that up, you know?"

Adam did know, and although it was a small thing, it made him even more convinced that something was going on with her. He was determined to talk to her as soon as he got a free moment. But when the foreman called for a break, she disappeared.

"Tina, where's Toni?" he asked, after searching the grounds in vain for several minutes.

"I think she's on the bus," Tina said. "She said she was going to rest for five minutes."

"Thanks," Adam said, already heading toward the direction of the bus.

"Adam?"

He paused to look back at Tina, and caught the concerned look on her face as she stepped toward him.

"I don't think she's okay," Tina said, lowering her voice. "Something's not right with her."

"Yeah, I've been having that feeling too," Adam said. "Let me go talk to her."

It didn't take long to find her. She was sitting outside on the ground, on the shady side of the bus, away from the crowd. Her head was rested against her knees, which were pulled up to her chest. He almost thought she was sleeping, except she was breathing way too fast, and he could see it.

"Toni?" He stooped down beside her. "Are you okay? What's going on?"

She moved slightly, but didn't answer.

"Toni." He placed a hand on her back. It was warm and damp.

"Go away, Adam," she said, her voice muffled since she never bothered to lift her head.

"Toni, talk to me," he said, unable to hide the concern in his voice. "What's going on with you?"

"Nothing."

"How about you look up and tell me that?"

She lifted her head and rubbed her palms over her face. "I'm fine," she said, finally turning her head to look at him. Her eyes were blotchy and her nose red. She was not fine.

"If you're fine, why are your eyes red?" Adam challenged.

"Grass allergies," she lied.

"They just showed up today?"

"Yes," Toni said, stubbornly looking away.

"No they didn't," Adam said. "You've been crying. Talk to me, please."

"There's nothing to talk about."

She took a deep breath and tried to stand up. But her legs wouldn't hold her and she began falling as she lost her balance. Adam stepped closer and grabbed her before her body slammed into the hard side of the bus.

"Okay, that's it," he said. "We're taking you back now."

"No, I'm okay," she protested, pushing away from him.

"You're not okay," Adam said. "And I'm not going to just let you run yourself ragged."

"Adam . . ."

"This is not a discussion, Toni," Adam said. He was mad at himself for not seeing how bad she was before. "Get on the bus."

She tried one of her scowls, but even that was weak. He breathed a sigh of relief when she finally gave in and got on the bus without protesting. He hoped some rest would help revive her. But he had a feeling it would take a lot more than that.

Chapter 13

Toni was exhausted.

Every jolt and pothole the bus hit reminded her of it. But it wasn't just her body that was exhausted. She felt tired on the inside.

As she leaned against the window, she was glad that she didn't have to share her seat with anyone. The thought of trying to muster up any sort of facade of decency was unbearable. She just needed to get through the next three hours and then she could be home and in her bed, and away from the images that were swirling in her mind.

She was stupid for coming here.

She knew it for sure two days ago when their bus pulled up in front of that house. That wretched house that looked just like the one she had grown up in. It was identical, down to the paint on the porch. If she wasn't sure before, she knew at that moment that the devil was real, and he was mocking her. It had taken everything in her just to stay there. And now she was drained.

She took another deep breath. Only three more hours.

"Is this seat taken?"

"Yes," she mumbled, without turning away from the window to respond to Adam.

"Too bad," he said, sitting down beside her anyway. "I just gave mine up to one of the boys so he could sleep. This is the only one left."

The only word that came to her mind was *whatever*. But she couldn't even muster the energy for that, so she closed her eyes and tried to sleep. Thankfully Adam seemed to get the point and didn't attempt to speak to her.

She should have known better than to choose the seat directly above the wheel of the bus. Sleep was almost impossible as every imperfection of the road vibrated through the window and into her head. She was on the verge of crying from misery, when she felt Adam's hand on her back pulling her toward him. Without even the slightest thought of resisting, she sunk gladly onto his shoulder, sleep claiming her almost immediately.

Toni's shoulder hurt. Really badly. She tried to move but the pain that shot through her was so intense it took her breath away. No, moving was not happening. She opened her eyes and blinked several times. Everything was blurry and too bright. She blinked again and it seemed to clear a little. She was looking at white.

Where was she?

Moving her fingers, she felt something soft beneath them. Carpet? She sensed something else. Like movement. But why couldn't she hear anything? Something was wrong with her ears. She could feel herself panick-

ing. Where was she? Wherever it was, she needed to get out of there.

She tried again to move, this time bracing for the pain. She managed to shift a little. Her shoulder felt heavy, and she reached her other hand over to try and lift it off the floor so she could sit up. That was when she felt the dampness. The panic became dread when she moved the mobile hand in front of her face and realized it was covered with blood. Her blood. She was bleeding!

She forced herself to sit up. Bile rushed to her throat as companion to the immense pain that swallowed her senses. If she wasn't dead yet, it certainly was happening now. Her vision was going blurry again, and her head was swimming, but she had to move. Had to get help. Somehow her brain had registered the fact that she was at her home.

Rolling to her side, Toni pushed herself onto her knees, then onto her feet, grabbing for the wall as a support. She took a step forward but her feet hit something heavy in the way. She looked down and another bout of panic and cold fear hit her as she caught sight of the body of her mother. She screamed, but it only came out as a hoarse rasp. But it was enough to solicit attention. She felt more than heard the pounding on the stairs, and the movement coming toward her. Stumbling back from her mother's body, she held onto the wall and limped her way to the kitchen, a trail of bright red blood on the pristine eggshell walls marking where she had been.

The footsteps were coming. Her brain screamed for her to move faster, but her body couldn't muster the strength to do it. She stumbled blindly backward into the kitchen. Through her cloudy vision she could make out a distorted figure in front of her now. Stumbling backward even faster, she tripped over the corners of the steps, over rugs, over walls and edges that on any other day she could navigate with her eyes closed. The figure moved and she heard the distinct click of metal against metal.

She was going to die.

She pushed back another step but this time her feet didn't touch anything. There was a loud explosion and the ground shifted from beneath her.

Toni screamed as her hands reached out to grab for anything to keep her from falling.

Her fingers found soft jersey material and she clung to it with everything inside her, hoping desperately that it would keep her anchored. But it was strong arms around her that held her firm instead.

"Hey, hey, hey, it's okay. Toni, wake up. It's okay. It was just a dream."

Toni's mind barely registered the voice whispering close to her ear. Her lungs ached as she sucked in huge violent gulps of air. And yet she still felt like she couldn't breathe. She still felt like she was dying.

"Toni, it's okay. You're okay."

No she wasn't. She knew she wasn't. But warm hands on the sides of her face insisted otherwise.

"Open your eyes, Toni," the voice said. "Open your eyes. Come on, it's okay. You're okay. Just open your eyes."

She opened her eyes and found herself staring into warm brown ones. Concerned warm brown ones. Nonetheless her heart kept pounding at an erratic pace. She took a deep breath. Then another. Then another.

"Adam?"

"Yeah," he said. He let out a deep breath he seemed to have been holding. "You scared me half to death a while ago and nearly woke up half the bus with that scream."

Toni blinked and looked around her, realizing, as she saw the curious faces watching her, that she had been asleep. She had only been dreaming. It had felt so real.

She also realized that she was still holding on to the front of Adam's shirt like it was a lifeline. She willed herself to let go. It took a couple moments for her brain to transmit the action to her hands. When she finally did, she slid back over to the window, sinking low in her seat in embarrassment.

"She okay?" she heard one of the boys whisper.

"Yeah, I think she's fine," Adam answered. "She just had a bad dream. Go back to your seats."

A few moments passed before she dared another glance at Adam."I'm sorry," she mumbled.

He shrugged it off. "You have nothing to be sorry for."

She nodded and turned her head away. But even though she stared out the window, all she could see were the images from her dream replaying in her mind. The blood on her hands, her mother's body on the floor. The gun aimed at her. The explosion when it was fired. Involuntarily her whole body began to shake.

Out of nowhere she felt Adam wrap his arms around her.

"Hey, hey, it's okay," he murmured, pulling her into his chest to hold her still. "It's over. You're here. You're okay."

She hated crying. But she was so exhausted that she

couldn't stop the tears. She silently wondered how long she would have to go through this. It felt like every year it got worse, instead of better. Every time she closed her eyes the memories became clearer and clearer. Her dreams felt more real than everything around her. More real than the bus she was sitting in. More real than Adam's arms around her. More real than life. And if this was how life was going to be, she wasn't sure she wanted it anymore.

"Was it your parents?" Adam asked after a long moment.

Toni nodded. She heard him sigh.

"Is this why you can't sleep?"

She nodded again.

"I'm sorry," he said from somewhere above her head. "I know it probably doesn't mean much, but I am."

It was something. Enough to start the quiet tears again.

"What happened?" he asked.

Toni knew what he was doing. He was trying to talk her out of her head. Connect her back to reality by engaging her. She remembered the technique from her brief time on a therapist's couch. She let him use it on her.

"I was sixteen when our parents died." Her voice sounded hoarse to her own ears. "Trey was in the middle of college. I was getting ready to graduate. And then everything fell apart.

"In an instant they were gone, and we had nothing."

"What about your other family?"

Toni sniffled and shifted away from Adam, back into her own seat. "We had one aunt living in California. She stayed with us for a while. But we were already grown and she didn't know what to do with us. She left after a month. Then Trey went back to school, and it was just me."

Toni sighed. Why was she even telling him this? Maybe because she still felt hazy about what was real and what was a dream. This could be either. And talking was making her feel better. Or rather, less insane.

"What did you do?" he asked after a moment.

"I got emancipated," Toni said with a sigh of release, her voice finally evening out. "I got a job. Did what I had to do. Plus there was some insurance to help. Trey finished school and got his commercial pilot license."

A weak smile lifted her lips as she thought of the day her brother got his wings. "He always wanted to fly. That was his dream."

"What about your dreams?" Adam asked.

Toni shrugged. She couldn't remember any of them.

The hum of the bus engine filled the silence that fell after that.

"I'm sorry," Adam said after a moment, the empathy in his voice reaching out and caressing her. "You deserved more than that."

She could feel his eyes burning into her, but she couldn't face them. So she turned away to the window. Empty, barren land rushed by them as they sped along the highway. There was nothing to see. But the nothing out there was better than the nothing Adam would see if she let him look into her like he was trying to.

It was a nothingness that had been there for a long time, and which had finally taken over completely.

The red letters stared mockingly back at Toni from her bedside table. 10:00 a.m. It had been twelve hours since she'd crawled into her bed. But she hadn't slept a wink.

The rest of the trip home had been uneventful. When the bus pulled into the Jacob's House parking lot at 8:30 p.m., Toni had made a beeline for her motorcycle and her apartment. A shower and two aspirins later, she had been in bed. However, sleep had been the one thing she'd been unable to tackle. Even though her bones were so exhausted they screamed for rest, her exhausted soul was what kept her awake.

She wished she could close her eyes and make it all go away, but her eyelids were painted with images from the past. Whatever box she had locked them in was now completely open, and they now had free reign all over her, running amok in her mind and wreaking havoc over her sanity. She couldn't shake the image of her mother lying still on the floor. Her blood, as it seeped slowly across the pale tiles.

Toni buried her face in the already soaked pillow and drew her knees up to her chest.

God, I don't know if you still know me, but if you are there . . . if you can hear me . . . please let me die. I can't do this anymore.

Though it was morning, darkness seemed to wrap around Toni like a cold, wet blanket. It weighed down her entire body, making it hard to move, or even breathe. She was drowning and she didn't know how much longer she could last.

Let Me help you.

The words echoed in the caverns of her battered mind more clearly than her own thoughts. With them came a flicker of hope that lit up the corners of her being for a brief moment. But almost immediately it was swallowed up by the darkness that was slowly eating her from the inside out. It was too late for her.

Let Me help you.

There was a buzzing in her ears. It kept going and wouldn't stop. Toni pulled the pillow over her head but she could still hear it. Maybe this was another symptom of her insanity.

Pounding soon accompanied the buzzing and Toni realized that it was the door. With energy she didn't know she had, she crawled out of bed and felt her way over to the door. She stopped a few times just to catch her breath. Her head was spinning and pounding at the same time. Each step felt like a hammer to her temples. When she finally got to the door, she had to brace herself against the frame to open it.

She barely remembered turning the locks when it swung open.

"Toni! I've been out here for like fifteen minutes. What took you so long . . . Toni?"

Every word from Jasmine was like a shard of glass through Toni's brain. Her head began spinning and she tried to grasp the door frame, but her hands were too weak. She was too weak. And tired. Too tired to think, too tired to breathe, too tired to live.

And so she just stopped trying.

She never even felt her body hit the ground.

Chapter 14

"**A**dam! Come quick! Oh God, she's dead!"

Adam dropped the plate in his hand. It shattered to pieces on the floor of the kitchen, but he barely noticed. "Jasmine, what's going on?" he shouted into his cell phone, jogging through the house toward the door. By the time Jasmine responded he was halfway into the car.

"It's Toni. . . . She's not breathing. . . . I can't reach Trey. . . ." Jasmine sobbed hysterically.

"Jasmine."

He had to repeat her name several times before she finally responded. Even though his heart was thundering in his chest, he forced himself to stay calm. If both of them were panicked, no one would be helped, especially not Toni.

Toni.

The thought of her being dead brought the weight of a ton of bricks down on his chest. He whispered a prayer and switched the car into a higher gear. It creaked and shuddered but it did what it was supposed to.

"Jasmine, are you sure she's . . . ?"

He couldn't even say the word.

"Have you checked for a pulse?"

"She's not breathing. I can't find a pulse. Adam . . ."

Adam floored the gas pedal, ignoring the speed limit. "Have you called the paramedics?" he asked frantically.

"Yes." There were more sobs from Jasmine. "Oh God, Adam, what if she's . . . ?"

Adam felt his jaw tense as the thought finished itself in his head. He turned the car onto the main street.

"I need you to take a deep breath," Adam said calmly, even as he bypassed two slow-moving cars and cut back into the left lane. "Can you do that for me?"

He heard Jasmine breathe in and out on the other end of the line.

"Yes." She choked back a sob.

"Good." Adam tried to keep the reassuring tone in his voice. "Now, Jasmine, you have CPR and First Aid training. You know what to do, don't you?"

"Yes," she said, with uncertainty first but then again with more confidence. "Yes. I know what to do."

"Good." Adam turned the car onto Toni's street. "You do what you need to do. I'll be there in a minute."

He clicked the phone shut as he pulled the car into a no-parking zone in front of Toni's building. As he jogged the last few yards up her front walk, he whispered a shorter more urgent prayer.

God, please let her be okay.

"Please sit down. You're making me dizzy walking in circles like that."

Adam stopped midpace and looked down at Jasmine, who was trying to find a comfortable position in a stiff waiting room chair at Saint Joseph's Hospital. That was hard normally, but became even harder when you were so pregnant you could barely see your toes.

It had been hours since the ambulance with Toni had arrived with them right behind, but they still had not been able to see her. All they knew for sure was that she was alive.

"Sorry, I didn't realize I was doing it." He sat down beside Jasmine and rubbed his hands over his face. "Still no word from Trey?"

Jasmine shook her head. "I left a couple messages on his cell phone but nothing. He had to fly to Florida today so his phone is probably off."

Adam nodded and leaned back, closing his eyes. The memory of the last time he was here flashed behind his dark eyelids.

It had been a Thursday night. He had been playing basketball late with Trey and some of the other guys who volunteered at the center. Then the call came that Khani was in the hospital. Khani had broken curfew and been hanging out in his old neighborhood, disobeying two of the center rules in one fell swoop. Something had happened and he had been stabbed several times in the stomach. By the time they had gotten to the hospital he was dead.

Adam clenched his jaw and took a deep breath. He hoped to God that the outcome tonight would be different.

He felt a small warm hand reach over and grab his.

"She's going to be okay," Jasmine said, squeezing his fingers. "Just pray."

He was way ahead of her on that one.

"Where is she?"

Trey's voice filled the quiet space of the waiting

room. The nap of his hair, normally flat and neat, was disheveled from what Adam assumed was the same nervous raking over his head that he had been doing for hours. But more obvious was the fear that locked his pupils. Adam realized if he was feeling this crazy about the possibility of Toni not making it, Trey had to be going ten times more insane.

As soon as Jasmine saw him her facade of strength crumbled. She burst into tears and collapsed into his arms.

"How is she? Is she alive?" Trey asked desperately as he held Jasmine and looked around for the doctors at the same time.

"Oh God, Trey, she wasn't moving, wasn't breathing." Jasmine threw herself against her husband's chest and another round of sobs erupted.

"She's alive." Adam rested a hand against his friend's back. "But she's not conscious. We're waiting for the doctors to let us know what's going on."

"Jasmine Shields?"

They all looked up at the tall, slim woman in a lab coat with a chart in her hand. "Are you here for Toni Shields?" the woman asked.

"Yes, I'm her brother, Trey, and this is my wife, Jasmine, and our friend Adam." Jasmine peeled herself off Trey long enough for him to shake the doctor's hand.

"Dr. Mornan." She smiled warmly and Adam's first thought was that nobody delivered news that someone was dead with a smile. He released a breath.

"Please, have a seat," she said, motioning to a circle of chairs nearby.

Like obedient family, Trey and Jasmine claimed chairs, but Adam was tired of waiting. He needed to know what was going on.

"How is she?" he asked.

"She's stable, but unconscious," Dr Mornan said. "Physically everything looks promising, but we are waiting for her to wake up."

"Do you know what happened?" Jasmine asked, leaning against Trey.

Dr. Mornan clasped her hands and paused. "We're not sure," she said carefully. "But we think she has stress-induced cardiomyopathy, which led to sudden congestive heart failure."

Jasmine gasped.

"She is very young and there is no history of heart disease in her records, which is why we think that it may be a temporary stress-induced condition," Dr. Mornan continued. "Our guess is that the weak condition of her heart affected the blood flow and lead to her loss of consciousness. We did an angiogram and we did not see any blockages in her heart, which is good. However, she is not out of the woods yet."

"Is she going to be okay?" Adam asked.

"We want to do some more tests to confirm," Dr. Mornan said. "But yes, she should be okay. Her condition is not deteriorating and we think with rest she should improve. We will have to observe her for the next few days to be sure."

"Can we see her?"

Dr. Mornan nodded. "Follow me."

Within moments Adam was standing inside Toni's hospital room. Tighter knots formed in his stomach as his eyes fell on her tiny frame, surrounded by white hospital sheets and connected to IVs and a heart monitor. Her dark hair spread out around her face like a halo, a stark contrast to the white pillow on which she lay. It had been barely two days since the last time he had seen her but somehow her face looked drawn and hollow. She looked like she was fading away.

Trey and Jasmine continued to talk to the doctor while Adam slipped into the chair by her bedside. He pulled her limp, cold hand into his, closed his eyes, and said a silent prayer. Her hand jerked and he opened his eyes to see if she'd miraculously awakened. If the intensity of his emotion could revive her, she'd be on her feet and doing a dance. But she had not stirred. He realized it was probably just an involuntary muscle spasm or something like that. He sighed heavily and forced words through the lump in his throat.

"I'm sorry, Toni."

"This isn't your fault," Jasmine said gently as she and Trey came to stand on the other side of Toni's bed.

"It is," Adam said, knowing better. "I knew something was wrong. I should have made her go home."

"No, this is my fault," Trey said. "I should have been taking better care of her. I should have been watching her. After the thing with the house . . . she wasn't okay."

"What thing with the house?" Adam asked.

Trey sighed. "With our parents' house. When she found out we were buying it, she freaked."

"Trey," Jasmine said, rubbing his shoulder, "I'm sure that wasn't the reason—"

"Yes, it was," Trey interrupted, his voice shaking. "You don't understand. That was the house our parents died in. That was the place they were killed. That was where Toni almost died."

"What?"

Adam's eyes opened wide as he looked up at Trey. Jasmine raised her eyes at her husband's. They were equally shocked.

"She never told you, did she?" Trey looked between Jasmine and Adam.

Trey sunk into the chair beside him, rubbing his hands over his face tiredly. It seemed as if he aged several years right before Adam's eyes.

"I barely know what happened. She only told me once and then refused to talk about it again, but from what I know, all three of them were home," Trey began heavily.

"Our dad was a parole officer for the state. He testified against some guys and because of his testimony, the guys ended up in prison serving extended sentences. When they got out, they came looking for all the people who were responsible for putting them away—including our father."

Adam watched the pain that marked Trey's features as he told the story. He knew talking about it was hurting his friend, but Adam wanted to know that truth. He needed to know what was going on with the woman lying in the hospital bed in front of him.

"Somehow they figured out where he lived and showed up. They got into the house, shot both our parents, and then shot Toni. She fell down the stairs into the basement."

Jasmine gasped and covered her mouth, tears springing to her eyes immediately.

Trey paused, and Adam could see it was becoming difficult for him to breath. Jasmine squeezed his shoulder.

"She lay . . ." Trey closed his eyes. "She lay at the foot of the stairs in the basement bleeding out for two hours before the police showed up. They said if she had been there even an hour longer she would have . . ."

Adam squeezed Toni's hand tighter and blinked

back the mist in his own eyes. He turned to look at her, lying peacefully in the hospital bed. The long lashes of her large beautiful eyes rested gently against her cinnamon-colored cheeks. Her pink flushed lips, which were usually shaped into a pout of some kind, lay silent and relaxed, as if she had a lot to say but chose not to. Adam was learning that there was a whole lot that Toni didn't say.

"She was in the hospital for about a week," Trey continued after he collected himself. "Then our aunt came and we stayed in a motel for a while. We couldn't go back to the house because the police were investigating, and then when we finally could go back we didn't want to."

"So what happened?" Jasmine asked. "Where were you? Where was Toni living?"

Trey shrugged, then looked down. "I'm ashamed to say I went back to school. Our aunt took care of Toni for a couple months but she didn't stay either. But at least she helped keep Toni from ending up under state care."

Trey shook his head. "She was only seventeen."

"I can't believe she never told me," Jasmine whispered, her eyes clouded with sadness. "I can't believe you didn't tell me, Trey."

"She never talks about it," Trey said. "After it happened she pretty much shut everyone else out."

He looked up at Jasmine. "I couldn't tell you. I couldn't talk about it," his voice wavered. "Because then you would know the kind of person I am—someone who would abandon his baby sister when she needed him most."

"Oh, honey, you didn't abandon her," Jasmine said softly as she wrapped her arms around Trey, who buried his face in her middle. "You didn't know how to handle it. You were dealing with your own grief."

"I should have been there for her," Trey said, his voice muffled with tears. "I was her brother. I should have taken care of her."

Adam didn't say anything. He agreed. Trey should have been there for Toni. And even though it would be years before he met Trey and Toni, Adam wished he had been there for her. She should never have had to go through that part of her life alone.

Trey kept talking. It was as if he had carried around the truth long enough and he needed to let all of it out. "After our parents died she was the one who took care of everything. She was the one who cleared up everything with the lawyers, got them to take care of selling the house. Most of the money paid for the rest of my tuition."

He laughed humorlessly. "According to her, both of us couldn't be dumb and broke." Trey shook his head. "You would have thought she was the older one the way she handled business."

He pressed his fist to his mouth and rocked back and forth a little. "I should have talked to her about the house. Even after the fight, I should have talked to her. Maybe if I had . . . Who knows?"

Adam looked at Toni and felt like he was seeing her for the first time. He was starting to understand her— the independence, the mistrust, the unhappiness. Trey was right. She wasn't over it. Not by a long shot.

The heart monitor seemed to beep too loudly in the room as they sat watching Toni breathe in and out slowly. Adam rested her fingers against his lips and closed his eyes. He felt Jasmine grab his arm. And then they did the only thing the three of them knew how to do. They prayed.

Chapter 15

"Okay, I've got Premiere Pink, Satin Sheets, and Shine On," Camille said, walking into the hospital room and emptying a small pharmacy bag filled with manicure supplies near the foot of Toni's bed.

Toni looked up from the morning's edition of the *AJC* at her friend, who began setting out supplies on what was supposed to be Toni's lunch table, but which had now turned into a cosmetics counter. "You know I'm not into the nail polish thing but, girl, your nails look a hot mess. What were you doing in Mississippi? Crawling through the mud?"

"Well, good morning to you too," Toni said with a laugh.

Camille slipped around the side of the bed and gave Toni a quick hug. "You know it's all good. So which one is it gonna be?"

Toni opened her mouth to answer but the words never made it out.

"Can you believe they wanted to search me out

front?" Afrika asked, stomping into the room. Camille and Toni exchanged a look and bit back smiles.

"Asking me if I got any weapons in my purse, just 'cause the metal detector went off."

"Afrika, did you forget to leave your box cutter in the car again?" Toni asked with a grin.

Afrika narrowed her eyes at Toni and put her hands on her hips. "You know, for your freshness I ought to make you stay up in here with your unibrow."

Toni's eyes widened in horror as she slapped her hand to her brow line. Camille burst into laughter.

Toni turned her alarmed eyes on Camille. "You couldn't tell me that I looked like a werewolf?" she screeched, grabbing the mirror Camille had set out on the table earlier. "What kind of friend are you?"

She scowled when she realized that Afrika had been exaggerating. She should have known. "You know you wrong for that," she said, pursing her lips at Afrika.

"Hmph." Afrika grinned as she came over and gave her friend a hug. "I got you good though, didn't I?"

"Whatever," Toni said, rolling her eyes. But as she looked back and forth between Camille, who was pulling out cotton and acetone, and Afrika, who had retrieved three different tweezers and thread from her purse, she couldn't help but laugh.

"You guys are crazy," Toni said, shaking her head. But she wiggled her fingers gratefully at Camille, glad to be pampered for a bit.

"So what's the deal anyway?" Camille held out all three bottles of nail polish to Toni. "When are they letting you out of here? It's been like what, a week and a half?"

Toni picked a bottle and Camille put the other two away.

"They say in a day or two I should be good to go." Toni pulled herself into a sitting position. "They're just keeping me a bit longer for observation."

Camille opened the windows to let out the smell of the polish and then sat on the edge of the bed across from Afrika, who was already using a tiny comb on Toni's thick eyebrows.

"Ouch!" Toni squealed as Afrika's thread pinched her skin. Afrika had recently learned to thread eyebrows. She wasn't perfect yet, but she insisted on using Toni as her crash test dummy.

"Shush," Afrika chided. "You didn't feel a thing."

"So I guess I must have imagined the pain a second ago," Toni said dryly.

"Mmm-hmm," Afrika said. "Just like Camille and I imagined a certain guy who doesn't wear suits, leaving as we were comin' in."

Toni bit her lip but said nothing.

"Was he here all night?" Camille asked casually, as she finished off the first coat of polish on Toni's left hand.

Toni sighed. "Yes, he was," she said wearily. "With Trey and his wife, and Naomi and a bunch of other people."

"I didn't see them this morning though," Afrika said slowly as she pretended to think back. "Did you, Camille?"

"Uh-uh," Camille said, shaking her head. "I don't think I saw them either. I think I would have remembered so many people."

"They came and went," Toni said defensively. "I was so drugged up last night, I barely remember who was here."

"And what's with this Trey-and-his-wife business?"

Afrika asked as she got up and switched sides with Camille. "You still got a beef with Jasmine?"

"She's still buying the house my parents were killed in, isn't she?" Toni snapped back.

"Look, I know Jasmine has passed her place a bunch of times," Afrika said. "And you know that usually I would be right behind you calling her crazy behind out on all the mess she pulls, but she's still your brother's wife. And you don't want to make him have to choose between the two of you. No matter which way that goes, it ain't gonna end well, you know?"

Toni shrugged. "He's already chosen her. So let them have each other and leave me out of it. Jasmine and I don't have to love each other for her and Trey to be together."

Camille and Afrika exchanged a look.

"You know she's the one who found you, right?" Camille asked quietly. She had been silent for a while, and even after she had spoken, she didn't look up at Toni. "Do you even remember what happened?"

Toni bit her lip and shook her head. She felt her stomach tighten as she watched Afrika and Camille exchange a look of concern.

Camille put the cover on the nail polish and let out a slow breath. When she finally turned her gaze on Toni, the fear in her eyes told Toni exactly how serious the situation had been.

"She had come to see you, to work things out," Camille said. "She buzzed and knocked for fifteen minutes. She was gonna leave, thinking you just didn't want to talk to her. But then you opened the door and collapsed right in front of her. She tried to wake you but you wouldn't respond. You weren't breathing, and they couldn't find a pulse. She thought you were . . ."

Camille swallowed and looked away. Even Afrika had ceased threading, and was holding on to Toni's other hand tightly.

"Jasmine called Adam screaming," Afrika continued. "Then she called me. Trey was on a flight so they couldn't reach him."

"T, she was so scared," Afrika said, shaking her head.

"*We* were so scared," Camille added, blinking back tears. "We didn't know if you were going to make it. I couldn't believe I got my friend back for a minute and was about to lose her again."

Toni blinked back the moisture in her eyes as she tried to forget those hours of misery.

"What happened to you, girl?" Afrika asked incredulously after a moment. "Was it something in Biloxi?"

Toni shook her head. She didn't want to talk about what had been happening to her over the past couple weeks. She had never told anyone. And why should she? She could take care of herself. That's what she had been doing since the day her parents died.

"I've just been dealing with a lot lately," Toni said, looking down at her newly polished fingers curled in her lap, but barely even seeing them.

A beat of silence fell among all of them before Toni spoke.

"It was the anniversary a month ago. I can't believe it's been ten years since they've been gone. It feels like yesterday."

She told them about her parents' deaths and everything that happened after, even about Trey's betrayal. When she was done, both of them looked like they needed a Hoyer lift to pull their jaws back up.

Camille was the first to speak. "I can't believe I

never knew all of this." She shook her head. "I knew your parents died and that it had been bad. It was all over the news. But I thought your aunt had been taking care of you. And then Trey wasn't around. . . ."

"How come you never told me any of this before?" A mix of sorrow and anger molded Afrika's features as she interrupted Camille. "Dang, Toni, we've been close for a couple years now. And I feel like I don't even know you."

"I know the feeling."

All three women looked up to find Trey leaning against the door frame.

"Can I come in?"

"Of course you can," Camille said. Toni pinched her hard and Camille jumped and snatched her arm away.

"I'm glad I finally caught you awake," Trey said, taking a few steps into the room, but not coming much further. His eyes looked relieved and sad all at the same time as he stared at Toni.

She felt something tug at her heart. She loved her brother so much. He was the only real family she had left, and she would do anything for him. But sometimes she felt like the feeling wasn't mutual. It hurt to give so much of yourself to someone and not have it returned.

Camille cleared her throat and slipped off the bed. Afrika quickly followed suit.

"We're, uh, gonna run down to the café, for a minute," she said, kissing Toni on the cheek. "We'll be back in a bit."

"Catch you later," Afrika said, squeezing Toni's hand before she followed Camille out of the room.

Toni and Trey watched them leave. And when they

could no longer avoid it, they both turned to look at each other.

Trey sighed. "So I know you're mad at me. And you have every right to be."

He came and sat in a chair near Toni's bed. "But you're my sister. And I hate knowing that we're fighting. You gotta know that I never thought buying the house would hurt you. You always acted like you were over everything. Like it didn't matter anymore."

Toni looked away from him, tears of anger burning her eyes.

"Toni, talk to me, please," Trey said, clasping her hand between both of his. "Tell me what you're thinking."

"I'm thinking that you should have known better," Toni said, turning toward him again. "I'm thinking that even if you thought it was okay, you should have at least told me about it before you announced it to the world. I know I can't tell you and Jasmine how to live your lives. I don't want to. But I never did anything that was going to affect you without telling you," Toni said. "When it came time to decide what happened to the house, I asked you if you cared if we sold it—"

". . . And you took care of me through all of it," Trey finished. "I haven't forgotten what you did for me, Toni. How you sacrificed everything so that I could have what I needed.

"I want to make sure that you have what you need, as well. But I can't if you never tell me. If you act like you're fine and you got it handled all the time, how am I supposed to know when something's wrong? Most of the time . . ." He paused and looked down.

"Most of the time I feel like you don't need me at

all," he said heavily. "Like your life would be just fine whether or not I was in it. Which sucks, 'cause I really need you."

"Trey, that's about the dumbest thing I ever heard you say," Toni said, as she pulled her brother into an embrace. "There's never going to be a time when I don't need you. You're pretty much stuck with me for life, buddy."

He laughed as he returned her embrace. When they both finally stopped hugging, Trey took her hands in his.

"You gotta talk to me, baby sis. You can't be Miss Independent all the time. Let me know what's going on with you. Can you do that?"

Toni nodded. "Yes."

"Are you sure? Do you promise?"

She laughed. "I promise"

"I love you, little sister," he said. "I don't tell you all the time 'cause it's weird. But don't ever forget it. Okay?"

She nodded.

"Good," Trey said, sitting back with a satisfied sigh. "Now let's talk about Jasmine."

"Trey, no," Toni said firmly, the smile disappearing from her face.

"Come on, Toni. You both are the most important women in my life," he said tiredly. "How am I supposed to survive if the two of you are always at war?"

Toni pouted but said nothing. How come she was always the one who got the lecture about getting along with Jasmine, like it was all on her? Jasmine was always the one making waves. Toni was always the one who would have to deal with it. But whenever Toni had something to say, she would get the lecture.

"Whose idea was it to buy the house, Trey?" Toni asked.

He grimaced. "It was a mutual decision. Jasmine and I came to it together."

"You didn't answer my question," Toni replied stubbornly, her eyes narrowed. "Whose *idea* was it?"

Trey sighed and rubbed a hand over his face. "It was my idea."

Toni and Trey both looked up to see Jasmine standing at the door. Toni felt every muscle in her body tighten. She turned her eyes back on Trey and said, "That's what I thought."

"Toni—"

"Trey, forget about it," Toni said, sighing. "Like I told you both before, do what you want to do."

"Toni, I'm sorry," Jasmine said, taking a step into the room. Toni could hear her sister-in-law's voice wavering but she kept her eyes on her brother.

"I never thought that you would be so upset about this. I just thought it would be great if Trey's children could be raised in the same house he grew up in."

She took a step further in. "If they'll never get a chance to meet their grandparents, at least they could be in the place where they once lived."

Toni's chest tightened as Jasmine's words sunk in. Trey's unborn child would never get the chance to meet her grandparents. Toni's own children would never get the chance to meet their grandparents. Though she had never thought of children of her own until this point, the idea that she would never be able to share them with her mother brought a crushing pain to her chest. She turned toward the window as fresh tears sprang to her eyes.

"Toni—"

"I'm tired. I think you should go," Toni said, trying hard to keep her voice in check. "Both of you."

She felt Trey's hand on her shoulder but she didn't dare turn around to face him. "You sure?" she heard him ask from behind her.

Not trusting her voice, she just nodded. There was a pause before she felt Trey stand up. A few moments later, she heard their footsteps fade away as they left the room. Then, when she was sure she was alone, she let herself cry.

Toni opened her eyes to blinding light streaming through her bedroom window. She groaned and pulled the sheet over her head.

"Well, it's about time," Camille said from somewhere over her head. "I was beginning to think we'd have to bury you in here."

"Who opened the curtains?" Toni moaned from under the blanket. "Too much light."

Camille snorted. "Not enough, if you ask me," she muttered, pulling the curtains together slightly.

Toni was grateful that Camille had been around to help her since she got out of the hospital. But the early mornings she could do without. She peeked out with one eye before pulling the whole blanket down to her chin. Camille was standing at the foot of the bed, hands on her hips.

"What?" Toni asked, stretching her arms above her head lazily.

"You've been out for almost ten hours, that's what," Camille said dryly. "When did you get so lazy? The Toni I know used to run on five hours a night."

"Guess I'm catching up then," Toni yawned. "I'm not as young as I used to be."

Camille looked like she wanted to argue but when she saw the strain on Toni's face as she tried to pull herself into a sitting position, her features softened. "Oh, honey, I didn't know it was like that," she said, coming over to the side of the bed. "Let me help you."

Toni slid to the edge of the bed, then put her arm around Camille, and with her help finally made it onto her feet. Still leaning against her friend, Toni made the slow trek from the bedroom to the living room. As soon as they got to the couch she called time.

"This is as far as I go today," she said, collapsing in one corner of the couch. The small bit of exertion had completely worn her out, leaving her feeling like age seventy-seven instead of twenty-seven. Camille sank down in the couch on her other side.

Out of nowhere Toni let out a loud laugh. Camille turned to look at her as if she had lost her mind. It only made Toni laugh louder.

"Remember when we were fifteen, and we decided that we were going to buy a beach house in Florida?" she asked between laughs.

Camille slapped her hand on her forehead. "Oh, geez. I can't believe you remembered that."

"Oh yes," Toni said, nodding. "You had broken up with Gary. . . ."

". . . For like the fiftieth time," Camille added, rolling her eyes.

"Uh-huh. And you swore you were done with guys. You said you would never ever get married. And that you were going to move to Florida, buy a condo, and live on the beach."

"And you promised to go with me," Camille said, wagging her finger at Toni. "I was going to be a fashion designer and you were going to be a celebrity publicist. Your first client was going to be . . ."

". . . Destiny's Child," finished Toni, rolling her eyes. "I was gonna get them to stop wearing Tina Knowles's basement creations. You know they were too fly for that mess."

"Girl, you ain't never lied."

They both laughed as the memories of their childhood flashed up before them like scenes from an old movie.

Camille sighed. "What ever happened to all those dreams?"

They both sat back on the sofa. The silence of the moment seemed to give greater life to the luminous rays of sun that charted a path through the living room curtains and found their aim on *Church in Port,* an original Herbie Rose. The painting, which was previously owned by Toni's parents, was worth far more to Toni than its unimpressive resale value. It hung on her living room wall, reminding Toni of Florida, and all the other plans she had that had died the day her parents had.

Camille sighed. "We should have stayed friends," she said quietly after a long moment. "I really missed you, Toni."

Toni turned her head to the side to look at the woman she had spent most of her early years with. "I missed you too," she said sincerely. She reached across and grabbed her friend's pinky finger.

Camille squeezed her hand. "At least we're here now. It's no condo in Florida, but it's something."

"Yeah, something like a shoe box apartment in Grove Park," Toni joked.

"Hey," Camille said. "Better than a room in your grandmother's retirement village. 'Cause that's where Gary lives."

Toni's eyes widened as she burst into laughter. "No way!"

Camille nodded, barely controlling her laughter. "I went with the Women's Ministry at church to visit some retired members. Guess who I ran into."

Toni doubled over in laughter, tears streaming down her face as she pictured a slightly older version of Gary on some old woman's porch wearing a wife-beater, shorts, and socks with slippers. She didn't know if Camille was picturing the same thing, but whatever it was, it had her friend rolling on the sofa with her too.

They were both laughing so hard that they almost didn't hear the buzzer.

"Looks like someone got her energy back," Camille said as she got up to answer the door.

"Hey, you ever let me see you with that crazy Texan again and you'll see some energy."

Toni was about to stretch and attempt a more comfortable position on the couch when Camille came back into the room, a strange expression on her face.

"You've got a visitor."

Toni stopped trying to move when Adam came around the corner into the living room. She stuck both her hands between her knees, resisting the urge to reach up and fix her hair, which she knew looked like a bird's nest atop her head.

"Hey." He stuck his hands in his pockets with all the ease of a teenager meeting his prom date's parents.

"Hey."

The three of them stood awkwardly in Toni's living room until Toni saw Camille motioning wildly behind Adam. Noticing the puzzled look on Toni's face, Adam turned to look back at Camille. She blinked her wide eyes at him innocently.

"Uh, let me get you guys something to drink," she said before disappearing into the kitchen.

Very smooth, Camille. If she was strong enough, Toni would have wrung her neck. But there were more pressing things at hand now. She forced herself to meet his eyes.

Adam.

He leaned against the entranceway to the living room, peering at her as if she was some strange new object he'd discovered in one of his boys' room.

She rolled her eyes. "It's still me, Adam," she said. "I still think you're an uptight control freak, and you still think I'm Jezebel reincarnated."

He cracked a smile. "I never called you that," he said. "Not to your face."

Toni tossed a cushion at him. He dodged it easily and chuckled.

"Come," she said, motioning to the space on the couch beside her. He accepted the invitation and she suddenly wished she hadn't extended it. He was too close for her to make jokes anymore. He would be able to see right through her.

The silence seemed endless as she watched him watch her. She wished she knew what he was thinking. But Adam's mind was a mystery to her, and even her best investigative skills got her nowhere.

She cleared her throat. "Thanks for, uh . . . visiting

me in the hospital," she said. "I think it really helped Trey to have you there."

"Why didn't you tell me?"

There would be no small talk with this one.

She dropped her gaze and shrugged. "I don't know."

"In Biloxi, when I asked you if you were okay," he began, "you said you were fine."

She sighed. But he wasn't done.

"On the bus back, you told me about your parents dying, but you never said that you were there," he continued. "You never said that you . . ."

He looked away for a moment, and Toni was almost sure she heard his voice catch. "You never told me you almost died too."

She could see the hurt in his eyes. She had hurt him. He thought she couldn't trust him. But he didn't understand. It wasn't even about that—wasn't about him. It was her.

Her eyes started to moisten. There was that annoying crying thing again. She looked away. "I don't like talking about it," she said. "Because I can't talk about it without . . ."

She blinked rapidly as inevitably, tears began to build behind her eyes. "I can't talk about it and not be emotional."

He shrugged. "So be emotional. I don't care."

"But I do," Toni said forcefully.

Adam didn't even flinch. "Why?" he countered.

His eyes watched her patiently. Expectantly. She wasn't sure if she was ready to tell him, though. To be that honest with him. She wanted to. But not like this. Not weeping all over the place like a twelve-year-old girl.

"Because," she said, her voice still steady, even though tears had already begun to slip down her cheeks, "I don't want to be that person who falls apart because of something that happened years ago."

Toni refused to sob. She refused to crumble. She was done with her parents' deaths controlling her and she had been done with it for a while. She was in control of her life. But that determination didn't seem to stem the flow of tears or even still her shaking hands.

Adam's eyes searched her face in concern. She could feel his empathy as if it was a tangible thing.

"I'm fine," she said unsteadily, swiping at her face. "Really, I'm okay."

"Okay," he said quietly, taking her shaking hands into his. "Okay, I believe you. It's okay."

But it wasn't okay. And at that moment she knew it for sure. She didn't resist as he gently pulled her toward him, but gladly buried her face in his chest, till her tears soaked his sweatshirt.

The wound was opened. It had never really healed anyway, but now it was wide and gaping. And all the meaningless things she had used to fill it were dissolving away, leaving only a shell of a person.

Let Me help you.

The words she had heard that day before she passed out came back to her. But she pushed them out of her head.

She didn't need anyone's help.

She didn't want anyone's help. But as Adam held her, she realized she missed having someone there who wanted to help. Someone like her mother. She hadn't let herself think about her in a long time and real sobs began to slip from her as she realized she was starting to forget. She couldn't remember the exact feel of her mother's touch, or the warmth of her eyes. Sometimes she would try to remember her and her face would be a blur. It was in those moments that Toni felt the most afraid—the most alone. Toni wanted to know what it felt like to be loved like that again. To have a family. To be in a place where she felt safe. At peace. Despite everything that had happened, she hadn't given up hope on having that.

She took a deep, shaky breath and inhaled Adam's fresh scent. It was like clean sun-dried laundry and autumn.

"He told me and Mom to go into the kitchen," she said quietly, still resting against him. "Daddy, he knew what was going on."

The words spilled out of her involuntarily, as if they were controlled by someone else. With her eyes closed she told him everything. From the moment they dragged her and her mother out of the kitchen, to the hollow sound of the explosions as they shot them, her mother first, then her father. The searing pain that pierced through her body when she was shot, and again when she fell down the stairs into the basement. She didn't die, but sometimes she thought she should have.

When she was done, Adam was the one who was shaking. She rested a hand on top of his.

"Don't," she said, without looking up at him.

"Don't what?" She felt his voice rumble in his chest.

"Don't be angry," she said, sighing.

After a moment he seemed to relax. Then he let out a heavy sigh. "Thank you for telling me."

She shrugged. "I think I needed to. For me."

He paused. "T, you know you gotta talk to someone about this, right?"

"I'm talking to you."

"You know what I mean," Adam said, his fingers gently smoothing a few strands of hair out of her face.

She sat up, untangling herself from him. "I don't want to do all that again," she said, looking away. "There's no point. People don't really understand. And after a while they get tired of trying. And then I'll just be back here trying to work it out on my own again."

"It won't be that way this time."

"You can't know that," she said, still not looking at him.

"Yes, I can. You're not doing it alone," he said, taking one of her hands. "You've got all of us here to support you, and we're not going anywhere. And even if we fail you, God will never fail you. But you have to let us in."

Toni shook her head. "No thanks."

Adam's eyes widened and he bent his head to get a better look at her face. "What?"

"I don't need a bunch of people up in my business," she said, shaking her head. "I'll be fine. I can handle this."

Adam's brows furrowed. "You mean like you were handling it several days ago when you were hooked up to machines in the hospital?" He frowned. "The woman I saw lying in a hospital bed barely conscious was not handling it."

Toni stiffened and drew away from him to the other end of the couch. "I'm fine, Adam," she said dryly. "Besides, I'm not your concern."

He let out a deep, frustrated breath. "You keep throwing up walls every time someone wants to help you. Why won't you let anyone in?"

She narrowed her eyes. "You mean why won't I let *you* in. Right?"

"Don't make this about me, Toni."

"Look." She ran a hand through her hair. "I'm really tired. Maybe you should go."

He stared at her for a long moment, then shook his head. "I don't get why you're fighting this so much." Confusion etched his voice. "Why do you so badly want to fix yourself on your own?"

"It's the only way I know how," she said.

"That doesn't mean it's the way it has to be," he said sadly.

"Adam."

He sighed and stood to his feet. "Okay. I'm going." He leaned over and kissed her cheek. "Take care of yourself."

As soon as she heard the door close behind him she felt a wave of weariness sweep over her. She curled her legs up under herself and closed her eyes, hoping that it would stop the tears that she felt coming again.

"Hey, you okay?" Camille asked from somewhere above her head.

With Adam crawling way up into that space inside her that she thought she had sealed off, how could she be? What he thought wasn't supposed to matter that much to her. But it did. And now she found herself wondering if he had been right about her needing someone else's help.

Toni sighed and opened her eyes. "No," she said tiredly. "And I think I'd like to go back to bed now."

Chapter 16

"**Y**ou sure you okay? I mean, I know I was on you to come today, but if you're still not a hundred percent . . ."

"I'm fine," Toni assured Jerome, as she walked up the steps to Immanuel Temple, her arm looped inside his. It was the middle of summer and over a week had passed since she had gotten home from the hospital. And despite a little residual weakness, she was starting to feel like herself again.

"Get me a seat in the back, and I'll be good to go. Just make sure that whatever you dragged me here to see is good. I don't come to church for just anybody."

"Don't worry," Jerome said with a grin. "It'll be good—I promise."

Toni gave him a doubtful look, but still let him lead her past the smattering of people in the lobby and into the church sanctuary. It was already pretty full, but they managed to find a couple seats near the aisle in the second to last row.

After Jerome made sure she was seated, he turned to leave.

"What? You're not sitting with me?" Toni asked, not necessarily wanting to do her first day back to church on her own.

"Nah," Jerome said with a mischievous smile. "If I sit with you, then you won't see the surprise."

She opened her mouth to protest, but he was gone before she could think of anything to say. She shook her head and slumped back in her seat. They were at the break in the program between the Bible study and the main service. She could see people making their way back to their seats from the outside, and watched the sound team setting up the microphones on stage for praise and worship. As she watched the band set up she couldn't help but smile. Even though she had been gone for a while, things still seemed the same.

"Excuse me, is this seat taken?"

Toni looked up and smiled. "Yes, but I was saving it for you."

Trey grinned as he slipped into the pew with Toni. He reached across and pulled her into a bear hug. "I'm so glad you're here, baby sis." The brightness in Trey's eyes echoed his words. "Is this the post-near-death-experience church visit?"

Toni rolled her eyes. "No, this is the Jerome-wouldn't-quit-bugging-me-to-come church visit. Apparently there is some surprise I need to see. Do you know anything about that?"

Trey made a zipping motion across his mouth. "My lips are sealed."

She rolled her eyes again, but leaned against her brother's shoulder as she turned back to the front. The full worship team was now on stage and about to start. Though there were quite a few new faces, Toni still recognized a couple of people from the days when she used to sing in the choir. Back then Toni's mother was the choir director and she would have the whole church up and on their feet from the first song. No one could rock the house like Alexandra Shields.

"Isn't it crazy how everything is the same as it was all those years ago?" she whispered to Trey. "Doesn't anyone ever leave this place? Move to another city? Switch churches?"

Trey shrugged. "Why would you do that if you're happy with where you are? This place is like family. Everyone here feels like they belong, like they're needed—and they are. That's why no one leaves."

Toni nodded but said nothing. *It must be nice to feel like that,* she reflected. *Like you belong somewhere, and you are important to someone's life.*

As if hearing her thoughts, Trey leaned over and whispered, "You know, even though you've been gone for a while, you still belong here. People still feel like you're family. While you were in the hospital there were a lot of people here praying for you."

Toni looked up at Trey. He nodded to confirm that everything he said was true.

"Don't believe me? It's right here."

Trey flipped through his Bible and pulled out a church bulletin—the one from the week before. He scanned it for a second, then handed it to Toni, pointing to the inside cover where there was a list of persons for special prayer. A lump formed in Toni's throat as she saw her name printed there in block letters. She ran her finger over it slowly. When she removed her finger, it was still there.

Memories of her childhood stole into her mind. People said you couldn't remember anything before the age of five. But Toni remembered kneeling by her bed with her mother's arms around hers, her hands clasped on top of hers, praying for her, praying with her, praying over her. It gave a new meaning to the idea of being covered in prayer. But with her mother gone, she had thought there was no one covering her anymore. Apparently she had been wrong.

She stared at the sheet for a long time before looking up at Trey. "Can I keep this?" she asked hoarsely.

He nodded, then reached for her hand, squeezing it tightly. Toni let out a deep breath. She didn't know she would miss this. It was almost as if being there, being in the church, had reminded her of something she hadn't known was missing. She felt happy and sad all at the same time. She blinked her eyes rapidly to keep from crying.

The praise team began singing and one by one members of the congregation began to get on their feet to join in. Trey was one of them. Toni was glad, however, to remain seated and just observe. The last time she was in church was years ago, when she was much younger. It was funny the things she noticed now—things she had not noticed then. Like the way people responded to the music and singing. Some of them swayed with the music, others stood still with their hands lifted to the ceiling, tears rolling down their faces. It was like they had forgotten everything else around them and were in a different place.

Even Trey stood singing with his eyes closed. Toni's eyes widened a little. Her brother was never one to show emotion in public. It was clear he was moved by what was happening. But Toni just felt disconnected.

They were singing about a God who loved them, who did great miracles, and there was none like Him. And a part of Toni ached to let herself be swept away with that conviction. But she couldn't. There had been no miracle for her parents when they needed it. There had been none for her when she was struggling afterward. She'd had to pull through that mess on her own. How could a God who loved her leave her alone like that?

She slumped lower in her seat and distracted herself with her iPhone, waiting for the service to be over. After all, she only came for Jerome.

A few moments later, however, Trey nudged her gently with his shoulder. He nodded toward the front. She looked up and saw Jerome walking across the platform.

"What's he doing?" Toni whispered.

Trey raised a finger to his lips and shushed her. "Just watch."

Toni's eyes followed Jerome, and widened in surprise when he sat down at the piano. Her mouth fell open when beautiful music flowed from the ivory keys, and Jerome's mellow voice drifted through the speakers. Her eyes stayed glued to him as he played and sang. She would never have guessed that the bandana-wearing, high-top rocking, stinky-attitude-giving boy she had grown to love the past few months had a hidden musical talent. And it truly was a gift, for Jerome's playing and singing was good. Very good.

He sang Smokie Norful's "I Need You Now" and played the song like it was his. But it wasn't his skill that had people getting to their feet and raising their hands. It was his heart. Even Toni felt her own eyes moisten as she listened to the intensity in Jerome's voice. She had never seen him like this, and instinctively she knew he wasn't faking it. How could this kid who had been through so much, have so much faith in a God who, by all accounts, had seemed to let him down?

When he had finally played the last note and walked away, Toni could barely speak, for fear that one word would send the unshed tears rolling down her cheeks. Instead of lifting her spirits, Jerome's surprise had left her hollow and empty, making her even more aware of the vacuum inside her. She felt her brother reach across and close his hand around hers. She closed her eyes and let the tears cascade down her cheeks.

The rest of the service went by in a blur. When it was over Toni escaped to the bathroom and locked herself in a stall. She crouched down in the small space and put her head between her knees, taking deep breath after deep breath. Nothing seemed to slow her racing heart.

"Get it together, girl. It's not that serious. You're just here for a visit." But somehow her whispered pep talk didn't work and her tears took the last of her makeup with them as they drenched her cheeks.

She didn't know how long she stayed hidden in the stall bawling her eyes out. It was at least a good ten minutes after the last visitor left the restroom. That was fine with her anyway. She didn't really want to talk to anyone.

She splashed some cold water on her face and attempted to fix her raccoon eyes, then slipped back inside the almost empty sanctuary and headed toward the exit. Toni noticed that the crowd had pretty much cleared out. In fact there was only one car in the back parking lot.

Adam's.

He was standing on the steps and she could tell he was waiting for her.

"Hey." He shifted his weight from one leg to the other.

"Hey," she echoed back.

"Jerome told me he saw you duck into the restroom, so I figured I would stick around and see if you needed a ride," he said. "Everyone's having lunch at the house."

Toni nodded and followed him to the car. The tension between them was so thick, it was making her claustrophobic. By the time he closed her door and got in on the driver's side, she could barely stand it.

"I'm sorry about the way I went off on you. . . ."

"I didn't mean to upset you. . . ."

They both stopped speaking, then laughed as they realized they had started to apologize at the same time.

Adam let out a breath he seemed to have been holding. "So I guess you're not mad at me anymore," he said with a grin.

Toni smiled back, relieved that the unease had disappeared. "Yeah," Toni said with a smirk. "For now anyway."

"Good," Adam said. " 'Cause no one else will let me pick a fight with them."

Toni laughed.

"So what was it like for you, being back here?" he asked as he started the car and pulled out of the parking lot.

"Scary," Toni said with a sigh.

He nodded. "That's a start."

She looked over at him, noting his strong profile, the cleft in his chin and the way the sun bounced off the angles in his face. She found it hard to look away.

"Thanks for waiting for me," she said after a long moment.

She reached out and squeezed his hand, which lay on the armrest between them, before folding her hands in her lap.

He kept his eyes on the road but smiled.

"Anytime."

The sun had just begun to dip below the horizon when Toni stepped through the back doors of her office building. She let out a tired sigh. She ended up clocking in a full workday on Sunday because she knew it was the only day that Naomi wouldn't be there to send her home. She felt fine and more than ready to get back to work. But for some reason, no one was buying it.

She walked the few feet to Trey's car leisurely. He had confiscated her motorcycle until she was better, and left her with his Neon as a consolation. It was nothing like her Honda CBR, but it would have to do.

Her stomach growled, reminding her that she hadn't eaten in a while. She flipped out her phone and dialed the first number that came to mind. Camille answered on the first ring.

"Hey, girl, what you up to?" Toni asked, as she dug through her purse for the car keys while balancing the phone.

"I was just about to sit down to eat," Camille said. Toni could hear her friend moving around pots and dishes in the background. Her stomach growled again.

"What's on the menu?"

"Chicken, macaroni and cheese, collard greens, red beans and rice . . ."

"Oh, girl, hold that thought," Toni said, jumping into the car and turning the engine. "I'm coming over."

"Well, you better get here quick," Camille said distractedly. " 'Cause I'm starving and I don't know how long I can wait on your late-for-everything behind."

"Whatever," Toni said. "I'll be there in thirty minutes."

She made it to Camille's place in twenty.

"Okay, so which man you got coming over?" Toni asked after she greeted her friend and stepped inside. "I know you didn't make all that food for just you."

"Girl, please," Camille said. "You should know me better than that. I don't need a reason to get going in the kitchen. I just felt in the mood to cook—lucky for you."

"You got that right," Toni said. "I was not trying to go home and cook anything this evening." She followed Camille through the apartment to the kitchen. "You have a nice place," she added, looking around.

Camille lived in a complete basement apartment near Powder Springs, west of Atlanta. With its own kitchen, laundry, and separate entrance, it was fully independent of the home above it. Camille had decorated the place nicely in bright blues and pale yellows that gave a feel of more light than there actually was.

"Thanks," Camille said, placing a large dish of food in front of Toni before sitting down at the small glass table herself.

Toni laughed. "You already made a plate for me?"

"I told you I was hungry, didn't I?" Camille said, an eyebrow raised.

They bowed their heads as Camille said a quick grace before digging in. It was a few moments before either of them spoke again.

"So where were you coming from anyway?" Camille asked after a few bites.

"Work," Toni said, taking a mouthful of Camille's macaroni and cheese. She closed her eyes. It was amazing. She was coming over here every Sunday from now on. "I was going stir crazy in my apartment."

Camille laughed. "You know Trey, Jasmine, your doctor, and your boss would kill you if they knew, right?"

"Yeah," Toni said, letting out a long breath. "But I'm not trying to be up under any of them. Especially Trey and Jasmine, who are turning cartwheels about me going to church. They think God is going to be the solution to all my problems."

"And you think differently?" Camille asked.

Toni bit her lip. "I think it's more complicated than that."

Camille shrugged. "Of course it is. But you've been through a lot, Toni. And if I know you like I think I do, you probably think you can handle it all on your own."

Toni pushed the food around on her plate but said nothing.

"But if ten years has taught you anything, it should be that you can't heal yourself. The only one who can bring you out of this is God."

Toni frowned. She felt like she was having the same conversation over and over. First with Adam. Now with Camille.

"You don't know what it was like, Camille," Toni said, putting down her fork. "When I was in that house with the bodies of my parents I felt like I was alone. I thought I was going to die. I remember thinking about God as I lay at the bottom of the steps in the basement bleeding and wondering where He was."

Camille reached a hand across and grabbed Toni's. "He was there, girl. Right on the floor with you.

" 'The Lord is close to the brokenhearted and saves those who are crushed in spirit.' That's Psalms 34:18. And in Hebrews where it tells us Jesus is our high priest, it also says we do not have a priest who is unable to empathize with our weaknesses."

She squeezed Toni's hand. "Everything we could possibly go through He's been through. And every time we go through something He is there with us. That's why we need Him, 'cause can't nobody else say that. And even if they can, they have no power to help us."

Toni pulled away from her friend's grasp. "I'll be fine, Camille. I'll get through this."

"And then what?" Camille asked.

Toni looked up at her friend in surprise.

"Okay," Camille said, sitting back. "Let's say you get it together on your own. It's unlikely, but let's say you do. You deal with all your issues. What happens after that?"

Toni cocked her head to the side. "Are you gonna get preachy?"

"Yes," Camille said without hesitating. "But you're eating my food so you can hear me out for thirty seconds."

Toni rolled her eyes.

"In the book of Matthew there's this story about this man who's controlled by an impure spirit," Camille begins. "Somehow the spirit is removed from him and the man is free. But then the spirit roams around, and finding nowhere else to settle, comes back to the man he was in before.

"This man had gotten his life together, but because he was still empty, because he hadn't filled the vacancy, the impure spirit left with something of more value. The impure spirit was able to again take hold of his life. And the parable says the second time around it was worse than the first."

"I'm not possessed, Camille," Toni said.

"No, but you're empty," her friend said. "And that's just as dangerous. And that space inside you, that gaping hole that you try to fill with work and everything else, that's the place where God needs to be."

Camille looked down at her plate. "Trust me, I know. I've walked that road."

Toni sighed. "You're talking about the abortion, aren't you?"

Camille nodded. Toni noticed that she didn't look up at her.

Toni put down her fork and sighed. "Look, Camille, I am really sorry about that. I shouldn't have gotten mad at you about having the abortion. I had no idea what you were going through and I had no right to judge you. I should have been there with you. I'm sorry—"

"It's okay," Camille said. She still hadn't looked up but she had put down her fork and stopped eating. "I should have listened to you when you told me not to do it. I was just so desperate. After I did it, though, I felt so terrible. I didn't sleep for weeks. I was so depressed."

A pained expression contorted her features. "I even tried to commit suicide."

"Oh, honey, I didn't know," Toni said, grabbing Camille's hand and holding it tight. "I am so sorry I wasn't there. I shouldn't have bailed on our friendship like that."

"You were going through your own stuff," Camille

said, shaking her head. "It was near when your parents died."

Toni watched her friend blink back tears. The memories of that time came flooding back to Toni. She remembered the horrible argument she and Camille had had about the baby. Toni had always thought abortion was wrong and so had Camille. But when she found out that she was pregnant and Gary broke up with her, denying the kid was his, she had felt like there was no other option. She had gone to Toni for support, but Toni had gotten mad at her and accused her of being selfish. They both had said some hurtful things.

"How did your mom take it?" Toni asked.

Camille shook her head. "She was so mad. She wouldn't talk to me for weeks. I think she was more upset about the fact that I had an abortion than about the pregnancy. She never threw me out or anything, but she might as well have. She wouldn't speak to me, and every time she looked at me it seemed like it broke her heart all over."

"That must have been horrible," Toni said, still holding on to Camille's hand.

Camille nodded. "Yeah, but Pastor and Sis Reynolds, and a lot of people from Immanuel were really there for me. I don't think I would have survived that year without them."

"You know when I saw you at Jasmine's place a couple months back, I was pretty surprised," Toni said. "I had thought for sure that you would have left the church a long time ago."

"I probably would have," Camille said. "If it wasn't for my Immanuel family, who knows?"

Toni nodded.

"That's why I'm going so hard with you," Camille

said, tilting her head so she could meet Toni's eyes. "I know you can get past this."

Toni bit her lip and blinked back the moisture from her eyes. "Thanks."

"So anyway," Camille said, sitting up with a little laugh and wiping her eyes, "my life is not totally depressing. After everything I went to college, got my nursing degree, got a job at the clinic, and here I am."

Toni nodded, going back to her food. "You look like you did good for yourself. You got it all together now."

"Well," Camille said, taking a forkful of chicken. "It ain't all together."

Toni watched her friend curiously but said nothing. Camille chewed a bit thoughtfully before speaking again.

"I've been thinking about moving."

"To a new place?" Toni asked.

Camille bit her lip. "To a new city."

Toni's eyes widened. "Really?"

"Yeah," Camille said. "I love Atlanta, but it would be nice to live somewhere else for a while, you know? Maybe LA or New York or Boston."

Toni's eyebrows went up. "Wow, you're serious."

"Of course I am," Camille said. "Why wouldn't I be? I'm twenty-seven, I've got no husband, no kids, no debt, nothing to keep me tied to the ATL. When else in my life am I going to be able to up and move? I'm surprised you sound so shocked. You were always the more adventurous one of the two of us."

"I know, but I don't know if I could just up and move," Toni said, shaking her head. "I've got a job here, and then there's Trey and Jasmine and the baby, and Afrika. . . ."

Camille made a sound in her throat and Toni looked up.

"What?"

"Nothing," Camille said.

Toni noticed her friend didn't meet her eyes. Toni put down her fork and folded her arms. "That's not a nothing sound. That's an I-don't-believe-you sound."

"Okay," Camille said, looking up, a small smile playing on her lips. "You sure those are the *only* reasons that you don't want to leave?"

"Of course those are the only reasons," Toni protested. "Why else wouldn't I want to leave?"

Camille looked at Toni for a long moment before putting down her own fork. "So you not wanting to go has nothing to do with Adam?"

Toni scowled. "Why would Adam figure into the equation?"

"I don't know," Camille said, in a voice that suggested otherwise. "You tell me."

"He doesn't figure," Toni said stubbornly. "I don't even know the guy. You probably know a lot more about him than I do."

"Not really. He's pretty private," Camille admitted. "You should probably ask Sabrina. They were dating for a while."

"Sabrina?" Toni repeated, her eyes widening. "Small-group Sabrina?"

"The very same," Camille said with a laugh. "Anyway, he's free and clear now, if you're interested."

"I'm not." Toni sawed away at a piece of chicken breast.

"Okay." Camille got up and took her plate to the sink. "But if you are, I'll just remind you of the vultures."

Toni laughed out loud. "You're terrible, Camille."

"Hey, I just speak the truth." Camille shrugged. "With those women at Immanuel circling, the good ones don't stay in the water long."

"Sounds like you have a little crush." Toni tilted her head to the side, considering her friend.

"Nah. Adam's like a brother to me." Camille turned on the water to wash her plate. "Besides, a lot of people at Immanuel in our age group know what happened with me."

She wrinkled her nose. "Maybe it's not so much that I want to move. I just want to be with someone who doesn't know my past before they get to know me."

Toni nodded. She definitely understood that feeling. And as she thought about herself, Camille, and even Jerome, she couldn't help but think it was amazing how so many people seemed to be looking for the same thing.

Chapter 17

A dam and Jerome walked up the front steps of the Westwood Towers and through the large impressive lobby to the front desk.

"We're here to see Dwayne Cartwright," Adam said to the poised young woman with a headset sitting behind the divide.

She smiled warmly. "Your names?"

Adam gave her their names and she gave him building passes and directions to Dwayne's office on the eighth floor.

"Thanks," Adam said, before heading in the direction she pointed. Jerome was busy looking around, and Adam had to tug at his arm to get him to focus.

Jerome let out a whistle once they were a distance from the reception desk. "Man, these people must be up to their armpits in cheese. Are you checking these floors, Bayne? They so shiny I can see my face in them. And do you see the swimming pool in the middle of the lobby?"

Adam chuckled. "It's not a swimming pool, it's a fountain."

"Yeah, well, I ain't never seen no fountain big enough for me to do laps in," Jerome said dryly, as they stepped into the elevator.

Even though Adam had laughed at Jerome's exaggeration, he had to admit that Westwood Towers did scream money. It was obvious that anyone who worked there must have it to spare—including Toni's lawyer friend Dwayne. As they walked down the hall to his office, Adam couldn't help but wonder how Toni knew someone like Dwayne well enough to pull the kind of strings she was pulling for them. Was he an old boyfriend? A current boyfriend? A lover? He felt the muscles in his neck tighten with every additional possibility. Maybe it was best he just not explore the thought at all.

Dwayne's door was open when Adam and Jerome finally found it.

"Come in," Dwayne said, standing from his desk when he saw Adam and Jerome lingering at the entrance. "Did you find the place okay? I know this isn't really your part of town," Dwayne said with a light laugh.

Adam frowned, and Jerome's eyes hardened.

"What's that supposed to mean?" Jerome asked.

"Nothing." Dwayne cleared his throat. "I just meant that most people don't come to this side unless they work in the towers. . . . . I never meant—"

"We found the place fine," Adam said, deciding to end Dwayne's discomfort. "Thank you for seeing us."

Dwayne ran a hand over the back of his neck. "No problem. Please, have a seat."

The three of them sat in uncomfortable silence as Dwayne shuffled through some papers on his desk. Adam's eyes followed the slim black man. He was tall, almost the same height as Adam, with smooth almond-toned skin. His curly brown hair gave away his mixed roots, however. Even though it was cropped close to his head, Adam could tell that he wasn't all black.

Shiny silver cuffs peeked through the sleeves of his gray pinstriped suit, which Adam could tell was expensive. Even though it was boiling outside, Dwayne was decked out in a jacket and tie. Adam figured the guy could pull that off working in a building so fully air-conditioned it felt like a New York winter.

Dwayne cleared his throat again and looked up at Adam and Jerome, who were both watching him. "So I wanted to talk to you both about the case," he began. "The prosecution is taking an aggressive approach but I still think we can get you out of this. The goal is to try and keep the case from going to trial."

Adam nodded. He had been reading up on similar cases, and he had arrived at the same conclusion. If they could somehow come to some kind of deal, or even get the case thrown out before they got in front of a judge, they had a better chance of ensuring Jerome got no prison time.

"So the key is to strike a bargain with the prosecution and get them to drop the case," Dwayne continued. "If we can give them something, they might be willing to go easy on you."

Adam sat forward a little. "What are you suggesting?"

"Well," Dwayne said, turning his focus toward Jerome, "I think if you agree to serve eighteen months, I can get you out on parole after a year—"

"You want me to serve time?" Jerome said angrily, jumping to his feet. "I thought you were supposed to be helping me stay out of jail."

"I'm helping you get the best out of this situation. And twelve months is better than three years," Dwayne said.

"But I didn't do nothin'!"

"You didn't do nothing?" Dwayne repeated, his eyebrows going up. He began flipping through Jerome's file in front of him. "It says here you were caught at the scene of an attempted car theft—"

"But it wasn't even my idea!"

"You resisted arrest—"

"The cop shoved my face into the ground, and put his foot on my neck—"

"You aided the escape of your two accomplices; you refused to cooperate with the police; and you were found with marijuana on your person at the time of arrest," Dwayne read from Jerome's rap sheet.

"I didn't help nobody get away. They left me," he said, beating his chest for emphasis. "And that weed thing was straight-up bogus. Even the cops at the station said that.

"Man, I don't need this," Jerome said, scowling and heading toward the door. "This is whack."

"Jerome." Adam's voice stopped Jerome short of the door, in no uncertain terms. *"Sit down."*

Adam could almost feel the hostility radiating off Jerome in waves, but eventually the young man turned around, walked back to his chair, and dropped into it. He shot a look so poisonous at Dwayne that the man pushed back from his desk a little.

Adam looked down at his hands folded in his lap. He had always known that there was a possibility

Jerome would end up serving time. It was just the way the system was. And if all that Toni had told him about the case was right, then the only way to appease the real people pulling the strings would be to make them feel like they had won a little—and Jerome in jail, even for a short period, achieved that. But that didn't mean Jerome planned to accept it. Even though it was hard to see, Adam knew the God he served was in control of the entire situation. If anyone could create a way out of this one for Jerome, it would be Him.

"What other options do we have?" Adam asked after a long moment.

"Not many," Dwayne said, his forehead wrinkling. "We could take our chances at trial, which we would probably end up losing; or we could agree to plead guilty to a charge of accessory to theft, which would carry a lighter sentence. It would still carry jail time, however."

"So basically, you're proposing that Jerome plead guilty and serve time for a crime he didn't commit," Adam said calmly.

"I'm saying that the prosecution wants Jerome in jail," Dwayne deadpanned. "They're going to try to get that one way or another. If we don't plead out, then they're going to take us to trial and go for at least five years. And they might be able to pull it off, given the other car theft they've tagged onto his case. Now I'll go with whatever you decide. The choice is yours. But if I was looking at eighteen months in jail versus five years, I would go with the eighteen months."

"Eighteen months and a police record that has Jerome listed as guilty of grand theft auto," Adam said. "A record that will follow him around for a lot longer than a year and a half."

Dwayne grimaced and sat back. "I can talk to them about keeping it off his record, but that might mean taking the parole off the table." He sighed. "I am just your lawyer. I can advise you of what's best but I can't make you do anything. At the end of the day it's up to you. What do you want to do?"

"We want you to come up with some better options," Adam said matter-of-factly. "Ones that involve no jail time for Jerome and don't have him in your system as a convicted felon. We told you what happened," Adam continued. "Jerome didn't do this. He knows that he shouldn't have been where he was that day, and that's why he admitted to criminal mischief. And he has been at Jacob's House for the last year and a half. He shouldn't have to serve more time. I heard you were good. Make the right thing happen for Jerome on this one. Please."

Dwayne ran a hand over his head. "All right. I'll talk to the DA and see what we can work out. But still, think about what we discussed. If it comes down to it, you should know what you're willing to accept."

They got to their feet.

"Thanks," Adam said, shaking Dwayne's hand. He nodded for Jerome to do the same. Grudgingly the young man complied, but then he made a beeline for the door.

As they waited for the elevator to come to their floor, Adam glanced back down the hall at Dwayne's office. The meeting had left him even more concerned about Jerome's fate than before, but it had also helped Adam to realize something that he had suspected all along.

It was going to take divine intervention to keep Jerome out of prison.

Chapter 18

"**M**r. Maxwell will see you now."

It was about time. Toni only had to wait three weeks to get on the man's calendar for an appointment, and then another thirty minutes in his lobby—even though she had been on time.

She wasn't going to be a diva though. Silver was in high demand. He was also very picky about the reporters he entertained meetings with. She had lucked out in getting onto his schedule at all—especially now that he had officially announced his plans to run in the coming election.

Silver Maxwell was Atlanta's celebrity mayor. Though he had only served one term, which ended almost seven years ago, the Atlanta people loved him so much that his name ended up on a ballot for something every election. He was in the news almost every week. It would be almost sickening if he wasn't so irritatingly charming. Even Toni, who couldn't stomach most politicians, had a little celebrity crush on him. He was exactly what she needed to take her story from good to great.

Smiling, she stood to her feet and followed the perky and impeccably dressed receptionist and her afro down a short hallway and around a corner into Silver's office. Like the rest of the floor, the spacious office was decorated in earth tones, with carved wooden sculptures, beaded rugs, handwoven wall hangings, and other pieces of African art. So it seemed Silver was in touch with his roots, from the hired help to the decor. Toni hoped that would work to her advantage.

Silver's desk was positioned in front of a large window that covered one entire wall and offered a panoramic view of the Atlanta cityscape. This is where she found him sitting.

"Ms. Shields, pleasure to have you stop by today," he said, rising from his plush office chair to shake Toni's hand. Even from where she was standing, she could tell that the thing was genuine leather and probably cost more than her whole sofa. Silver might be about the working class people, but he definitely wasn't living like one of them.

"The pleasure is mine, Mr. Maxwell," Toni said, her lips curving into a smile. "And please, call me Toni."

"Well, then I must insist that you call me Silver," he said, his eyes sparkling mischievously as he smiled back.

Toni shook her head. There it was—that Silver charm. It didn't hurt also that Silver didn't look a day over thirty-five even though he was well into his forties. And from the photos, Toni knew that his coffee-colored skin, chiseled features, and rugged handsomeness were the same as they were twenty years ago. Toni didn't know who was hanging on Silver's arm these days, but she was one lucky woman.

She accepted the seat he offered her across from his

desk and tried to remember she was a veteran reporter and not a seventeen-year-old schoolgirl with a crush.

"So, what can I do for you today, Toni?" Silver asked, once she was seated.

"Well, I am actually working on a series for the *AJC* on one of our local youth facilities," Toni said, easing into the topic. "You might have heard of it, the Jacob's House Young Men's Center?"

Toni watched Silver carefully. But if he recognized the name of Jacob's House at all, he didn't show it.

"I am a little familiar with it," he said, nodding for her to continue.

"Yes, well, there is a young man at the center, Jerome Douglas, who about eighteen months ago began to serve out time there because of a carjacking that he was alleged to be involved with. He has almost completed his time but his case has been reopened in court and there seems to be an attempt to have him resentenced so he ends up serving hard time.

"There have also been questions at high levels about the effectiveness and value of the center as an alternative sentencing option for young men who pass through Atlanta's justice system. There have even been suggestions about having it shut down."

Toni paused, waiting for Silver to say something. Anything.

"This is all quite interesting, Ms. Shields," Silver said, a small, cautious smile still playing at his lips. "I am just not sure what this all has to do with me."

Toni sat back. So he wasn't going to give away anything. She would have to pull it out of him. That was fine. She could do that. She could do that very well.

"We've been doing a lot of research on Jacob's House and have found out that over the more than twenty years that it has been around, it has helped a number of young men within this city," she said purposefully, her eyes still fixed on him. "Many of whom have gone on to be outstanding citizens, loved and respected by the Atlanta community."

Silver leaned back in his chair.

"We were hoping to interview one or two of these men for our series," Toni said, smiling. "Men like you."

Silver rocked back in his chair thoughtfully and considered Toni for a long moment. "I've always loved your stories, Toni. For a while your front page pieces used to be the first thing I would read in the morning when I got to the office."

He chuckled. "That exposé you did on the mayor a couple weeks ago was actually what made me reconsider running in the next mayoral election. You seem to have a knack for finding the most elusive information."

Toni smiled tightly. "I just do my job, Silver."

"Yes," Silver said, nodding. "That you do. And very well, it seems."

"Haven't seen you on the front page for a while now, though." He cocked his head to the side as he considered her. "But a story like this, about a current mayoral candidate's potentially seedy past, that just might put you in the headlines again, right?"

Toni's smile faded a little. "That's not why I'm doing this. The young man in question, Jerome Douglas, I have met personally. He's a good kid who was just in the wrong place at the wrong time. And I know it sounds clichéd but it's the truth," Toni said earnestly. "I've also met a lot of the boys in that home, and others who have gone through it. Most of them are good people who just needed a second chance. If they shut down

Jacob's House, a lot of young men now and in the future will suffer because of it."

He continued watching her but said nothing.

"I just want people to see that something good can come out of this place—that it's worth keeping around," Toni finished.

Silver pressed the tips of his fingers together thoughtfully before swiveling his chair around to face the window. He sat there looking out a long time, until Toni began to wonder if he had forgotten that she was in the room.

"Let me tell you a story." He was still facing the window, with his back to Toni. "There once was a young boy who grew up in the projects in Atlanta. His mother was sixteen when she had him and was in no condition to take care of herself much more a child. So the city took him. He bounced around for a while and ended up in a wonderful foster home where his foster father would pay him five dollars for every cocaine drop he would make for him. By the time this young man was fifteen he was making his own drops independent of his foster father, who happened to have been shot for being stupid."

Toni grimaced. If she had a dollar for every time she heard a story like this, she could buy herself some designer shoes. She had lost her parents, but while they were alive she had been very fortunate. They had been good people.

"This young man was out doing one of his drops one day when he got caught by the police in a raid," Silver continued, still staring out the window. "He got taken to the station and was crowded into a cell with a bunch of other pushers and hard criminals. Most of them went to jail, but a social worker who knew his case took pity on him and got him into a special center where he could serve out his time instead of becoming another statistic."

Silver turned his chair back around to look at Toni. "I think you know the place they sent him."

Toni nodded.

"During those two years, he was fortunate enough to meet people who showed him that there were paths his life could take that wouldn't end with him dead or behind bars before he turned twenty-five," Silver continued. "He got cleaned up, finished school, went to college, and eventually became a mayor of Atlanta."

He gave a sad little smile. Toni could tell that talking about his past brought up a lot of difficult memories for him.

"That is quite a story," Toni said honestly. "One that I am sure the people of Atlanta would love to hear—especially about one of their favorite politicians."

Silver sat forward and folded his arms decisively. "That may be true, Ms. Shields, but that is not a risk I am willing to take."

Toni tensed. He had gone back to calling her *Ms. Shields*.

"I love the people of this city, but I have known them for many years. They don't want mayors with shady pasts. They want a clean, spotless image that can stand up against that of the mayors in New York, Chicago, and the other major US cities. If this hits the press I don't have a chance."

"I think you underestimate your supporters," Toni tried.

"Maybe," Silver said. "But I would rather err on the side of caution."

Toni sighed, starting to feel a little frustrated. Silver

had been her golden ticket to securing major coverage for this story. Having his story would almost guarantee that the right attention would come to Jerome's case. As she sat there looking at a pleasant but unyielding Silver, she realized that things again would not work out as she had hoped.

"I respect your desire to have this part of your past remain confidential," Toni said. "But if I could find this information, so could someone else. Wouldn't you like to have the opportunity to decide how this story is told when it goes to the public?"

"That's a bridge I think I'll wait a while to cross. Especially since I never had to cross it the last time I ran for mayor." He looked at his watch, and Toni knew the meeting was over. She shook her head and stood to leave.

"Oh, and Ms. Shields?"

Toni turned around.

"I may be charming, but don't cross me. You print one word of what I just told you, or connect my name with your story in any way, and I will sue you and your entire newspaper," he said easily. "And this time, sweetheart, you won't be able to sweet talk some ten-dollar cop out of jail time."

So he had done his research on her. She was impressed. If he was a couple years younger, she might have been tempted to break her no-politicians rule just for him.

He flashed her a campaign smile, and Toni couldn't help but shake her head. Only Silver could make a threat like that sound as smooth as butter.

As she headed toward the door again she stopped short to look at a photo hanging on the wall.

"Is that a Cessna Citation Mustang?" she asked.

Silver looked up from his desk, surprised. "Yeah. You know about planes?"

"A little," Toni said.

"Is that one yours?" she asked, pointing to the picture.

A nostalgic look slipped into Silver's eyes as he leaned back in his plush leather chair to admire the photo of the top model aircraft. "I wish," he said. "I just got my pilot's license about six months ago. I've flown a couple small crafts, but this baby here, I can't wait to get in the cockpit for."

Toni bit her lip thoughtfully. "You know, my brother uses one of those all the time on his small private trips. He's a pilot. . . . He could probably let you take one up if you want."

Silver's eyes widened like a child's on Christmas morning. "Really?"

"Yeah," Toni said, shrugging. "He does it all the time." She dug into her purse and pulled out one of Trey's business cards, handing it to Silver. "Give him a call. He's been giving lessons for about a year now, so he could probably arrange something for you."

Silver looked at the card as if it was made of gold, then looked back up at Toni. "Thanks," he said hesitantly, still a little in awe.

Toni smiled. "No problem."

She knew he probably expected her to try and bargain for what she wanted with what she had just offered him. But she was too smart for that.

"Have a great day, Mr. Maxwell." She walked out of the office, pulling the door closed behind her.

So much for that.

Chapter 19

"**W**ho's this Ann Armour chick and why is she stealing our byline?"

Toni cracked an eye open and glanced at her bedside clock. "Afrika, it's six o'clock in the morning," she said, her face still in the pillow. After playing tug of war with her sheets for most of the night, she had finally fallen asleep at 2:00 a.m. And she had been enjoying those few golden hours until her cell phone rang.

"I had an early client and she came in with the paper, talking about some kid getting fleeced by the city for the sake of some extra votes," Afrika said. "You couldn't even tell me the story was coming out today?"

Toni hadn't even been sure when it would be out herself, after Silver refused to be a part of things. However, she had still been able to write the articles with some less glamorous names included instead. She had been exhausted by the time she ran the whole thing through the fact checkers, made some last minute edits, and sent it to Naomi, but she had been satisfied.

"And who's this Armour person?" Afrika asked again.

"It's me," Toni said, rolling over in bed and pulling the covers closer around her. "I had to write under a moniker. If Gordon knew I was behind this, I would be lining up downtown collecting unemployment about now."

"Oh, it's like that?" Afrika asked, the hostility leaving her voice.

"Yeah, it's like that," Toni said. "But don't worry. I got something for you."

"Okay," Afrika said. "Did you tell Thug-Life that he's a celebrity for the day?"

"No. I was gonna wait and bring the paper over to Jacob's House this morning," Toni said, sitting up.

"Well, you better get on top of that," Afrika said. "'Cause by the time Miss Paula here tells the whole world about the story, it will be fully sold out."

Toni yawned. "Okay, will do. Thanks again for your help, girl."

"Yeah, yeah. Holler at me later."

Toni hung up the phone and glanced at the night table. It was barely 6:10 now, but she was fully awake. Plus she was more than a little curious about the story.

Getting out of bed, she slipped on some sweats and a pair of slippers and took the stairs down to the front of the building where she knew she could get the paper. The cold air nipped her but she didn't even notice as she flipped through the sections. There it was. Front page of the Metro section: **17-YEAR-OLD TAKES A HIT IN ELECTION CROSSFIRE.**

A picture of Jerome sat parallel to one of city councilman Jim Wilson addressing the media. Toni knew that picture. It was taken at the press conference where Wilson had announced his intention to run for mayor in the coming election.

As a member of city council, Wilson was directly connected to the decisions that had led to the reopening of Jerome's case. The article even included statements Wilson had made about the case at several different occasions. A few staff from the councilman's office had also provided comments about how the councilman felt about the case. He'd had no mercy for Jerome, and in turn, Toni had had none for him. So when she had written the story, she hadn't spared any details. Needless to say, it wasn't looking good for Wilson.

Toni smiled and got a second copy of the paper before heading upstairs. She could already tell that it was going to be a great day.

She had just opened her apartment door when she heard the phone ringing again. She barely managed to pull the door closed behind her before dashing over to the nightstand where the phone still sat.

"Hello?"

"Toni, I'm so sorry."

Toni didn't like the way this phone call was starting.

"Who is this?" She glanced at the caller ID but the number was private. She started to feel even more apprehensive.

"It's Tricia, and I have some info you're not going to like. I hope you're sitting down."

Toni had started pacing. Tricia almost never called her. And the fact that she was calling before seven on the morning that Toni's story broke was more than a little disconcerting.

"What's going on, Tricia?"

She heard the young woman take a deep breath. "It's Adam Bayne. Remember I told you his name came up and I was waiting on some more info?"

"Uh-huh," Toni said. "That was weeks ago. I figured since I didn't hear from you that it turned out to be nothing."

"I'm so sorry, Toni," Tricia said, irritating Toni with her multiple apologies. "I thought I had sent the info to you, but when I saw the story this morning, I realized I must not have. I know you would have never run the story the way you did if you knew—"

"Knew what?" Toni rushed her to the point.

"Adam Bayne," Tricia said. "Turns out he has open warrants in the state of Maryland. And not just one."

Toni felt her heart stop. "Please tell me that you're talking about unpaid speeding tickets."

"No," Tricia continued. "These are felony warrants. Breaking and entering, assault, accessory to robbery, possession of firearms. Plus my contact dug a little deeper and found Adam's name on a bunch of other cases involving criminal gangs in the area."

Toni shook her head. "You've got it wrong, Tricia. That's impossible. Not the Adam Bayne I know. I mean, how could the army have even taken him with all those charges?"

She heard Tricia snort. "Are you serious? You remember what was happening ten years ago, right? They were shipping troops out to Afghanistan so fast that they pretty much enlisted anyone with ten fingers and toes who was willing. The charges that were actually on his record at that time probably got waived. My guess, though, is that a lot of the others showed up after the fact. You know how people start implicating others when they're in a tight spot.

"I'm sure about this, Toni. We have his social security number. It's him."

Toni wanted to curse. This was really bad.

"Do you have the files?"

"Yeah, I had already scanned them. Check your inbox. I just sent them to you." Tricia's voice began to crack. "Oh God, I feel so horrible."

The girl was so distressed that Toni almost felt sorry for her.

"Toni, I'm so, so—"

"I know." Toni cut her off. "Look, I gotta go."

Toni hung up the phone before Tricia could respond and turned on her laptop. She continued to pace as she waited for it to boot up and for her wireless to kick in.

Adam was a fugitive?

This was bad.

How could she not have known this? She knew everything about Adam. She knew he was originally from Baltimore. She knew that he was involved with gangs when he was younger. But really, what young man growing up in the projects wasn't? She knew he was ex-army. She even knew the exact dates he was in Afghanistan. But she had missed this. The most important part. She had missed it.

This was really bad.

What was she going to tell Naomi? She had burned Jim Wilson like bad fried chicken on the morning's story. No doubt he would be looking for a way to defend his actions. And if Tricia could find this info on Adam so could someone else. Before they knew it, the *AJC* would be accused of defending an institution run by a fugitive of the law. The *AJC* would look bad. And then they would want to know who the Ann Armour behind the story was. When they found out it was Toni Shields she would be an outcast. It wouldn't be a Stephen Glass *New Republic* type scandal, but it would be close.

The little wireless icon finally popped up in the corner of her screen and Toni clicked into her mail and downloaded the attachments. She couldn't believe what she was seeing. She hit print and heard her Canon spring to life. She had to see this up close.

She paced the living room again as her eyes read the two pages of charges and connections over and over again. She looked at them so many times she was sure the images were burned onto her brain.

This was real. Adam could go to prison for this mess.

She stopped suddenly, sitting down hard on the sofa as the reality hit her full force.

Adam could go to prison.

For some reason the thought made her really angry. How could he be so irresponsible with his life? How could this be true? Why didn't he tell her? She had asked him all about his past, about his time in Baltimore, but he had never mentioned being charged. And he had to know about them. You didn't get charged for breaking and entering and not know. So he had lied to her.

She got up and began to get dressed. She needed an explanation. And this time he would tell her the truth.

Chapter 20

"We need to talk. Now."

Adam looked up from his desk into eyes of fire. Toni was not happy.

But Jerome, who had been on cloud nine all morning, didn't seem to notice. "Toni, how come you didn't tell me this would be coming out today?" He was grinning like a candidate for public office as he held up the newspaper. Adam had summoned him after breakfast to show him the article and he had been there ever since.

"Wanted to surprise you, kid," Toni deadpanned, barely taking her eyes off Adam. "Can I talk to Adam alone for a minute?"

"Yeah, sure," Jerome said, jumping up and heading through the door with the paper in his hand. "I gotta get ready for a summer class anyway. But you gotta tell me who this Ann Armour is later."

"Sure," Toni said with a smile that didn't move past her lips. It disappeared as soon as she closed the door behind Jerome.

Adam braced himself. "Something wrong, Toni?" he asked, even though he instinctively already knew the answer.

"You lied to me," Toni said, glaring at him. She hadn't even bothered to sit.

"When did I—"

"I asked you about your past," Toni said. "I thought you told me everything."

Adam blinked as the cold fingers of apprehension began to creep up his spine. "I did tell you everything," he said.

"Liar," Toni said. Her face was contorted with anger, but her eyes burned with something else.

Hurt? He had hurt her? He folded his hands in his lap. "I told you everything that you needed to know."

"You told me there were always gangs where you grew up but you never told me you were involved in one," Toni snapped. "I had to find that out on my own."

Adam's heart began to hammer in his chest. What else had she found out on her own? He clenched his jaw. "It was none of your business," he said coldly.

He knew he was getting defensive, but he was mad at himself. He should never have let her so close to him. With everything that had happened hidden ten years in the past he had thought that he would be able to forget it when he came to Atlanta. But finding a needle in a haystack was a breeze for Toni. He should have known that she would find out about his mess. The only question was exactly how much she knew.

"And that's where you're wrong, Adam. It is my business. Because I was the one who wrote the story about you. So right now, you are my business.

"And so is this."

His apprehension turned to cold fear as she tossed the folder onto his desk. It landed right on top of everything, demanding his immediate attention.

His hands trembled in his lap as he involuntarily stared down at it.

"Go on," she taunted, hands on her hips. "Open it."

Adam felt frozen behind his desk, unable to move even if he wanted to.

"Can't do it, can you?" she snapped. "Still not man enough to face up to your own mess. Well, let me help you."

She stepped forward and flipped the file open, forcing Adam to come face to face with the police report he thought had been buried in another state.

"Attempted robbery, breaking and entering, assault, possession of illegal firearms," she said, running down the charges on the front page. "There was nothing you *didn't* do, was there?"

She snorted. "Do the people you work for even know the real extent of your mess?"

Adam had confided in Pastor Reynolds the day he had accepted the offer to work at Jacob's House. He knew he couldn't start the first day without letting his boss know about his past. He had mentioned some of the things he had done in Baltimore, and Pastor Reynolds had encouraged him to deal with his wrongs and be open with the boys and with himself about his past. But Adam resisted. Pastor Reynolds had hired him anyway. Adam wasn't sure why.

But he couldn't tell Toni that. He couldn't even look up at her.

"How could you do this?" Her voice dropped as her anger faded to something else that had an even more crushing effect on him. "How could you keep this from me? After I told you everything about me."

Toni's words were like a noose around Adam's heart, being pulled tighter and tighter.

"I thought it was different with us. I thought . . ."

She thought what?

That their friendship was more than that? To him it was. That's why he couldn't tell her. He suddenly understood why Trey never told Jasmine about how he had left Toni on her own after their parents died. Jasmine would have seen how weak he was. No man wanted to look that weak in front of a woman. Especially one he cared about too much.

"And the boys." Her anger was back. "How can you look at them every day and tell them to face up to their consequences when you aren't even facing up to yours?"

She shook her head. "They worship the ground you walk on, Adam. But they don't even know the real you."

He knew she was baiting him, waiting for him to say something. Anything. But all his senses had shut down, and he couldn't even bring himself to look up at her. His worlds were colliding and he didn't know how to handle it.

He felt her eyes roam over him with disgust, before she shook her head.

"You're a fraud, Adam Bayne." Her disdain was so potent it seemed to hang in the air like humidity. "No better than those politicians using Jerome to win a campaign. Instead you're using him to clear your conscience."

She left through the door, slamming it hard behind

her. But Adam never saw her. His eyes were still on his desk, where his past sat mocking him on photocopied Baltimore Police Department letterhead. He had known he couldn't hide forever. Despite his best efforts, his past had caught up with him.

He had no choice but to face it head on.

Chapter 21

Toni was freaking out.

She had hoped that talking to Adam would make her feel better. But he had barely said anything. More importantly he hadn't denied anything. She had hoped for an explanation. He had a lot of brothers. Maybe one of them had committed all those crimes, and not him. Maybe it was a case of mistaken identity.

But her hopes had been for nothing. And now she was in trouble. Big trouble.

She turned her CBR onto Donald Lee Hollowell Parkway and headed in the opposite direction of her apartment. She had to think and she couldn't do it at home. She felt her cell phone vibrate but ignored it. The last call she had taken had turned her world upside down.

It was almost 8 a.m. She should be getting ready for work. But how could she go to work knowing what she knew? How could she face Naomi? How could she explain why she didn't know about Adam's past before now?

Her heart began to beat faster as panic swallowed her. She felt like she was suffocating inside her helmet. She had to talk to someone.

Taking the next exit off the parkway, Toni headed west. When she finally got to her destination, she stumbled off her bike and tugged off her helmet, gasping for air. She would not cry.

She rang the doorbell. When Camille finally opened the door, she burst into tears.

"Dang, girl, what's wrong with you?" Camille asked, alarm all over her face as she pulled Toni into her arms.

Even though the woman was already dressed in her uniform and looked like she was about to step out, Camille led her inside and into the living room as if she had all the time in the world.

"Girl, what's the matter, talk to me," Camille said as she sank into the sofa and Toni buried her head in the woman's lap.

"It's a mess. . . . He might go to prison. . . . He can't because I already told him everything. . . . And Naomi's gonna kill me when she finds out . . . he has all these charges. . . . I'm probably gonna lose my job. . . ."

Toni knew she wasn't making much sense but her world wasn't making much sense right now either, and she was upset that she was more concerned about what might happen to Adam than about her job or the stories in the paper.

"Okay, honey, it's okay," Camille said, rocking her gently. "It's going to be okay."

Toni didn't believe her.

Then Camille started praying.

"He that dwelleth in the secret place of the most high shall abide under the shadow of the almighty. . . ."

The 91st psalm. Toni remembered that. Her mother used to pray it also. In fact she had made Toni memorize it when she was ten.

". . . He shall cover thee with His feathers, and under His wings shalt thou trust. . . ."

She tried to focus on Camille's voice, and not the thoughts that were wreaking havoc on her sanity.

". . . for He shall give His angels charge over thee, to keep thee in all thy ways. They shall bear thee up in their hands. . . ."

She began to repeat silently as the words began to come back to her memory like an old song she had forgotten she loved.

When it was over Toni sat up and took a deep breath.

"Adam has open warrants for his arrest in Baltimore."

Camille could have swallowed a full-size frog the way her mouth fell open.

"I did a story for the *AJC* about Jerome Douglas and Jacob's House, and slammed the city for their handling of the case," Toni continued. "But Adam is a major part of the article. If the people I wrote about decide to defend their actions, all this stuff about Adam might come out. And my boss will probably can me for not knowing this info about Adam beforehand."

Camille let out a whistle. "Wow. That's heavy."

Toni nodded.

"What are you really worried about though?"

Toni looked up at her friend. She should have known Camille would see through her. She shifted her eyes away. "If this all comes out in the open, Adam may end up going to prison." She managed not to choke on the words, but the tears had sprung to her eyes again.

"It would be my fault," Toni said, picking at her

nails. "He never wanted to do the interview, but I convinced him. He never even wanted me to do the stories in the first place. And now he might go to prison because of me."

"I know you care about him, honey, and I know you are worried, but you can't blame yourself for that, T," Camille said, cutting Toni off. "It sounds like this whole thing is a lot more complicated than just the stories. Don't blame yourself for this."

"But—"

"But nothing," Camille said, shaking her head. "I know the temptation is there to take this on with everything else, but resist it. You can't help Adam or yourself if you're suffocating under a whole pile of guilt."

Toni nodded and bit her lip. "I hear you. But I feel like I have to do something."

"Like what?"

Toni stood up and began pacing the living room. "I don't know. I should tell Naomi, my boss. But she is gonna be really mad about this. The *AJC* will look stupid if someone else publicizes this info and we aren't prepared to deal with it.

"But I should have known before. And Gordon already has me on watch. This will probably be it for me. I'll probably get the ax."

Toni sat down hard. "Camille, what will I do? All I have is my job."

The pity in Camille's eyes at her friend's words made Toni aware of how pathetic that really was. Her whole life was her job. She had nothing else of worth. No real family, no strong relationships, only a spattering of friendships. Her job was her world. If she lost it she would have nothing.

"Your job is not all you have and it's not all you are,"

Camille said. "You are a sister, a daughter, a friend. You are so many things, and your life is worth more than your byline at the *Atlanta Journal-Constitution,* no matter how good a publication it is."

But Camille was wrong. Toni didn't have anything else. That's why she couldn't tell Naomi.

"Maybe it will all blow over," Toni said. "Maybe no one will even notice the stories. I can't let Naomi know how big I screwed up. If I lose my job . . ."

Toni stood up to go. She had made her decision.

"Toni, are you sure about this?" Camille asked, worry and caution in her voice.

"I'm sure," Toni said, hugging her friend. "Thanks for listening."

"And what about Adam?" Camille asked as Toni headed to the door.

Toni stopped but didn't turn around. "What about him?"

"He hurt you by keeping all this from you," Camille said. "You should tell him that."

Toni shrugged and pulled out her keys. "He didn't hurt me."

But even she knew she was lying. However, she couldn't think about that right now. She had to get home and get to work.

"Thanks again," Toni said, opening the front door and letting herself out.

She heard the woman sigh in disappointment. "That's what friends are for."

Even though she had decided not to tell Naomi, Toni knew she couldn't face her yet. So she called in sick and had her assignments e-mailed to her.

There were quite a few. Since she had put in so much time writing the Jacob's House series, she had fallen behind on the research she needed to do for her regular assignments. At least they would take her mind off her present troubles. Thoughts of Adam and the stories kept popping up in her mind, but she pushed them away and eventually got so wrapped up in her work that she managed to forget.

Then the phone rang.

"What did you say to him?"

"Jerome?" Toni glanced down at the caller ID to confirm that it was who she thought it was.

"This morning, when you came by," he continued. "You and Bayne got into a fight, didn't you? I could hear you from the other side of the door. What did you say to him?"

Toni wasn't liking his tone and the day had already drained all the patience she had in stock. "That's none of your business," she said. "You shouldn't eavesdrop on grown folks."

"He's gone, Toni."

"What?"

"We got back from school this afternoon and some old guy was in his office, said he was the replacement."

Toni got up from her chair and walked around the living room as she tried to make herself breathe.

"Replacement?"

"Yeah, replacement," Jerome spat, like it was a dirty word. "He said Bayne would be gone indefinitely. Now he's got the place on lockdown and none of us can't go nowhere for no reason. Everything was fine until you came over and started hollerin' at him this morning, so I wanna know, what did you say?"

Toni needed to process what Jerome was saying logically, but before she could even start she heard banging on her front door.

"Toni . . ."

"Jerome, there's someone at the door," she said, heading toward her front door, with the phone still attached to her ear.

"If that's Bayne tell him I wanna talk to him. He can't just bounce like that without letting a brother know."

But it wasn't Adam.

"What's going on with Adam, Toni?" Trey stormed into the apartment still dressed in his pilot's uniform.

"Is that Bayne?" Jerome shouted in her ear.

"No."

Why was everyone asking her for Adam? What was going on?

"Who's on the phone?" Trey asked. "Is that Adam?"

"No, it's Jerome. . . . Look, Jerome, I gotta go. Let me call you back."

She hung up before he could respond. The phone rang again immediately. It was Jerome. Toni tossed it onto the couch.

"What are you talking about, Trey?" Toni asked, suddenly exhausted.

"He called this morning while I was flying and left a message," Trey said, pacing the floor. "He said he's going home to turn himself in. What's he talking about, Toni? He said you would know."

"He's turning himself in?" Toni's ears began to ring. "Oh God, he can't."

She began pacing the living room again. Adam couldn't turn himself in. He didn't deserve to be in jail. And what if he did go to jail? She might never see him again.

Breathe, girl. Breathe.

But she couldn't. This could not be happening. Not now. Not today.

"Toni!" Trey was trying to get her attention. He had been asking her something but she hadn't heard it.

He grabbed her shoulders, stopping her midstride, and turned her around to face him. "Why is he turning himself in?"

She went over to her desk and pulled the copy of his record from under a pile of papers and handed it to Trey. Then she sat down on the sofa and buried her face in her hands.

"I just found out this morning," Toni said quietly after a moment. "I went to see him, and we got in a fight. Now Jerome just told me that there's a new director at the center and Adam's gone. He must have gone to Baltimore."

Trey sat down on the sofa beside her, still staring at the two sheets of paper. He kept switching back and forth from one to the other. Toni understood his disbelief perfectly.

He ran a hand over his head. "Adam had told me he'd been into some bad stuff. But I never knew. . . ."

Trey shook his head, still memorizing the record.

Adam was going to the police. He was going to give himself up and probably submit to all the charges. They would lock him up immediately, and he would sit in prison until his trial. What would happen to him there, only God alone could know.

Toni couldn't breathe again.

No.

This was not happening. She wouldn't let it.

She stood up suddenly and began grabbing her keys and her purse.

"Where are you going?" Trey asked, suspicion lacing his voice.

"To Baltimore."

"Toni—"

"If he left this morning, then maybe I can catch him before he ruins his life."

"Are you crazy?" Trey said, jumping up. "It's Baltimore, Toni, not Buckhead. You can't just jump on your motorcycle and ride there. That's an eleven-hour drive."

She grabbed her leather jacket from the coat closet. "I can make it in ten."

"Look, I get that you're upset," Trey said. "He's my best friend. I'm upset too. But this was Adam's choice. And if you get on that metal death trap and try to ride it all the way to Baltimore, that will make two people I'll have to worry about."

Toni turned back to face her brother. "Then maybe you should get me on a flight."

"Toni, I can't let you do this."

"Trey, I am going, with or without your help."

They stared at each other a long time. Toni was serious, and nobody knew better than Trey how determined she could be, except for Adam. She looked into her brother's eyes and saw the raw fear in them. Trey was not accustomed to discomfort, and she hoped that would work in her favor.

They held their positions in the standoff for a few more moments before he sighed and pulled out his phone.

"Let me make some calls."

Chapter 22

When Adam pulled up to Federal Hill Park in South Baltimore, Jonah's car was already there. Parking behind him, he shut off the engine and closed his eyes.

Ten hours of thinking about what he had to do had done nothing to settle his nerves. But ten years of guilt was something he was tired of living with. On the surface, his decision to turn himself in seemed spontaneous. But the truth was, he had been thinking about it for a while. Especially since the legal situation had gotten intense for Jerome.

Opening his eyes, he got out of the car and walked across the grass toward the bench under the tree where his brother was sitting. He remembered the last time they were here like this. It was after Noah died. The decade between then and now felt like a day.

"How was the drive?" Jonah asked when Adam sat down.

"Not long enough," Adam answered.

Jonah nodded. "You don't have to do this, Q," he said after a moment.

"Yes I do," Adam said. "I gotta take responsibility for everything that was on me. I think that's the reason I haven't been able to come back here. Because I knew that my mess was out here, about to catch up with me any minute."

Jonah chuckled. "You know what Momma always said. . . ."

"Be sure your sins will find you out," they both said at the same time.

Adam shook his head. His mother had always been right about that. He didn't know why he had thought in this one instance it wouldn't have been true.

"Have you talked to her?" Jonah asked.

"No," Adam said, shooting a sharp look at his brother. "Have you?"

"Easy, bro," Jonah said, noting the tension in Adam's tone. "You told me not to tell anyone you were coming and I didn't. But you know, ain't nothing stay secret around here. She's bound to find out before the week is out.

"Plus Tiffy was with me when you called this morning, and she's been side-eyeing me all day. I know it's because I wouldn't tell her who was on the phone," Jonah added. "I love you, bro, but you ain't the one I gotta share a bed with, you know what I'm sayin'?"

Adam smiled. "Okay, I hear you," he said. "As soon as you drop me off you can tell her everything."

"Good, 'cause I'm gonna need someone to drive your piece o' junk to my house anyway."

"Don't hate on Sunshine," Adam said, referring to his eight-year-old Pontiac Sunbird. "She's one of the most loyal women in my life."

"What about the other woman in your life? The one you left in Atlanta," Jonah said.

Adam got up and began to walk to the car. "Don't wanna talk about her."

"Did you tell her about all this?" Jonah asked, as he followed him.

Adam shook his head. Apparently the don't-want-to-talk-about-her part had not registered. He got into his car and started the engine, not waiting for Jonah to catch up.

"We talking or we driving?"

"Okay," Jonah said, getting into the passenger side. "Don't talk about it. But don't call me at two in the morning when you're at the hospital freaking out about her either."

"As long as you quit whining to me about Tiffy maxing out your credit cards," Adam threw back. "Actin' like you never knew she was high maintenance when you met her in a Chanel store."

"Hey, love is blind," Jonah said, grinning.

Adam snorted. "And broke too."

But even that couldn't wipe the silly grin off his brother's face. Without a doubt he was thinking of his beautiful wife, Tiffany, with whom he had two equally beautiful children—children who had not spent much time with their Uncle Q. Adam's brow furrowed as he thought of all the things he had missed being away from home. His brother's wedding. His stepdad's funeral. His sister's graduation from university. The birth of several nieces and nephews. Countless birthdays and family reunions. His choices had stolen so much of his life from him. That's why he had to do this, because he didn't want to miss any more.

"Hey, I know you've made up your mind about this,"

Jonah said as he pulled his door closed. "But you mind if we say a quick prayer?"

Adam closed his eyes as Jonah started to pray.

"Dear God, I don't know what Q is doing or what You're doing with him. But I know You changed him, and I know his heart belongs to You. If You lead him into this, You will take him through this. So I pray You give him strength to face all that is before him. Help him to know that we are always there for him, but more importantly, that You are always there for him. Bring him back to our family safe and soon. In Jesus's name, amen."

Both men opened their eyes but neither of them moved. They sat in the car a long moment before Adam sighed. "You feel that?" he asked wearily.

"Yeah," Jonah said, nodding. "You got to talk to Momma before you do this."

Adam frowned. He hated when God changed up his plans like that. But he wasn't about to not listen to what the Spirit was telling him to do. His heart told him he needed to go see his mother before he went to the police station. Especially since he wasn't sure when he would see her again. He had been trying to avoid hurting her one more time. But it wasn't to be.

He waited as Jonah got out of the car and headed to his own vehicle.

"All right," Jonah said. "Guess we're going home."

Adam shook his head. "Lead the way."

Chapter 23

Even though Trey had pulled some strings to get them on an afternoon flight to Baltimore, Toni still felt anxious. She didn't want to think of what would happen if Adam walked into a station and turned himself in. She had seen the charges. She knew they were serious. And who knew what else Adam was planning to admit to. Why did he have to be so irritatingly honest?

"Hey, it's going to be okay," Trey said, grabbing Toni's hand as they sat waiting for the plane to come to a stop on the runway. But Toni couldn't even muster a weak smile. She wasn't so sure.

There was a rental waiting for them at the airport in Baltimore, and Toni had already Googled the directions from the airport to Adam's mother's house, the address she got from Trey. She offered to drive, but Trey wouldn't let her, mumbling something about her breaking the speed limit and getting them a ticket. She rolled her eyes but got into the passenger seat without argument.

The drive was only twenty minutes, but it was too long. By the time they got to the address it was late afternoon. They were in a suburb outside Baltimore. The street was quiet for the time of day, with very little traffic. Toni climbed out of the car and took in the blue and white house that was supposed to be their destination.

"Are you sure this is the place?" Toni asked, looking down at the directions, then back at the house number.

"It's the right place," Trey said, shading his eyes as he looked up at the house.

There was one other car parked in front of the house, but it wasn't Adam's.

They were too late.

As if reading her mind, Trey grabbed her hand again. "Don't start jumping to conclusions yet," he said. "Let's see if anyone is here first."

Toni hung back as he walked up the steps and rang the doorbell once. They waited, but no one answered. Trey was about to ring it again when two cars came up the street and stopped in front of the house. Toni's heart beat hard in her chest. One of the cars was Adam's.

A tall guy with glasses who was unmistakably Adam's brother got out of the other car. He walked toward them slowly, a curious expression on his face. Before he could open his mouth, however, Adam stepped out of his car and came toward them.

Relief flooded through Toni as she watched him approach her. However, in almost the same instant it was transformed into hot anger.

"Toni? What are you doing here?" he asked, the look of shock on his face reflected perfectly in his voice.

"What am I doing here?" she snapped back. "What are you doing here, Adam? Are you crazy? Don't tell me that what Trey told me was right—you're turning yourself in?"

Adam glared at Trey, who was still standing on the steps. "You let her come here?"

"I didn't have a choice," Trey said, holding up his hands defensively. "You know how she is."

"Were you even thinking about anyone other than yourself?" Toni shouted at Adam.

"Of course I was," Adam retorted, his eyes blazing. "I was thinking about the boys. I was trying to be real about my mess, for them."

"For the boys! How does your being locked up help them?"

"You were the one who told me to be honest!"

"When did you start listening to me?"

"Uh, guys, can we take this inside?" Adam's brother said, looking around to make sure no one else was on the street and hearing them.

"Look, Toni," Adam said, his voice dropping as he took a step toward her and reached for her hands. "You were right."

"No, I wasn't," she said, pulling away.

"Yes, you were," he insisted, gently taking her hand again. "I have to do this. I can't carry this around anymore. I have to come clean so I can move on with my life. . . ." His eyes were pleading with her to understand, but she couldn't.

"No," Toni said, pulling away, stubbornly blinking back the moistness that was filling her eyes. "You can't. How can you do this to Jerome? You know he needs you. You know he doesn't have anybody else. How can you just leave him like this?"

"Jerome's in good hands. He has a great support system around him," Adam said. "He'll be fine."

"Okay, fine, I'm sorry," Toni said, shaking her head. "Is that what you want me to say? I take it back. Everything I said. I didn't think you would do this—"

"I'm not doing this just because of what happened with us," Adam said, reaching out and wiping a renegade tear from her cheek before sticking his hands in his pockets. "It's been on my mind for a long time. I have to do this—"

"What in heaven's name is going on out there?"

Four pairs of eyes looked toward the door where an older woman stood, watching the drama unfold in front of her house.

"Momma . . ."

"Q?" Adam's mother blinked several times and took a step forward. "My word, it is you!"

The sound of sirens interrupted anything else she planned to say. Before any of them knew what was happening, two cop cars had pulled up to the gate. Toni could see windows opening along the street, and even a person or two on porches nearby.

Two officers got out of one of the cars and walked toward the group.

"We got a call about a disturbance here." The officer's voice seemed to rumble through his tree trunk frame as his eyes scanned the scene before him.

Jonah stepped forward quickly. "No disturbance, officer. We were just going inside."

"Is there an Adam Bayne here?" the other, smaller, wiry officer asked.

"No," Toni lied.

"Yes," Adam answered at the same time, stepping forward.

"Mr. Bayne, do you know that there are open warrants for your arrest in the state of Maryland?" the larger officer said. He set a hand on his belt. "We're going to have to take you in."

"Officers, do we really have to do this now?" Jonah began.

"Please step back, sir." The goliath officer stepped in front of Jonah.

"Sir, I'm gonna have to ask you to place your hands behind your head."

With a look of resignation, Adam stepped away from Toni. His mother had started wailing at the door, but Toni barely noticed. Her eyes stayed glued to Adam's as they slapped the cuffs on his wrists.

"Let's go."

The officer began to lead him away, but Toni grabbed the edge of his shirt.

Adam shook his head. "Don't."

"No," she whispered angrily. "You can't do this."

"It's already done," he said simply, an expression of acceptance slipping over his features.

"Ma'am, I'm going to have to ask you to let go of him."

Toni didn't even look at the skinny white officer.

"Ma'am, if you don't let go we're going to have to arrest you for obstruction."

The larger uniform began to step forward.

"Trey," Adam called, without taking his eyes off her.

"Toni, let go," Trey said softly, stepping between his sister and his best friend. "I know this is not the way we wanted things to turn out, but it is what it is."

Pushing past her brother, Toni grasped Adam's face between her palms and kissed him, her lips finding his easily, as if they had done it a thousand times before. As she was about to pull away, she felt him lean in and kiss her right back with an intensity that took her breath away. It was like someone hit a mute button. In that moment there was no one else but her and Adam. But within seconds, it was over and they were pulling him away, ducking him down and locking him in the back of the squad car.

She felt glued to her position on the concrete as she watched the squad car until it turned a corner and she could no longer see it. She could hear commotion around her. Her brother was talking to Adam's brother. His mother was still crying on the steps and it sounded like more people were joining the fray.

But all that registered to Toni was exhaustion. She had been halfway around the country and it wasn't even 6:00 p.m. Without waiting for Trey, she walked over to the rental and slipped into the passenger seat. She was about to shove the paper on the seat onto the ground when she saw Jerome's face staring up at her from the front page. Her stomach lurched.

"Trey!" she screamed, jumping out of the car.

"Hey, is everything okay?" Trey asked, alarm written all over his face.

"No." Toni shook her head, her mind already spinning as she realized how things could get so much worse. "We have to go back to Atlanta. Right now."

Chapter 24

"We have to pull the stories."

The words flew off Toni's lips before she was fully inside Naomi's office. It was after eight Monday evening and Naomi was standing by her desk with her jacket on and her keys in her hands. She would have already been gone except Toni had called her and asked her to wait.

Naomi sighed and sat down. "Close the door." Before Toni could even sit, Naomi said, "Okay. What's going on? Yesterday you were thrilled with the stories. And the first one turned out amazing. We've been getting calls from local news channels all day. We even got a mention on the evening news. This is your dream."

Or her nightmare.

"There is a situation at Jacob's House now," Toni said.

"What kind of situation?"

Toni tried to think of the best way to explain what was going on. So much had happened in less than twenty-four hours that she could barely piece it together herself.

She must have paused for too long. Naomi stood and came around the front of her desk. Toni feared Naomi was now close enough to choke her.

"Let's pretend for a moment that I'm not your boss." Naomi's concerned eyes roamed over Toni's face. "What's going on, T? Are you involved with this guy?"

Toni's eyes widened. Had she mentioned Adam? Why would Naomi automatically go there?

"You've been spending a lot of time there for the story, and doing the interview with him. In situations like this, sometimes the lines get blurred," Naomi said, as if reading Toni's mind. "Plus, I read what you wrote about him. So are you?"

"No." Toni pushed her words out quickly. She wasn't involved, at least not in the way Naomi was thinking. Unless that kiss counted for something. And come to think of it, a kiss like that should.

"Toni!"

Naomi startled her out of her musings. "Adam Bayne is in jail. He was taken into custody in Baltimore this afternoon."

"Are the charges legit?" Naomi was nothing if not about the facts.

"Yeah." Toni handed Naomi a copy of Adam's rap sheet. "And he's not denying most of them, so he's probably going to be in lockup for a while."

Naomi let out a little whistle as her eyes scanned the sheet. "How did the cops find out about him anyway?"

"He turned himself in." Toni prayed that Naomi wouldn't ask her anything else about that part.

"Why?"

Toni paused. "We had a bit of a misunderstanding about the charges."

Naomi's eyebrows shot up. She got up and walked

back around to her side of the desk. Toni guessed she
was trying not to choke her.

"You knew about these beforehand?"

Toni bit her lip so hard she tasted blood. She nodded.

"And you didn't say anything? Toni! How could you
be so irresponsible?"

"I just found out this morning," Toni said.

"Why did you just find out this morning?" Her editor's
blue eyes turned dark and stormy. "Why did you not know
this information three weeks ago when you came into my
office begging for the front page? Furthermore, you knew
at least twelve hours ago and you said nothing?"

"I was still trying to figure out what we should do,"
Toni stammered.

"That's my job," Naomi said. "I'm the editor. I control how things work out on the paper. Your job is to
give me complete up-to-date information as soon as it
is available."

"I know." Toni dropped her head into her hands.

"This was a stupid, reckless rookie reporter mistake,
Toni." The disappointment in Naomi's voice cut Toni to
her core. "I'd never expect this kind of thing from you."

That made two of them. Toni raised her eyes and
took her thrashing like a woman.

"Do you realize the kind of repercussions this could
have? Not only for the paper, but for Jacob's House and
for that kid Jerome? Not to mention both of our ca-
reers."

Toni knew. She had spent the entire flight back to
Atlanta and the drive from the airport thinking about
all of that. And every time she did, she felt her heart
beat faster. One negligent act on her part could affect
the lives of so many people. She should have been

more diligent about her research. How could she have been so careless?

"I'm so sorry." Toni hoped her sincerity was obvious. "I really am. You can tell Gordon that this was my idea, my story, my error. Whatever happens, I'll take it. I deserve it anyway."

"We don't have time to think about that now." Naomi took off her jacket and sat down. "We have to fix this."

"So you're pulling the rest of the stories?" Toni asked hopefully.

"No," Naomi said. "That's not an option. We've already said that this is a weeklong series so we have to keep it that way. Plus, if we pull the plug as is, that would just send even more attention to the situation. Our only chance is to rewrite the stories, make the slant more neutral, and take Adam Bayne out of them."

"That might work for tomorrow's piece, but Wednesday's is based on the interview I did with him," Toni said. "That would mean writing a whole new piece."

Naomi barely glanced at Toni as she powered up her computer with one hand and picked up the phone with the other.

"Then you'd better get your laptop and start typing 'cause I need to see that new piece before any of us walks out of here tonight."

She shook her head as she dialed. "Now I gotta call Larry and tell him we have to make changes to tomorrow's edition. You know he hates the last minute shenanigans."

That was her cue to leave. Toni headed to her own desk and got comfortable. It was going to be a long night. But it would be worth it, if it helped allay even a little of the damage that was likely to come from her very foolish mistake.

Chapter 25

"Toni, there are camera crews here at Jacob's House. They're interviewing the staff and trying to talk to some of the boys. What's going on?"

Her worst nightmare, that's what.

Toni slid lower in her chair and rubbed her temples in an attempt to ease her three-day headache. "It's Jerome's story," Toni said. "Looks like a lot of people are interested."

"You got that right," Jasmine said. "And I don't know whether I should kiss you or strangle you."

Right then, Toni preferred the latter.

"Look, just remember not to tell anyone that I was the one there working on the story, okay?" Toni said.

"Yeah, yeah . . . Excuse me, you can't be in here!" Jasmine said. "It's getting crazy. I have to go. Let me call you back later."

Toni sighed and closed her eyes. Despite her hopes, and even a few stilted prayers, the story hadn't died. In fact, it was more like a snowball rolling down a mountain. It kept gaining more momentum and getting bigger and bigger with each turn. Toni wished it would all go away.

The only good thing about it was that she spent so much time worrying about the stories that she spent only half her time worrying about Adam. She had been getting information on his status thirdhand from Trey, who was getting his information from Adam's brother. There was still no word on what would happen and how long Adam might be sitting in jail.

Toni was still new to the prayer thing but she had found herself sending words upward more often than not. She closed her eyes again and sent up another silent petition.

God, I hope you're hearing me. Please take care of Adam and get him out soon. And if You could kill this story and help Jerome while you're at it, I would really appreciate it.

"Hey, everyone, we're on the midday news again." Suddenly the volume on their small office TV went to its maximum, and everyone was sliding their chairs over to the coffee corner where it sat.

". . . Citizens continue to weigh in on the case of Jerome Douglas, the seventeen-year-old young man who is being prosecuted a second time by the state and essentially forced to serve a double sentence for acts he allegedly committed almost two years ago."

Anchor Tasha Carr was standing at a busy corner in downtown Atlanta doing the day's report. Almost every day that week since the story broke she had been covering it for Fox 5, Atlanta's local news.

"However, mayoral candidate Jim Wilson still holds his position that Jacob's House should not have been considered as a valid sentencing option for Douglas. In a statement made just a few hours ago, he explains why."

The scene on-screen changed to one of Jim Wilson in front of the city hall building. Toni felt her stomach tighten.

"You know, I think we all should take the time to look at the kind of institutions we are using as rehabilitation options for offenders of the law and the staff we have working at these institutions," Wilson began. His usual arrogance was like nails on chalkboard for Toni's nerves.

"Take this Jacob's House Center, for example. The director of the center, a Mr. Adam Bayne, was recently arrested in the state of Maryland and is now sitting in a Baltimore jail because of felony charges laid against him several years ago. Why hasn't the *Journal-Constitution* told us that? This man was essentially a fugitive from the law, but we have him running a center that was supposed to rehabilitate young men in trouble with the law. What kind of rehabilitation could these young men possibly be getting under those conditions? Is it any wonder we have to examine each case again?"

A pin could drop and Toni would hear it. Everyone turned to look at Naomi, who stood off to the side with a cup of coffee in her hand, and Gordon, who stood at his office door. The two looked at each other before they both headed into Naomi's office. The door closed and immediately the decibel level went up.

Toni closed her eyes as her head began to throb.

"You think Naomi knew about this before she ran that story?" Tammy, a features writer, stopped by Toni's desk to gossip.

Toni shrugged. "How would I know?"

"She must have known," Michael, a newbie reporter, added from across the aisle. "Naomi never lets a story run without checking all the facts."

"Yeah, but she can't always know everything." Toni couldn't help the defensive edge that crept into her voice. "She's only human."

"And then there's this Ann Armour person." Tammy chewed her lip thoughtfully. "I wonder who she is. I haven't seen anyone new here in a while. I bet it's Naomi."

"Actually, I would have guessed you, Toni. Feels like your voice." Michael chuckled. "Only Gordon has you so busy chasing puff pieces that I don't know when you would have found time."

Toni glared at Michael from across the aisle. What was with this little snot-nosed kid anyway? He looked like he was barely out of high school. Because they were both in general assignment he thought they were on par now? Toni had probably been writing stories when he was just learning about complete sentences.

"Nah, Toni would never miss something as important as a criminal record." Tammy's confidence was like a punch to the gut. "She's much too thorough for that."

Tammy's words, though meant as a compliment, made Toni feel like melting into the carpet. She desperately wished they would go away.

As if on cue, Naomi's office door opened, and Gordon stepped out. His presence sucked the sound out of the room.

"Okay, listen up, everyone," Gordon said. "We took a hit today, but we're not going down. However, we are making some changes. As of today, until further notice, all content comes to me first. I will approve all story ideas before you proceed with them." He let his eyes sweep the room to make sure his point was emphasized. "And that goes for everybody."

Heads bobbed understanding. When Gordon was satisfied, he said, "That's all. Back to work."

Tammy disappeared without further comment, and Michael turned back to his desk.

Toni watched as Gordon returned to his office and closed the door. He had essentially assumed the editor in chief role and everyone knew it. He had taken Naomi's job.

Moments later Naomi's office door opened and she walked out with her purse and laptop and headed to the elevator. She must have known that all eyes were on her, but she didn't talk to or look at anyone. As soon as the elevator doors slid closed behind her, the buzz went up again. Everyone had the same words on their lips.

Had Naomi been fired?

Chapter 26

"Bayne. You got a visitor."

The hopelessness that hung in the air like a mist seemed to cling to Adam as he followed the guard out of his cell and down the hallway. Each day of the past two weeks had made the halls a little more familiar to him, the sights and smells a little more tolerable, the orange jumpsuit more normal. It was almost as if he was acclimating. And maybe he should. Maybe he shouldn't be making his brother waste his two-hundred-dollar-an-hour time on his case. He may have never fired a shot that killed someone, but he had been responsible in other ways.

Another guard passed him on his right, shoving him hard with his shoulder. Adam winced and gritted his teeth against the pain that shot through his shoulder and arm. The prison nurse had done her best, and the swelling in his left eye had gone down somewhat, but the deep two-day-old gash in his right shoulder was still extremely painful. Both injuries had been gifts from Gully, one of many old colleagues from his gang days who had made him feel welcomed since his arrival.

The guard led Adam through three sets of security doors, down some stairs, and through another set of doors before he saw her. As soon as her eyes met his, she started crying. Adam sighed. This is why he didn't want her coming here. She was strong but she couldn't take this, and he couldn't take seeing her like this. She had been through enough already. But he had known she would come as soon as they started letting him have visitors.

"You've got fifteen minutes," the guard said.

Adam heard the door to the tiny space close behind him and the guard take up position inside the door. And then he had no choice but to face his mother, for the first time in almost ten years.

He slumped into the only chair in the room. She watched him for a long moment through the glass before she motioned for him to pick up the receiver.

"What did they do to you?" She motioned to his eye. The strength of her voice was inconsistent with the tears on her face.

"It was nothing," Adam said. "I'm fine, Mom."

"Adam Quentin Bayne, I don't see you for almost a decade and the first sentence out of your mouth to me is a lie?" She frowned. "Boy, you lucky I can't reach across this glass to you."

Adam knew she was serious but he couldn't help but chuckle. He had missed her threats. They had been worth a lot more when he was younger, but even when he and his brothers had become grown men towering over her, she used to throw them around. And every now and then, for good measure, she would act on one.

"Mom, I don't want you to worry." Adam's smile

dried up quick when he saw that his mother was not equally amused. "I'm okay."

She sighed as her eyes inspected him. "Jonah told me that you talked to the detective for your case. That you confessed to a whole bunch of other things that they didn't accuse you of."

She shook her head and Adam looked away.

"Q, baby, why are you doing this?" She searched his eyes for an answer. "I know you've changed. Jonah's told me you're not the same person you used to be, and I could hear it in your voice the few times we've spoken. You know you don't gotta prove nothing to nobody. Why you putting yourself through this?"

"Because, Mom, you always taught us to face up to our wrongs, and I have to do that."

"But, baby, don't you know that God has already forgiven you? He's thrown your sin to the bottom of the sea, never to be remembered. Why can't you forgive you?"

"I know God's forgiven me." Adam let out a tired breath. "But my heart was telling me I needed to do this. I have missed too much time with you and Esther, and Jonah and the kids. It's hard being afraid to come home for Christmas, or holidays. I just need to deal with this and be over with it. I don't want to feel like I have this weight on me all the time."

"Q, serving time ain't gonna lessen that weight for you." She shook her head. "You've got to forgive yourself and let it go. Stop punishing yourself for what happened to Noah."

Adam looked down at the desk. He knew in his mind that everything his mother had said was right, but somehow he couldn't convince his heart.

"I just need to do this and then everything will be

right." The words came out barely audible. He didn't need to look up at his mother to know she was shaking her head.

"Q, you been stubborn since the day you were born," she said. "So I know that nothing I can say is gonna change your mind when you're set on a certain path. But just promise me that you'll use the time you're sitting in here to talk to God about this. Really talk to Him. Let Him heal you of this pain you're carrying around. 'Cause if you don't you'll walk away from this place just as miserable as when you came in." His mother pressed a palm against the glass. "Promise me."

Adam rubbed his hand over his face and braved a look at his mother. She stared at him expectantly.

"Q . . ."

He sighed. "I promise, Mom."

She nodded in approval. He closed his eyes and prayed that he would be able to keep his word.

Chapter 27

Toni paced the dirty concrete, wringing her hands as she waited for them to clear him through.

It had been three weeks, three days, and seventeen hours since she last saw him. Since then she had almost lost her job from her story gone bad, almost lost her boss's job from her story gone bad, almost lost her mind as she watched the story go on and on, and lost almost three pounds worrying about Adam.

Thankfully she still had her job and Naomi was still editor in chief at the *AJC*. The Jacob's House/Adam story had died a week and a half after it broke when the attempted suicide of a state senator's wife took front page, and Toni had started eating again when Trey called and told her Adam was being released.

Adam had finally made it before a judge who, upon examining his current circumstances, his tour with the army and his clean record over the past ten years, had determined that he was no longer a risk to society. After three weeks of thinking that he would be behind bars for the rest of his life, Toni was more than a little relieved to hear he was getting out. She had almost cried when Trey told her the news.

She stopped moving when the gate began to slide open. She watched as all the barriers between them were removed until he was standing just a few feet away from her.

"Hey," he said, his voice husky with the weariness she saw in his eyes. "You didn't have to—"

Before he could even finish the sentence, she closed the space between them and threw her arms around his neck.

He smelled like cheap soap, the stubble on his cheek scratched her face, and his swollen left eye and stiff right arm were throwing her for a loop. But she didn't care. She didn't even care that she had started sniffling like a twelve-year-old. All she cared about was that he was out, free.

"It's okay." His words fell like warmth into her hair. "I promise. I'm fine."

She pulled away and looked at him, and the crooked smile playing on his lips as his eyes drank in hers.

Then she whacked him hard with her purse.

"Oww!"

"Don't ever do that to us again," she scolded. "Do you know how worried the boys and Jasmine and Trey were these past weeks?"

"But I—"

"I didn't say you could talk." With her hands on her hips, she glared at him. "What kind of stupid reckless thing is this? I know you're all about honesty and whatever, but there are limits, Adam Bayne. And confessing to crimes you did umpteen years ago that nobody even cares about—What are you smiling at?"

The mischievous grin that played on his lips didn't even waver as she glared at him.

"You missed me, didn't you?"

Her mouth fell open. "I did not!"

"Admit it, you were thinking about me every day," he teased. "I bet you even like me."

Toni spun on her heel and walked toward the exit. "In your dreams, Adam Bayne." She could hear him chuckle behind her as he followed.

"Not my dreams, but maybe yours."

She stopped suddenly, whacked him again with her purse, and then kept going.

"Oww! What do you have in that thing? Lead?"

Toni didn't pause to wait for Adam as she walked through the main doors toward the parking lot where Trey was waiting by the car. When he finally caught up to them she was already in the backseat.

"Good to see you, man." Trey embraced his friend. "You had us all worried there for a while." Trey glanced back at Toni. "Some of us more than others."

"So I see." Adam's smile was all teeth and confidence.

Toni ignored them both.

"So we ready to bounce or what?" Trey shifted his weight from one foot to the other, then back again, all the time jingling the car keys in his pocket.

Toni watched her brother in amusement. No one liked jail, but she was sure she didn't know anyone who hated it as much as Trey. You would think that he had been on lockdown at some point the way he avoided going anywhere near a jailhouse. The mere fact that he drove across several states to a place like this to pick up Adam proved just how deep their friendship was.

"Definitely," Adam said, motioning for the keys. "Let me drive."

Trey raised an eyebrow. "You sure you remember how?"

"Man, I was in there for three weeks, not three years." Adam laughed as he grabbed the keys from Trey.

"So where we going?" Trey asked as they pulled away from the Baltimore City Correctional Center.

"Home," Adam answered simply.

Toni understood more clearly what he meant by home twenty minutes later when she found herself back in front of the two-story blue and white house where she had last left Adam three weeks earlier. They had barely stopped the car and gotten out when the front door flew open.

"Q, is that you?"

Long cocoa-colored arms and legs with a mass of curly weave attached came flying down the steps and jumped on Adam. He seemed just as happy to see the woman as he swung her around easily, laughing.

"It's so good to see you!" she exclaimed, cupping his cheeks and grinning when he finally set her down. "Jonah told me you saw him before everything went down and I was actually jealous. We've missed you so much. It's been so long."

"I know, I missed you guys too." Adam grinned at the woman in his arms. She gave a little scream and then threw her arms around him again.

Toni looked over at Trey, who just shrugged.

"Trey, Toni, this is my sister, Esther." Adam managed to extract himself from his sister's embrace long enough to make the introduction.

"Nice to meet you," Trey said, reaching out his hand.

They had all barely greeted each other when a voice cut the meeting short. "You gonna bring that boy inside or what?"

Esther rolled her eyes. "Comin', Momma."

"Well, you heard her." She linked her arm with Adam's and pulled him toward the steps. She smiled at Toni and Trey. "Ya'll better come on too."

As soon as they stepped through the door they were hit by a blast of music and activity. It seemed like they had crammed the entire neighborhood into this little house for Adam. Toni watched as Adam was almost immediately swallowed up in a group of people hugging him, laughing, and asking a million questions at once. She stepped closer to Trey.

"Guys, I want you to meet the rest of my family." Adam pulled away from the crowd and pointed to some guys behind him.

"You already met my sister, Esther, outside. This is my oldest brother, Jonah," Adam said, grabbing the shoulder of the tall, wiry guy with a sprinkling of gray hair and a toddler sitting on his shoulders. Toni remembered him from her first time in Baltimore.

"That's Benji." He nodded to a shorter, stout guy who looked like a bouncer.

"And Jacob."

The last brother, who wore glasses and was about the same height as Adam, gave her a warm smile. Toni liked him instantly.

"Man, you got a lot of brothers," Trey said with a whistle.

"And this isn't even all of us," Jonah said with a grin, as he balanced the boy who was unmistakably his son on his head. "Israel isn't even here."

"He's Jacob's twin," Esther supplied.

"Guys, this is my other brother, Trey, and . . . his sister, Toni."

Toni continued to smile, but the wind had been knocked out of her. *Trey's sister?* She didn't even rate being called a friend. But before she could overthink it, she felt the wind knocked out of her again as she got swallowed into a hug. Before she knew what was happening, she lost Trey as they both were swallowed up into the welcomes and embraces of Adam's family and friends, who had barely known them for five seconds but treated them as if it were five years.

"Nice to meet ya'll," Benji said, not too long after his large, hulking frame had simultaneously embraced Trey and Toni. "Ya'll staying for dinner, right?"

"Are you sure there's enough?" Trey asked, looking around skeptically at the overflowing living room just beyond the hallway.

Benji laughed. "Momma ain't never run out of food yet. There's always enough." He nodded toward the kitchen. "Just let her know you're here."

Adam's mother had to be close to sixty but she easily looked ten years younger. When the three of them entered the kitchen she was busy giving instructions to a younger woman on how something was to be done. Whatever it was, it was clear that Miss Thing hadn't done it properly the first time.

The moment she saw Adam, however, all was forgotten as she pulled him into a big hug. The love was so strong it filled the kitchen like a thick aroma. Toni didn't miss the dampness in the older woman's eyes as she held on to her youngest son.

When she finally let him go, Adam turned toward them. "Mom, these are the people I was telling you about."

Adam's mother wiped her eyes and smiled.

"This is my buddy Trey and his sister, Toni."

"I've heard a lot about you." The older woman took Trey's hands into hers. "It's a pleasure to finally meet you."

"It's great to finally meet you too, Momma Bayne," Trey said, grinning. Other people's mothers loved Trey, and he loved them right back. Toni could already tell that he had taken to Adam's.

Momma Bayne turned to Toni. "It's good to have you." She squeezed Toni's hand. "Any friend of Q's is welcome here."

Except that apparently she wasn't a friend—only Trey's sister.

"Thank you," Toni said, forcing a smile.

She was about to pull away but Momma Bayne pulled her closer and whispered in her ear. "And I like you. You got spunk."

Toni's mouth fell open as she realized Adam's mother must have remembered her from the day Adam was arrested weeks earlier. But Momma Bayne only winked at Toni before turning her attention back to the bustle in her kitchen.

"We're almost ready," Momma Bayne said, going back to the stove. "Ya'll wash up. Q, tell the rest of them to get ready, and tell Esther to come help me get these things on the table."

Toni handed her purse to Trey, and gave him a warning look before he could protest. Then she turned to Momma Bayne. If she was going to be here, she might as well be useful.

"How can I help?"

Chapter 28

"W here is it you said we were going?" Trey asked from the passenger seat. It had been almost twenty-four hours since Adam had been out of jail, and he was enjoying freedom more than he ever had before in his life. Their plan was to leave Maryland and head back to Atlanta later that day, but there was something Adam needed to see first.

Adam grinned. "I didn't say. But that was slick."

"Come on, Adam, now that you actually got me out of bed and into the car, the least you can do is let a brother know what's up," Trey protested, still rubbing the sleep out of his eyes.

Adam laughed out loud. "Trey, it was ten a.m.! You should have been up hours ago."

"Man, between my job and Jasmine's to-do list for baby-proofing the house, I haven't slept late for a long time." He yawned. "When I can get it I take it. And why didn't Toni have to get her behind up too?"

Adam sobered up a little and turned the car off the

main road onto a narrower street. "Because she can't know about this yet."

Trey raised an eyebrow. "About what?"

Instead of answering, Adam pulled the car over to the side of the road, shut off the engine. He opened the door and climbed out. "We're here."

He looked across the street at the long two-story building with the for-sale sign still on the lawn. He heard Trey come around to stand beside him.

Trey yawned again. "What's here?"

Adam stuck his hands in his pockets as his eyes took in the slightly overgrown lawn, the thick foliage at the back that needed to be dealt with, the cracked windows on the second floor, the peeling paint and the rusted gate posts that had long parted ways from an actual gate.

"This, my friend, is House of Judah."

"Q, my brother, I can't believe you beat me here."

Adam turned toward the sound of the voice and grinned. He had been so focused on evaluating the building that he had not heard his old friend pull up a few feet behind him.

"Chauncey," Adam grabbed his friend by the hand and pulled him into a quick man hug. "Man. It's good to see you after so long. E-mails are just not the same, you know."

"Yeah." Chauncey grinned. "I always meant to get down to Atlanta to see you, but you know how crazy the church gets up here."

"Yeah. And I know that there is no way Natalie is letting you out of her sight either," Adam said with a laugh.

Chauncey raised an eyebrow. "You know my wife well."

"Chauncey, this is my brother from Atlanta, Trey." Adam introduced his friends to each other. "Trey, this is the youth pastor for my old church, Chauncey Brown."

"Nice to meet you." Trey reached out to shake the man's hand. "Adam mentioned you a few times."

Chauncey accepted the offer. "Same here. I'm glad to know he's got some brothers looking out for him in Atlanta."

"Chauncey and I go way back. Fortunately, he took a better path than I did," Adam said. "Instead of running the streets he stayed clean, went to college, and eventually became a pastor."

"Hey, it was just the grace of God." Chauncey rested a hand on Adam's shoulder. "And you've come a long way. If that wasn't true we wouldn't be standing here today, talking about getting you involved with this place once it gets started."

Adam glanced at Trey, whose eyes were throwing up all sorts of questions. He knew he needed to tell his best friend what was going on. But sometimes it was easier to show someone your vision than talk about it. Hence the reason he dragged Trey out of bed and brought him here.

"Hey, nothing's been decided yet." Adam grinned. "Let's get a look at this place before any of us start making promises."

The three men crossed the empty street and walked through the open gateway of House of Judah. The property, like those around it, was quiet and seemingly abandoned. Its closest neighbors were a hilly grassy field on one side, and what looked like a storage yard on the other. Behind it was a high wall, every inch of which was covered by leaves and vines. Chauncey told Adam that there was a high school on the other side.

"Wow," Trey said. "This place looks like it lost a fight with a bad storm."

"Yeah, it needs a lot of work," Chauncey said. "The previous owners fell into financial difficulties and weren't able to manage the upkeep. But the location is amazing. And we've had a few assessors come by and they've all said the foundation and the structure are sound. We would just need to do some upgrading and some work on the aesthetics."

Adam heard his friend, but he hadn't needed a structural engineer to help him see the potential in House of Judah. From his count of the windows, he suspected that there were about fifteen units on the second floor. That was room for at least thirty boys. And then there was the first floor. He was itching to find out what kind of facilities were down there.

"Can we go in?" Adam took a few steps ahead of his friends toward the front doors.

Chauncey grinned and shook a bunch of keys. "That was the plan."

The front lobby looked shabby but not terrible. It was nothing some new furnishings and paint couldn't fix. The lobby led straight to a long hallway that ran the width of the building. Chauncey led them through a tour of the lower level of the building, which came with a huge kitchen, a gymnasium, computer room, laundry room, and offices.

Trey whistled. "This place came fully equipped."

"Yeah." Chauncey nodded. "We got really lucky. It was almost as if it was built with a Jacob's House type project in mind."

Adam heard Trey stop walking. He glanced back, already picturing the "what's-going-on?" look on his best friend's face even before he saw it.

Chauncey, being the wise man that Adam always knew him to be, seemed to sense the tension. "Uh, I gotta make a few phone calls," Chauncey said, already backing away to the lobby. "Just holler at me when you want to head upstairs, okay?"

Adam nodded.

"All right, Adam," Trey said as soon as they could no longer hear Chauncey's footsteps. "Start talking."

Adam watched his friend leaning against the wall eyeing him, a look of soberness, with the slightest hue of anger, resting on his features. He had a right to be mad. Adam knew he should have told Trey what was going on before now. But with everything so uncertain on so many levels, he hadn't wanted to rock the boat unnecessarily.

"Remember about a year and a half ago when my mother's pastor came down to Atlanta to visit the center?" Adam began after a moment.

"Yeah," Trey said. "He asked a lot of questions and spent a lot of time at the center. He was a pretty cool brother."

"Well, he was pretty impressed with what he saw and was inspired to start a similar project," Adam said. "He's been in touch with the center's leadership board at Immanuel and with me about it for a while."

Trey frowned. "And you didn't say anything to any of us?"

Adam shrugged. "It wasn't a big deal. They just wanted information on our operations. I figured all they wanted from me was research."

"But then?" Trey prodded.

"But then about six months ago they asked me if I would be willing to join the team." Adam began pacing the narrow hallway. "Since I already knew the program inside out, the possible problems, and the needs, they figured I would be a good person to help lead in a similar kind of program here—at least in the initial phases."

"I thought we were tighter than that, Adam." The frown lines in Trey's forehead had deepened. "Why am I just hearing about this?"

"Because it wasn't even an option for me," Adam said. "There was no way I was moving back to Baltimore with all those charges hanging over my head. Furthermore, I had no desire to leave Jacob's House. And I told them all of that."

"But that's changed?" Trey asked.

Adam ran a hand over his head, as if it could help shift away some of the confusion and weight there. "A lot's changed, Trey. The charges are being taken care of, so that's not an issue anymore. And even though the board members know everything about me being in jail, they still want me to be a part of things here."

"Adam, this is a big decision," Trey said.

"I know." He sighed. "And I'm still making it. I haven't said yes yet."

"But you're looking really interested." Trey narrowed his eyes at Adam. "Is it the fancy facilities? Are they offering you more money here? Is it 'cause Jacob's House doesn't have all this?"

"Come on, Trey, you know I don't roll like that." Adam was disappointed his friend could even think that way about him. "You've known me for how many years? Have you ever heard me trip over a salary? Yes, I talk about what's lacking at Jacob's House, but only because I know the boys could do better with so much more."

"Yeah, about the boys," Trey said. "How you think this is gonna affect them?"

"I haven't said yes yet, Trey."

But as they both stood in the hallway in silence, they both knew that Adam was a lot closer to yes than to no.

Adam was the first to speak. "So what do you think?"

Trey stared at Adam for a long time. "I think you're running." Trey's gaze didn't waver as he said the words.

Adam's eyebrows shot up. "What?"

"I think now that everything about you is in the open in Atlanta, it's not the hideaway it was for you before," Trey said simply. "I think you're afraid to face everyone now that you're not as spotless as you appeared to be before."

Adam's face hardened. "I never thought I was spotless."

"But you were okay with people thinking you were," Trey said. "You know that things would have been different if everyone knew the full details about your past. You knew the boys would look at you differently. And you know you're going to have to answer their questions now. I think that scares you."

"If that was the case I wouldn't come to Baltimore," Adam said coldly. "Who I am is no secret here."

"Exactly," Trey said. "Your face was never on the front page of a newspaper here. You never needed to explain to anyone who you were—they already knew. But you're still going to have to explain to the young men you work with here who you are. And you're still going to have to work to gain their trust just like you had to at Jacob's House."

"I know that," Adam said. "I've been working with those guys full time for years."

Trey narrowed his eyes, and Adam knew his friend

had caught his jab at the fact that Trey only volunteered at the center on a part-time basis. Adam appreciated the hours Trey gave to the center, but it was just a side activity for Trey. Jacob's House was Adam's life. Adam knew all about having to gain the boys' trust. That was his everyday goal.

"Yes," Trey said. "And this is your opportunity to show them how to handle things when their past comes to the surface. Are you going to teach them to run and keep hiding who they are? Or are you going to teach them to stand strong and prove to those around them that they have changed?"

"You think you know everything about me, Trey, but you don't," Adam said.

"You might be right," Trey said. "But whose fault is that?"

The words stung, and Adam realized that his friend was more right than he wanted to admit. But he pushed the thought away. This new House of Judah project in Baltimore was a good one. It would help a lot of young men who needed direction, and Adam knew that he could do good work there. What could be wrong about that?

"Have you even prayed about this decision?" Trey asked. "Are you sure this is what God wants?"

"Baltimore is my home, Trey," Adam said. "I don't need God to tell me this is where I need to be."

"So, you haven't," Trey deadpanned.

"So you think He's going to tell me something different?" Adam's eyes challenged Trey.

"I think the fact that you haven't asked is a sign that you already know the answer."

Adam's eyes fell to the floor as a heaviness slipped over him. This was not how he had hoped the conversation with his best friend would go. He had needed Trey to support him. Needed him to understand why he wanted to do this.

"Look, Adam, I know this is a good project," Trey said quietly. "And I know it will help Baltimore. I even think that done properly it will bring honor to God. But it's like David building God's temple. His heart was in it, but God said no.

"Sometimes we want to do things for God—good things. But God says no, because it's not for us. Usually it's 'cause He has something else for us to do. Or because we are going after it for the wrong reasons.

"I don't know if that's the case here, but I know that you'd better know before you make a big move. Especially one like this that can affect the lives of a lot of young men not just here in Baltimore but also in Atlanta."

The drive back to Adam's mother's house was quiet, with neither man saying much to the other. It was only when they pulled up to the gate that Adam turned to his friend.

"Let's just keep this quiet for now, okay?" Adam asked.

Trey snorted. "Not like it's good news or anything."

They got out of the car just in time to see Esther's car pull up at the front gate.

"Little brother, where you been?" Esther and Toni got out of the car. They had so many bags attached to each arm that Adam wasn't quite sure how they had managed to fit them all in the car.

"The better question is where have you been?" Adam asked with a smirk, though he could probably guess.

"She's been showing me around town," Toni answered. "Since my brother and his best friend ditched me this morning."

"Yeah, well, it looks like you kept yourself and your Visa quite busy." Trey moved toward the house.

Adam was about to follow suit when Esther's voice stopped him. "You never answered." She was still pulling things out of the backseat. "Where were you guys?"

Adam looked back and caught Toni watching him for the answer. He felt his stomach tighten a bit and he looked away.

"Nowhere special."

He headed inside. Not special yet anyway.

Chapter 29

Adam took the long way into the center. It was the end of August and between his jail time and clearing things with the church board and the city so he could resume his position at Jacob's House, it had been almost five weeks. As he walked up the back steps and through the hallways of the place he had called home for the past three and a half years, his eyes eagerly took in each detail. He realized he had missed the place more than he imagined he would.

Adam stopped short of the common room. The door, only a few steps away, was open. The sound of the boys drifted out to meet him in the hallway. It was the sound of young men who could almost never be silent when they were together.

However, as soon as he stepped over the threshold into the room, all talk ceased. He could feel their eyes follow him as he strode slowly to the front of the room.

God, now what? You didn't tell me about this part.

Adam looked around at them, all twenty-one of them. They were rarely all in the same room together, but today they crowded in, perched on desks, leaning against the wall, clad in baggy jeans, baseball caps, and graphic T-shirts, staring at him, waiting for him to tell them something he never planned to share.

His eyes drifted to the right side of the room. Trey gave him a nod from the back corner, where he was leaning against the door. Adam nodded back. This was it.

"So, a lot of you are probably wondering what exactly happened to me these past couple weeks." He rubbed his palms together. "I know you've seen it all on the news, so I'm just going to tell you like it is." He took a moment to glance at all of them.

"I was arrested in Baltimore, my old hometown."

He saw the widened eyes and the raised eyebrows and could almost hear the whispers behind them.

"And it wasn't a mistake," he continued, moving across the front of the room. "It wasn't racial profiling. It wasn't five-oh trying to keep a brother down. It was all on me. It was because I messed up a long time ago, and it was time for me to own up to my mess."

Adam saw Rasheed shake his head. To Rasheed's left, Jerome sat eyeing Adam as if he had just taken off a mask and revealed himself to be someone else. Tarik was perched on the edge of a table on Rasheed's other side. The smirk on his face concerned Adam more than the judgment he saw in the eyes of Jerome and Rasheed.

"When I first got here, I told you guys who I was, but I didn't tell you everything. You knew I came from the streets like you, but you didn't know that I was in the streets, that I ran the streets. Harder than a lot of you in here. I didn't want to tell you that, 'cause to me that didn't glorify God. That wouldn't help you be better than who you were."

Adam paused as Toni and Jasmine slipped in the

back door. Two of the boys at the back got up, giving them their seats. Adam swallowed hard. He hadn't planned to talk about this in front of her.

But the voice in his head told him to forget that plan: *Tell them the truth. The whole truth.*

Her eyes caught his, but he couldn't read her. He took another deep breath and kept going.

"But as I was lying in that cell, I realized I'd been wrong and I promised God that if I got out, I would tell you all the truth. Let you know the real me."

Adam rubbed his chin. "When I was sixteen my brother and I got mixed up with some gangs. Not your small time, selling-crack-to-the-kids gangs. These brothers were about the big business, selling semis and automatics, stealing cars, moving kilos of drugs. You name it, we were up to our elbows in it. And my brother and I were right in the middle. A lot of people got hurt because of us. People died because of us. Because of me. One of those people was my older brother, Noah."

Adam took a moment to breathe as the image of Noah flashed before his mind. A day didn't go by that he didn't think of his brother. An hour didn't pass where the guilt of his brother's death didn't weigh on him. Today it felt even heavier. Pushing away the painful memories, he kept going.

"Being greedy, I had tried to con some guys out of some money we owed. But of course, you know you can't steal from other criminals and get away with it," Adam said. "They found out, it came down to the line, and my brother ended up taking a bullet for me."

Adam shoved his hands into his pockets, the muscles in his jaw tensing. He glanced over at Trey, and his friend nodded for him to continue.

"Everything changed after that. My mom decided

she wouldn't watch another of her kids die. It was either enlist or go to jail; she said she would call the police herself and tell them everything she knew. It wasn't much of a choice. I enlisted. Did my time, and then came here. I never went back home. And you know the story from there."

Adam took another deep breath. "A couple weeks ago, a friend of mine called me a fraud after she found out about my past." He looked over at Toni, who was still watching him, the same closed expression on her face. "God told me it was time to own up. So I went home, and I did what I had to do."

"Why'd you go to the cops?" a voice called out. Adam looked up to find Tarik glaring at him with a mix of confusion and anger. "If God forgives, like you said, then once you ask for forgiveness it's over."

"If we confess our sins, He's faithful and just to forgive us our sins and cleanse us from all unrighteousness," Adam said, understanding the boy's anger, only because it had once been his own. "Confession has to come as part of repentance and forgiveness, Tarik."

"But why?" Tarik asked in frustration. "Isn't it enough to be sorry?"

"Confession shows that you're ready to face the consequences of your actions," Adam said simply.

"Man, that's whack," Tarik grumbled, reclaiming his position against the wall.

"Maybe, but it's what God told me I needed to do."

"What? Now you expect all of us gonna walk up to five-oh and be like, 'Oh, I stole a car last year. My bad.'"

A few of the boys chuckled.

"So why you telling us all this, Mr. B?" Sheldon asked from under a baseball cap pulled so low that Adam couldn't see his eyes.

Adam shook his head. "I'm telling you for two reasons. One, because I felt like I owed you all an explanation. And two, because I want you to think about why you're really here. I spent the last ten years hiding in different places. Is that what you're doing here? Hiding? Waiting until the coast is clear so you can go back to the regularly scheduled program? Or do you recognize that this is a second chance for you? This is an opportunity for you to start your life over in a better way, the right way, the way God wants you to."

Adam paused and looked around at them, letting the words sink in.

"Either way, we'll help you, 'cause that's what we're here for. But a lot of you are turning eighteen soon. You know after that you're on your own. What you gonna do then? We can help you start a new life. But I've seen a lotta cats just like you go right back to where they were. Within less than a year they're back in jail. Now that doesn't have to be you—it's your choice."

He looked around at the young men in front of him. Some of them were nodding; others already had their earphones plugged in. Adam sighed. He had done all he could do. He dismissed them and watched as they streamed out of the room. He caught a glimpse of Toni as she walked out with them and wondered how she would see him now that she knew everything.

"I know that was hard." Trey's presence at the front beside him distracted him from his previous thoughts. "You did good."

Adam shrugged, unconvinced. "Sometimes it doesn't feel that way."

"I know, but it's not about what they say." Trey put a hand on his shoulder. "By their fruits you will know them."

Adam nodded even though he wasn't as sure. He had seen too many leave and end up right back where they started. He had faith, but he was running low on hope.

"So how does it feel to be back?"

Adam looked up from his desk at Jasmine, who was standing at the door, barely balancing the weight of her pregnant belly. He hadn't been keeping count but it wasn't hard to tell that she was due any moment.

It had been his second full day back at the office. The church had stood by him through everything, and like Pastor Reynolds had promised the day Adam had told him he needed to go back to Baltimore, his job was waiting for him when he returned.

"It feels strange," Adam said, looking around his tiny office. "When I was sitting in jail I actually never thought it might happen."

"Yeah, I never got a chance to talk to you about that," Jasmine said, sinking into the chair across from his desk. "What happened to you in there?"

Adam smirked. "I'll tell you about it when you're not pregnant," he said.

She rolled her eyes. "Well, with that long list from the city auditors I can already tell you're going to have your hands full," she said, rubbing her belly.

Adam grimaced. Thanks to all the publicity from Toni's articles and his stint in jail, the city was auditing Jacob's House. They were looking over staff, programs, funding, and anything else they felt like. Adam had already met the team, and their list of requests increased every day.

"Yeah," Adam said with a sigh. "And now I have to

look for new staff too, since a certain someone won't be here."

"Actually, I've been talking to a therapist who works in my building," Jasmine said brightly. "I think she might be willing to help out for a couple months until I get settled with Baby Shields."

Adam laughed. "Baby Shields? You guys have had eight months and that's the best you can do?"

"The naming of a child is not something to be rushed, Adam Bayne," Jasmine said with a wag of her finger. "When you have one of your own you'll understand."

"Yeah, well, that's looking like a long time off," Adam said, flipping through the mail on his desk.

"Really?" Jasmine batted her eyes and stood to leave. "I thought for sure you'd have a few offers while you were in Baltimore. I hear they're really friendly up in corrections."

He heard her laugh as she waddled out of the office before he could toss a wadded up piece of paper at her. She moved pretty quickly for a pregnant woman.

He went back to the envelopes, flipping through the regular fare of bills and apology letters. He wasn't sure which was worse: being asked for money or being rejected for it. He was almost at the end when he came upon a gray envelope.

Curiously, Adam slit the envelope open and shook out its contents. A check was the only thing that slid out of the envelope, and Adam's mouth fell open when he saw the number of zeros attached to it. He turned it over in his hands and held it up to the light just to make sure it was real. Then he checked to make sure that it was really for Jacob's House. Yep. That was their name all right. Adam didn't know who the Platinum Foundation was, but at that moment he could have kissed every member.

Just as he was checking the envelope to make sure nothing else was in there, the phone rang. "Hello?" Adam answered absently, holding the envelope up to the light and peering inside.

"Adam Bayne, please."

"Speaking."

"This is Joyce Hardaway calling from Dwayne Cartwright's office."

Adam froze. "Yes, how can I help you?" he said, apprehension increasing his response time.

"Mr. Cartwright would like to meet with you and Mr. Douglas as soon as possible. Are you able to come in within the hour?"

"What's going on?" Adam asked, the morning's joy already forgotten. It was never a good thing when your lawyer wanted to meet with you immediately about an open case. Adam wasn't liking the sound of things.

"I'm afraid I'm not at liberty to discuss that. Mr. Cartwright will explain when you come in. Can you make it today?"

"Uh, Jerome's in summer school," Adam said, considering but then quickly abandoning the idea of pulling Jerome out of classes for the day. There was no sense in rushing bad news. "We can stop by at about three p.m., after he gets out."

"Okay, I will let Mr. Cartwright know."

"Thank you."

A sense of foreboding hung over Adam as he pushed through the next couple hours. Not even the joy of the morning's six figure donation could remove the apprehension of what he was sure was about to happen.

He was about to lose Jerome to the system. He had failed him—just like he had failed Noah.

Adam was waiting for Jerome when the school bell rang.

"Yo, Bayne, what's poppin'?"

"We gotta go see your lawyer."

No further explanation was needed and no further conversation was worthwhile. They drove in silence over to Dwayne's offices.

They were about to take the elevator up to the office when Adam put a hand on Jerome's arm. "Hey, no matter what happens, I want you to know that I'm proud of you, okay?" Adam said.

"Okay." Jerome's face was expressionless. "Let's just get this over with."

Dwayne's office door was already open when they got there. Adam tried to read the man's expression, but it was almost impossible.

"Have a seat," Dwayne said, motioning to the chairs in front of his desk.

"What's the emergency?" Adam asked, getting straight to the point.

"I got a call from the DA this morning," Dwayne said, folding his arms on his desk. "They're dropping the charges. Jerome's free and clear."

"What?" Adam asked, echoing the confusion in Jerome's face. "I don't understand."

Dwayne shrugged. "Me neither. The DA just called and said the case has been dismissed. I received the official papers from the court this afternoon. This is real."

"Did they say why?"

"No."

"So that's it?" Adam asked, looking back and forth between Jerome and Dwayne. "It's over?"

Dwayne nodded. "Yup. Jerome will finish his time at Jacob's House, under the terms of his original sentence, after which his record will be wiped clear if he stays out of trouble for three years."

"Yes!" Jerome jumped up. "That's what I'm talkin' 'bout."

Adam stood up, trying to stay composed. "So I guess this is it then," he said. He reached across the desk to shake Dwayne's hand. "Thank you."

Dwayne shrugged. "I didn't do anything. You guys must have friends in high places."

Jerome was still hooting and hollering like a maniac all the way out of the building and into the parking lot.

But Adam could barely speak. He had known that it would take something unusual to free Jerome from the weight of this case, but to see it happen was almost too much for Adam. He thought about how hopeless he had felt just the day before as he talked to the boys about their future. The discouragement he had felt that he hadn't shared with anyone. But today's experience had given him new hope.

Thank you, God. Thank you for this gift to Jerome. We know it's from You.

"Yo, Bayne, this is awesome!" Jerome shouted. "Man, I can't believe this."

"Yeah, this is crazy," Adam said, tossing the keys to the car to Jerome. "Let me call Toni."

Her number rang twice before she picked up and said hello.

"Hey, you will never believe this," Adam began. "We just walked out of Dwayne's office. All of Jerome's charges have been dropped. Every single one of them. He's been cleared. It's over!"

"That's amazing!" Toni screamed so loud Adam had to hold the phone away from his ear.

He laughed. "Yeah, I know. You should see Jerome out here. He's doing the happy dance, like he just won the lottery."

He could hear Toni's laughter on the other end. "I can't even believe this is happening, Toni," he said. "There were times when I thought . . ." He couldn't even finish his sentence.

"I know." He could hear the smile in her voice. "Sometimes the things we pray for seem impossible. But when God answers, it's overwhelming."

He nodded, then remembered she couldn't see him. "Yeah."

"We have to celebrate!" she said, her voice going up several decibels again.

He laughed. "I was thinking the same thing," Adam said, keeping his eye on Jerome as he followed behind him to the car. "What are you doing tonight?"

"Meeting up with you guys," Toni said cheerily.

"All right then. I'll call Jasmine and Trey and let you know where it will be."

"Okay," Toni said. "I'm so glad things are working out."

"Yeah, they are," Adam said, grinning. He wasn't really ready to get off the phone yet. "I got some more big news too."

"Oh yeah?"

"Yeah, this morning we got—Jerome, don't even think about it!"

"Huh?"

"Uh, sorry about that, Toni," Adam said distractedly. "I gotta go. Jerome just got in the driver's seat and started my car."

She laughed. "Oh yeah, you better go then. See you later."

"Yeah," Adam said, breaking into a jog as he hung up the phone. "Jerome! Get your butt out of the driver's seat!"

Chapter 30

By the time Toni got to Applebee's, where they had agreed to meet, it was seven-thirty and everyone was already there. "Sorry I'm late," she said with a sheepish grin, once she had maneuvered through the other diners and reached the small corner of the restaurant where Jerome's celebration was taking place.

On the phone Jasmine had said it would only be a couple of people. But a couple seemed to have turned into about fifteen. Along with Jerome, Trey, Jasmine, and Adam, a huge chunk of the staff from the center had turned out, as well as Afrika, Camille, Rasheed, and a couple of Jerome's other friends. They had pulled three tables together, and even then few people seemed to notice when Toni showed up.

"What took you so long?" Jerome asked. "We been waitin' on you to order."

"Yeah, girl." Afrika smirked. "What took you so long?"

Toni didn't miss the way Afrika's eyes purposefully

met hers and then dropped to her dress and shoes, and back to her face.

"I got caught up in something and time got away from me." She sent Afrika a warning glare, telling her to behave.

The truth was Toni had gotten caught up trying to figure out what to wear. She had gone through three different outfits before going back to the one she had picked out first. She had told herself she just wanted to look nice to celebrate an important moment for Jerome—it had nothing to do with Adam. But she wasn't that good at lying to herself. And from the amused look on Afrika's face, it seemed like her friend knew the real reason she was late too. Toni hoped that she wasn't as transparent to everyone else.

"So where do I sit?" She smiled brightly, looking around.

"You're over here," Afrika said, nodding to a chair across from Camille. "On the other side of Tina."

"So who's sitting there?" Toni asked, pointing to the chair beside hers, which happened to be at the end of the table.

"Me," Adam said, appearing from nowhere and pulling out Toni's chair for her. "And, no, you can't have the seat at the end."

"Why not?" Toni asked. "What happened to chivalry?"

"It got tired of waiting on you and left," Adam said, seating himself beside her. "Besides, if you sit here, you'll have to get up every time Jasmine needs to go to the restroom."

"It's true," added Trey, who had also just returned and taken his seat at the head of the table, adjacent to Adam on one side and Jasmine on the other. "She's already gone twice, and we've only been here half an hour."

"Okay I concede," Toni said. "Are we ready to order?"

Afrika laughed. "We already ordered. You're on your own, hon."

"No problem," Toni said, glancing at the menu. "I already know what I want."

As if hearing her, the waitress, a slim young woman with honey blond hair and eyes the color of graphite, appeared at their end of the table. Once Toni had ordered she turned to Adam. She caught him staring at her and felt her cheeks grow warm.

"What?"

He smiled and leaned close to her ear. "You look nice."

She ducked her head down to hide the instant smile that broke her lips. Three outfit changes and thirty extra minutes getting ready for one compliment from Adam. So worth it.

"Thanks."

She dared a look up at him and found herself trapped in his dark chocolate orbs. They conjured up memories of Sunday mornings, Christmas treats, chocolate Easter eggs, and a lot of other things that reminded her of home.

"Okay, so what's the big news?" Jasmine's voice brought Toni crashing back into the present.

"There's more news other than the charges for Jerome's case being dropped?" Camille asked, looking back and forth between Toni and Adam.

"Yeah," Adam said, sitting up. "Thanks for reminding me. You will never believe what came in the mail this morning."

"A straight-A report card for Rasheed?" Sam asked, tuning in to the conversation for the first time from beside Afrika.

Trey snorted. "He said big news, not big miracles."

"Hey, I heard that," Rasheed called from the other end of the table.

"Well, you'll want to hear this too," Adam said, his eyes taking in everyone at the table. "Today we got a check in the mail. You'll never guess how much."

"Forty grand," Jerome threw out.

"One hundred K," another one of the kids guessed.

"Try two hundred and fifty thousand," Adam said, grinning.

Shrieks and cheers went up from the table as everyone started talking at once.

Toni couldn't believe her ears. Two hundred and fifty thousand dollars. That was enough money to do a lot of the things that desperately needed to be done at Jacob's House. It could transform the whole center.

"That's amazing, Adam!" Toni exclaimed. "Where did it come from?"

"I don't really know," Adam said with a laugh. "All that came in the envelope was the check. And the sender was the Platinum Foundation. I've never even heard of them before."

"Did you look them up?" Jasmine asked.

Adam nodded. "Nothing online that I could find. All I have is their return address, which is some random Atlanta PO box."

"That's really strange," Toni said.

"I know," Adam said, nodding as he looked at her. "But I prayed about it. And until God shows me differently, I am just going to take it as a gift from Him."

At that moment their food came, via a new waitress.

They were deep in conversation on what the money could be used to do at Jacob's House when Adam's phone rang. Toni watched him excuse himself from the table to take the call, immediately feeling the cool absence of his presence beside her.

Even though Camille was saying something to her, Toni couldn't help but find her eyes drifting over to where Adam stood a few feet away from the table. His back was to her but she saw his shoulders tense. A few moments later, her curiosity was further piqued when he came back to the table and said something quietly to Trey. The subtle change in Trey's expression was all the confirmation she needed. Something was wrong.

"You're leaving?" Jasmine asked, as Adam grabbed his jacket off the back of the chair.

"Yeah," he said, attempting a smile that did not reach his eyes. "I have to take care of some things. But you guys stay and finish up. Sam, can you make sure all the boys get back okay?"

"No problem, boss," Sam said with a nod.

Everyone seemed content with Adam's explanation. Everyone but Toni.

She grabbed his wrist before he could walk away and turned questioning eyes on him. He shook his head in silent answer, but that wasn't good enough for her either. She waited a moment before excusing herself discreetly and following him outside.

"What's going on?" She almost had to jog to keep up with him as he walked to the car.

"It's nothing you need to worry about," he threw behind him.

"Let me decide what I want to worry about," Toni said.

His jaw tightened.

"Adam."

He finally stopped walking and turned to face her. The frustration, anger, and defeat that played games with his features made her heart turn over. She touched his arm and his eyes shifted to some point beyond her head even as the muscles in his jaw flexed again.

"Tarik's in trouble," he said after a moment.

The face of the young man who had been on the roof with Toni and Adam flashed in Toni's mind.

"The police caught him trying to bum a ride across state lines," Adam continued. "They have him in custody."

Toni squeezed Adam's arm. "I'm sorry. That does kind of put a damper on the night. So you're going to pick him up and take him back to the house?"

Adam frowned and looked at Toni, his eyes meeting hers for the first time since they'd gotten outside. "No, Toni," he said quietly. "I'm going to talk to the police. Tarik won't be going back to Jacob's House. This is his third strike. Now he goes to jail."

Toni's eyes widened. "But he's a kid."

"He's nineteen," Adam corrected. "The state considers him an adult and he will be treated that way."

"Oh God . . . Adam, I'm so sorry. I never realized . . ." Toni's voice faltered.

"These things happen," Adam said. "You can take the kid out of the hood and you can show him life outside it, but sometimes . . ." He shook his head. "Sometimes it's not enough."

His voice was completely devoid of emotion, and that scared Toni almost as much as the hopeless resignation sitting on his face. He turned to head back to his car but Toni grabbed his arm again.

"Adam . . ."

"I have to go, Toni. The cops are waiting for me," he said. But he didn't pull out of her grasp. Toni took that as a sign and slipped her arms around him. He let her hold him for a few moments before she felt him pull back slightly.

"This is not your fault," she said, her hands resting gently on his tense shoulders. "I know you're thinking it, but it's not."

He didn't even meet her eyes. "I have to go." His voice was so low she barely heard it.

She let go of him and watched him walk away. Then she whispered a prayer that God would protect Adam's heart. There was only so much a man could take.

Chapter 31

A dam followed the custody officer down the halls of the police precinct that had over the past three years become all too familiar to him. He silently wondered how it was that his day could go from 100 to 0 in only a few moments, but that was what had come to be his life at Jacob's House. Every high moment, every achievement, was merely the calm before the next storm. And now that he was standing in the eye again, he was wondering how far-reaching the bands of this particular catastrophe would be.

The court officer hadn't been interested in much of what Adam or Immanuel's lawyer—the one who occasionally helped out Jacob's House—had to say. Technically this had been Tarik's fourth strike. The first time he had been caught hanging out in his old neighborhood Adam had managed to squash it and keep it off his file. But the second time, the police had been there and so there was no hiding it. First strike.

After that it was suspension from school for fighting. Second strike. Adam remembered sitting Tarik down and explaining how serious his record was. If he got in trouble again before his term was done, there would only be one option—real jail time. Three to five in a state facility. Tarik had said he understood, but as Adam followed the custody officer into the small windowless visitors' room, Adam began to doubt that the young man in fact had.

"Please be reminded that you are not allowed to touch the prisoner," the officer said as he directed Adam to a chair on one side of the single table in the room.

"Any sudden movements will be regarded as hostile and lead to an immediate termination of the visit. A guard will be in the room at all times. Any questions?"

Adam shook his head and sat down. A few moments later, a door on the other side of the room opened and Tarik shuffled in with restraints on his wrists and a scowl on his face. When he looked up and saw Adam, a flash of something that he suspected might be regret passed over Tarik's features. But it was gone before Adam had time to be sure, and replaced with the default emotion for most of the boys at Jacob's House—indifference.

Tarik slumped into the chair across from Adam as the guard took up position at the door. The two men looked at each other for a long time, neither saying anything. Adam had questions, and yet none of them really mattered, none of them would change the current situation.

"So what, boss? You got something to say to me, or you just wanna get one last look at my mug before they lock me up and throw away the key?"

"I'm not your boss anymore," Adam said.

Tarik nodded. "Yeah, you must be glad about that."

Adam narrowed his eyes, trying to understand what was going on in Tarik's head. "Why are you here, Tarik?" he asked.

"You know why," he said dryly. "'Cause five-oh picked me up."

"Yes, I know that part," Adam said. "What I don't know is why you were trying to hitch a ride out of state."

The young man curled his lip and shifted his eyes away from Adam.

"You knew the rules," Adam said. "You knew that if you ever tried to leave the state without a judge's permission that it would be over. You knew you were down to your last strike."

Tarik continued to give Adam attitude.

"I don't understand you, man. You had what, seven months left? By this time next year you would have been free and clear."

Tarik shrugged. "I wasn't feeling the Jacob's House vibe anymore. I'm nineteen. I can't be hanging around a bunch of kids just waitin' for something to happen. A brother needs to live his life."

"How were you planning to do that?" Adam asked angrily. "Did you even think it through? Don't you think you would have been on the police radar once they realized you had skipped the program? How were you going to live your life with a sentence hanging over you?"

Tarik shrugged and turned cold eyes on Adam. "The same way you did."

Adam felt his insides turn to stone as Tarik's words slammed into him. He blinked several times and tried to recover, but he knew everything he was feeling was all over his face.

Tarik laughed. "What, you ain't got nothing to say now?" he asked, sitting forward and placing his cuffed hands on the table. "I thought you had all the answers, man."

Adam's mind fumbled for a response but he was still reeling.

"You gotta admit you got a pretty sweet deal though," Tarik continued, his eyes narrowing. "Get all you can out of your crew, but when the hustle gets too hot, and the cops get too close, just bounce. Run off to the other side of the country until things cool down. The church scene is a nice touch too. I bet that's why they let you out so quick in B-more. I mean, you got Jesus now, so you must be really different." Tarik laughed again, shaking his head.

"Is that how you think it is?" Adam asked.

"Hell yeah," Tarik said. "You might fool them other little niggas, but I know what's up. And if you weren't stupid enough to turn yourself in, none of us would ever know anyway."

Adam felt his jaw tense. He wanted to reach across the table and shake Tarik until he got some sense in him. Tarik thought this was a game, but it wasn't. He had no idea how sorry Adam was for everything that he had done in his past.

"I turned myself in because I regretted what happened and because I was tired of running from my past," Adam said through his teeth.

"Nah, man," Tarik said with a shake of his head. "You turned yourself in 'cause them niggas downtown found out about you. And don't even try to say it ain't about that. 'Cause you had what, ten years to feel sorry 'bout what you did, but you never felt like talking to five-oh back then."

Adam looked down at the table. He couldn't deny the truth there. He had had many opportunities to do the right thing, many times when God had spoken to his heart. But he had delayed, until he couldn't delay any longer.

"You're right. I should have come clean before. But I didn't. And I regret that too. I know you probably don't believe me but it's the truth," Adam said.

"But just so you know, Tarik, it was never easy for me. And if you had disappeared like you wanted to, it wouldn't have been easy for you either. It would be day after day of trying to stay under the radar, wondering if when people looked at you too closely they were remembering you from your old life. It would be worrying every time you applied for a job that your boss would run a check on you and find out your history. It would be that tightness in your chest every time you saw red and blue lights in your rearview mirror. Even when you weren't doing anything wrong, you would always wonder if they were coming for you.

"That's not living life. That's not being free."

Tarik smirked. "You did it for ten years. It can't be that bad."

"Two minutes," the guard at the door said.

"I'm sorry, Tarik," Adam said, his brow furrowed.

"For what?"

"For failing you."

The remorse Adam had seen before flashed across Tarik's face again, lingering only a moment longer this time than before.

"Whatever," Tarik said, when the indifference had returned. "It was good knowing you, Bayne. Guard?"

Adam watched as the guard by the door moved to Tarik's side. Without a look back, Tarik walked out of the room and out of Adam's life. But Adam knew the young man's words would stay with him for much longer. Just like the feelings of failure that they had brought with them.

Chapter 32

"Hey, man. How's it going?"

Adam turned away from his computer screen to the window so he could give Chauncey's phone call his full attention. It's not like he had been getting much work done anyway.

"It's been better," Adam answered with a heavy sigh.

"That bad, huh?"

"It feels that way," Adam said. "We just lost another one to the system."

Adam gave his friend the Cliffs Notes version of the Tarik story. Even though it had been over a week, his disappointment in the young man and in himself still felt fresh. The other boys had seemed to sense his foul mood and were giving him more space than usual. He felt bad for neglecting them, but he just needed a minute to recover. Before Tarik it had been almost eight months since they had lost a young man from the program. He had almost forgotten what that kind of failure felt like.

"Man, I keep going over the last year and a half and

wondering what we could have done differently."
Adam leaned back in his chair and rubbed his eyes.

"Don't beat yourself up, Adam," Chauncey said.
"There's only so much you all can do, and if I know
you like I think I do, you probably did all of it and a little more. At the end of the day those young men have
to make up their own minds. I know nobody could
have told us anything when we were actin' a fool and
playing like we were grown."

Adam nodded. "I know that's right."

"And like you said, Tarik's been the only one this
year so far. That's something to give God thanks for. In
fact, I've been checking around and the success rate for
Jacob's House is unprecedented. The YMCA tried to
start something like this in Detroit back in the nineties
and they shut it down within three years. They weren't
the first either. A bunch of other groups have tried similar setups all over but most of them go under within a
couple years."

"Yeah, Pastor R. clued me in on the YMCA and a
few other programs when I just got here," Adam commented. "He said when he became pastor at Immanuel
one of his top priorities was to make sure that the center stayed open and stayed successful."

"Well, he should be proud of himself," Chauncey
said. "I don't know what it is, but somehow you guys
have stumbled onto the winning formula."

Adam sensed his friend's pause.

"Which leads me to the reason for my call."

Adam chuckled. "And here I was thinking you just
wanted to check in on a brother."

"Yeah, that too," Chauncey said. "But I'm hoping
that some time in the near future I'll be able to do these

check-ins face to face, like in the office we're preparing for you at House of Judah."

Adam had known that sooner or later he would have to give his friend a definite answer. The weeks since he had left Baltimore had flown by, but throughout House of Judah had stayed a constant in the back of his mind. If he didn't know better he would have thought Chauncey had been reading his mind. He sure had picked an opportune time to call.

"I'm still thinking about it," Adam said. "It's not going to be easy to pick up and leave this place."

"I know," Chauncey said. "You put a lot of your heart into those boys. But if those couple weeks you were away proved anything, it was that they can manage without you."

"Is this your way of making me feel special, Chaunce?" Adam asked, only half jokingly.

"No," his friend answered. "This is my way of telling you that they could use you there, but we really need you here. You've got the background and experience to run this program in its pilot phase. And being native to Baltimore, like most of the young men in the program will be, will definitely give you an advantage connecting with them."

Chauncey was saying all the right words at the right time. Running a pilot project would be challenging. But at the moment it seemed easier to Adam than staying at Jacob's House, especially now that he'd let the boys down so badly.

"Give it to me straight, Adam," Chauncey pressed. "What's holding you back?"

"I don't know, man." Adam closed his eyes for a moment. "Atlanta's all I've known for the past three plus years. I haven't even lived in Baltimore in almost ten. I'm sure the scene has changed since then."

But Chauncey wasn't buying Adam's diversion. "Adam, you're holding out on me. It might have been a while but I still know you well enough to know that. Give me the truth. What's making you hesitate?"

Adam looked up as the door to his office eased open and dark inquisitive eyes peeped in at him. "Busy?" She silently mouthed the word, immediately drawing his attention to her pink-hued lips.

"I just need more time, Chaunce." Adam's eyes never left Toni. "Let me give you a shout at the end of the week."

"All right, brother," Chauncey said. "Talk to you then."

Adam hung up the phone and watched as Toni let herself into his office completely.

"So the boys tell me you've been channeling the Grinch this past week." Her arms were folded and her face set in the almost-annoyed expression she seemed to reserve only for him. She was wearing another of those shirtdress things with leggings. He wondered if she knew the kinds of problems he had when she did that.

"The boys or just Jerome?" he asked.

"No, Rasheed mentioned it too, on Saturday at church," Toni said. "Hence the reason I had to sacrifice my lunch break to come down here."

"So what's your plan?" Adam asked. "You're gonna beat me back into a good mood with today's copy of the *AJC*?"

Toni wrinkled her nose. "Is that the best you've got? Wow, you are in a funk."

Adam rolled his eyes.

"I had a feeling this was going to require a big sacrifice on my part," she said with a shake of her head. "But I'm willing to do it, for the sake of the boys. . . . I'm going to let you ride my baby."

Adam's eyes widened and his mouth fell open. Even when she held out the keys to clarify what she meant, his shock only moderately decreased.

"What?"

"You heard me," she said, jingling the keys to the motorcycle in front of him. "I've seen you checking her out. I know you want to."

He closed his mouth and hoped he hadn't drooled all over his desk. "But Trey says you never let anyone ride it. You barely let him get on it."

"Yes," Toni said, a hand on her hip. "Consider yourself lucky. So are you coming or what?"

She didn't have to ask him twice. He grabbed the keys from her outstretched fingers and was up and around the desk before her hand even fell to her side. He could hear her laughter behind him as he strode quickly through the house to the parking lot.

However, when his eyes landed on the gleaming red and silver high power sporting machine, he couldn't help but pause. It was almost as beautiful as its owner.

"You do know how to ride one of these things, right?" Toni asked, coming up behind him.

Adam grinned as he got on the motorcycle and slipped the key into the ignition. "Get on." He watched her eyes turn into saucers.

"But I only have one helmet," she almost stammered.

"We won't go far."

Without further protest, she got on behind him, resting her hands on his waist. Her grip tightened once he started the motorcycle and pulled out onto the road.

He had almost forgotten what it was like being on two wheels on the road with the wind directly against him and the world right up close. Even with the dangerous distraction of Toni's body so close to his, he could still appreciate the feeling of freedom that came from the experience. He was almost sad to have it end minutes later when he pulled back into the Jacob's House parking lot after going around a couple blocks.

He set down the kickstand but let the engine idle. He knew Toni had to get back to work, but he appreciated her letting him take her baby out. It really did make him feel better, if only for a moment.

"I'm kinda mad," she said with a pout, after getting off and removing her helmet. "You've only known her for a minute and she already seems to like you better. Where did you learn to ride like that?"

"Back home," he said with an easy smile, still straddling the bike. "And then in the army."

She smiled. "Was it as good as you remembered?"

"Better." He shook his head as his eyes roamed her face. "How did you know I would enjoy this?"

She shrugged. "Just a feeling I had."

"Thanks," he said quietly, hoping she saw the sincerity in his eyes.

"You're welcome," she said with a wink. "But get a scratch on her and I'll kill you."

He raised an eyebrow as she handed him the helmet. "She's yours for the afternoon."

His mouth fell open again. "You're going to leave me alone with her?"

"Yeah," Toni said. "I think you need her right now. Don't worry. I'll get a cab back to work."

In that moment all Adam wanted to do was pull her into his arms and kiss her senseless. But instead he dug into his pocket and pulled out his keys. "Take my car," he said. "And don't worry if you scratch it. I probably won't notice anyway."

She grinned and accepted his offer. "Duly noted."

"Thanks again." He stood up to put on the helmet and put back the kickstand. "I think Baby and I are gonna take the afternoon off."

"Well, get on with it then," Toni said mischievously, giving him a quick slap on the butt. "And while you're out there try to relax and have a good time."

Adam grinned as he gunned the engine. That he could definitely do.

Chapter 33

"I'm here to see Silver Maxwell," Toni said, walking up to the reception desk, ignoring the two other persons sitting in the lobby. One of them, a heavyset caramel-colored woman with pretty eyes and a mean scowl, glared at Toni.

"Relax, I'll only be a minute," Toni said with a smile.

"Excuse me," the receptionist said, the attitude apparent in her voice and in the movement of her neck. "Do you have an appointment?"

"No," Toni said. "But I think he'll want to see me."

"Miss, if you don't have an appointment then you can't—"

Toni cut her off. "Tell him it's about the Platinum Foundation."

"Ma'am, you can tell him yourself when you make an appointment."

Toni sighed and tried not to roll her eyes. "Look," she said, lowering her voice and trying a smile. "Just pick up the phone and tell him Toni Shields is standing in the lobby asking about the Platinum Foundation. If he doesn't want to see me, I promise you I'll leave."

"Ma'am . . ."

"Uh, Michelle," Toni said, glancing down at the nameplate on the desk," it's just one call. Please?"

Toni tried a bigger smile, and it seemed to work. The receptionist glared at her for a moment longer, before reluctantly picking up the phone and punching several numbers.

"Mr. Maxwell, I have a Toni Shields in the lobby? She is here from the Platinum Foundation? I told her to make an appointment but . . . Oh."

Toni smiled as the woman looked up at her curiously.

"Okay, I'll let her know," the receptionist said, her voice dropping. "Thank you, sir. No problem, sir."

Michelle hung up the phone and cleared her throat, shuffling a few papers around on her desk. After she had made Toni wait long enough, she looked up again. "Mr. Maxwell will see you now," she said in a clipped tone.

"Thank you." Toni resisted the urge to gloat.

When she got to Silver's office he was already waiting for her. "Hello again, Ms. Shields," he said with a small smile from behind his desk. "It seems I underestimated you."

"Most people do," Toni said with a smile.

Silver laughed. "I can only imagine how well that works for you. Please, have a seat."

"That's okay. I'll stand," Toni said. "I know you have other visitors waiting, so I won't stay that long. I just wanted to come by and say thank you."

Silver leaned back in his leather monstrosity and clasped his fingers together in front of him, but said nothing.

Toni continued. "I had to go down a lot of rabbit holes, but I know what you did. I know you're the Platinum Foundation, and that you're the one who made that big donation to Jacob's House."

Silver continued to smile at Toni, but said nothing. She had suspected that he wouldn't admit to anything. He had gone to great lengths to detach himself from the charity organization, which was nothing but a name registered in city documents. But once she discovered the truth, she knew she would have to see him personally.

"I also know that you were the one responsible for Jerome's case getting dropped." She lowered her voice as she stepped closer to the desk and leaned forward. "You have no idea how many people you made happy," she said sincerely, hoping he understood the full depth of her gratitude. "Thank you very much. I really really appreciate it."

"I'm sorry, Ms. Shields, I'm afraid I don't know what you're talking about," Silver said quietly, in a tone that told her the exact opposite. In his eyes she saw the "you're welcome" that would never reach his lips.

Toni nodded. "Okay. I haven't mentioned it to anyone and I'll keep it that way, if that's what you want."

Silver nodded and Toni knew that they had somehow reached an agreement.

"Thanks for your time, and for . . . everything." She turned to leave.

She was halfway to the door before she gave in to the urge to say her last words. "I don't understand you, Silver." She shook her head. "Any other politician would have gotten a camera crew and called up every major media house to be there when they handed over a check like that. But you—you don't even want the people you helped to know."

Silver looked down at his desk for a long moment before he spoke, then said, "Tell your brother thanks for taking me up. I really appreciated it."

Toni smiled as she headed toward the door once more. "It was great seeing you again, Silver."

"Always a pleasure, Toni."

Toni nodded at Michelle as she headed out of the office. As soon as she got to the parking lot she pulled out her cell phone.

"Hey, it's me. Okay, you can go ahead and run it, and leave Silver out. Like we suspected, he doesn't want any recognition."

Toni ended the call and got into Adam's car, a feeling of satisfaction suffusing her. It was almost over.

Chapter 34

"Yo, I know this ain't none of my business, but I gotta ask. Why you holdin' out on Bayne?"

Toni looked across the shirt rack at Jerome and put her hands on her hips. "You're right," she said, "it isn't. Didn't your momma ever teach you not to stick your nose in grown folks' business?"

Jerome's face darkened as he turned away from Toni and headed to another rack of shirts. "Nah," he threw behind him. "She was too busy workin' for all of that."

Toni bit her lip, wishing instantly that she could have taken back her words. They were in Sean John trying to find a suit for Jerome to wear to Immanuel's summer banquet. The annual youth event, which ended the summer, was the biggest thing next to the prom. Their shopping day had been going well so far until Toni mentioned Jerome's mother.

"Have you spoken to her lately?" Toni asked as casually as she could. She kept flipping through shirts so that it didn't seem like such a big deal.

"Not much," Jerome mumbled, wandering over to

another rack. "I called her the other day to tell her about my grades from last semester and about the case."

Toni glanced over at him. "What did she say?"

Jerome shrugged. "She said that it was about time I started doing well at something."

Toni gritted her teeth and tried not to let the annoyance show on her face. "Have you thought about going to see her?" she asked.

Jerome waited a long time before he answered. So long that Toni almost thought he hadn't heard the question. "I don't think she wants to see me," he said quietly after a moment, avoiding Toni's eyes.

"Did she tell you that?"

"No."

"Then why do you think that?" Toni asked, coming over to stand near him.

Jerome braved a look at her and Toni's heart almost broke with the sadness she saw in his eyes. She would have given anything to take that away.

"She's never asked to come see me, or asked me to come visit," Jerome said. "If she wanted to see me, she would have said something."

Toni sighed and pulled Jerome down on one of the cushioned seats in the store. "Sometimes, people who have been angry for a long time have a hard time knowing how not to be angry," Toni said slowly. "They care, but they're so used to not using their emotions, that they don't really know how to tell someone that they care about them."

"You mean like you and Bayne?" Jerome asked.

Toni rolled her eyes. "I mean like you and your mom. She probably doesn't know how to tell you she misses you since she hasn't seen you in such a long time. She might feel like you're doing so well here, that you don't need her anymore."

"That's dumb," Jerome said with an air of annoyance. "She's my mother. Of course I need her. I'll always want her around."

"Yeah, well, things that are clear to you might not always be so clear to another person, you know?"

Jerome nodded and looked down at his hands. "You think I should ask her if I can come visit?" he asked nervously after a long moment.

Toni shrugged. "It's up to you. There's a chance that she might say no. But there's also a chance she might say yes."

Jerome bit his lip thoughtfully. "Okay," he said with a nod, looking up at Toni earnestly. "I'll tell her I'd like to come visit, if you tell Bayne that you're feeling him."

"Boy! Go try on these shirts before I knock you upside the head," Toni said in mock annoyance as she pushed two shirts into Jerome's hands. "The nerve!"

"Is that a yes?" Jerome threw behind him as he headed toward the changing rooms.

"Don't make me get up off this seat!" Toni threatened. She shook her head as she watched him scramble into the dressing room.

Crazy kids.

Toni had barely parked the car in front of Jacob's House two hours later before Jerome jumped out, suit in hand. In a couple strides he was up the steps and at the front door. Only then did he seem to remember Toni.

"Hey, Toni, hurry up," he called, his hands on the door. "I gotta show Bayne this. He's gonna flip."

"I'm coming!" Toni said, laughing at the boy's enthusiasm. She had never seen Jerome act so excited. He seemed to have forgotten how uncool it was to get worked up about anything. Grabbing her bags and locking the doors, she barely made it up the steps before Jerome darted inside.

"So what do you think?" he asked, walking backward in front of her. "Think I should wear the pink tie, or the purple one?"

"It doesn't matter," Toni said, stepping up her own pace just to keep up with him. "You'll look good either way. Just make sure your shoes match your belt."

"You're gonna come over and check me out before I leave, right?" Jerome asked. "You always look like a million dollars. So if you say I look good, then I'll know I'm on point. . . ."

"Why you stopping?" Jerome asked when he realized Toni had paused at the bottom of the stairs.

Toni bit her lip. "I can't go up there. That's where you guys live."

Jerome rolled his eyes. "It's not that big a deal. You can come up," he said. "I'll just holler and let everyone know we have a visitor."

Toni still hesitated. "I don't know, Jerome. Doesn't Adam have a rule on that or something? I don't want to overstep, you know?"

Jerome pounded the banister impatiently. "The rule is no females upstairs after six p.m. and without a chaperone."

"See . . ."

"I'll be your chaperone," Jerome said. "Quit arguing and come on."

Toni sighed. "Okay, I'm coming. No need to bust a blood vessel."

"Don't know what you worried about, anyway," Jerome murmured as he continued up the stairs. "It's not like the two of you gonna do nothing."

"Hey, I heard that!" Toni called after him.

Somehow the dorm area was cleaner than Toni expected. Most of the boys had their doors open and from what she saw, everything looked pretty neat. Well, as neat as could be expected from teenage boys. It seemed like most of the guys were out of the house. But those who were in their rooms merely nodded to Toni as she passed by. Others barely gave her a second look.

Adam's apartment was at the end of the hall on the second floor. The door was half open when they got to it. Without hesitation Jerome barged in.

"Yo, Bayne, guess who's gonna be rockin' the latest Sean John style next weekend?" Jerome yelled, disappearing inside the apartment.

"Jerome! Don't you know how to knock?" Toni scolded from the doorway.

Jerome poked his head out. "Don't worry. Bayne doesn't mind. You can come in."

"I don't think so," Toni said, taking a step back. There was something very personal about entering Adam's living space. Almost intimate.

Only moments later Adam appeared at the doorway, dressed in jeans, a T-shirt, and socks. "He's right, it's no big deal. Come on in."

Toni took a couple delicate steps into the apartment, directly into what appeared to be a common area. It was larger than she expected it to be. Just opposite her, a huge window took up most of the wall, running almost from floor to ceiling. It was covered with light white curtains and darker orange drapes, with the drapes pulled back to let lots of natural light into the room.

A large, soft neutral couch sat along the back wall, with orange cushions scattered on it that matched the curtains. Opposite the couch was an entertainment center with a modest television, a less modest sound system, and an insane amount of CDs that Toni immediately wanted to riffle through. A brown rug with scattered patterns in cream lay in the space between the couch and the entertainment system, along with two medium-sized ottomans that matched the couch.

A huge picture of a Baltimore cityscape hung on the wall behind the sofa. She nodded as her eyes quickly took it all in. She felt like she had seen a part of Adam that she had not known before. She liked it.

"So what's the verdict?" Adam asked.

She realized he had caught her doing her visual inspection. She grinned. "Very impressive. Who knew a guy from the projects could set up a room?"

Adam laughed. "What? I can't have taste?"

"Yeah, you can," Toni said with a smirk. "But since Trey can't even put together an outfit without help, I have pretty low expectations of men when it comes to visual arts."

"Well, I have to be honest." His eyes sparkled as he stared at her. "This isn't all me. When I just got here Esther visited and decided to set this place up for me. I only picked out the couch and the picture. She did everything else."

"Really," Toni said, folding her arms knowingly. "You didn't pick out that top-of-the-line five-CD-changer sound system I'm looking at?"

Adam bit back a grin. "Well, maybe I had a hand in that too. But that's my one indulgence. The music has to be right. Sometimes it's the only thing that keeps me sane around here."

Toni nodded, her eyes lingering on him. There was something about him today. She couldn't quite put her finger on it, though.

"What?" he asked, looking down, then behind him, then back at Toni. "Do I have something on my shirt? My face?"

Toni shook her head. "No," she said with a puzzled smile. "There's just something about you, that's all. Something different. Like you're more relaxed. Did you do something?"

Adam smiled. "I caught the midday news on Fox with Tasha Carr. She had quite a story."

Toni smiled. She had seen Tasha's broadcast herself while having lunch at a deli near work. It had been a follow-up report to the Jacob's House exposé. Tasha had talked to a number of the men in Atlanta who had gone through the center. All of them had nothing but positive things to say about Jacob's House and gave their support about keeping it open. A few of them even had a few positive things to say about Adam.

"How did you manage to pull that off?" he asked.

Toni shrugged. "Tasha and I went to college together back in the day before she turned big time. When I pitched the idea to her she was all over it. I think they're going to rerun it as a special feature on the nightly news."

"Thank you," he said. The appreciation in his eyes warmed her all the way through.

"I brought the mess to your door," she said. "The least I could do is try to leave a positive impression of this place at the end of things."

"You are full of surprises, aren't you?" Adam said, chuckling as he walked over to where she was standing.

"You have no idea," Toni said with intended mis-chief.

Her flirting wasn't wasted on Adam. His eyes widened and he opened his mouth to respond, but Toni never heard it as Jerome came out of what she assumed was Adam's bedroom that very instant. Before Toni had even gotten inside, Jerome had disappeared into the bedroom to change into the suit she had just bought him.

"Okay, check this out," he said, striking a pose. "What do you think?" he asked, striking a new pose. "Am I killing it or what?"

Adam raised an eyebrow. "Pink tie?" he asked from beside Toni.

Toni whacked him playfully on his chest with the back of her hand. "What's wrong with a pink tie?"

"Isn't that a bit girly?"

"It is not," Toni said, rolling her eyes. "It looks great."

"I don't know," Adam said. "Next thing you know we'll be getting you a pink flower to go in the pocket of your—"

Toni slapped her hand over Adam's mouth and felt him laugh against her fingers.

"Don't listen to him," Toni said, trying to reassure a worried-looking Jerome. "You look hot. The girls will be falling all over you, especially Keisha."

Jerome looked down at his tie skeptically. "I'm gonna go try on the other one." He disappeared into the bedroom again.

Toni turned to Adam, a disapproving glare on her face. "See what you did," she chided softly. Adam opened his mouth and bit Toni's fingers gently. She felt a flutter in her stomach at the sensation of his warm lips against her fingers. She pulled her hand away quickly.

"Something wrong, Miss Shields?" The amusement in his eyes told her he had caught the nervousness in hers.

"Nothing." Toni's voice came out more high pitched than she intended.

"Are you sure?" He stepped closer and Toni was surrounded by his scent. Adam was so not playing fair.

"Sure." She cleared her throat.

They stared each other down a long time, the space between them so charged that Toni was sure that the tiny pricks she felt on her heated skin were from it. Toni stepped back and found enough air to breathe.

"When did he decide he was taking Keisha?" Adam asked, tearing his eyes away from her. "I thought he was going with Rochelle?"

"Uh-uh," Toni corrected. "Rochelle was the one who asked him. But he always wanted to take Keisha. He was just afraid to ask her. He has the hugest crush on her. Don't you pay attention?"

"I pay attention to you," he said, his eyes smiling at her. "Why'd you cut your hair? I liked it at your shoulders."

Toni lifted her hand to her new shorter do, and instantly regretted saying yes to Afrika when she had suggested a change only days earlier. She would never cut it again.

"Okay, what about this?" Jerome said, coming back out in the purple tie. This time he was looking to Adam for approval.

Toni sent Adam a silent warning that she knew he read loud and clear.

He nodded. "That's what I'm talking about," he said. "Now you look like a man."

Toni rolled her eyes.

"Thanks, Toni," Jerome said, grabbing her in a hug and easily swinging her around. "You're the best."

Before she could stop laughing he was through the door.

"Don't be walking around all afternoon in that suit," she called after him. "Go hang it up in the closet and don't get it soiled! I'm not paying for dry cleaning."

Adam laughed. "You are going to make a wonderful nagging mother for some kid someday."

Toni pursed her lips. "Since that's as close to a compliment as I think I'm gonna get from you, I'm gonna go ahead and say thanks."

"That was a lot of money you spent on Jerome." He had moved into her space again, enveloping her with his warmth, making her nervous. She fiddled with the ends of her hair.

"There're only so many outfits I can buy for my unborn niece. Jerome did really well in school this year and he deserved to be treated."

Adam nodded. "I know. But it was still really nice, what you did for him. It probably means more to him than you know. You mean more to him than you know."

As Toni's eyes met Adam's she got the distinct impression he hadn't just been speaking for Jerome. He was close enough to kiss her, but he didn't. So she shrugged it off. It was probably her imagination hard at work.

She cleared her throat. "By the way, I got you something." She retrieved the shopping bag on the floor and held it out to him.

Adam's eyes widened in surprise as he took the bag from her. "You didn't have to . . ."

"I know," she said, sinking down on the couch. She had to put some distance between them. His cologne was messing with her head. "I saw it and I thought of you, and once I see something I like, I have to get it."

Adam took a tentative peek in the bag.

"Go ahead. Open it." She was eager for his response.

He glanced at her a moment longer before reaching into the Sean John shopping bag and pulling out a box. Opening it carefully, he peeled back the tissues, revealing a purple dress shirt, only slightly darker than Jerome's tie.

Adam looked down at it for a long time without saying anything. Toni began to panic a little.

"I saw a red one, but I figured this color would look better against your skin," she said nervously. "I wasn't sure of your size, but I figured you were a little bigger than Trey since you're taller. If it's the wrong size, I have the receipt. I can get it exchanged."

He was shaking his head. Still not looking at her.

She sighed, her heart feeling crushed in her chest. "You don't like it."

"No . . . I like it," he said, struggling for words. "It's just that . . ."

She saw his jaw tighten and relax, then tighten again. Then he was pacing the ground, one hand on his waist, the other rubbing the back of his head.

"You can't do this," he said, dropping his hands to his sides and turning to face her, his brow furrowed in frustration.

"I can't do what?" Toni asked, confused. "Buy you a shirt?"

"Yes, buy me a shirt."

"Why?" Toni asked incredulously. "I saw something that I liked for you, and I bought it. It's not a big deal."

"It is a big deal!" Adam protested.

"It's just a shirt, Adam!"

Toni couldn't believe they were arguing over this. They had gotten into fights over some stupid stuff before, but this took the cake.

"It's not just a shirt."

"What?"

Adam blew out a breath. "No one has ever bought me a shirt before—no one other than my mother."

"So?"

"So you can't just buy me a shirt and walk away."

Toni's face wrinkled in confusion. "But I'm not walking away."

"But I am."

Toni sighed and closed her eyes. "Adam, you're not making sense."

"I'm leaving."

Toni blinked several times, not sure if she had heard him right. "I'm sorry," she said, shaking her head after a moment. "For a minute I thought you just said you were—"

"Leaving," Adam finished. "Yes, that's what I said."

Cold fingers of panic began to creep up Toni's spine. "Leaving, like going to Baltimore for a visit?" she asked weakly.

Adam shook his head sullenly as he watched the truth unfold in her mind. "Not for a visit. For good."

Toni gripped the side of the couch and took a deep breath. Then another. Then another. It wasn't helping. She still felt like she couldn't breathe.

She looked out the window at the bright sky, till the

sunlight seemed to burn her pupils. Then she looked down at the ground. None of it helped. She couldn't make sense of it. Adam was leaving? How could this be happening?

She braced herself against the couch and forced herself to stand, though her legs were more than a little unstable. "I h-have to g-go."

"Why?" Adam asked, stepping closer, his eyes searching hers desperately.

"I can't," Toni said, shaking her head as she still held on to the couch. "I just can't—"

"Toni, please. Talk to me," he pleaded.

What did he want her to say? That she didn't want him to leave? Did he want her to beg him to stay?

How had this happened anyway? One minute her life had been neat and organized. Okay, so she had a few issues. But she had been getting by. And then Adam had come along and stirred up the pot. He had come into her life and turned everything upside down, only to turn around and leave. She blinked back the tears that were already springing to her eyes.

"How can you do this to me?" she demanded, turning hurt eyes on him. He was so close that she wanted to reach out and slap him. "How can you just leave me like this? After everything we—"

Adam took the rest of the words right off her lips when his mouth descended on hers. One hand caressed the length of her arm, tracing a burning path across her already flushed skin. The other slipped to the nape of her neck, easing her closer with sweet, gentle pressure. Her body melted toward his and her lips parted, inviting him home. She had played their first kiss over and over in her mind a million times. But the memory had nothing on the reality.

He began to pull away, but Toni wasn't having it. She buried her fingers in the front of his shirt and pulled him back to her, tipping on her toes to return his kiss with one of her own. She didn't think about the fact that he was leaving. She didn't think about the fact that she was already too attached to him. She didn't even think about how massively complicated he made her life. All she thought about as she stood in his apartment kissing him, her heart syncing in rhythm with his, was the fact that she was exactly where she belonged.

"Adam."

His name slipped from her lips like a whispered request. In answer he slanted his mouth across hers, deepening the kiss. Every nerve in Toni's body felt like it was on fire. Even her ears were ringing.

It wasn't until she heard the second distinct ring of Adam's phone, that she realized the sound she had been hearing was not in her head, but in her purse.

"Adam . . ." Toni whispered, her eyes still closed. "Phone."

He swept his lips over hers. "Forget it."

She wrapped her arms around his neck.

For once, she had no argument.

Chapter 35

Toni rushed through Northside Hospital, following the signs until she found the maternity ward.

"I'm here to see my sister-in-law. She just came in with contractions and her husband isn't with her," Toni said in one quick breath to the nurse on duty.

It had taken her and Adam almost twenty minutes to get to the hospital after they realized the calls they had been ignoring were from Jasmine and Trey. Once they had finally gotten to the hospital, Toni hadn't even waited for Adam to park before jumping out of the car and rushing inside.

"No problem," the slim older woman said with a bright smile. "If she's not already in the delivery room you should be able to see her. What's her name?"

"Shields. Jasmine Shields," Toni said, trying to peep over the desk at the nurse's computer screen. She didn't understand how the woman could be so calm when her sister-in-law was about to have her first child, probably all alone.

"Oh, her," the nurse said, her smile drying up. "Yes, she's still here all right. But she's not alone."

"Oh," Toni said, noticing the change in the nurse's tone. "I guess my brother got here quicker than he thought."

"Oh no," the nurse said, shaking her head with a smirk. "I don't think that's her husband. But you can see for yourself. She's in room one-forty-five."

Toni headed down the hallway, not giving the nurse's words much thought. However, once she rounded the corner into Jasmine's room, everything made sense.

"Can you move it a little over to the left, please? That way we can capture anyone who comes through the door."

"Jasmine, what's going on?" Toni asked incredulously. "I thought you were in labor. Why is there a cameraman in your hospital room?"

"You got here finally!" Jasmine exclaimed, pulling herself upright in the hospital bed. "Thank God! I am so glad to have some family here with me."

"I don't know. It kinda looks like you have everything under control," Toni said, nodding toward the kid marching to Jasmine's tune with the tripod in his hand.

"What? This?" Jasmine asked. "Jon's just setting up the camera for me and then he'll be gone. You know I have to capture the birth of my first child on film."

"Yeah, I should have known your drama wouldn't stop just because you were in labor." Toni dropped into the chair by Jasmine's bedside. "But the way you were hollering on the phone, I thought we would miss the whole thing."

Jasmine grimaced. "Well, I am actually in labor, but the contractions are still pretty far apart, and I am only dilated four centimeters. It's probably going to be a wh—ahhh!"

Toni shrieked as Jasmine grabbed her hand and squeezed it hard. She felt as if every bone in her hand had been crushed. Once Jasmine loosened her grip, Toni pulled her hand away.

"Have mercy, Jasmine," Toni said, rubbing her fingers.

Adam appeared in the door. "Hey, I just got off the phone with Trey; he's on his way." He looked over at the wiry young man to the side. "Who's that?"

"The cameraman," Toni said, shaking her head, a "don't ask" expression on her face.

"Where is Trey?" Jasmine demanded, her forehead glistening with sweat. "Call him back and tell him he needs to get his narrow behind here right now!"

Adam's eyes widened with a touch of fear as he looked at Jasmine. "Uh, how about I just get out of your way," he said. He backed out of the room and nodded to Jon to follow him. The frightened-looking teenager didn't hesitate.

"Dios mío, Toni, I can't do this," Jasmine said, gripping Toni's hand tightly. "What was I thinking? I can't have a baby. I can't be someone's mother."

"Yes, you can, Jasmine," Toni said calmly, squeezing her sister-in-law's hand. She could see the worry etched all over Jasmine's face. "You can do this. You might be a pain in the butt, but I know you are an amazing and caring person. This baby is gonna be blessed to have you as a mother."

Jasmine began to cry. "Do you really mean that?"

"Yes, I do," Toni said sincerely, as she blinked back tears of her own. "You are one of the best things that ever happened to my brother. And you're an amazing sister."

"I'm sorry I'm a little crazy sometimes," Jasmine sniffled, wrapping her other hand around Toni's.

Toni laughed. "It's okay. You fit right in with the rest of us."

"I'm scared, Toni," Jasmine said, her eyes widening.

Toni smiled and patted Jasmine's damp forehead gently with a cloth. "Don't be. You are going to have this baby and everything's going to be fine. Okay?"

Jasmine nodded, even though her eyes still looked wide and uncertain. "Okay."

"Okay, how's everyone doing in here?" a chirpy nurse asked, floating through the hospital room's door.

"Ahhhhh!"

Another shriek from Jasmine shot searing pain through the joints of Toni's hand.

"Okay, looks like someone's ready to have a baby," the nurse said with a small laugh.

Toni glared at her. There was nothing funny about the pain in her fingers. Trey had better show up soon.

As if on cue, her brother rushed through the door.

"Baby, sweetheart, I'm here," he said breathlessly, slipping in beside Jasmine and grabbing the hand that Toni quickly abandoned.

"Oh, thank God," Jasmine said as she started to cry again.

"Okay, we're gonna have to examine you again to check how dilated you are," the nurse said, uncovering a nearby metal tray with medical tools. "Let's just get your feet up in these stirrups and we'll be ready to go."

Toni stood up at the word *stirrups*. That was a lot more of her sister-in-law than she wanted to see.

"Uh, I think you guys have everything under control," she said. "I'll just be outside."

Jasmine and Trey barely noticed her as she left.

She found Adam sitting outside the door. "Coward."

"Hey, I know my limits," Adam said unapologetically. "And unless I'm the father, I don't need to be in there. I'll just hang out here and they can let me know when it's over."

"Well, from the look of things that might be a while," Toni said, sitting down beside him.

"Then I guess we'll be here a while," he said, turning to look at her. His gaze heated her from the crown of her head to the soles of her feet. She could barely make herself sit still.

Toni let out a deep breath. "Then we should probably talk about what you said earlier."

Adam sighed and leaned his head back against the wall behind them. "What do you want to know?" he asked.

"Well, for starters, you could tell me why you're leaving Jacob's House, and Atlanta," Toni said. "I never thought you would leave the guys like that, especially now when things seem to be going well with a lot of them."

"It's the right thing to do," Adam said, crossing one leg over his knee casually.

"Convince me."

He glanced at Toni, then folded his arms. "Okay. While we were in Baltimore," Adam began, "I went to see House of Judah. It's a former retirement home that a union of churches in Baltimore have bought. They plan to renovate the building and run a similar Jacob's House project out of it."

Toni listened, intrigued as he explained how the seeds for the project had started a year earlier, and how he had been providing advice and consultation ever since.

"When I think of all the kids I grew up with in B-more, I know that we could have been so much better if we had gotten a second chance. Maybe if we'd had an opportunity to grow in a community where people believed in us, things would have been different." He looked down at his hands.

"You're thinking about Noah, aren't you," Toni said.

Adam laughed sadly. "I don't think I ever stop thinking about him. Every time I look at a young man going in the wrong direction, I see Noah."

"So why would you leave Jacob's House now and abandon all the young men here?" Toni asked. She watched Adam open and close his mouth several times before answering her.

"I can't be with them forever," he said quietly after a moment.

"No one expects you to," Toni said. "But you've only been here three years. You know how long it takes to form trusting relationships with these young men. Everyone else in their lives has given up on them, and they assume that everyone in their future will be the same. How can you just up and leave as soon as you've started to make a connection?"

She saw his jaw tighten.

"There'll be other counselors."

"True," Toni said. "But that doesn't mean your time is up here. Jerome has one year left. This year he should be applying to college. So should Rasheed and a couple others. You think some new guy who doesn't know them will be able to motivate them to do that?"

Toni let out a long sigh. "I'm pretty new to this whole talking to God thing, but are you sure this is what He wants you to do? Because this feels like it's coming out of left field."

Adam sat forward, frustration all over his face. "So now you think you know everything about me?" His tone had an edge that told Toni the conversation was not going well. "I've been working with these people a long time. I helped them put together the initial proposal for the Baltimore project. We've been in contact for months. Just because I didn't tell you, doesn't mean I haven't been thinking about it."

"Adam, I didn't mean to imply that—"

"And in case you've forgotten, Baltimore is my home," Adam continued, cutting her off. "My mother, my brothers, my sister, nieces, nephews, they're all in Baltimore. Is it wrong for me to want to be where they are?"

Toni looked down at her hands and closed her eyes. *God, please give me the right words to say to him. I'm not trying to upset him. But I feel this isn't right. If I am being selfish please let me know.*

"I know Baltimore is your home," Toni said quietly, without looking across at him. "I know you miss your family. If you feel that this is what God is calling you to do, then do it. But remember that for a lot of these boys you and the staff at Jacob's House are the only family they have left to count on."

"I thought you of all people would have understood." He shook his head as he stood up. "I can't talk to you about this right now."

Toni felt the temperature drop between them as Adam walked away. She kept watching him, but he didn't look back even once, didn't even slow his pace. It was the first time he had shut her out so completely. She prayed that conversation hadn't just damaged what had become one of the most important friendships of her life.

Chapter 36

Isabel Alexandra Shields came screaming into the world at 2:45 a.m. on Friday morning after eight hours of labor. Toni thought she was the most beautiful thing she had ever seen, but she was too exhausted to be sure. After kissing her brother and sister-in-law good-bye, she headed into the lobby with dreams of her bed on her mind. That was when she remembered she had come in Adam's car.

After their disagreement over him leaving, she had spent most of the late night and early morning avoiding him. It wasn't that hard. Northside was a huge hospital. And once news of Jasmine's delivery had spread around, a lot of other people, like the pastor's wife, Camille, Afrika, and a few relatives of Jasmine had shown up. Many others had come and gone through the night. But now that the show was officially over, the crowd had begun to thin out, and Toni's options were few.

"Hey, you ready to go?"

It was Adam.

"Uh, actually I was just going to get a cab," she said, already moving toward the huge glass doors. "I figured you might still be mad at me."

Something she couldn't read flashed across his face, but was quickly replaced. Toni didn't like the new blank look. At least when he was upset she could see some kind of fire in his eyes. But now the eyes she loved to lose herself in were cold and still, giving her nothing.

"There's no need for that," he said. "I'll take you home."

She noticed he didn't say he wasn't mad.

"Really, Adam, it's not a big deal," Toni said, already glancing at the door.

"Toni, it's almost three a.m." Frustration. At least she had managed to evoke something. "There is no way I am letting you climb into a cab at this time of morning."

"She can ride with me," Afrika said, appearing out of nowhere. "I'm headed that way anyway."

Toni breathed a sigh of relief. She was never so happy to see her friend in her whole life. Adam looked back and forth between Afrika and Toni. He frowned a little, but shoved his hands in his pockets tiredly and headed toward the doors without further protest.

"Good night, ladies," he threw behind him.

Toni watched him, until the darkness swallowed him up and she could no longer make out his form. She wanted to run after him. Put her arms around him. But instead she stayed rooted in the lobby.

"Okay. Let's move," Afrika said, digging her keys out of her purse. "You can explain in the car."

They managed to get out of the parking lot and onto

the main road before Afrika began her interrogation. "Spill it."

"Adam and I had a fight," Toni said. She decided to leave out the part about him kissing her. She wasn't ready to talk about that yet.

"No joke." Afrika smirked. "What happened?"

Toni sighed and turned toward the window. "He's leaving Jacob's House."

"Word?"

"Yeah," Toni said. "He got an offer to head up a similar project in Baltimore and he's thinking about going."

Afrika let out a whistle.

"I can't believe he's doing this, Afrika," Toni said. She could feel herself getting annoyed. "It's so irrational."

"And I'm guessing you pretty much let him know that, right?"

Toni pouted. "Just barely. I hardly got a word out before he started going off on me. He actually accused me of not wanting him to be with his family. Me. The one who lost her family and knows what it's like to be without them."

When Afrika didn't say anything, Toni turned to look at her. "What? You think I was wrong?" Toni asked.

Afrika shrugged. "Hey, the two of you have been tight for a good minute. You know him better than I do, but what would be so bad about him helping the kids in Baltimore like he's doing here?"

"Nothing," Toni said with a sigh. "I just feel like . . . like maybe he's going because of everything that happened here with his story in the news. It's almost as if he's running."

"Did you tell him that part?"

"Like I said, I barely got a word in."

"Then you gotta holler at him again," Afrika said. "Give him some time to cool off and then go talk to him. When there's feelings involved it's easy for things to get outta control."

Toni's eyes widened. "Who said I have feelings for him?"

Afrika rolled her eyes. "Seriously, T?" Afrika asked with a laugh. "The two of you are so hot for each other you're about to burn the rest of us up with your heat."

Toni shook her head vehemently. "That's crazy."

"Nah, girl, what's crazy is him setting up camp at your bedside when you were in the hospital," Afrika said. "Crazy is you flying across the country to try and stop him from going to jail. . . ."

"Baltimore is hardly across the country," Toni said dryly.

". . . And don't forget that ten-hour trip to pick him up when he got out of jail. I ain't never done that for no brother—not even when it was good like that."

"Trey asked me to go with him. . . ."

Afrika laughed. "All right, girl. Stay in denial. But I've seen you two together, and from the way you been eyein' a brother, I wouldn't be surprised if you were already in lo—"

"Don't even think it," Toni said quickly, knowing exactly where her friend was going. It was impossible. There was no way that she could be in love with Adam.

Absolutely no way.

Now if she could only get her rapidly beating heart to believe that.

* * *

When Adam stepped into Pastor Reynolds's office on Wednesday morning for their weekly meeting, he already knew exactly what he was going to say.

"This is probably going to be one of our last meetings," he began before Pastor Reynolds could even get a word in. "I've decided to take the position in Baltimore."

Pastor Reynolds straightened a few files on his desk before acknowledging Adam. "I'm glad you could make it this early," he said after a moment, glancing at the clock on the wall to his left. "I know seven a.m. is a bit unreasonable, but I also know you have long days, and I figured you could get this out of the way. I was just going through my morning devotions. You mind joining me?"

Adam knew the man of God well enough to know that he had heard his statement about leaving. But Pastor Reynolds had the patience of the saints, and he wouldn't get to it until he was good and ready. Or until God told him it was time. And so Adam nodded and followed Pastor Reynolds's tall former-NBA-player frame over to the side of the huge office where there was a small sofa and two armchairs surrounding a coffee table.

"Where are you reading from today?" Adam asked.

Pastor Reynolds didn't do devotional books. According to him, God's Word was so rich that you could read the same chapter every day and get something new from it every time.

"Today I've been reading First Chronicles," Pastor Reynolds said, choosing the armchair that already had the Bible open in front of it.

"I thought you were just done going through the book of Second Samuel?" Adam asked, making himself comfortable in the other chair. "Isn't it pretty much the same thing?"

Pastor Reynolds chuckled. "It covers the same period, but it's not the same. The perspective is different. Besides, you know David is one of my favorite Old Testament brothers."

Adam nodded. He knew that was true.

"I'm in chapter seventeen, where David tells God he's going to build the temple for him," Pastor Reynolds said. "After all, God had done so much for David. He had brought him a mighty long way. He had forgiven David for all the evils in his past. And David wanted to do this great thing to honor Him. Even Nathan the prophet thought it was a good idea."

"But God said no," Adam said, already familiar with the story.

Pastor Reynolds nodded. "That's right. He sent the prophet Nathan back to King David, to let him know that the building of the temple wasn't his work to do. It was to be left to his son Solomon.

"I especially love verse sixteen. After David's request is denied he doesn't sulk like a child. He goes to God and says, 'Who am I, O God, and what is my house that You have brought me so far.' He humbles himself and accepts God's decision. Even though it must have disappointed him—even though it must have frustrated him to have all the wealth and resources but not the permission to build—he received God's message with gratitude and went on to renew his covenant with God."

Pastor Reynolds paused and shook his head. "I don't know if I could have taken it as well as David. It's like me wanting to build a bigger Immanuel Temple over in the southeast and God saying, 'No, Reynolds. That's not for you.' Building a temple is a good thing. How could God be against something like that?"

Adam knew where Pastor Reynolds was going.

"But you know what I realized when I read this? It's about letting God choose our work. If we are going to claim to be totally submitted to God, we have to be just that, totally submitted. We have to remember that our ways are not His ways. And sometimes, He refuses our seemingly noble intentions because they aren't best for us and for His cause.

"It's a hard lesson for many of us to learn, but sooner or later we must. Especially those of us in ministry. Not everything benevolent that we want to do for God is ordained by God."

"Me going to Baltimore is not like that," Adam said stubbornly, his brow furrowing.

"I didn't say anything about Baltimore," Pastor Reynolds said, sitting back. "I was just sharing my morning devotions."

"But you were thinking it." Adam frowned. "I don't understand. I thought you thought me helping with this project was a good idea."

"I do," Pastor Reynolds said calmly. "But helping with the project and moving to Baltimore to head it up are two different things."

"But I know all about it," Adam insisted. "Plus the experience of being at Jacob's House gives me a practical advantage to helping it work well."

"I am sure it does."

"Baltimore is my home," Adam argued.

"That's true too."

Adam sighed when he realized he was running out

of explanations. "I've done all I can do here in Atlanta," he said, looking down at his hands. "I have nothing left to offer these boys."

Pastor Reynolds said nothing, and Adam knew he was waiting for the rest. He always had a way of pulling every last bit of truth out of the core of Adam's being.

Adam stared across the office at the floor-to-ceiling bookshelves without really seeing any of it. "You were right three years ago when you told me to go deal with my issues in Baltimore," he said after a moment. "I didn't do that right away. Now I feel like maybe I'm not the kind of leader these boys need anymore. I have nothing left to teach them."

"You can teach them it's never too late to take ownership of your past," Pastor Reynolds said, sitting forward. "You took responsibility for your mistakes. You might have taken a long time to do it, but you did it. That's a powerful lesson for young men to learn."

Adam's stomach was in knots. He was starting to feel unsure about his decision and he hated that.

Pastor Reynolds continued. "In the past few weeks you have faced up to what happened. You've been upfront and honest with the boys, with the church, and with the world. These boys need to learn how to do that. All of them have tarnished pasts. And even if they clean up and become amazing men, one day, someone's going to throw that tarnished past back in their faces. They have to learn how to deal with that. Do you want them to learn how to acknowledge their past and show that they are changed? Or do you want them to learn that they should change locations every time their past comes to the surface? Should they find a new job every time a coworker finds out they were convicted of a crime? Should they abandon every relationship once their criminal history becomes known? What about their children? Should they hide who they used to be from them?" Pastor Reynolds let out a long breath and shook his head.

"Adam, this is still about honesty and personal responsibility. Running every time your past comes up is the same as hiding from it."

"I'm not running," Adam said strongly. He was tired of everyone implying that he was. "I'm going back to Baltimore, to the place where all my mess happened. How is that running?"

"Your face was never on the front of a newspaper in Baltimore," Pastor Reynolds said. "Plus all those years ago when you lived in Baltimore you weren't ashamed about being a criminal. You weren't in touch with Christ yet. You didn't have people who respected you and who might be disappointed in your past."

Adam sunk lower in his chair.

"But you have that here. And facing it is hard," Pastor Reynolds said gently. "But part of letting Christ forgive us of our past, is letting go of the shame of that past. It means having the humility to acknowledge where God brought us from to where we are now, knowing that none of that could have happened without Him.

"Until we do that we will struggle with knowing which decisions are of God and which ones are just reactions to our own fears."

"So you're saying I shouldn't go," Adam said, unable to hide the disappointment in his voice.

"No," Pastor Reynolds said, shaking his head. "I'm

saying, don't build the temple unless you're sure God has given you the green light."

Pastor Reynolds closed the Bible in front of him. "Adam, you know that you're like a son to me. I know in your heart you love God and want to serve Him. I want you to make the right decision on this. Can I pray with you?"

Adam nodded and lowered his head. Pastor Reynolds's prayer was quick and to the point.

"Kind and compassionate Father, thank you for your salvation and grace. We would be nowhere without them. Take Adam into your care, and lead him down the path You have for him. Give him true freedom from the guilt and shame of his past. Help him see Your vision for his future. All these things we ask in Your Son's name, amen."

And with the end of the prayer came the end of the discussion. Even though they met for over an hour afterward about administration matters related to Jacob's House, the topic of Adam's leaving never came up again. Nonetheless, the uncomfortable feeling in Adam's stomach had seemed to intensify since the moment Pastor Reynolds prayed on him. He didn't want to make the wrong decision.

There were many good reasons why he should go, and he had named all of them to Pastor Reynolds. But there were also just as many convincing reasons to stay, one of them being a petite five-foot-four beauty who was the reason he'd finally had the courage to face his past in the first place. A part of him was willing to ditch the whole idea of leaving just to see what could happen with the two of them. But he couldn't base a life decision like this on a woman he had known for only a few months—even if she was the kind of woman he could imagine knowing for a lifetime.

Regardless of where he went, someone would get hurt. But at the end of the day, everything would resolve itself if he was where God wanted him to be.

Now if he could only figure out where that was.

Chapter 37

"I'm not going," Toni said stubbornly, returning to her couch and plopping down on it, as she pulled a pillow to her chest.

Jerry Springer was on television and she was watching two pregnant women fight over a man who wasn't worth half their energy.

"What do you mean you're not going?" Afrika asked, closing the front door to Toni's apartment and following her to the living room. "You have to go. It's the boys' end of year barbeque. Plus it's Adam's last night. You remember him? The man you're in love with."

Toni pouted. "You've been talking to Camille, haven't you?" she said, switching the channel to *Law and Order*. But not even the antics of the SVU team could keep her distracted.

"No," Afrika said, coming to stand in front of the television. "I've been watching you. I see the way you look at him. You're slick, but you're not that slick. I know you done gone and caught feelings over him."

Toni scowled.

"Look, honey, I get that you're upset he's leaving, but if you don't go you won't forgive yourself," Afrika said. "So go get dressed."

Toni pouted. "He's making a mistake."

"Maybe," Afrika said. "But being a real friend to him means being there for him even when he does something dumb."

A knock on the door interrupted whatever else Toni wanted to say. Afrika went to get it, and came back with Camille. She frowned as her eyes took in Toni's sweats and T-shirt.

"Why aren't you dressed?" Camille asked, placing a hand on her hip. "Do you know what time it is?"

"I'm not going," Toni repeated. She flipped the channel again. *The Real Housewives of Atlanta* reruns.

"You have to go," Camille said. "Adam's going to be there."

"Is there an echo in this room?" Toni asked, annoyed.

"What's her problem?" Camille asked, turning to Afrika.

"She's still mad that Adam is leaving," Afrika answered, sitting down in the armchair next to the coffee table. She turned to Toni again. "Did you even go talk to him like we discussed?"

Toni scowled and turned up the volume on the television.

"I'm guessing that's a no," Camille said.

"Okay, Toni, we're about to keep it real here." Camille reached over and turned off the TV to show her friend she meant business. "I know you won't admit it, but you have deep feelings for Adam. Nothing's wrong with that. But this is his life and he's made this choice for himself that quite frankly has nothing to do with you. How can you be so mad about it?"

"Because I don't think it's the right choice," Toni said stubbornly.

Camille shrugged. "So what? So because you don't agree with him, you're not going to talk to him? Even if it's not the right choice, is that a reason to end the friendship? I hate to bring this up, but are you not feeling déjà vu on this?"

Toni's mouth fell open and she looked across at her friend. She knew Camille was talking about what had happened to their friendship after Camille's abortion. But the look on her face wasn't a spiteful one. She wasn't bringing it up because she was still angry at Toni for leaving. She was mentioning it because she loved her and didn't want her to make the same mistake again.

"I'm sorry, Camille," Toni said. "I should never have walked out on our friendship back then. But this is different."

"Really?" Camille asked gently. "How? You didn't agree with the choice I had made, and it ruined our friendship. Now you are about to distance yourself from Adam because you don't agree with what he's doing. How is that not the same?"

"She's right, T," Afrika said. "And if we're keeping it real, that's what you did with Jasmine after the house thing too."

Toni bit her lip as she suddenly saw her pattern.

"Look, honey, you were mad at God for a long time because you didn't understand how He could take your parents away from you; you were mad at me for a long time because of what happened; you were mad at Jasmine because she hurt you," Camille said.

"I'm glad that you are starting to repair all those friendships, but don't make the same mistake again. Don't cut off the people who love you because they sometimes disappoint you. Loving someone means taking the good with the bad. What if God cut us off every time we did something that He didn't agree with? Can you imagine where we'd be?"

Toni rested her head on the cushion as she thought about her friends' words. She knew they were right, but she was so used to cutting the painful things out of her life, that she wasn't sure she knew how to do things any other way.

Toni sighed and shook her head. "I guess you have a point. But am I just supposed to act like what he's doing is okay?"

"No," Afrika said. "You don't have to agree with what he's doing. But you have to support him—show him that you're still there for him even though you think he's going the wrong way. That's what you do when you love someone."

"I don't love him," Toni said quickly.

Camille rolled her eyes.

"Yeah, we don't have time to argue that with you right now," Afrika said, standing up. "We're already late. Get dressed. We're leaving in five minutes."

Toni pouted. "I'm a grown woman. You can't just barge into my apartment and tell me what to d—"

"Get dressed," Camille and Afrika said together.

Toni scowled but got up and headed to her bedroom, wondering when she had lost control of her life.

The party was already in full swing by the time Toni, Afrika, and Camille showed up. Smells of barbecued everything greeted Toni as she followed Afrika and Camille out of Jacob's House to the lawns and basketball court in back. Some sound equipment was borrowed from the church and speakers were set up around the perimeter of the event. Rasheed was over by the turntable spinning tracks while a guy Toni recognized from church stood nearby overseeing.

As Toni had expected, the event was packed. Apart from the boys and the Jacob's House staff, there were a few parents, friends from the school, and many of the members from Immanuel. She laughed as she caught sight of Pastor Reynolds trying to keep up as he played three on three against a few of the boys with Sam and another brother Toni didn't recognize. A few feet over on the sidelines, his wife, First Lady Loretta Reynolds, stood with her son, Joshua, taking in the action.

Slipping away from her friends, Toni headed over to where they were standing. "Sister Reynolds!" Toni called out to the older woman, who was stylishly dressed in skinny jeans that weren't tight but looked amazing on her. The short-sleeved white jacket and matching inset blouse that finished the ensemble made her look casual but elegant.

"Hey, Toni," Loretta said, warming her with a smile. "How are you?"

"I'm good," Toni said, smiling back. She turned her gaze to the tall man beside Loretta. "How's it going, Josh? Where's Samantha?"

"She's over by the benches, swapping baby stories with Jasmine," Joshua answered, giving Toni a half hug.

Joshua and Trey were about the same age and had been very close growing up. However, they had gone to different colleges and Joshua had moved to a suburb an hour outside Atlanta with his wife, Samantha, after he had graduated. He and his family often came out to Immanuel to visit his parents and catch up with old friends.

"Foul!"

Toni turned to the court where there was a bit of a scuffle. Pastor Reynolds was groaning and holding his back while the other players crowded around him.

"Oh no." Sister Reynolds cocked her head to the side like she was inspecting damage. "Looks like your father has gone and injured himself again."

"Again?" Joshua asked. "Has he hurt his back before playing with the boys?"

"Not his back," she answered, heading onto the court. "Just his pride."

Joshua and Toni chuckled as they watched the First Lady rescue her husband.

"Josh, brother, you should be out there on the court." Trey appeared at their side with three sodas.

Joshua laughed. "No way," he said, taking the soda Trey offered him. "I can't even handle my dad. You want me to go up against those boys too?"

"I'm getting you on the court before you leave today," Trey said. Then he directed his attention to Toni. "Baby sis. How you holding up?" He put an arm across her shoulder and handed her a drink with the other.

"I should be asking you that question," she said, popping the tab on the can. "I feel like I've barely seen you outside the house since the baby was born."

A look of weariness slipped over Trey's face. "Don't ever have kids, Toni. They are beautiful little creatures until they start crying. Then they just turn into howling monsters that refuse to let you sleep."

Joshua and Toni both laughed.

"I'm serious," Trey said, shaking his head tiredly. "I've been sleeping like three hours a night since Isabel came home. And Jasmine's decided that since she has to take care of her all day I get to take the night shift."

Toni raised an eyebrow. "So she's not breast-feeding her at night?"

"Breast pump," Trey and Joshua answered at the same time.

Toni laughed.

"Yeah, been there, done that," Joshua said with a chuckle. "Welcome to parenthood, brother."

"I know." Trey stifled a yawn. "Tell me about it."

"Man, are you yawning at our party?" Adam asked with a laugh.

Toni hadn't even seen him come up.

"Bro, I'm about to find a couch inside and crash," Trey said, swallowing back another yawn. "I am beat."

"I understand," Adam said with a laugh. "But know that for bailing out early you're gonna have to come visit me soon in Baltimore."

"Yeah," Trey said. "You'll need to ask my kid about that, since she's the one running my life now."

"Will do," Adam said with a laugh. "Can I steal this one from you guys for a minute?" He had a hand on Toni's back and was already easing her gently away.

"Sure," Joshua said with nod.

"Steal her for as long as you like," Trey said with a mischievous grin. She watched a look she didn't understand pass between Adam and Trey. But she didn't have time to think about it as he pulled her in the direction he was going.

And then she was alone with Adam—or as alone as

she could be in a yard full of people. She had only been walking with him for a minute but he had already been stopped by three people who had come by to greet him. Once word had got out that he was leaving, everybody wanted to say their good-byes.

He must have realized that any kind of conversation would be impossible where they were as he led her off the court, across the grass, and toward the sidewalk of the road that marked the end of the Jacob's House property. Toni could still hear the music as they walked, but it seemed to be more of a lull in the background.

"So, I know it's been more than two weeks," he began when they were a good distance away. "But I just wanted to apologize for what happened at the hospital."

Toni glanced at him. He had his hands shoved deep in his pockets and was staring at the ground as he spoke.

"I know you were only telling me how you felt and I shouldn't have gone off on you like that," he continued. "I really value our friendship and I don't want to leave with us fighting like this." He gave a nervous laugh. "I'm actually surprised that you even showed up today."

Toni was ready to tell him that she just came for the boys, but something inside stopped her. "I actually wasn't going to come," she said. "I still don't fully get why you're doing this. But it's your life, and I respect that this is something you feel you need to do."

He nodded. "It is."

She sighed. "Can you tell me why?"

His jaw tightened and she reached out a hand to

touch his arm. "I don't want to fight, Adam, I just want to understand," she said softly. He glanced at her, and she saw him relax.

"Baltimore is my home, Toni," Adam said after a moment. "I feel a responsibility to the community there. I feel a responsibility to the people there who got hurt because of me, and to those who helped me even though I hurt them. I feel a responsibility toward their kids, their nieces, their nephews, their neighbors.

"I look at Jerome and Rasheed and the boys here, and I see Benji's son and my cousins' kids, and my mother's neighbor. And I worry about them, because it's so easy for them to go the wrong way. And if they do mess up, what options are there for them?"

His jaw had tightened again, and Toni could see the frustration coursing over him in waves. She took his hand and squeezed it gently and he seemed to come down a little.

"I know a place like this can do amazing things for the youth in that area," he continued. "And I know how to make it work. Not just theoretically, Toni; I know how to make it work practically."

Adam shook his head. "How can I have the information, the opportunity, the spiritual desire to do it and not act on it?"

Toni let his question hang between them as they continued walking, her hand still in his. She was still learning things and one thing she had learned in the past couple months was that it was okay to not say anything sometimes—even when you felt like you were right. And so she was content to let the silence hang between them. Adam didn't seem to mind either.

A cool evening breeze met them as they walked the path down to the end of the road. Toni smiled as she remembered this was the same road where she and Adam had caught Rasheed and his girlfriend making out. Moments like these made her feel like Adam had been in her life forever, instead of less than a year. She wondered what she had done with all her time before she met him and the boys at Jacob's House. It seemed now that they were a regular part of her routine.

"I've been thinking about how to be a good friend," Toni said after a few minutes. "I tend to . . . distance people when they do things that I don't agree with." Toni smiled. "Not a great way to maintain friendships, I know."

Adam smiled but said nothing.

"Anyway, the new Toni is trying not to do that anymore," she said with resolve. "I am going to miss you though—no one else can pick a fight with me like you do."

His whole face relaxed and his eyes took on golden highlights as he laughed.

"But whether you're here or in Baltimore, you can count on our friendship," she said.

He grinned. "Does that mean I can call on you to help fix a roof in Baltimore, friend?" he asked.

"The friendship is free, the roofing services aren't," Toni said. "A sister's time is expensive."

They both laughed again, and Toni felt like whatever tension had been left between them had disappeared.

"So we're good?" he asked.

Toni smiled. "Yeah. We're good."

He pulled Toni toward him into a warm embrace. His fresh scent surrounded her like a mist. She felt her heart speed up a little.

Darn.

She had hoped those feelings would have been gone.

His arms stayed wrapped around her and she didn't pull away. She knew that they couldn't stay that way forever, but she wanted to remember this moment. It might be the last one she had with him.

He finally let her go, but his hands caressed her arms and shoulders as he searched her eyes. "If I was here . . . it would be different, wouldn't it?" he said in a low voice.

Toni nodded and smiled sadly.

"I wish I had met you sooner," he said. His eyes bore into hers, adding a lot of things that his lips would never say because he was leaving and therefore had no right to. But Toni understood them anyway.

She shrugged. "I guess we just had bad timing."

He ran a hand across her cheek. "I never wanted to be another one to leave you."

Toni shook her head. "You're not. I'm not losing you. You're just moving. Besides, both of us have things we need to work through before we can think of being with someone else," she added.

He nodded. He looked at her a long time, and Toni knew that he was memorizing her face, because she was doing it too.

"You ready to head back?" he asked after a moment, his fingers still intertwined with hers.

She nodded and turned toward the direction of the party. And then, before she could take one step, he pulled her to him quickly and crushed his lips against hers. His hands slipped to the back of her neck and she felt the air leave her body as she took in his intensity. But before Toni could get invested in the kiss, he pulled away.

"I'm sorry," he said, his forehead pressed against hers. "I shouldn't have done that."

"You're right. You shouldn't have."

But she tipped up and kissed him back gently. And then he wrapped his arms around her again, and she buried her face in his chest. It was good-bye.

But it was okay. She was learning to live with good-byes. She was learning they weren't the end.

Chapter 38

"**A**re you sure you're ready for this?" Trey asked from the driver's seat.

Toni looked out the window at the house where her life had both begun and ended. She shook her head. "No, I'm not ready," she said after a long moment. "But I'm tired of waiting."

She opened the car door and stepped out onto the sidewalk, taking in everything before her. It wasn't exactly the same as it had been ten years ago. For one, someone had gone ahead and erected a low white fence around the perimeter of the property. Her mother had never liked fences—even when the neighborhood dogs would come and leave their gifts on her front lawn. She said it made her home feel like a prison. She had been satisfied with the large uncut stones that used to line the front, separating the front yard from the sidewalk. Apparently those that came after her hadn't had her level of tolerance.

The walkway to the front steps also looked like it had had some help from the previous owners. And there also looked to be a new roof and gutters. But other than that, it more or less looked exactly how she remembered it, down to the light blue paint on the outside walls.

Toni stood in front of the gate feeling stuck. She was stuck, and had been for a long time. She had been standing at the threshold of her life, unable to go back but too paralyzed to move forward. She heard Trey get out of the car behind her. He would stay with her, but he wouldn't force her to do anything. This had to be on her. She had to do it on her own or not at all.

A cool September morning breeze moved up the quiet street, rustling the trees in the front yard and moving the light wooden gate slightly open. It swung lazily on its hinges as if to ask what the big deal was. Sometimes Toni asked herself that same question.

Shoving her hands into the pocket of her jacket, she made the short trek up the walkway to the house. The porch steps creaked as she took the first step. They were pretty old. In fact the whole house was old. It was the first home her parents had lived in after they got married, and even then it hadn't been new. But it had stood the test thus far.

The faded red front door gave easily. Toni stepped inside and memories assaulted her. It had been more than ten years since she had been back here. There was no furniture now, but she knew exactly where everything should have been, from the overstuffed beige sofa, to the tiny end table beside the television where her mother used to stash magazines. She walked through the living room space, touching the walls, remembering everything exactly as it had once been.

She had been afraid to be here. This was where her parents had died. She had thought that all she would

see were the images from her dreams—them lying
dead on the floor. Dead. The stain of blood on everything they had touched in those last terrible moments
vivid. But what she saw were the things that she had almost forgotten. The four of them watching television
on the couch on Saturday nights; her father asleep with
the paper in the large armchair; her mother trying to
get Toni to stand still as she measured her for the next
sewing project; she and Trey staying up late to watch
movies while their parents were asleep. Good things
had happened in this house. So many things worth remembering, but her pain had stolen those memories
from her.

"Remember when we used to fight over the television remote in here?" Trey asked from the doorway.

Toni laughed. "Yeah. You used to hide it in the
morning before you went to school so you could have
it in the evening when you got home after me."

Trey chuckled. "Yeah, but no matter where I hid it,
you always found it."

Toni smiled and shook her head. She walked over to
the window, pushing it open so she could lean out.
"The first time you took the car out on your own, I remember Daddy standing here," she said. She laughed
as she remembered how her father had paced the
ground all evening until Trey came back.

"He didn't sit down once, just watched that road
until he saw the VW Jetta turn the corner."

Trey laughed. "Really? I never knew that." He
shook his head. "But now that you mention it, that does
sound like Dad."

Trey suddenly slapped a hand to his jaw. "You remember the first time I got into an accident?"

"How could I forget?" Toni asked, her eyes widening. "I thought Mom was gonna have a heart attack. She was freaking out, thinking you were hurt."

Trey snorted. "I was freaking out too. I thought Dad was gonna kill me."

"I thought so *too*," Toni said with a nod. "For sure, I thought you would never get behind a steering wheel for the rest of your life."

"But he was so cool about it," Trey said. "I think that made me feel worse. But I remember thinking"—Trey paused—"how cool he was for caring about me more than the car. He was amazing."

Toni nodded. "They both were."

She walked across the living room, her footsteps echoing softly through the empty space. Somehow being there was filling the emptiness in her heart. Instead of hurting her, the memories that kept washing over her like the ocean were healing.

The sun streamed through the empty kitchen like it had many mornings in Toni's childhood. She let her hand slide down the wall as she tried to remember all the images of her mother in this room. Her fingers hit a snag on the wall and she gasped when her eyes caught what it was.

"Trey, get in here," she called, now running both her hands over the jagged surface.

"What is it?" Trey asked from behind her.

"Look," Toni breathed. "It's still here."

Trey whistled. "I can't believe it. I thought someone would have painted over that or sanded it down for sure."

But there on the kitchen door frame were the marks where their mother had measured them when they were kids. They were worn and faded in some places, but they were still distinguishable in the aging wood.

Toni ran her fingers over the etchings and realized that she didn't want to let it go. "You have to buy this house," she said.

Trey looked at her as if she had sprouted another head. "What?" he echoed.

"You have to buy this house."

Trey folded his arms. "I thought you never wanted to see this place again. I thought you wanted to burn it to the ground."

Toni sighed and pulled herself up onto the kitchen counter. "I thought so too," she said, biting her lip. "I thought that when I came here all I would see were images of what happened to Mom and Dad."

"And what happened to you," Trey added.

Toni nodded. "Yes. That too. But it hasn't been like that," she said, shaking her head. "It's strange. I'm remembering a lot of the good memories too. And even the bad ones." She shrugged. "They still hurt, but I feel like I can handle them."

She turned to her brother. "I am afraid that if we lose this house again we will lose those memories. I don't want to forget them anymore, Trey."

He nodded. "Yeah. I know what you mean. He stuck his hands in his pockets. "I know it's just a house. But I feel like a lot of who we are and who they raised us to be is still here. I just felt like, if I could raise my kids here, I could raise them as well as Mom and Dad raised us. You know?" Trey shrugged. "I'm hoping."

Toni nodded and slipped off the counter. "I know." She put her arms around her brother. He returned the embrace.

"So this is okay with you?" he asked. "I just want to be sure."

Toni nodded and headed toward the front door. "It's okay with me."

She had her hand on the front door before Trey realized what she was doing. "You're ready already?" he asked. "You haven't even checked out the upstairs."

Toni gave a small smile as she opened the front door. "Baby steps, Trey. Rome wasn't built in a day."

He nodded and followed her out, understanding.

Things had gone better than she had expected. She wasn't about to push it. There would be many more days in this house ahead.

And that thought made Toni smile.

Chapter 39

"Get dressed. We're going out."

Toni put down the book she was reading to give Camille her full attention. "When? Now?" she asked, adjusting the phone against her ear.

"Yes now," Camille said. "Forever Jones is performing tonight at C-Room. And I've actually convinced Afrika that she won't die of boredom from gospel music, so get your butt in something cute and meet us there."

Toni sighed. "Thanks for the offer but I really don't feel like going out."

"I noticed," Camille deadpanned. "In fact for the past three weeks, all you've been doing is moping around that apartment like you've lost your best friend."

Some days it felt like she had.

"I have not been moping."

"Really?" Camille said. "When was the last time you went out?"

"I was at church today." That sounded lame even to her and she could see her friend rolling her eyes.

"That doesn't count and you know it. Get dressed."

"Camille—"

"This is not optional, Toni," Camille said. "Get dressed, get on your bike, and meet us at the doors in forty-five minutes. The show starts at exactly eight, so you better not be late."

"Camille. Camille?"

The beeping on the other end let Toni know she was talking to herself. She sighed, hung up the phone, and pulled herself off the couch. Normally she would have jumped at a chance to see the new band, Forever Jones. She hadn't actually seen them live since they came on the music scene. But she wasn't really in the mood for people. Especially since the one person who she wanted to see most was so far away.

But since that was unlikely to change anytime soon, she might as well pull herself out of her funk and pretend to have a life.

She headed to her closet and looked around. Her choice of clothing certainly had changed over the past year. She glanced at her mini dresses and skinnies, which hadn't been touched for a while, and moved past them again, opting for a pair of gray boot-cut pants. She added a cute white top, a broad red animal print belt, and matching heels to the mix. A few touch-ups to her face and hair and she stood in front of the mirror satisfied with what she saw. Not bad for someone who wasn't really trying.

She glanced longingly at the unfinished novel on her sofa before grabbing her red leather jacket and heading out the door.

If nothing else, she was proud of herself for being on schedule. When she finally got on the 1-75 south heading toward Forest Park, she had just enough time to make it to the venue before Camille started calling again. However that hope faded when she saw a cop flash his lights and step out into the road ahead of her.

She did a quick mental check.

Speed limit? Check.

Helmet? Check.

Lights?

Oh no.

Toni pulled her motorcycle onto the shoulder and came to a stop. "Good evening, officer," Toni began. "I know my lights were off but honestly I just—"

Toni's voice trailed off as she took off her helmet and came face to face with the officer. He shook his head and Toni's heart fell into her stomach.

"So we meet again, Miss Shields," Officer Powell said.

Toni sighed. She should have stayed home.

"License and registration please."

Toni produced the documents and sat back on her motorcycle as she waited for Officer Powell to come back with her ticket. So much for being on time.

However, when both doors to the cop car opened and Officer Powell returned with a second officer in tow, Toni knew that she probably wouldn't be seeing Forever Jones anytime soon.

"Miss Shields, do you know that you have a warrant out for unpaid fines?" Officer Powell asked, a smug look on his face.

"What unpaid fines?" Toni racked her brain trying to figure out what he could be talking about. But when he started reading out a list of traffic tickets and parking violations, she knew she was in trouble.

"Okay, yeah, that was me," Toni admitted. "But can't

I just pay them now? Come on, Officer Powell, do we really have to go through the whole arrest thing?"

Apparently she did, as the handcuffs on her wrists only moments later suggested. Feelings of déjà vu washed over her as she rode to the station in the cop car, and later heard the metal bars close with a clank behind her.

She really should have stayed home.

"Hey, don't I get one call?" Toni asked through the bars of the cell. Officer Powell only chuckled before disappearing down the hallway. She knew she could get someone to post bail for her once she made the call, but she had a feeling Officer Powell was going to make her sweat it out for a while.

It figured that the one time she was actually trying to stay out of trouble would be the time when she would get arrested.

Karma was a mean old heifer.

Toni sank down onto the hard metal bench and looked around the holding cell. There were three other women this time. Toni did a double take when she realized that one of the three was the same thick red-skinned woman who had been there the last time Toni was locked up.

"You here again?" Toni asked when she caught the woman looking at her.

"So are you," the woman slurred. "You must like the hospitality."

At first Toni had thought the woman was old. But on second glance she looked like she could be the same age as herself. When she heard her speak, Toni knew that she was probably younger.

"Something like that," Toni said. "What's your excuse?"

"What's it to you?" the young woman snapped.

"Nothing," Toni said with a shrug. "Just making conversation."

The woman was wearing fishnets with tiny shorts, and a tight black corset top that made her breasts look bigger than they actually were. It was clear what she had been doing when she got picked up. Half her face was hidden under blond hair, and Toni couldn't help but wonder what she would look like without the wig.

"What's your name?"

Toni was surprised. She hadn't expected her to speak again. "Toni. You?"

"Beth," the woman said after a moment. "Where you going in them fancy clothes?"

"I was going to meet up with some friends, but five-oh kinda interrupted my flow."

She nodded. "I know what that's like."

A banging on the bars interrupted whatever else Beth might have said.

"Shields, you're up," a custody officer said as he opened the gate. "Time to use your lifeline."

Toni called Camille, Afrika, and Trey, but no one picked up. She finally ended up just leaving a message on Trey's voice mail at home. At least then maybe he or Jasmine would get it. However, Toni wasn't sure when exactly that would be.

By the time they escorted Toni back to the holding cell, the two other women were gone, and it was just her and Beth.

"You got someone coming for you?" Toni asked.

"Nope," Beth said, lying back on the metal bench. "It'll be me and the Atlanta PD."

Toni raised an eyebrow. "So how are you going to get out of here?"

Beth shrugged. "They'll let me out tomorrow morning when I've dried out."

The way she said it told Toni that being picked up while soliciting drunk was something of a regular occurrence for Beth. For some reason the thought twisted Toni's heart. Maybe because she knew what it was like to be alone and not have anyone to depend on but yourself.

"What you do, anyway, that got you in here all the time?" Beth asked. "I didn't know they started arresting people for being rich."

So she thought she was rich. Toni almost laughed.

"I'm a reporter," Toni said. She explained that she worked at the *AJC* and sometimes doing her job got her in trouble. She even told her how it amused her friends and family. She wasn't sure why she was telling Beth all of this. But she did anyway.

"What about you?" Toni asked. "What's your deal?"

"You can't guess?" Beth asked cynically, motioning to her outfit. "I provide late night services."

"Why?" Toni asked.

"Because all of us can't be reporters."

She walked right into that one.

"I was in foster care for most of my life," Beth said. "When I turned eighteen they kicked me out of the system. I had no family and nowhere to go. And since a girl's gotta eat . . ." Beth let her guess the rest.

"What happened to your family?" Toni asked, frowning.

Beth shrugged. "I don't remember none of them. And I got moved around so often that I can't recall most of the foster families either. And trust me, with everything I done been through, that's probably a blessing."

Toni didn't know what to say. She had thought her life was rough. But there were always people who were worse off. She had lost a lot but God had still blessed her abundantly. Despite her past, she had so much to be grateful for. And that made her future something worth looking forward to.

"I'm sorry you had to go through all of that," Toni said after a long moment.

Beth snorted. "Yeah, me too."

They chatted some more and Toni found out that Beth was only twenty-five. And she was actually quite funny when she wasn't being cynical. Toni had been lying back on the metal bench laughing at one of Beth's jokes when the banging on the bars came again.

"Shields, you're out. Someone just posted your bail."

Toni sat up, a little surprised. She had expected to end up spending the night.

She was about to leave when she remembered Beth.

"Hey, if I leave my number out front for you, will you call me if you need anything?" Toni asked.

"You ain't gotta feel sorry for me," Beth said coldly, not even bothering to look at Toni. "I'll be fine."

Toni heard echoes of herself in the woman's voice. Echoes of her old self.

"I know, but maybe you can call me anyway," Toni said. "Maybe we can grab some food or something."

"Whatever."

That was better than she expected. Following the custody officer down the hall, she made a mental note to leave her card and number at the front for Beth. When she finally reached the exit, however, she forgot everything.

"So I leave you for a month and you go get yourself locked up," Adam said, leaning on the counter.

Toni's mouth fell open. She searched for words but she couldn't find any. All she found was a flood of emotions that she thought had begun to fade away.

"Sir, please sign here," the custody officer said, motioning to a form on the counter near Adam.

Toni watched him, speechless. She couldn't believe he was there, standing in the police station, posting bail for her. It must be a dream. But the cuffs cutting into her wrists told her it wasn't. They suddenly felt like million-pound weights and she shook them impatiently at the guard. She needed them off now.

"Sir, please note that we are releasing Miss Shields into your care," the officer said as he unlocked the handcuffs. "It is your duty to ensure she appears in court on the stipulated date. Failure to do so will lead to a forfeit of the cash bond posted."

"What are you doing here?" she asked a little breathlessly, her eyes fixed on him.

He smiled. "I came to post your bond."

"But . . . how?"

"Trey's flying and Jasmine couldn't leave the baby," he said, stepping closer to her. "So she asked me to come."

Toni shook her head, confused. "But you live in Baltimore."

"I did. For a while," he said, taking another step toward her.

"But now?" she asked, helping to close the distance.

"Now I'm here."

And there were no more words for a while as he pulled her close and she wrapped her arms around him, holding tight. She buried her face in his chest and tried not to cry as she realized how much she had missed him. It was like a piece of her heart that she didn't know had been gone was suddenly filled.

"So I guess it's safe to say you missed me too?" he asked, pushing a lock of hair behind her ear as his warm brown eyes roamed all over her face.

Toni smiled. "You have no idea."

His mouth covered hers, and as he kissed her, Toni knew exactly how much he had missed her over the past month. She had almost forgotten exactly where they were when she heard a throat clear from somewhere behind her.

"Miss, your things?"

Adam let her out of his embrace, but kept her hand firmly in his as she retrieved her purse, jacket, and the keys to her motorcycle.

They were about to leave when she remembered Beth. Pulling out of Adam's grasp, she dug into her purse for a business card.

"Can you give this to the woman in holding when she gets let out?" Toni asked. "She said her name was Beth."

The officer nodded and looked over the card. "I'll put it with her things."

"What was that about?" Adam asked, slipping an arm around her as they walked out of the precinct.

"Nothing for you to worry about," she said, snuggling closer to him.

The night air felt cooler and fresher as she walked hand in hand with Adam across the parking lot back to his car.

"So you want to tell me the real reason you're here?" Toni asked, pulling herself up onto the hood of his car. " 'Cause if you just kissed me like that only to take off to Baltimore again, I'm going to have to hurt you."

He laughed. "You don't have to worry about that," he said, leaning back on the neighboring car across from her. "I'm staying here."

Toni cocked her head to the side. "What happened?"

He looked down for a moment. "Things didn't turn out the way I thought they would."

Toni bit her lip. "I'm sorry. You know, even though I didn't agree with your decision, I would never wish anything bad for you or the project."

"I know," Adam said, nodding. "And the project was great. Things were going well. But I just . . ."

Toni didn't speak, but let him find his own words.

"I guess I realized that it wasn't where I was supposed to be," he said finally, with a sigh.

"How long did it take you to figure it out?" Toni asked gently.

Adam laughed. "About a week. And the rest of the time was just me being stubborn and fighting what I knew God was telling me.

"And then Pastor Reynolds called and told me they still hadn't found a replacement here, and that if I ever changed my mind, I could come back."

"So was that the only reason?" Toni bit her lip and watched him watch her. "If Pastor Reynolds hadn't offered you your job back, would you still be in Baltimore?"

Adam looked at her for so long Toni felt like she would evaporate under his gaze. When he finally spoke, his eyes never left hers.

"I told them I was leaving before Pastor Reynolds even called."

Toni felt her heart beat faster. "Why?"

"Well, there was this woman in Atlanta I couldn't get out of my head." He took a step toward her. "And I realized that it would be pretty difficult for me to be useful if she was all I could think about."

Her heart was pounding so hard now that she could feel the pulse in her throat and hear the beat echo in her chest.

"It was like I needed to be where she was, almost like we belonged together." He was standing right in front of her now, his hands resting on the car, on either side of her.

"Must be some special woman." She couldn't tear her eyes away from him. Mercy, he was fine. She had almost forgotten.

"Really special." He leaned in closer. "Amazing, actually. Beautiful inside and out. One in a million."

Toni felt the tears brim her eyes and when he brushed his lips against hers gently, she let them roll down her cheeks.

"And I'm absolutely crazy about her."

She slipped her palms up to cup his face and brushed light kisses over his lips before pulling him into a tight embrace. This man owned her heart and he didn't even know it.

She laughed and wiped the moistness from her face as she let him go.

"Well, I sure am glad Pastor Reynolds held out for you."

He laughed. "You and me both. I guess he knew it would take me a little while to figure things out. He was right. Just like you and Trey. You can go ahead and say, I told you so."

"No," Toni said thoughtfully. "I like the other part better. The part where I'm right. Can you say it again?"

He laughed and let his hands rest on her waist. "You were right, beautiful."

"You know I don't really care about being right, right?" she asked, resting her arms around his shoulders. "I just don't want you having any more regrets about the decisions you've made. I want you to be happy."

"Yeah, I know," he said. "That's one of the things I love about you."

Toni beamed. He had said the L word. At least she knew she wasn't the only one thinking about it.

"You know, if a relationship between us is gonna work, you're gonna have to stop getting arrested," Adam said after a moment. "I can't afford to be posting bond for you every week."

"I wasn't even doing anything this time, babe, I promise," Toni protested.

Adam rolled his eyes. "Yeah, sure."

"Seriously, I got pulled over for not having my lights on, and then I find out that I have a bunch of fines from unpaid traffic stuff," Toni explained to a laughing Adam. "Isn't that crazy? They're locking me up for traffic violations."

"You gotta try and stay clean, beautiful," he said, shaking his head. "I got enough to deal with handling the boys; I can't have the cops on my woman too."

Toni cocked her head to the side. "When did I become your woman?"

"What, you have an objection?" he asked with a grin.

"Nope." She shook her head. "Not as long as you promise not to run off to some other state and leave me."

"Deal," he said, shaking her hand in a mock agreement. Then he pulled her toward him and kissed her again, and Toni was sure that she had walked away with the better end of the bargain.

She knew in her heart she loved this man. She also knew he loved her. God had purposed for them to be together. Despite all their running away—from their pasts, their mistakes, and the pain of losing people they loved—God had still brought them home and there was no place like it.

Don't miss Rhonda Bowen's latest,

Hitting the Right Note

On sale in April 2014!

Chapter 1

"He asked me to marry him! We're getting married!"

According to a recent report on ABC's *Nightline*, 70 percent of professional African American women over the age of twenty-five are unmarried. As JJ held the phone away from her ear to avoid Sydney's screams, she realized that her older sister had joined the 30 percent and left her stranded.

JJ Isaacs set the phone on hands-free and began applying mascara to her lashes. Though the news was not entirely surprising, it was not what she had expected to hear when she saw her sister's number pop up on the caller ID. Not on this night, anyway.

"Ohmigosh, JJ! He wants to marry me. Hayden Windsor wants to spend the rest of his life with me. Can you believe it?"

Could she believe that ex–NBA star Hayden Windsor, one of the first professional basketball players to figure out how to retire from the game and not go broke, wanted to marry her sister? Of course she could.

Who wouldn't want to marry her tall, gorgeous, successful-business-owning sister? In fact, if they weren't related, JJ would have married her.

"Congratulations, hon," JJ said, pushing back a thin layer of irritation to find the genuine happiness for her sister that was camouflaged underneath. "I'm guessing you said yes?"

JJ grimaced and reached for her lipstick as Sydney screamed her response in the affirmative. She had never seen—okay, heard—Sydney like this. Her older sibling was usually the sane one in the craziness that was their big, dysfunctional family. Whereas everyone else was content to fly by the seat of their pants, Sydney was always the one with the plan. Getting married to a man she had dated for less than a year was not like her at all. But that's what happened when people fell in love. Or so JJ assumed. Having had no firsthand knowledge of the being-in-love experience, she couldn't say for sure.

"That's great, Syd," JJ said, reminding herself that she was happy for her sister. "Hayden's a prize."

"He is amazing, isn't he?" Sydney said, managing to modulate her voice to a less ear-splitting volume. "JJ, you should have seen his proposal . . ."

JJ rolled her eyes and mouthed a silent *no, thank you*.

"It was perfect," Sydney began. "He took me to . . ."

A banging on wood saved JJ's sanity.

"Five minutes to curtain, ladies," a booming voice called from the other side of the dressing room door.

JJ had never been so happy for a curtain call. She loved her sister and really was happy for her, but the last thing she wanted to hear from her sister, who had yet to remember what JJ was doing that night, was how her perfect boyfriend had done the perfect proposal to set off their perfect engagement.

"Syd, I gotta go." JJ jammed her feet into heels and swiped a layer of gloss over her lips as the scramble of women around her picked up speed. "I'm about to go onstage."

"Oh, honey, I'm so sorry! I completely forgot you had a show tonight."

JJ tried to ignore her annoyance.

"It's okay." JJ stood and straightened her dress. "I wouldn't have wanted to wait till tomorrow for this news. In fact, you can call me back later tonight and tell me all the details."

By then she wouldn't be as anxious and cranky as she usually was the last few minutes before a performance.

"Okay, sure," Sydney agreed.

A hand tugged at JJ's arm.

"We gotta go, JJ," Torrina said, nodding toward the door.

JJ picked up the cell phone to end the call. "Gotta go, Syd. Love you."

"Love you, hon. Have a great—"

JJ didn't hear the end of her sister's sentence. She barely got to toss her phone on the dressing room vanity before Torrina, her fellow backup singer, dragged her through the door and down the narrow backstage passageway. Sturdy iron beams holding the stage in place, and swiftly moving black-clothed men and women holding the show in place, barely registered with JJ as she hurried behind the other singers to her place near the second curtain.

"Everyone on your marker Curtains go up in five, four, three, two . . ."

JJ didn't hear the end of the countdown. Just the drummer's intro as the band started up Jayla Grey's "Sunday to Sunday." JJ was already up onstage with the rest of the backup vocalists as the curtains rolled up. Jayla would make her entrance in only a few seconds as she sang the first verse to one of the most popular songs off her Juno Award–winning album, *Desire.* JJ remembered when the "Sunday to Sunday" single first started blowing up the airwaves a couple years back. She never dreamed that she would be part of the performance for that song, but here she was at the Festival Place with hundreds of eyes watching her perform. Okay, so they weren't really there for her, but she was part of the show.

Jayla's strong, sultry contralto voice came in with the first few lines of the song, about a woman who was willing to slave for her man because she loved him. The crowds began to clap in rhythm and cheer.

JJ's own hips began to move to well-choreographed steps as the song progressed. Beads of perspiration began to dot her forehead and chest as the hot strobe lights shone down on her and everyone else onstage. But it just energized her and set her blood pumping as her voice came in strong for the pre-chorus. Her body began to feel the music, catching its own rhythm, making the steps her own. The sweet melodies curled out of her, blending with those of her fellow singers to bring a rich, lush harmony that cushioned Jayla's flawless voice. The screams of the crowd soaked into her like a light, warm drizzle on a humid day. JJ was in heaven and she never wanted it to end.

But eventually it did. Much quicker than she expected, with the fifty-minute set feeling like only fifty seconds. Her body still buzzed with energy as she skipped down the steps from the stage, her five-inch platform heels clicking gracefully. At first she could barely walk in the things. But after four months of wearing them onstage, she could manage a sprint if she needed to.

"Good show tonight, guys," Coley, the show's producer, said as he met JJ and the rest of the singers at the bottom of the steps. He pushed the mouthpiece of his headset up to his ear. "You guys were awesome, as usual."

"Good to know," Donald, a fellow singer, commented as he uncapped a bottle of water. "Especially since I felt like I was melting underneath those lights up there."

"Yeah," Torrina agreed, with a cheeky smile. "Plus I almost broke my neck on the wires on the floor back there in our little area."

"I guess it's a good thing I work with professionals then," Coley said, returning his mouthpiece to the right position as he began to walk away. "Lesser singers would have complained."

They all laughed as they headed back to the dressing rooms. Jayla, who was already in her robe, met them at the doorway.

"Thanks a lot, guys," she said, hugging each of them. "I was just telling Philip and the rest of the band, everything was almost perfect tonight. Couldn't have asked for a better show."

"Does that mean we get a raise?" Mark, the other male singer, asked with a grin.

Jayla smiled. "You better talk to Todd about that. He's the one signing your checks, not me. I just dish out the praise. You guys enjoy the rest of the night and this week. On Monday we'll start rehearsals for the tour."

JJ smiled but said little. Though everyone had been really nice to her, as one of the newest members of the team of backup singers, she still felt a little on the fringes. Truth was, she was only there because one of Jayla's original singers, Amina, got in a tiff with management and quit. Torrina had shared the dramatic details with her not long after JJ joined the crew.

However, her newness meant she didn't get all the inside jokes and she didn't always get invited to all the social events. But over the past two months, as she spent more time with the team, she was starting to feel like one of the family.

"I'm gonna head out but just wanted to say you were amazing tonight, Jayla," JJ said, squeezing the older woman's arm. She was about to turn away when Jayla grabbed her.

"You weren't too bad yourself," Jayla said with a smile. "I caught you doing your thing out there. You're coming on tour with us, right?"

JJ's eyes widened. She knew Jayla was going on a major tour in a couple weeks, but she had assumed that the main three would be going as backup. No one had talked to her about being a part of that team, and she honestly hadn't even considered it.

"Uh, I . . . I don't know," JJ stammered.

Jayla nodded thoughtfully. "Let me talk to my people and have someone get back to you. But keep your calendar open."

JJ opened and closed her mouth a couple times to answer and just ended up nodding.

Jayla chuckled. "See you next week, JJ."

JJ stumbled through the dressing room, barely able to focus as she gathered her things and exited the building. As soon as she stepped through the door into the cool, dark night, a hand grasped her upper arm, yanking her forward.

"Did I just hear what I thought I heard?" Torrina asked, her voice several pitches higher than usual and her eyebrows arched several inches higher than normal.

"She wants me to come on tour with her!"

Both women squealed and jumped around in the parking lot, holding on to each other. JJ wasn't normally a screamer, but maybe there was something in the water tonight. She couldn't help herself.

"Jayla Grey wants me to come on tour with her!" JJ shrieked again. "She told me she was going to talk to her people. She invited me to rehearsal on Monday. She wants me to come on tour with her!"

"Oh, that's amazing," Torrina said, still bouncing even though her feet were planted firmly on the ground. "It would be so much fun to have you with us. I mean the other guys are great, but it would be great to have a girlfriend on the bus."

"I know," JJ said. "And, girl, I'm gonna need you to have my back. Someone's gonna have to keep me from making an absolute fool of myself when I see Angie Stone."

"Girl, I don't know if I can help you there," Torrina said, slapping a hand on her hip. "Last year I saw John Legend backstage at a show I was doing and I near lost my mind."

JJ burst out laughing.

"I'm serious!" Torrina said, eyes widening and hair flashing in the normal dramatic way in which she told her stories. "I was trying to climb over the barriers from our backstage area to his, nearly ripped my thousand-dollar dress. I almost got to him too, except his security guard got to me first."

"Oh no!" JJ covered her mouth. "That must have been embarrassing."

Torrina grinned. "Just a little. But I could take a little embarrassment for some John Legend. You know what I'm sayin'?"

JJ laughed. Only Torrina.

The door swung open again, letting out a blast of sound and another round of musicians and performers, some of them from Jayla's team.

"JJ, Torrina, you guys heading out with us?"

"Where's everyone going, Sam?" Torrina asked the short, stout guy wearing a spiky Mohawk and sunglasses.

"Probably going to grab a bite to eat in the hotel restaurant, then hit a couple bars downtown. One of the other guys says he knows a spot where they have a live band all night. Wanna come?"

"Sure," Torrina said with a nod. "I could eat. You too, JJ?"

"I'll head back with you guys to the hotel, but I've gotta crash," JJ said. "I'm exhausted. I think my body's still reeling from the excitement of these last couple nights. Plus I feel a headache coming on."

"Not used to life on the road yet, are you?" Donald asked. He threw an arm around JJ, tugging her against him as he joined their circle.

"No not yet," JJ said with a tight smile as she casually eased herself out of Donald's uninvited embrace. "Still a newbie."

JJ followed the group over to the two huge, black

SUVs that would take them back to the hotel where they had been staying for the past two days, making sure to be seated between Torrina and the door. As the vans pulled out of the parking lot, Torrina leaned over and whispered in JJ's ear.

"It's okay. You can come with us tonight. I'll keep Donald out of your way and make sure they lay off you at the bars. No one will give you a hard time."

JJ was grateful for Torrina's concern. She knew that Donald's unwelcome attention created an issue for JJ, especially when they all hung out socially. In any other situation she would have just told him to back off. But she was trying to make a name for herself in the industry and didn't want to stir up drama over what might just be a minor issue. The fact that she opted not to party like a rock star already made her stand out. She didn't want to be called a whiner on top of it too.

"Thanks, but I really am tired," JJ whispered back. "Three shows in three days is crazy."

Torrina's lip curled. "I know that's right."

"Plus my sister got some big news today and she's supposed to call me back tonight, so I really want to catch her," JJ added.

"Gotcha." Torrina nodded. "If you change your mind though, just text me and I'll let you know where we are. We'll probably be out till four a.m. anyway. When we finish a set of shows like this, these guys like to go hard and then crash for a couple days."

JJ chuckled. "I can imagine."

The SUVs pulled up to the hotel entrance and they all got out. JJ waved to the others as they split up in the lobby; she headed toward the rooms, they headed to the hotel restaurant.

"Call me if you need someone to scrape you off the bar floor," JJ called.

She grinned as the sound of Torrina's laughter followed her across the lobby.

Pushing the door to the stairwell open, she began her trek up the steps to the sixth floor. She spent most of her life bypassing elevators for the stairs, so her thighs were used to the workout. Once inside her room, adjacent to Torrina's, she slipped off her jacket and sank down onto her bed to take off her strappy shoes. She had just freed her toes from their confines when she heard a knock on the door.

"Room service."

She grinned and hurried to open the door. Her bellhop was dressed in a gray ribbed sweater and leather jacket instead of a uniform, and carried several takeout containers and a bottle of something sparkling instead of pushing a hotel dinner cart. Plus she was sure it was illegal for someone to look that deliciously handsome.

She grabbed the lapels of his jacket and pulled him inside.

"Perfect timing," she murmured before his lips met hers. He managed to kick the door closed and wrap his arms around her without dropping any of his packages.

JJ snuggled closer, slipping into the familiar place where her body fit in his arms. Okay, so she may not be getting married, and her sister may have just abandoned her in the single zone. But at least she wasn't hanging out there alone. Being in the 70 percent might not be so bad after all.

Chapter 1

Sydney was never big on sports. It wasn't that she was athletically challenged. It was just that chasing a ball around a court, or watching other people do it, had never really been high on her list of favorite things.

However, as she stood at the center of the Carlu Round Room, surveying the best of the NBA that Toronto had to offer, she had to admit that professional sports definitely had a few attractive features.

"Thank you, Sydney."

Sydney grinned and folded her arms as she considered her younger sister.

"For what?"

"For Christmas in October." Lissandra bit her lip. "Look at all those presents."

Sydney turned in the direction where Lissandra was staring, just in time to catch the burst of testosterone-laced eye candy that walked through the main doors. Tall, muscular, and irresistible, in every shade of chocolate a girl could dream of sampling. She was starting to have a new appreciation for basketball.

Sydney's eyebrows shot up. "Is that . . . ?"

"Yes, girl. And I would give anything to find him under our Christmas tree," Lissandra said, as her eyes devoured the newest group of NBA stars to steal the spotlight. "I love this game."

Sydney laughed. "I don't think it's the game you love."

"You laugh now," Lissandra said, pulling her compact out of her purse. "But when that hot little dress I had to force you to wear gets you a date for next weekend, you'll thank me."

Sydney folded her arms across the bodice of the dangerously short boat-necked silver dress that fit her five-foot-nine frame almost perfectly. It was a bit more risqué than what Sydney would normally wear but seemed almost prudish compared to what the other women in the room were sporting. At least it wasn't too tight. And the cut of the dress exposed her long, elegant neck, which she had been told was one of her best features.

"I'm here to work, not to pick up men," Sydney reminded her sister.

"No, we're here to deliver a spectacular cake." Lissandra checked her lipstick in the tiny mirror discreetly. "And since that cake is sitting over there, our work is done. It's playtime."

"Focus, Lissa." Sydney tried to get her sister back on task with a hand on her upper arm. "Don't forget this is an amazing opportunity to make the kinds of contacts that will put us on the A-list. Once we do that, more events like this might be in our future."

"OK, fine," Lissandra huffed, dropping her compact

back into her purse. "I'll talk to some people and give out a few business cards. But if a player tries to buy me a drink, you best believe I'm gonna take it."

Sydney smirked. "I wouldn't expect otherwise."

"Good." Lissandra's mouth turned up into a naughty grin. " 'Cause I see some potential business over there that has my name etched across his broad chest."

Sydney sighed. Why did she even bother? "Be good," she said, adding a serious big-sister tone to her voice.

"I will," Lissandra threw behind her. But since she didn't even bother to look back, Sydney didn't hope for much. She knew her sister, and she'd just lost her to a six-foot-six brother with dimples across the room.

Sydney eventually lost sight of her sister as the crowd thickened. She turned her attention back to their ticket into the exclusive Toronto Raptors NBA Season Opener event.

The cake.

Sydney stood back and admired her work again, loving the way the chandelier from above and the tiny lights around the edges of the table and underneath it lit up her creation. The marzipan gave the cream-colored square base of the cake a smooth, flawless finish, and the gold trim caught the light beautifully. The golden replica of an NBA championship trophy, which sat atop the base, was, however, the highlight.

She had to admit it was a sculpted work of art, and one of the best jobs she had done in years. It was also one of the most difficult. It had taken two days just to bake and decorate the thing. That didn't include the several concept meetings, the special-ordered baking molds, and multiple samples made to ensure that the cake tasted just as good as it looked. For the past month and a half, this cake job had consumed her life.

But it was well worth it. Not only for the weight it put in her pocket, but also the weight it was likely to add to her client list. Once everyone at the event saw her creation, she was sure she would finally make it onto the city's pastry-chef A-list, and Decadent would be the go-to spot for wedding and special-event cakes.

She stood near the cake for a while, sucking up the oohs and aahs of passersby, before heading to the bathroom to check that she hadn't sweated out her curls carrying up the cake from downstairs. She took in her long, dark hair, which had been curled and pinned up for the night; her slightly rounded face; and plump, pinked lips; and was satisfied. She turned to the side to get a better view of her size six frame and smiled. Even though she had protested when Lissandra presented the dress, she knew she looked good. Normally she hated any kind of shimmer, but the slight sparkle from the dress was just enough to put Sydney in the party mood it inspired. OK, so Lissandra may have been right—she was there for business—but that didn't mean she couldn't have some fun, too.

By the time she reapplied her lipstick and headed back, the room was full.

She tried to mingle and did end up chatting with a few guests, but her maternal instincts were in full gear and it wasn't long before she found her way back to the cake. She was about to check for anything amiss when she felt gentle fingers on the back of her bare neck. She swung around on reflex.

"What do you think you're doing?" she said, slapping away the hand that had violated her personal space.

"Figuring out if I'm awake or dreaming."

Sydney's eyes slid all the way up the immaculately toned body of the six-foot-three man standing in front of her, to his strong jaw, full smirking lips, and coffee brown eyes. Her jaw dropped. And not just because of how ridiculously handsome he was.

"Dub?"

"Nini."

She cringed. "Wow. That's a name I never thought I would hear again."

"And that's a half tattoo I never thought I'd see again."

Sydney slapped her hand to the back of her neck self consciously. She had almost forgotten the thing was there. It would take the one person who had witnessed her chicken out on getting it finished to remind her about it.

Hayden Windsor. Now wasn't this a blast from the past, sure to get her into some present trouble.

She tossed a hand onto her hip and pursed her lips. "I thought Toronto was too small for you."

"It is."

"Then what are you doing here?"

"Right now?" His eyes flitted across her frame in answer.

"Stop that," Sydney said, her cheeks heating up as she caught his perusal.

"Stop what?" he asked with a laugh.

"You know what," she said. She shook her head. "You are still the same."

He shrugged in an attempt at innocence that only served to draw Sydney's eyes to the muscles shifting under his slim-fitting jacket.

"I can't help it. I haven't seen you in almost ten

years. What, you gonna beat me up like you did when you were seven?"

"Maybe."

"Bully."

"Jerk."

"How about we continue this argument over dinner?" he asked.

"They just served appetizers."

The corners of his lips drew up in a scandalous grin. "Come on, you know you're still hungry."

He was right. That finger food hadn't done anything for her—especially since working on the cake had kept her from eating all day. But she wasn't about to tell him that.

Sydney smirked. "Even if I was, I don't date guys who make over one hundred thousand dollars a year."

He raised a thick eyebrow. "That's a new one."

"Yes, well," she said, "it really is for your own good. This way you won't have to wonder if I was with you for your money."

"So how about we pretend like I don't have all that money," he said, a dangerous glint in his eyes. "We could pretend some other things, too—like we weren't just friends all those years ago."

"I'm not dating you, Hayden," Sydney said, despite the shiver that ran up her spine at his words.

"So you can ask me to marry you, but you won't date me?"

"I was seven years old!"

"And at nine years old, I took that very seriously," Hayden said, his brow furrowing.

Sydney laughed. "That would explain why you went wailing to your daddy right after."

He rested a hand on his rock-solid chest. "I'm an emotional kind of guy."

"Hayden! There you are. I've been looking all over for you!"

Sydney turned to where the voice was coming from and fought her gag reflex. A busty woman with too much blond hair sidled up to Hayden, slipping her arm around his.

"This place is so packed that I can barely find anyone." The woman suddenly seemed to notice Sydney.

"Sydney!"

"Samantha."

Samantha gave Sydney a constipated smile. "So good to see you."

Sydney didn't smile back. "Wish I could say the same."

Hayden snorted. Samantha dropped the smile, but not his arm.

Sydney glared at the woman in the red-feathered dress and wondered how many peacocks had to die to cover her Dolly Parton goods.

"So I guess you two know each other?" Hayden asked, breaking the silence that he seemed to find more amusing than awkward.

"Yes," Samantha volunteered. "Sydney's little bakery, Decadent, beat out Something Sweet for the cake job for this event. She was my main competition."

"I wouldn't call it a competition," Sydney said, thinking it was more like a slaughtering.

"How do *you* know each other?" Samantha probed.

Hayden grinned. "Sydney and I go way back. Right, Syd?"

Samantha raised an eyebrow questioningly and Sydney glared at her, daring her to ask another question. Samantha opted to keep her mouth shut.

"So this is where the party is," Lissandra said, joining the small circle. Sydney caught the flash of recognition in Lissandra's eyes when she saw who exactly made up their impromptu gathering.

"Hayden? Is that you?"

"The very same," Hayden said, pulling Lissandra into a half hug. "Good to see you, Lissandra."

"Back at you," Lissandra said. "Wow, it's been ages. I probably wouldn't recognize you except Sydney used to watch your games all the—oww!"

Lissandra groaned as Sydney's elbow connected with her side.

"Did she?" Hayden turned to Sydney again, a smug look in his eyes.

"Well, it was nice to see you all again," Samantha said, trying to navigate Hayden away from the group.

"Samantha, I can't believe you're here." Lissandra's barely concealed laughter was not lost on Sydney or Samantha. "I thought you would be busy cleaning up that business at Something Sweet."

Sydney bit back a smirk as a blush crept up Samantha's neck to her cheeks. Samantha went silent again.

"What business?" Hayden looked around at the three women, who obviously knew something he didn't.

"Nothing," Samantha said quickly.

"Just that business with the health inspector," Lissandra said, enjoying Samantha's discomfort. "Nothing major. I'm sure the week that you were closed was enough to get that sorted out."

Hayden raised an eyebrow. "The health inspector shut you down?"

"We were closed temporarily," Samantha corrected.

"Just so that we could take care of a little issue. It wasn't that serious."

"Is that what the exterminator said?" Lissandra asked.

Sydney coughed loudly and Samantha's face went from red to purple.

"You know," Samantha said, anger in her eyes. "It's interesting. We have never had a problem at that location before now. It's funny how all of a sudden we needed to call an exterminator around the same time they were deciding who would get the job for tonight's event."

"Yes, life is full of coincidences," Sydney said dryly. "Like that little mix-up we had with the Art Gallery of Ontario event last month. But what can you do? The clients go where they feel confident."

"Guess that worked out for you this time around," Samantha said, glaring at Sydney and Lissandra.

"Guess so," Lissandra said smugly.

Sydney could feel Hayden eyeing her suspiciously, but she didn't dare look at him.

"Well, this was fun," Sydney said in a tone that said the exact opposite. "But I see some people I need to speak with."

Sydney excused herself from the group and made her way to the opposite side of the room toward the mayor's wife. She had only met the woman once, but Sydney had heard they had an anniversary coming up soon. It was time to get reacquainted, and get away from the one man who could make her forget what she really came here for.

By the time the hands on her watch were both sitting

at eleven, Sydney was exhausted and completely out of business cards.

"Leaving already?" She was only steps from the door, and he was only steps in front of her.

"This was business, not pleasure."

Hayden's eyes sparkled with mischief. "All work and no play makes Sydney a dull girl."

This time her mouth turned up in a smile. "I think you know me better than that."

His grin widened in a way that assured her that he did. "Remind me."

She shook her head and pointed her tiny purse at him.

"I'm not doing this here with you, Dub."

He stepped closer and she felt the heat from his body surround her. "We can always go somewhere else. Like the Banjara a couple blocks away."

Sydney scowled. Him and his inside knowledge.

"If we leave now we can get there before it closes."

She folded her arms over her midsection. "I haven't changed my mind, Dub."

He grinned. "That's not what your stomach says."

Sydney glanced behind him, and he turned around to see that Samantha was only a few feet away and headed in his direction. Sydney wasn't sure what string of events had put Samantha and Hayden together that night. The woman was definitely not his type. Or at least she didn't think Samantha was.

"I think your date is coming to get you," Sydney said, her voice dripping with amusement. "Maybe *she* wants to go for Indian food."

"How about I walk you to your car?"

Without waiting for a response, he put a hand on the

small of her back and eased her out the large doors into the lobby and toward the elevator.

"What's the rush?" she teased.

"Still got that smart mouth, don't you."

"I thought that was what you liked about me," she said innocently, as he led her into the waiting elevator.

"See, that's what you always got wrong, Nini." He leaned toward her ear to whisper and she caught a whiff of his cologne. "It was never just one thing."

Sydney tried to play it off, but she couldn't help the way her breathing went shallow as her heart sped up. And she couldn't keep him from noticing it, either.

His eyes fell to her lips. "So what's it going to be, Syd? You, me, and something spicy?"

He was only inches away from her. So close that if she leaned in, she could . . .

"Hayden!"

A familiar voice in the distance triggered her good sense. Sydney stepped forward and placed her hands on his chest.

"I think you're a bit busy tonight."

She pushed him out of the elevator and hit the DOOR CLOSE button.

He grinned and shook his head as she waved at him through the gap between the closing doors.

"I'll see you soon, Nini."

For reasons she refused to think about, she hoped he kept that promise.